DRAMATIC STRUCTURE AND MEANING IN THEATRICAL PRODUCTIONS

DRAMATIC STRUCTURE AND MEANING IN THEATRICAL PRODUCTIONS

Thomas Price

EMText
San Francisco

Library of Congress Cataloging-in-Publication Data

Price, Thomas, 1937-
    Dramatic structure and meaning in theatrical productions / Thomas
Price.
      p. cm.
    Includes bibliographical references.
    ISBN 0-7734-9897-4
    1. Drama--Technique. 2. Drama--History and criticism. I. Title.
PN1661.P69 1992
808.2--dc20
                                                      92-21128
                                                              CIP

Excerpts from *Luigi Pirandello, Six Characters in Search of an Author*, translated by Felicity Firth, in *Luigi Pirandello Collected Plays*, vol.2, copyright ©1988, by permission of Riverrun Press; Sophocles, *Oedipus the King*, translated by David Grene, in *The Complete Greek Tragedies*, edited by David Grene and Richmond Lattimore, copyright ©1958, by permission of The University of Chicago Press; William Shakespeare, *The Tragedy of Othello the Moor of Venice*, edited by Tucker Brooke and Lawrence Mason, copyright ©1965, by permission of Yale University Press; Anton Chekhov, *Three Sisters*, translated by Ann Dunnigan, in *Chekhov: The Major Plays*, copyright ©1964 by Ann Dunnigan, by permission of New American Library, a division of Penguin Books USA Inc.; François Truffaut, *Jules and Jim: A Film*, translated by Nicholas Fry, copyright ©1986, by permission of Don Congden Associates, Inc., agents for Simon and Schuster; Molière, *Tartuffe, or The Imposter*, translated by Richard Wilbur, copyright ©1963, 1962, 1961 by Richard Wilbur, by permission of Harcourt Brace Jovanovich, Inc.; Betolt Brecht, *Mother Courage and Her Children*, translated by Ralph Manheim, in *Bertolt Brecht: Collected Plays*, vol. 5, edited by Ralph Manheim and John Willet, copyright ©1972, by permission of Vintage Books, a division of Random House, Inc.

Editorial Inquiries and Order Fulfillment:

The Edwin Mellen Press
P.O. Box 450
Lewiston, NY 14092
USA

Printed in the United States of America

To Anita Sorel

And in memory of Howard Laws

CONTENTS

Foreword   xi

Acknowledgments   xv

Part I   The Dialectic

INTRODUCTION   5

DIALECTIC OF ACTION   7

Theorem 1: Action/Counteraction

2: The Order of Ends

3: Deeds, Not Words

4: Hidden Players

5: Misdirection

6: Unidirectionality

DIALECTIC OF IMAGERY   51

Theorem 7: Figurative Opposition

8: Functional Units

9: Equality of Image & Symbol

10: Shifting Images

11: Mirror Images

12: Verification of Action

IMPLICATIONAL DIALECTIC   59

Theorem 13: Descriptive Reduction

14: Qualitative Opposition

15: Verification of Action & Imagery

16: Terms Extraordinary

17: Sub-plots

18: Relative Complexity

19: Dominant/Recessive as Wish/Fear

20: Irony as Negative Dominant System

IDEOLOGICAL DIALECTIC   63

Theorem 21: Drama/Auditor Dialectic

Part II   The Seven Structural Models

INTRODUCTION   69

FIRST MODEL: STATIC   75

Definition & Schematic

General

Analysis: Pirandello, *Six Characters in Search of an Author*

SECOND MODEL: APOSTATIC-POSITIVE   105

Definition & Schematic

General

Analysis: Sophocles, *Oedipus the King*

THIRD MODEL: APOSTATIC-NEGATIVE   135

Definition & Schematic

General

Analysis: Shakespeare, *Othello, the Moor of Venice*

FOURTH MODEL: METASTATIC-POSITIVE   185

Definition & Schematic

General

Analysis: Chekhov, *The Three Sisters*

FIFTH MODEL: METASTATIC-NEGATIVE 223

    Definition & Schematic
    General
    Analysis: Truffaut, *Jules and Jim*

SIXTH MODEL: SYNTHETIC-REALIZED 269

    Definition & Schematic
    General
    Analysis: Moliere, *Tartuffe, or The Imposter*

SEVENTH MODEL: SYNTHETIC-IMPLIED 309

    Definition & Schematic
    General
    Analysis: Brecht, *Mother Courage and Her Children*

Afterword 351

FOREWORD

This work offers two things: (1) a general dialectical theory of dramatic structure and (2) a comprehensive methodology for the analysis and critical understanding of plays, screenplays, and opera libretti. It is based on the assumption that a drama's argument does in fact carry a specific meaning independent of any particular reader or spectator, and that it is possible to abstract this argument into the language of values using the ground-rules and structural models here developed. These methodological principles may be learned and employed by any reasonably intelligent person or group of students, and will yield results that can be replicated and verified by others.

The text is addressed to the generally educated reader, whether the academic who seeks a new way of comprehending the implications of dramatic form, the theatrical director or designer who needs a firmer grasp of the play's argument and imagery, or the amateur who simply wishes to understand more clearly why certain plays and films affect him or her the way they do. I have therefore tried to avoid obscure language in general, and the jargon of contemporary "meta-criticism" in particular. The few technical terms I have found necessary to employ are clearly defined at the outset, and redefined in context, with frequent cross-references to methodological principles and structural models elaborated elsewhere in the text. I have attempted to make this book as suitable for the university classroom as for the theatrical director's office or the private library of the stage and film devotee.

The work is divided into two parts. Part One (the shortest section) presents the theory and basic methodology in a series of numbered theorems, beginning with the governing hypothesis and extending to twenty corollary principles addressing, in order, (1) the dialectic of action, (2) the dialectic of imagery, (3) the implicational dialectic (descriptive reduction of 1 and 2), and (4) the ideological dialectic between play and auditor. Each theorem is presented in a brief paragraph typed in italics, and then followed by an essay elaborating on the principle in question or, in the case of imagery, by one or two instances of how the principle operates in specific dramatic texts. In order to touch the experience of as many readers as possible, I have drawn my examples from a broad sampling of Western drama, ranging from the ancient Greeks to contemporary film, and from acknowledged dramatic masterpieces to more popular recent works.

Part Two of this study demonstrates the practical application of the principles set forth in Part One, analyzing at length specific well-known dramatic texts according to these protocols, and developing a series of structural models clearly implicit in the theorems of Part One. It is my belief that these models (seven in number) are adequate for the description of all dramatic texts; in other words, that the dynamics of any play or screenplay will best be understood as conforming to one of these structural classes. Full-length analyses of six celebrated plays and one screenplay (each conforming to one of the major dynamic models) are preceded by brief italicized definitions of the model, together with general discussions of the mythical and modal tendencies of each dynamic type, and examples of various plays, screenplays, and opera libretti that fall into the same class.

The theory and resulting methodology are based on the single hypothesis elaborated in Theorem 1. In brief, this hypothesis proposes that dramas are essentially binary structures whose two parts function dialectically. One side of the argument objectifies a complex wish, while its complementary opposite side objectifies a proportionally complex fear. These opposed voices may be understood as the dominant and recessive functions of the authorial mind at the time of composition. The key to this argument lies in the drama's action and counteraction—a conflict which ultimately resolves itself into a radical distinction between those characters who are permitted to achieve their overriding will and those who are not. Consequently, the three-stage analytical process begins by addressing the drama's dialectic of action. Only after that critical task has been completed does it proceed to the supporting dialectic of imagery and symbolism, and thence to a descriptive abstraction of the results of the first two stages—the implicational dialectic. If the initial two steps are negotiated successfully, the resulting abstraction will give a clear, intellectually satisfying, and often astonishingly revealing picture of the superior and inferior voices objectified in the drama's argument. This last stage of analysis is particularly fascinating in connection with controversial works, or the works of dramatists about whose life and personality little is known.

The original hypothesis as to the drama's essentially binary form led to the discovery of several previously unnoticed characteristics of dramatic fantasy, and these new insights eventually became corollary theorems of signal import to the whole process of dialectical analysis. Among these was the realization that the drama's argument cannot be accurately determined without regarding as full members of the cast all offstage characters who serve as motives for onstage figures. Another discovery was that characters who change allegiance, and therefore shift between dialectical poles, always move in the same direction in any particular drama. This latter principle implied that there was a strictly limited number of dynamic possibilities within the drama's binary system, and this in turn led to the development of the seven structural models elaborated in Part Two. Evolving as offshoots of the original hypothesis, these new principles were not only theoretically interesting in themselves; their obvious analytical value also provided additional proof of the validity of that hypothesis.

During the many years of developing and refining this work I have introduced its theory and methods to undergraduates and postgraduates in English and Theatre Arts, both here and abroad, and have found it immensely useful not only because it enhances abstract understanding (though that would be justification enough), but also because it encourages a heightened respect for the objective integrity of the text, close attention to the specific details of the drama under discussion, spirited group dialogue, and, at the end, a refreshing consensus as to the nature of the drama's argument. Students can be taught to use the principles of dialectical analysis independently and to verify or correct each others' findings. I have also been called upon by two professional directors to employ this method in assisting them to stage plays both classical and modern at the Old Globe and Cassius Carter Theatres in San Diego, and was assured by them that it provided substantial help in making critical decisions as to overall production and design concepts, casting, the management of specific scenes, and the supplying of motives for actors.

These and many other signs encourage me to believe that the present study has the basic earmarks of a good theoretical model: it is based on a simple and elegant hypothesis, it throws a great deal of unexpected light on the subject of investigation, it yields results that are replicable, and it has practical value for workers in the field. Moreover, I am of the opinion that this model may also apply, with certain methodological adjustments, to the novel and other forms of dramatic literature, indeed, to anything with a plot.

It will be appreciated from the above that the work here described is "counter-trendy" in the extreme. It treads on the forbidden ground of intentionality in assuming that the dramatic text has inherent meaning, and in the belief that it is possible to abstract that meaning in a reasonably objective manner. Such projects have been anathema to the critical establishment for some little while now—although there seems to be growing reaction against systems of criticism that are fundamentally eccentric and therefore not replicable independently of their authors. I therefore submit the present study without apology, confident both in the validity of its governing hypothesis and in the efficacy of its resulting theorems and structural models as tools for general use.

Having said this, I should add that the present system embraces most of the principal critical modes—formalist, archetypal, psychological, socio-historical, and reader-response. Indeed, it could itself be regarded as a metacritical system, but at the opposite end from so-called high criticism and allying itself rather with the perspectives of Frank Ellis, Frederick Crews, and Gerald Graff (*Literature Against Itself*). Moreover, the present work offers a most sensitive way of "deconstructing" the text in that it is geared to the detection of inherent contradictions, which it assumes are fundamental to the nature of dramatic action and therefore key to the interpretation of the drama in general.

ACKNOWLEDGMENTS

In thanking those who contributed in various ways to the creation of this book, I must first of all acknowledge my deep obligation to Robert T. Knighton, Professor of English at the University of the Pacific, for reading this work in its various stages, offering painstaking and insightful advice on matters of both substance and style, and consistently encouraging me in this undertaking during the many seasons of its writing. To numerous others I am also variously and gratefully obliged: Minerva Marquis, who afforded me the opportunity to test my method with her on productions at the San Diego Old Globe and Cassius Carter Theatres; Diana Friedman for assistance in working out the dialectics of numerous plays and screenplays; and Seamus O'Connor, who was willing to discuss my analysis of his play, *The Cure*. I am equally indebted to Professor Mark D. Edwards of Stanford University for his comments on my analysis of *Oedipus the King*; Prior Robert Hale, Cam., O.S.B., for helping me to work out the structure of a screenplay and urging me to complete the manuscript; Marcia Price, Professor Glenna Matthews, and Jennie Graves for their helpful comments on portions of the text; and Susan Gilner for astute editorial suggestions. To the late Professor Norman Philbrick I will always be grateful for assisting me to resume my work at a point when that had apparently become impossible; and equally to Anita Sorel, the late Howard Laws, and the late Dr. Tom Smith for moral and material assistance at other critical junctures. For various other courtesies I am indebted to Edith Carlson, Christina Chanes, Professor Una Chaudhuri, Nancy Fox, Candice Fuhrman, Donald Holtzrichter, Richard and Lea Hunt, Kuang Li,

Deirdre Reynolds, Jerry Mabie, Anne O'Connor, William and Jean Rich, Donald Snowdon, James Templeton, and Maurice Wong. Nor must I omit to offer thanks to the many former students both here and in China who were my collaborators in this work throughout its development. My thanks also to the Editor-in-Chief of Mellen Research University Press, Dr. Robert West, for his helpful suggestions, keen wit, and gambler's instinct. And finally to my comrade and fellow windmill tilter, Fritz Hamilton, my gratitude for his good humor and unflagging encouragement.

Part I

The Dialectic

A truth in art is that whose contradictory is also true.

Oscar Wilde, *The Truth of Masks*

This spirit of duality which . . . distinguishes Dionysus and his realm, in its epiphany, from everything which is Olympian, returns over and over again in all the forms of his activities. . . . His duality has manifested itself to us in the antitheses of ecstasy and horror, infinite vitality and savage destruction; in the pandemonium in which silence is inherent; in the immediate presence which is at the same time absolute madness. All of his gifts and attendant phenomena give evidence of the sheer madness of his dual essence: prophecy, music, and finally wine, the flamelike herald of the god, which has in it both bliss and brutality. At the height of ecstasy all of these paradoxes suddenly unmask themselves and reveal their names to be Life and Death.

Walter F. Otto, *Dionysus Myth and Cult*

Duality is a basic quality of all natural processes in so far as they comprise two opposite phases or aspects. When integrated within a higher context, this duality generates a binary system based on the counterbalanced forces of two opposite poles. . . . The mystery of duality, which is at the root of all action, is manifest in any opposition of forces, whether spatial, physical, or spiritual. The primordial pairing of heaven and earth appears in most traditions as an image of primal opposition, the binary essence of natural life. . . . [The] eternal duality of Nature means that no phenomenon can ever represent a complete reality, but only one half of a reality. Each form has its analogous counterpart: man/woman; movement/rest; evolution/involution; right/left—and total reality embraces both. A synthesis is the result of a thesis *and* an antithesis. And true reality resides only in synthesis. . . . These [oppositions] are therefore not so much an expression of the duality of the forces involved, but rather of the *complementary* nature within the binary system.

Juan Eduardo Cirlot, *A Dictionary of Symbols*

There is only a limited number of plots, recurring down the ages, derived from an even more limited number of basic patterns—the conflicts, paradoxes, and predicaments inherent in man's condition. And if we continue the stripping game, we find that all these paradoxes and predicaments arise from conflicts between incompatible frames of experience or scales of value, illuminated in consciousness by the bisociative act.

Arthur Koestler, *The Creative Act*

INTRODUCTION

The first part of this study elaborates a general theory of dramatic structure and meaning. Its argument is presented in a series of theorems, beginning with the fundamental hypothesis and proceeding to twenty corollary principles. These propositions serve at once as theoretical framework for the whole and as methodological ground rules for the analysis of specific dramatic texts. Hence, there is virtually no separation in what follows between theory and practice; for although the general principles have been derived inductively from observation, their deductive value as analytical tools should become immediately apparent, provided one accepts the governing hypothesis as valid.

The theorems presented here are divided into three major sections corresponding to a three-stage process of textual analysis. Thus, the first group of propositions addresses the paramount subject of action (*praxis*), the second treats of supporting imagery and symbolism, while the third outlines a method of abstracting implication or motive from the parallel structures of action and imagery. A final theorem, implied in the preceding ones, proposes new, value-based criteria for assessing variations in reader response to individual texts.

Each of the initial "action" propositions (nos. 1–6) is followed by an essay expanding on the principle in question and adducing specific instances of its operation in the plots of various dramas. The subsequent theorems relating to imagery (nos. 7–13) are each followed by one or two brief illustrations of corresponding figurative processes in representative plays. The final propositions relating to the abstracting of implication (nos. 14–20) are presented baldly, without further commentary or example, because these theorems are more or less self-explanatory; moreover, this final stage of textual analysis will be elaborated in great detail in Part Two. The reader will thus notice an acceleration in the exposition of Part One as the text progresses from action through imagery to implication. This speeding-up not only reflects the decreasingly arduous nature of the theory and practice involved but also corresponds to an actual quickening of the exegetical process itself. For once the most difficult and crucial job of action-analysis has been accurately completed, the structures of imagery and implication begin to fall into place almost of their own accord. Everything hinges on the correct assessment of action.

I must emphasize that the theorems offered in Part One provide merely an introduction to a critical approach whose full development and validation are reserved for Part Two, where these principles are systematically applied in detailed analyses of specific dramatic texts. Thus, matters which may seem at the outset somewhat novel or abstract (despite the illustrations) will come together later in an orderly, concrete, and highly pragmatic fashion. If Part One is the foundation, Part Two is the finished structure; neither is fully comprehensible without the other.

DIALECTIC OF ACTION

THEOREM 1
HYPOTHESIS: ACTION/COUNTERACTION

Dramatic fantasy constitutes the projection of an internal argument. This argument is essentially binary in character, expressing the tension between opposing yet complementary mental functions. COROLLARY 1: During the course of the fantasy one side of the argument eventually asserts its dominance over the other. The dominant voice speaks for the superior function of the authorial personality and expresses a complex wish, while the recessive voice speaks for the inferior function and expresses a proportionately complex fear. COROLLARY 2: Those characters of the drama who are permitted to achieve their overriding wish make up the fantasy's dominant function; those who are not allowed to attain their overriding objective comprise its recessive function. The former are here designated as "protagonists," the latter as "antagonists."

Rationale. It is a truism that drama cannot exist without conflict. Such conflict may be regarded literally as a dispute between the contending characters of the play's action, or more precisely as the representation of an argument within the mind of the dramatist at the time of composition. In this second aspect dramatic conflict must be understood as an objective correlative for an internal struggle which originates not with the characters of the play but with their author. That the play's argument or plot is fundamentally the projection of a spiritual struggle within the soul of its creator was clearly understood by medieval and early Renaissance thinkers, who as a matter of course used the Latin phrase *bellum intestinum* (internal war) or the Greek *psychomachia* (mental conflict) to designate such literary expression of inward strife.

During the late Renaissance, however, the concept of *psychomachia* began to drop out of currency owing, ironically, to the development of psychological realism, which deflected attention away from the spiritual struggle of the dramatist to focus instead on the spiritual struggles of his characters. Over time writers became less interested in the allegorical nature of their fictional personages than in treating them as if they were in fact human beings, to be invested with all the complex social and psychological motives impelling actual mortals. Instead of asking auditors to believe in the reality of the general principles their characters stood for (The Flesh, The Five Wits, Temptation, The Devil, and the like), playwrights began asking them to believe in the reality of the characters as *independent agents*. This shift in dramaturgical focus no doubt seemed a great aesthetic advance to societies caught up in the ambition of the new natural science to describe phenomena with rigorous objectivity. That such objective treatment, with its focus on external realities, should pass over into the delineation of dramatic characters was natural enough, as indeed was the tendency to ignore the subjective determinants of literary fantasy.

The "science" of dramatic realism, as it later developed, was especially prone to deny these subjective factors because, in its passion for the appearance of "reality," it tended to forget the "as if" clause that must attend any mimetic illusion. With a subtle and no doubt unconscious hypocrisy, dramatic realism demanded of its audience a "willing suspension of disbelief" in order to invest *virtual* beings with the dignity of *actual* ones. Thus lured into the trap of psychologizing about fictional personages as if they possessed the motives of flesh and blood humans, spectators and critics naturally began to ignore motives that could be inferred from analysis of the dramatic structure as a whole, and as an allegory for a deeper, more subjective conflict. In short, realism forced the dramatic character to "take the rap" for his author. Henceforth playwrights could, and usually did, deny that their characters referred to any meaning beyond themselves; authors could even deny their own comprehension of that limited meaning, because the characters were, after all, mysteriously independent agents. From here it was but a short way to the belief that the dramatic text and its characters possessed no truly comprehensible motives, aside from those projected onto them by the reader or spectator. This isogesic project reduced the text to a sort of Rorschach test, and the briefly discredited school of "impressionistic criticism" was not only revived but ultimately apotheosized in the name of reader response theory. In this light, the abandonment of the quest for inherent textual meaning by modern projective criticism can be understood, at least in part, as the logical culmination of realism's misdirected search for motive in character rather than author, and in its concentration on action at the literal rather than the allegorical level.

The ancient notion that drama is a product, not of more or less "real" characters acting somehow autonomously, but rather of an argument (*dialektikos*) within the mind of the playwright was revived in the nineteenth century by Hegel. "The true course of dramatic development," he asserted, "consists in the annulment of *contradictions* viewed as such, in the reconciliation of the forces which alternately strive to negate each other in their conflict."[1] The key phrase here is "*contradictions* viewed as such," for it implies that the dramatist is aware, at some level, that the argument between his characters objectifies contradictions within his own soul, that the whole dramatic enterprise is in fact the allegory of an internal conflict or *bellum intestinum*. The forces (or characters) "which alternately strive to negate each other in their conflict" are thus schematic projections of interior forces struggling to negate each other in the author's consciousness. Hegel goes on to say that

> Dramatic action . . . is not confined to the simple and undisturbed
> execution of a definite purpose, but depends throughout on conditions of
> collision . . . and leads therefore to actions and reactions, which in their
> turn call for some further resolution of conflict and disruption.[2]

Here the modern philosopher proposes a critical modification to Aristotle's famous dictum that "the soul of drama is action." A dramatic action must not only have a beginning, middle, and end, or, as we should say, a "through-line" focussed upon the purposeful deeds of a central character; it must also have a "counteraction," a definite collision of forces in order to make it truly dramatic. Thus, the story of Oedipus only makes theatrical sense because the definite purpose of the young king is in direct conflict with the equally definite purpose of other characters in the drama, whose spokesman is Tiresias. And the collision that results from these cross-purposes must ultimately be understood as the objectification of spiritual contradictions "viewed as such" in the mind of the dramatist.

---

[1]Friedrich Hegel, *Hegel on Tragedy. Edited, with an Introduction by Anne and Henry Paolucci* (New York: Doubleday), 1962, p. 71. See also pp. 12–16, 18, 45, 64 ff, 84, 89, 98, 112–129.
[2]Hegel, p. 65.

Hegel postulated two ways in which the collision of forces at the center of a drama may be "annulled" and the argument thus brought to a satisfactory conclusion. The first way is a "reconciliation" between the contending sides. The philosopher favored this outcome because it satisfied his desire to find a synthetic resolution for all dialectical oppositions. Nevertheless, he was forced to concede that in some dramas "the twofold vindication of the mutually conflicting aspects is no doubt retained, but the *one-sided mode* is canceled."[3] In other words, of the two diametrically opposed dramatic impulses, the one sensed as unbalanced and therefore dysfunctional is somehow overcome, rejected rather than assimilated.

Reintroducing the medieval concept of drama as a collision between polar forces or attitudes, Hegel thus added two corollary postulates: first, that the fantasized argument (plot) seeks a "reconciliation" or compromise, and second, that if such synthesis does not occur, the recalcitrant, unacceptable force will be destroyed or, as he put it, "canceled." Tantalizingly close to the mark, Hegel's theory nevertheless fails to account satisfactorily for the reason why dramatic conflict seeks only one of two possible resolutions—synthesis or cancellation.

It was Freud who supplied the answer. Working inductively rather than deductively, studying the dream rather than the drama, Freud came to the conclusion that nocturnal fantasies "are invariably the product of a conflict" and that they therefore constitute "a kind of compromise structure" between opposing impulses.[4] Similar to Hegel's observations regarding dramatic fantasy, Freud's theory went further to posit a motivating force behind the conflict expressed in dreams. This force, he determined, is always a *wish*. Conflict arises because of internal resistance to the wish in the form of guilt—hence, the usual compromise structure that permits the wish to be expressed only in the distorted and disguised form peculiar to the language of dreams. Occasionally, however, in the nocturnal fantasies of children and in the less guilt-arousing dreams of adults, the wish easily overcomes all resistance and consequently appears as a transparent fulfillment. This process is even more obvious in the patently wishful character of day-dreams.[5]

---

[3]Hegel, p. 71. See also pp. 49, 87.

[4]Sigmund Freud, *An Outline of Psycho-analysis. Translated and Newly Edited by James Strachey* (New York: Norton), 1969, p. 27.

[5]Sigmund Freud, *The Interpretation of Dreams. Translated from the German and Edited by James Strachey* (New York: Avon), 1965, p. 155ff.

Freud's theory therefore makes room for two basic types of dream. In the first the wish expresses itself in a cryptic synthetic formation owing to high internal resistance. In the second the motivating desire is clearly fulfilled because of low resistance. This is strikingly parallel to Hegel's theory of drama, for the latter's concept of reconciliation between the contradictory forces can be expressed in Freudian terms as a compromise structure resulting from the collision between a wish and the resistance to it, while the idea of cancellation of the one-sided mode can be translated as an overcoming of relatively weak resistance by a forceful wish. Moreover, both theorists emphasize the allegorically meaningful nature of human fantasy, whether nocturnal or diurnal. The dream is not visited upon the dreamer, willy-nilly, by mysterious external forces, any more than the dramatist's characters wander into his consciousness from the outside as independent agents (no matter how stubbornly Pirandello would have us believe otherwise). In both cases, the opposing characters and images are understood to be metaphors for a conflict that reflects the deepest personal aspirations and fears of dreamer or dramatist.

Despite these suggestive parallels between the Hegelian and Freudian theories, it might seem premature to extend Freud's hypothesis regarding dreams to the highly conscious fantasy called drama, had not my own study of dramatic structure already led me to the conviction that plays also invariably express a wish, and that this wish always meets with resistance—the source of all dramatic conflict. Furthermore, my investigations have led me to the conclusion that, although there are several specific patterns of dramatic action and counteraction, each of these dynamics falls into but one of two broader categories: first, the simple bi-polar collision in which the wish overcomes resistance either by sheer force of weight or else by effecting advantageous alterations in the balance of power; and second, the synthetic dynamic that permits the wish to emerge dominant only after exposing the terms of the original argument to have been false from the beginning.

Aside from their peculiar idioms, dream and dramatic fantasy seem to differ largely in the fact that the majority of the latter develop the simple two-sided collision from which the wish emerges dominant with little or no modification, thereby canceling its antagonist. True synthetic or compromise formations are scarcer in drama than in dream, as Freud himself hinted when he claimed that "what determines the production of the imaginary figure in waking life is the impression which the new structure itself is intended to make."[6] This may be paraphrased for our purposes by saying that, because he possesses greater conscious awareness of the effect he desires to produce, the dramatist must in some measure comprehend his own wish. And because he does so, the always implicit obstacle or resistance to that wish is also apprehended with greater clarity and therefore more readily marked for defeat. As a result, dramatic fantasies usually constitute more obvious examples of wish-fulfill-ments than do most dreams. Yet Freud may have been overly sanguine about the fiction writer's clarity of intention, for drama finds many ways to disguise (or hide from) its true wish—notably by the employment of irony, in which the victors are made to appear unacceptable in varying degrees. However, this fact does not vitiate the hypothesis that dramatic fantasy expresses a wish; it merely indicates that, as with most dreams, many waking fantasies seek means by which to disguise their essentially wishful nature.

I have therefore accepted the Hegelian and Freudian concepts of fantasy as a collision between dialectically opposed mental forces, and have also followed Freud's additional lead in assuming that these forces objectify (1) a wish, and (2) the resistance to it. I must now supplement these postulates by proposing my own central hypothesis, namely, that the dramatic fantasy's motivating wish always emerges victorious, always overcomes the resisting opposition. In psychological terms, dramatic action thus constitutes a successful battle by the ego-syntonic function (conscious wish) for dominance over its opposed recessive function (resistance or feared obstacle). In plain theatrical language, this struggle between dominant and recessive functions means that the entire cast of a play divides itself into just two camps: those who eventually dominate and those who are eventually dominated. From an economic point of view, therefore, no drama contains more than two "characters"; for the dominant and recessive functions operate within the closed world of the fantasy as single dynamic principles. The individual characters of the drama thus comprise fragments or "splits" of one or the other of these two functional units.

Characters become members of the dominant unit if their author permits them to achieve their overriding wish, or of the recessive unit if he does not allow them to achieve that wish. This is so because the wishful impulses of the fantasized conflict

---

[6]Freud, *The Interpretation of Dreams*, p. 359.

are objectified, appropriately, by those who succeed in attaining their goals, while the fearful impulses are objectified by those who do not succeed in so doing. The collision of such blocs constitutes the essence of all dramatic conflict; and the inevitable victory of one warring faction over the other can best be understood as the symbolic triumph of one syndrome, or constellation of related impulses, over a dialectically opposed syndrome within the mind of the dramatist at the time of composition.

Sometimes plays include at the outset a third functional unit, whose possession is the issue at context between the primary combatants, or whose modus vivendi represents an acceptable alternative to an otherwise stalemated conflict. But in such "triangular" situations this apex unit invariably comes to rest in one of the two major warring camps, or else itself assumes the role of dominant function by drawing one of the initial contestants to its side. Therefore, all plays, including those which begin in triangular configurations, remain fundamentally bi-polar, with one of the two dialectical forces ultimately dominant at the end of action. Part Two of this study will elaborate on the various structural possibilities within this binary system, including the several initially triangular situations. My present task, however, is to expand on the principle of dominant and recessive functional units.

To suggest, as I have done, that the dramatis personae of any play should be grouped into just two general categories—the victorious and the vanquished—may at first seem an injuriously reductive proposal. And it may appear to be rubbing salt in the wound to add that, from an economic point of view, no play contains more than two "characters" or "functions." Yet although a masterful dramatist may stamp each of his characters with unique and distinguishing features, even his most lifelike personages do appear, in the final analysis, to represent nothing more nor less than fragments of a single attitude or set of values. Consequently, by dividing a play's cast into victors and vanquished we will discover that the characters comprising any one of these two economic units do in fact share many essential qualities in common. Moreover, we will notice that these features always stand in clear dialectical opposition to the principal qualities shared by the characters of the opposing economic unit. The most important common attribute of the victors, of course, is that they all succeed in attaining their overriding motive. But beyond this, the dominant characters also share many other secondary attributes—beliefs, moods, mannerisms, attitudes of mind and body—that permit them to emerge victorious from the struggle. Thus, not far beneath the surface of these somewhat differentiated "personalities," we will begin to make out the features of a single, larger "character." This figure is none other than the dominant side of the authorial personality, fulfilling its wish symbolically by projecting it onto these externalized creatures of fantasy and permitting them to achieve "their" wish. The recessive or shadow side of the authorial mind, its fears and dreaded attributes, is simultaneously projected onto the opposing group of characters and, through them, symbolically suppressed by denying them the fulfillment of "their" wish.

What, then, is the most expedient method of distinguishing the dominant from the recessive characters, of segregating those who achieve their overriding wish from those who do not? Since the abstraction of common qualities for each separate functional unit can only occur after the dust of battle has settled and the lines between victor and vanquished have been clearly demarcated, it will be necessary to examine the actions of each character separately in order to determine his ultimate allegiance; for the loyalty of a character may sometimes alter during the course of the drama, and his overriding motive as well as his success or failure in attaining it will therefore depend most critically on his final actions relative to the other characters. The job of "dialectical placement" presents fewer difficulties than might be expected because, unlike human beings, dramatic characters have no will of their own. Although parts of a larger, more complex motivational structure, the individual characters are in themselves relatively simple: they remain fragments of an argument within the mind of the dramatist, who usually invests even the most complicated of his fictional personages with but one driving wish. This is true also of naturalistic drama that attempts to create the illusion of complexity inherent in actual life; for whatever an author may hint as to manifold and convoluted motives for a specific character, the operational motive invariably remains single, and can always be determined by careful attention to the character's action. The most expedient methods of dialectical placement through action analysis will be set forth in the following theorems. Before proceeding to that subject, however, I should like to propose a modification of conventional terminology, at least for the purposes of the present system.

Because my major concern is the distinction between the dominant characters who are permitted to attain their overriding wish, and the recessive characters who are not allowed to do so, it would be convenient to have a one-word generic name for each of these two types. Although "winner" and "loser" might seem simple and straightforward enough, I prefer to avoid these terms because they are loaded with emotional resonances that can be distracting, even misleading in the present context. Instead, I have become accustomed to using the more neutral terms "protagonist" and "antagonist" for dominant and recessive character, respectively. Yet because even these venerable words are only relatively neutral, some further discussion of them will be helpful at this point.

To the ancient Greeks "protagonist" meant "first combatant," that is, the first actor to enter the stage during a performance. "Antagonist" meant "second combatant," or second actor to enter. In the time of Aeschylus, when all the parts in a play were represented by only two actors who changed characters by leaving the stage and changing masks, it was important to keep track of who entered first and second in order to know which actor was playing which role. That need has long since vanished; and two millennia later the term "protagonist" has come to assume the meaning of "central character" or "hero," while "antagonist" has come to denote "adversary."

Unfortunately, the current meaning of "protagonist" is extremely muddy and imprecise because its equivalents of "central character" and "hero" are equally so. Aside from disagreements over which character is truly the "hero" of a particular piece, and the dangerous tendency to identify the largest role with the author's persona, we are left with the awkward fact that some leading figures triumph in the dramatic collision while others of like prestige fall to defeat. For every victorious Sigismundo, El Cid, and Mirabell, one can always oppose an unlucky Faustus, Antony, or Wallenstein, who are also protagonists in the popular sense. Conversely, the victors of many plays cannot be accounted protagonists or heroes in any conventional reckoning. Indeed, we have no really adequate term to designate such "secondary" figures as Fortinbras in *Hamlet*, Cassio in *Othello*, Aricia in *Phaedra*, or Mrs. Elvsted in *Hedda Gabler*, even though these characters head the dominant units of the plays in which they appear. "Supporting character" will not do because, economically speaking, such figures do not support, they command.

The term "antagonist," as it is normally employed, likewise presents ambiguities; for although it has the denotation of "adversary," it carries no indication whatever of adversary *to whom*. Consequently, both sides of the dramatic collision may be antagonists to each other. But although a protagonist may be an antagonist to any other character, his adversaries can never be protagonists. In other words, the leading character may have the glory of functioning as both protagonist and antagonist simultaneously, while his opponents may not. This ridiculous state of affairs would not exist if "protagonist" and "antagonist" had not become quite useless as precise terms for analytical discourse. Yet it would be a pity if such venerable and euphonious words were to wind up on the junk heap of the lexically exhausted.

At the risk, therefore, of raising the eyebrows of theatre historians and etymologists, I have chosen to continue employing "protagonist" in the sense of dominant character or victor, and "antagonist" in the sense of recessive character or loser. Thus invested with new meaning, these terms provide immediate and precise information as to the dialectical status of the characters to whom they are applied. Used in this way as antonyms, "protagonist" and "antagonist" also regain something of their original meaning of "combatant." Moreover, stripped to their root word of "agon," denoting "combat" or "conflict," these terms bare the sense of collision between dialectically opposed forces which is the quintessence of dramatic action.

THEOREM 2
THE ORDER OF ENDS

A drama's dialectical meaning depends upon its ending, that is, upon the specific composition of its bi-polarity at closure. The alignment of its characters (and of the images that accompany them) in either the dominant or recessive units as they are finally segregated provides the key to the fantasy's wishful and fearful motives. Great care must therefore be exercised to determine the ultimate allegiance of each and every character at the end of action; and special vigilance is required in the case of characters whose last acts occur off-stage or prior to the drama's concluding scenes.

Rationale. Aristotle's laconic statement that plays must have a beginning, a middle, and an end has perplexed many readers of the *Poetics*, partly because the point seems too obvious for comment, and also, paradoxically, because much drama since Chekhov appears to have neither beginning nor end but only a sort of middle, during the course of which nothing is truly concluded. In an era that could regard as emblematic of its temper such apparently plotless dramas as *Waiting for Godot*, the ancient insistence on some kind of dramatic resolution, or even a clearly defined argument, seemed somewhat irrelevant. But the irrelevance, like the plotlessness, was only seeming. For almost any drama, no matter how apparently obscure or devoid of obvious conflict, will yield under attentive scrutiny a concrete and definable opposition of forces; in short, an argument.

I say "almost any drama," for a small minority of works written in dialogue fail to produce an argument, properly speaking, but instead employ the outward clothing of dramatic form to express an essentially lyrical statement uncomplicated by conflict. This is particularly true of certain one-act plays and monologues, whose brevity permits lyrical utterance or self-revelation for its own sake, without the necessity of developing a radical conflict in order to sustain interest. Other theatre pieces, such as Buñuel's film *The Discrete Charms of the Bourgeoisie*, dramatize a series of thematically connected anecdotes which, however "dramatic" in themselves, fail to bring all the characters of the various sketches together into a single action and counteraction. And finally, there is the serial drama or "soap opera," which, like Aristotle's dragon, is so long that we cannot see the beast's head and tail at the same time; nor, if the producers have their way, shall we ever see its tail. All such works usually imply a dialectic of some sort; but because their arguments either fail to manifest themselves directly in action, lack a unified plot, or attempt to sustain an action without end, these types are best analyzed by methods suited to poetry, psychology, or sociology rather than to drama proper. It is most important, however, to emphasize that such plotless works are exceptions to the rule. The vast majority of dramas, including most short plays and monologues, do in fact develop a radical collision at the level of action.

The outcome of this collision, the final alignment of characters in either the dominant or recessive camps, puts the seal on the drama's dialectical meaning. For having once determined the order of ends at the critical level of action, we are then in a position to discern the action's supporting figurative opposition; and when these two steps have been completed, it will be possible, by deriving the polarities of both action and imagery, to abstract the drama's motivational opposition. However, the initial task of establishing a drama's radical collision by separating protagonist from antagonist, dominant character from recessive, is not always a simple one. Much stage and screen drama has become highly cryptic, owing in part to the influence of expressionism, and in part to the post-Freudian awareness that, like any other kind of fantasy, dramatic fiction lies open to analytical methods that may uncover sensitive material. On the whole, modern drama has become more secretive and defended, thus often making it harder to draw a distinction between victors and vanquished. Yet such obscurities have the salutary effect of forcing us to be more attentive to the fundamental ingredient of the art, namely, action.

Now this action cannot but contain a beginning, a middle (in the sense of episodes or scenes), and an end—an end not only for the drama as a whole but more specifically for each separate character in the action. The character's ultimate allegiance is the critical issue, for a drama reveals its motives by the way in which it achieves closure; and the final segregation of the characters into dominant or recessive camps provides the essential clue to the work's wishful and fearful impulses, for which its polarities of action and imagery stand as metaphors. Analysis of a play's structure must therefore determine, foremost among all other things, the allegiance of every character at the final curtain.

Accurate determination of each character's final position relative to the opposing forces of the dramatic collision may be hindered by several kinds of distraction peculiar to various sorts of plays. I shall touch upon the most common of these difficulties separately, reserving for last the thorny problem of irony and the even more vexing temptation to fantasize beyond the end of action.

Perhaps the most common obstruction to the ordering of ends is the tendency of many characters to disappear before the drama's conclusion. Because these slippery figures are often minor personages, their failure to appear at the grand sorting out of the final scenes may easily go unnoticed. Yet their status as mere supporting characters does not warrant neglect; for each addition, however small, to the camps of protagonist or antagonist contributes to full, accurate derivation of the essential characteristics common to each of the colliding forces. Moreover, some figures who disappear before the final curtain are not minor at all; consequently, their omission from a dialectical chart of action would gravely impair understanding of the traits common to the camp to which they belong.

Shakespeare's *Macbeth* affords specimens of both major and minor disappearing characters in the figures of Banquo and Fleance. Banquo is murdered in Act Three, and last appears as a ghost in Act Four. Although his prominence in the first half of the action makes it improbable that he should be forgotten entirely in the final reckoning, the elapse of nine highly charged scenes after his last appearance might well obscure the specifics of that moment, especially as it is represented only in dumb show. Yet the vision of Banquo's ghost in a procession of eight future kings establishes him as the ancestor of a new royal house, thus presaging the frustration of Macbeth's ambition to retain the throne for himself and his descendants. Moreover, Banquo's last appearance places him squarely among the action's protagonists by showing that, within the Christian ethos of the drama, death does not constitute defeat for those who successfully resist temptation. Banquo's son, Fleance, appears only three times during the entire play; yet the child's escape from the murderers in his second scene, and his appearance as crowned king in the dumb show of Act Four, also foreshadow the usurper's downfall. Moreover, the boy's tender age will contribute to the implicational term "innocence," a key derivation qualifying the godly protagonists of this tragedy. Neglect of either of these disappearing characters would therefore considerably diminish our view of the play's dominant function at the primary level of action, and thus later constrict our picture of the drama's dialectics of imagery and implication.

The task of establishing an accurate order of ends always becomes more acute in plays with large casts, not only because such works often contain disappearing characters, both major and minor, but also because in the crush of events that ends an epic drama it is often most difficult to keep track of each character's final commitment relative to the work's radical conflict. Shakespeare's history plays provide sufficiently tough object lessons for the sorting out of ultimate allegiances at the bustling end of action. Thus, although Bagot, Surrey, and Another Lord may not be the most memorable figures in *Richard II*, special attention to their final commitments to the camps headed by Richard or Bolingbroke will add details that complete the overall picture of the protagonists' and antagonists' units.

Another type of character who often eludes accurate final placement is he who pays lip-service to one cause while supporting another by deeds. More shall be said on this subject in a later section; but it is prudent to observe here that in such cases the ultimate betrayal may be forgotten after all the ringing protestations of initial fealty, especially if the character in question be endowed with attractive qualities. *Richard II* again supplies an example in the curious figure of the Duke of York, who baulks at deserting Richard's standard for that of the usurper, Bolingbroke. York makes many declarations in favor of the Divine Right of Kings, and at first courageously resists the uprising; yet in the end he bows to the inevitable and becomes Bolingbroke's man. His dialectical shift is so quiet that it could easily be ignored; however, his guilty apostasy serves to highlight qualities in Richard so dysfunctional as to make even the staunchest pleader for the Divine Right desert the royal standard. A similar apostasy in Brecht's *Galileo* will be overlooked if one does not sufficiently credit the title-character's recantation and return to the fold of the Church. His emphatic statement, "Any man who does what I have done cannot be tolerated in the ranks of science," drives home the central fact that Galileo has actively betrayed his science by treating it as a commodity in the marketplace, that his theories have been formulated primarily in the service of a bourgeois love of comfort. Therefore, no amount of admiration for the physicist's genius, his lust for life, or even his belated but impotent self-awareness should obscure the point that Galileo has compromised the forces of progress and by so doing has become one of the chief antagonists of the drama. In the final event he remains, albeit guiltily, on the side of the Church, with its fear of being destroyed by the New Science. Failure to assess Galileo's deeds realistically and to observe the end of action leads to a sentimental perversion of Brecht's play, and makes a hero out of an anti-hero.

Equivocators like York and Galileo always render the dialectical ordering of ends more troublesome because they begin in one camp and move to the opposing side. Although I shall treat the subject of shifting characters at large in a later section, it is well to offer advance caution in the final placement of characters who switch allegiance during the course of action. Such wariness is particularly advisable in the analysis of dramas of suspense or attrition, where defections often occur so early in the action that subsequent events may cause them to be forgotten entirely.

The difficulties of placement by ends of action touched upon so far appear relatively trifling by comparison to the problems that arise in the analysis of ironic drama, which depicts the triumph of morally dubious or even repugnant characters. While in its milder forms irony produces a bittersweet flavor by representing the protagonists as all-too-human, more intense irony grows less palatable by conceding victory to figures who are thoroughly malign and sub-human. The more acrid the irony, the more readers or spectators hesitate, on both logical and moral grounds, to grant victory to symbolic forces of such degraded nature, to an argument so unsatisfactorily resolved; and this natural reluctance is uniformly encouraged by writers of irony, most of whom seem equally repelled by the characters dominating their fantasy. Thus, a sort of double resistance is set up at both the sending and receiving ends against recognizing irony for what it is, namely, a negative wish.

In order to avoid the confusion in dialectical placement that this sort of denial encourages, it is necessary to take two somewhat unusual precautions. First, we must temporarily "bracket" our private response to both protagonist and antagonist; that is, we must suspend, insofar as possible, all emotional, moral, or aesthetic judgments in the face of an argument of which both sides will be found unacceptable in some important respects. Second, we must revert to the most elementary criterion for determining victors and vanquished: *He who is permitted to accomplish his will, no matter whether we approve of him or not, must be numbered among the protagonists.* The corollary to this proposition is that certain other characters will have to be placed with the antagonists, even though they may possess appealing qualities that are nevertheless represented as dysfunctional in a mad world. The pathetic romanticism of Blanche DuBois is not an advantageous quality in a fictive society brutalized by the crass materialism of Stanley Kowalski. Nor does the fact that a play's entire cast may inhabit an infernal scene, allowing less freedom of action than that possessed by the most miserable soul in the audience, invalidate the principle that one functional unit will eventually dominate in the sense of retaining greater control. One has only to recall Genet's *Deathwatch*, in which, though all the characters are imprisoned, the manacled Green Eyes still manages to accomplish his perverse will. Or Sarte's *No Exit*, whose principals find themselves trapped forever in a "hell" whose management consists of the off-stage "they" and "their" visible representative, the Valet. Even such cryptic pieces as Beckett's *Endgame*, with its garbage can dwellings, or Robbe–Grillet's *Last Year at Marienbad*, with its suffocating baroque corridors and apparent plotlessness, will be obliged to reveal the secret of who ultimately dominates, who is dominated.

The writer of irony may not consciously approve of the characters dominating his fantasy; yet, ugly though they are, these commanding figures objectify the superior side of an internal argument for which no better answer has been found. In this sense, irony constitutes a gesture of despair, a concession to impulses and attitudes sensed as degrading. There are, as we shall see, certain forms of irony that end in stalemates so obvious that they strongly imply a synthetic third term which provides an acceptable alternative to equally undesirable antinomies (see Part II, Ch. 7). However, most ironic dramas end not in stalemates but in checkmates. That we may disapprove of black, white, or both, must not make us inattentive to the moves, the pieces taken, or especially the endgame during which the superior force closes in for the kill.

Undoubtedly the most serious impediment to separating victors from vanquished according to their final deeds lies in the natural inclination of readers and spectators to continue fantasizing beyond the drama's concluding scene, thus wishfully altering its true ending. The more powerful and disturbing the play, the more ambiguous the fates of its principal characters, the greater our desire to append imaginary sequels to the dramatist's own fantasy. Will Dr. Stockman be able to survive and re-educate the youth of his corrupted town? Will Nora create a new and better life for herself once she has left her doll's house? Will Barbara and Cusins be able to modify Undershaft's crude philosophy of power? All such questions, and the various possible fantasized answers to them, though pleasant and perhaps educational diversions for the uncritical spectator, are quite inadmissible for analytical purposes because they constitute independent poetic acts that have nothing to do, strictly speaking, with the drama under consideration. For to project a continuance of action beyond a play's conclud-ing scene is to disrupt the final stasis that determines the work's ultimate dialectical structure, and as a consequence to falsify that structure at all levels, from action through imagery to implication.

Similarly, the introduction into stage directions of novelistic description or rationalization, a technique for which Shaw is notorious, can be truly dramatic only when capable of translation into visible action or scenery. Otherwise such digressive material is quite immaterial—at best a hint for directors and actors, at worst a secret the audience cannot share. Moreover, this sort of intrusion often lays down a smokescreen which structural analysis must blow away in order to render visible the concrete details of dramatic action, and most particularly the order of ends. The same necessity for caution applies to lengthy philosophical prologues and epilogues which may induce us to view the action and its supposed implications in a way that is not really supported by the drama's authentic structure. Thus, in his preface to *The Devil's Disciple*, Shaw claims that, as an Irishman, he has been able to take an impartial view of the American War of Independence; yet the action of his play reveals an author overwhelmingly sympathetic with the Americans' cause and equally outraged, as perhaps only an Irish author could be, at the arrogance of the British imperialists. Although Shaw's arch claim to neutrality is transparently disingenuous, other dramatists seem truly embarrassed by their own fantasies; as a consequence they often defensively manipulate their readers into a course of analogizing that distracts them from the actual events onstage, and especially from the ends of action upon which rest the play's real implications, the author's true motives. "The end crowns all."

THEOREM 3
DEEDS, NOT WORDS

The dramatic character's overriding wish must be deduced from a realistic assessment of his actions, just as his success or failure at attaining that wish must be determined from his deeds within the larger context of action and counteraction. Errors in dialectical placement will otherwise often result from taking too seriously either the character's own rationalizations for his actions, or statements made about him by other characters. Facts must in all cases take precedence over claims, deeds over words.

Rationale. Man, according to Aristotle, is the sum of his actions. That is why the choruses of Greek tragedy repeatedly warn against judging a person's life to be happy or otherwise until the last of its events be accounted for. Such philosophical realism—the assessment of moral character on the basis of actions—has been undermined in large part by long centuries of Christian belief that a person's thoughts and intentions are of equal importance with his deeds; that if he is guilty of murder in the imagination, he is as culpable before heaven as if he had in fact committed the offense. Nineteenth-century romanticism contributed to this attitude by favoring the vagaries of the imagination over fact, and by elevating the inner life of the spirit above the mundane behavior of individuals in the humdrum routine of daily life. Nor did twentieth-century existentialist thought entirely forswear the romantic tradition, for it continued to focus on the individual as creator of his own ethical norms in the face of a universe perceived to be indifferent and therefore, ultimately, absurd. In sum, we have long been schooled in a cult of the personality that taught us to judge men at best by their individual styles, and at worst by their mere expression of intention.

As any competent jurist knows, however, intentions expressed in words are of secondary importance to the cardinal *facts* of the case; *what* was done, to whom, by whom? Only after these questions have been answered does the issue of motive assume the slightest importance. The "reason" for an act must come last in sequence because motives without consequent actions are of no practical significance in a social context. This, of course, reflects the attitude of the jurist, not the detective. The latter may interest himself in character and possible motive as clues leading to a determination of the person (agent) who committed the crime (act). But the detective would be out of business were it not for criminal acts, and we should all be in jail were the motive alone sufficient cause for arrest. Only after crime and criminal (act and agent) have been clearly established beyond reasonable doubt (verdict) may the court allow its assessment of motive or intention to affect its final determination of the degree of guilt (sentence).

The realistic stress upon act, as distinguished from agent or motive, is as essential to the analysis of drama as it is to the law. The dramatist must project his internal argument through characters in active conflict if the spectator or reader is to derive satisfaction from his investment of concentration; and the practical implications of this conflict must be demonstrated lest the argument remain purely academic. Thus, when Aristotle rated "action" above both "character" and "thought" (i.e., the character's thought expressed in dialogue), he meant that the moral quality of the dramatic character resides primarily in his deeds rather than in his "personality" or in his verbalized rationalization of those deeds. Therefore, in order to assess the actions of dramatic characters with exactitude, it is necessary to assume an attitude of legalistic realism; for the moment we must put aside our ingrained fascination with character and motive in order to concentrate, initially, on deeds.

This is not to suggest that acts are motiveless, or that motives are unimportant; indeed, since the dramatic character's success or failure at achieving his overriding wish provides the primary criterion for dialectical placement, it is obligatory in every instance to determine the precise nature of that wish. The difficulty is that a dramatic character does not always openly express his driving wish; on the contrary, his own words may disguise, or the words of other characters may falsify his true intent, thus forcing us to rely on the touchstone for determination of motive in all cases, namely, action.

One can adduce no more blatant instance of focusing on words rather than deeds than the great number of essays attempting to picture Hamlet as a character disinclined to action. Such misguided labors were the result of taking the Prince at his word when he says that he is a procrastinator, given over to thought when deeds are required. The *facts* that during the course of the play Hamlet concludes a pact of silence, feigns madness, murders Polonius, drives Ophelia to her grave, eludes two men hired to shadow him, forges state documents, escapes a band of pirates, browbeats his mother, directs a stage play, engages in fisticuffs with Laertes (whom he later kills in a duel), and finally stabs King Claudius to death, cause one to marvel that in the pauses between these activities he has time or energy left to descant on being a dawdler. Hamlet's own warning, "Seems, seems, nay I know not seems," might have been taken as a useful hint by critics who judged him to be irresolute because his own statements *seemed* to indicate that he was so.

This is not to say that dialogue and action are categorically separate. Speech does indeed sometimes constitute action, but then only in the legal sense of incitement or conspiracy; that is, whenever it demonstrably effects subsequent events. Thus, while Lady Macbeth's hectoring her reluctant husband into committing regicide constitutes dramatic action of the first order because her exhortations are successful, Macbeth's own arguments against the deed are ultimately invalidated by his eventual complicity in the murder. Yet these examples seem rather obvious by comparison to many others in which, by sheer weight of words, characters tend to elude accurate dialectical placement on the basis of their deeds. One such instance is *King Lear*'s Edmund, whose lengthy and memorable asides openly advocating villainy, coupled with his many real crimes, may completely overshadow his brief dying act of contrition. Yet the sincerity of Edmund's "Some good I mean to do, / Despite of mine own nature" is immediately validated by his revelation of the death writ for Lear and Cordelia, and also by the offer of his sword as token for the remanding of the warrant. Thus, the erstwhile villain's final words constitute positive action because the contrition is accompanied by atonement. Failure to plot Edmund's dialectical shift, however sudden and "unmotivated," to the side of the godly would not only impoverish the protagonists' unit in its final stasis but also result, at the second stage of analysis, in omission of his weapon from the dominant imagery of the sword (as reversed cross) qualifying the victors of this thinly veiled Christian allegory. In line, therefore, with our "Order of Ends" theorem, it is particularly important to determine whether a character's final words, however undramatic in the popular sense, do in fact lead to actions that occur before the final curtain falls.

Perhaps even more common is the reverse situation: moments when dialogue carries great emotional impact, yet does not constitute action in the strict sense. Such moments create particularly hazardous traps when attractive characters rationalize their deeds in such a way as to make actual defeat appear to be moral victory. Dramas of both romantic and ironic tone often contain figures whose ultimate destruction arouses powerfully ambivalent sentiment, no doubt reflecting the playwright's own mixed emotions when faced with the task of suppressing them; indeed, instances of this type of dramaturgical complication (or subterfuge) abound in such profusion that the job of selecting examples becomes largely a problem of elimination. Elizabethan and Jacobean plays, for instance, bustle with leading characters who, though their fates be disastrous, nevertheless often seem to possess higher motives, or at least more rhetorical bravura, than many of the morally weak and suspect figures surrounding them. Marlowe's Tamburlaine, Shakespeare's Antony, Chapman's Bussy D'Ambois, Ford's Anabella all address so strong an appeal to the auditor's romanticism that he may incline to discount the calamitous effects of their actions, and thus to view their deaths as triumphs of the spirit and therefore also as dialectical victories. For although the death of a character does not automatically place him in the antagonists' column, neither is it safe to presume a victory in death unless the play's social or religious ethos compels recognition of martyrdom as an actual triumph. High-sounding and possibly touching last speeches, like those of Cleopatra and Othello, must be treated with great circumspection, lest one be lulled by the rhetoric of self-vindication into mistaking vanquished for victor.

Cleopatra is an excellent case in point, for her elaborately staged suicide has elicited countless tears from spectators and many admiring words from critics. Aware that the conquering Octavious Caesar intends to lead her and her children in triumph to Rome, Cleopatra chooses death rather than ignominy, rationalizing her "escape" as a moral triumph:

> 'Tis pity to be Caesar;
> Not being Fortune, he's but Fortune's knave,
> A minister to her will; and it is great
> To do that thing that ends all other deeds;
> Which sleeps, and never palates more the dug,
> The beggar's nurse and Caesar's. (V, ii)

A. C. Bradley reacts to this final pathos in typically romantic fashion:

> ... the moment, though tragic, is especially one of exaltation.... We are going to see Cleopatra die, but she is to die gloriously *and to triumph over Octavius*.[7]

Like Bradley, more recent commentators have also allowed their judgment of the drama's action to be distorted by the Egyptian queen's eloquence. Thus, the Polish critic, Jan Kott, writes with sentimental fervor in the very face of admitted fact:

> Antony and Cleopatra become great lovers only in Acts IV and V. And not just great lovers. They pronounce judgment on the world. At the close

---

[7]A. C. Bradley, *Shakespearean Tragedy*. 2nd Edition. (Basingdale: Macmillan), 1974, p. 315. Italics mine.

> of the play the theme of the exposition returns. Heaven and earth are too
> small for love. . . . The funeral oration over the corpses of Antony and
> Cleopatra is spoken by *the victorious triumvir, Octavius, the future
> Augustus Caesar. . .* He is still talking, but the stage is empty. And the
> world has become flat.[8]

Both of these approaches to the play are predicated on two unspoken assumptions, namely, that poetical rationalizations for deeds are more important than the deeds themselves, and that the love–death motif automatically infuses the work with an ethos that elevates Cleopatra and her concubine to the status of true martyrs. Slighting the drama's actual events, such critics choose to discount the unromantic Octavius' dialectical victory.

Structural analysis of *Antony and Cleopatra* yields no evidence of a pervasive ethos requiring us to view the lovers' death either as moral or dialectical triumphs. Neither does it confirm the romantic picture of Egypt's queen as a person caught in events over which she has no control. Her deceitful message to the estranged Antony is the direct cause of his own suicide, an outcome that the emotionally erratic Cleopatra fails to anticipate. Moreover, her claim that she had rather die than be Caesar's slave loses its benign appeal once it is recalled that she is willing to make terms with Octavius even after Antony's suicide. Indeed, she demands that control of Egypt remain in the hands of her sons, from whom she does not wish to be "unfolded." To this end she falsifies the royal inventory in order to retain half of her possessions, part of which are to serve as bribes for Livia and Octavia to induce their "mediation." Only after Dolabella secretly informs her for the second time that Octavius has no intention of honoring his word to keep her on the throne of Egypt does Cleopatra make final preparations for the least painful possible of suicides. In no way does she attain her overriding desires to remain Egypt's queen and Antony's lover. For it is she who has destroyed Antony, and with him her chance of remaining on the throne. Nor is there evidence that Octavius and the other protagonists possess any particularly dysfunctional traits; on the contrary, abstraction of their essential common characteristics yields a string of temporal virtues only equalled by the gross faults of the ill-starred lovers and those few cohorts who remain with them to the bitter end.

To recommend circumspection in the face of self-proclaimed moral victories is not tantamount to advocating cynicism. Indeed, dramatic literature abounds in figures

---

[8]Jan Kott, *Shakespeare Our Contemporary*. Translated by Boleslaw Taborski (New York: Norton), 1966, p. 176. Italics mine.

whose suffering for religious or social causes puts the seal on their triumph. A brief list of such moral as well as dialectical victors would include Sophocles' Antigone and Oedipus at Colonus, the Jesus of the Corpus Christi cycles, Shakespeare's Cordelia, and Corneille's Polyeucte. Modern drama, too, includes many figures whose martyrdom constitutes dialectical victory: Ibsen's Dr. Stockman, Eliot's Beckett, O'Casey's Juno, Brecht's Kattrin, Betti's Argia, Sartre's Orestes, and Kubrick's Spartacus all fall within this large and distinguished company. In such cases as these, however, moral and dialectical victories coincide for both of the following reasons: (1) such martyrs manage to achieve their overriding will, either by actively shaping or passively accepting their destiny; and (2) the play's religious or social ethos implies a teleology with which the character's actions are consistent. Furthermore, these martyrs are often joined in the dominant unit by powerful offstage figures, divine or human, who must be viewed as triumphant.

In sum, we are back to Aristotle's quite accurate observation that plot, not character, is the soul of drama, and to the legalistic realism that regards the act to be the surest gauge of intent. Thus, what a fictional personage is caused to *do* must be our main concern; any speculations about the whys and wherefores of his actions are of secondary importance. Even the character's open declarations of purpose must be treated with caution; for express motives may often obscure or belie the acts for which they are intended as justifications, while what are taken for implied motives may reflect nothing more than the reader's own projections onto the dramatic text. Such displacement of interest onto possible motive only increases the chance that action may be overlooked or distorted, with the likely result of errors in the dialectical positioning of characters strictly according to their deeds. Fortunately, however, action is much more objectively apprehended than motive; indeed, in every case it is the true indicator of motive.

> The flighty purpose never is o'ertook
> Unless the deed go with it.
>
> *Macbeth*

THEOREM 4
HIDDEN PLAYERS

Offstage characters become active participants of a drama's argument whenever they materially affect the course of events by functioning as motives for the actions of onstage characters. These "hidden players" are often the most powerful, some-times the most numerous, and occasionally the sole members of the fantasy's dominant or recessive units. Consequently, their omission from a chart of action will obscure the drama's binary structure, and thus also its dialectical meaning.

Rationale. Most stage-plays contain exposition referring to events that have occurred either anterior to dramatic time proper or else offstage during the time of representation. Screenplays also include similar expository action; but since the cinema can easily encompass this sort of material in the lively form of flashbacks or spatial cross-cutting, it usually appears as an unmistakable unit of dramatic time. The film can easily show what has happened in the past or in another locale, thus forcing its spectators to pay equal attention to "now" and "then," as well as to the onstage "here" and the offstage "there." By comparison to film, however, the legitimate theatre finds itself severely handicapped because it must convey its own exposition chiefly by means of dialogue; the playwright is hard put to make an audience visualize his offstage action with anything like the clarity and immediacy afforded by cinematic techniques. Consequently, spectators and readers of stage drama are less inclined to lend their fullest attention to antecedent or offstage events that are represented only indirectly, and sometimes awkwardly as apparent interruptions of action.

Symbolic acts of this class are performed by agents who, because they are absent from the immediate scene of action, seem to be at one further ontological remove from reality than the characters who appear onstage. As a consequence, such absentee figures are regularly discounted or, when they are counted at all, relegated to the status of mere imagery. Yet although these "hidden players," as Lorca suggestively called them, are rarely listed among the *dramatis personae*, they often palpably affect the plot by influencing the behavior of characters onstage. Whenever they do this, whenever they operate as motives for other characters' actions, offstage figures must be regarded as full-fledged actors in the drama, presences whose omission from a dialectic of action would materially weaken our picture of its structure. Indeed, because these hidden players often comprise the drama's major protagonists or antagonists, their omission from a chart of action would completely falsify its binary structure.

The Ghost of Hamlet's father can be taken as a crude ancestral type of such penumbrae, which in works of later vintage often make their presence felt as invisible spirits of the dead, hovering over the action to inspire, to haunt, or even to destroy the living. Ibsen's *Ghosts* provides signal examples in Captain Alving and Joanna, the dead lovers whose past actions are revealed to have critically influenced the destinies of Oswald and his half-sister, Regina. The same author's *Hedda Gabler* is haunted by the spirit of General Gabler, who continues to exert a powerful influence over the behavior of his neurotic daughter. Similarly, Camus predicates the madness of Caligula upon the death, anterior to dramatic time, of the emperor's sister, Drusilla; for so unbearable to Caligula is the severing of the incestuous bond with her that he endeavors in vain for symbolic reunion through his dreams of the "Impossible," of possessing the moon, and of carrying evil's logic to its illogical conclusion. Although plays like these overtly predicate the behavior of living characters upon that of the dead, other works allude more fleetingly and obliquely to invisible agents; but whenever such hidden players substantially influence the onstage course of events, they must be included in a chart of action as effective constituents of the fantasy's dominant or recessive functions, and therefore as full-fledged actors in the drama.

If ghostly presences must be added to the *dramatis personae* under the denomination of "hidden players," certainly it will be necessary to account for still other figures from the past either alluded to in exposition or implicit within the mythos of the particular drama. But, if so, precisely which characters? The history of the House of Cadmus is obviously relevant to an understanding of Sophocles' Theban plays, yet surely it is not obligatory to include all the characters of the myth, and its variants, in a dialectical chart of *Oedipus at Colonus*. Similarly, it would seem unnecessary to expand an action-chart of the same author's *Trachiniae* to include all the characters associated with the twelve labors of Heracles when the issue in question is the hero's final suffering and death. Between the error of slighting expository action and the tedium of attempting to trace onstage character's fates back inferentially to various myths of the Creation runs a practical middle course. This way lies in following the assumption that only those characters either specifically evoked in dialogue or clearly implicit within the context of action are of interest in the search for hidden players. And even then one may reasonably exclude any figures whose acts do not form tangible intersections in the matrix of events shaping and modifying the collision taking place onstage. Passing allusion to absent figures is not always sufficient reason for including them in a graph of action, especially when the reference comes merely by way of illustration, exclamation, or for purposes of figurative or comic effect. If personages thus introduced cannot be shown to modify the drama's complexion beyond the purely rhetorical, then one is obliged to account for them at the second stage of analysis as images, rather than at the primary level as actors. Yet it must be added at once that most characters referred to in expository dialogue, as well as certain others alluded to fleetingly by way of exclamation or invocation, do in fact form causal links in the drama's action by supplying motives for events that take place under the glare of the stage lights.

Hidden players are not, of course, confined to figures who are supposed to have died anterior to dramatic time. Many offstage characters are very much "alive" and influential during the course of action; they just never make an entrance. Lorca's *The House of Bernarda Alba* provides an excellent case in point, for not a single one of this work's antagonists ever appears onstage. This highly oblique manner of representing dramatic collision—in which Lorca took pride—may easily divert the inattentive into mistaking a purely internal struggle for the radical one; but if this happens, the onstage arguments between Bernarda and her daughters will be misconstrued as the play's central conflict, which in fact consists in the opposition of Bernarda's household to those outsiders who violate sexual or class taboos. This confusion is bound to occur if one fails to account for all the absentee characters, both living and dead, with whom Bernarda has come into conflict—the unfaithful husband, Antonio, who dies before the curtain rises; Pepe el Romano, Adela's unconventional suitor; Paca la Roseta, the prostitute; the lustful harvesters; and the pregnant girl murdered by the villagers. The distinction between radical and subsidiary conflicts in *The House of Bernarda Alba* can be represented graphically by enclosing the hidden players' names in brackets (a procedure I shall employ henceforth) and by using the symbol "X" to designate those characters who die either before or during dramatic time:

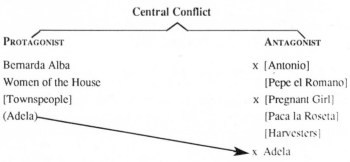

Central Conflict

PROTAGONIST	ANTAGONIST
Bernarda Alba	x [Antonio]
Women of the House	[Pepe el Romano]
[Townspeople]	x [Pregnant Girl]
(Adela)	[Paca la Roseta]
	[Harvesters]
	x Adela

Following this procedure one is obliged to view the struggle between the women inside Bernarda's house as a purely internecine conflict, of secondary importance to the successful war by the matriarch and townspeople against "free spirits" and sexuality in general. Thus, Adela's suicide will be seen in its proper light as the result of her negative apostasy to the camp of the despised antagonists; for her clandestine affair with Pepe outside the repressive walls of Bernarda's domain cannot prosper in a fictive society that offers ostracism or death as the sole alternatives to obsessively strict, conventional rectitude.

The House of Bernarda Alba is not alone among plays whose action focuses on only one of the two major colliding forces. If that work obscures the radical conflict by screening all of the antagonists from direct view, a heavier occultation is produced by even more radical economy in O'Neill's *Long Day's Journey Into Night*, which cannot be dialectically understood without perceiving that every single one of its protagonists as well as several of its antagonists are hidden players. Thus, the soul-wrenching battle between the members of the Tyrone family constitutes merely an internal conflict among the visible losers of a struggle to maintain health, hope, and dignity. For this autobiographical work contains no less than eighteen offstage characters whose actions, during or prior to dramatic time, have the cumulative effect of isolating the Tyrones and inducing them to retreat ever further into a world of resentment, illusion, and addictive stupor.

Allowing one whole side of the collision to be viewed fleetingly through the dark glass of expository dialogue, and offering only an incomplete glimpse of the other side, O'Neill encourages the inattentive to seek the drama's meaning in the actions of the living members of the Tyrone family alone. As a result, the play's radical conflict between the unfortunate Tyrones and their associates on the one hand, and the successful outsiders who profit from the Irish family's weaknesses on the other, will go relatively unremarked. However, careful attention to the actions of the Tyrones' offstage fellow antagonists reveals that James' father abandoned his wife and children to flee back to Ireland, thereby implanting in his son a terror of poverty that keeps him land-poor and prevents him from seeking proper medical care for his family. Further, it reveals that Mary's father gave her notions of gentility that rendered her incapable of surviving a nomadic life as wife of a matinee-idol, a man to whom her father was nevertheless incautious enough to introduce her. Among the characters on the uniformly occulted protagonists' side, one finds the hotel physician whose liberal dispensations of morphine started Mary on her career of addiction; Dr. Hardy and the druggist, who both profit from allowing her to continue on this path; the real estate agent who sells James over-priced land; and so on, through the barkeeps and brothel owner who minister to the character failings of the sons, Jamie and Edmund. This by no means exhausts the list of hidden players on either side of the conflict in *Long Day's Journey Into Night*, as an action-chart, again bracketing offstage characters, reveals at a glance:

Central Conflict

PROTAGONIST		ANTAGONIST
[Yankee Shop Owner]	x	[Tyrone's Father]
[Edwin Booth]	x	[Tyrone's Mother]
[Mother Elizabeth]		[Mary's Father]
[Convent Girls]		James Tyrone
[Hotel Physician]		Mary Tyrone
[Dr. Hardy]	x	[Eugene]
[Druggist]		Jamie
[Real Estate Agent]		Edmund
[Oil Millionaire]		[Bridget]
[The Chatsfields]		[Smythe]
[Mamie Burns]		Cathleen
[Barkeeps]		[Shaughenessay]
		[Fat Violet]

Thus, although the cast of O'Neill's play includes only five characters, these visible players comprise less than a fifth of the personages, living or dead, who make up the work's dialectic of action; and if these lonely five command the stage, it cannot be said that they truly dominate the action because twelve of the offstage figures must be listed as protagonists, as victors in this secretive drama that focuses relentlessly on but a portion of the losers. Failure to recognize the full extent of this work's *dramatis personae*, and to determine its members' placement within the fantasy's binary system, will render it dialectically unintelligible, and therefore—to the extent that a work's purport depends upon its oppositional structure—meaningless.

Thus far I have limited my discussion to plays that screen one entire functional unit from direct representation. Yet this sort of misdirection, this squinting view of dramatic conflict is comparatively rare. Much more common is the employment of varying numbers of hidden players in one or both units, while at the same time allowing other characters from each side of the conflict to tread openly upon the boards; and in fact the majority of plays contain at least some offstage actors whose alignment with either the dominant or recessive units assists in rendering the fantasy dialectically comprehensible. The problematical title-character of Beckett's *Waiting for Godot* is an obvious instance of this type. Similarly, the strange play-within-the-play of Pirandello's *Henry IV* requires the inclusion of Pope Gregory VII, even though this figure is alive only in the demented imagination of Henry. Strindberg's *Miss Julie* remains largely inexplicable if one fails to identify the offstage Count as the chief protagonist, just as the same author's *Dance of Death* cannot be dialectically understood without recognition of the absent Colonel as principal support of the drama's dominant unit.

The plots of many comedies turn upon absentee characters, both dead and living. The most usual comedic patterns are (1) the last-minute intercession of an offstage human or divine authority figure; and (2) the convenient death of a hidden player who functions as a "blocking character" while alive. In both cases the hidden player's effect upon the action is transmitted through a second party who enters to bear the glad tidings. Moliere's *Tartuffe* furnishes an illustration of the first type when its comedic stalemate is broken by none other than the offstage Louis XIV, whose Officer brings word of the impostor's criminal record and a warrant for his arrest. More ironically, Brecht saves Macheath through the "glorious messenger" who announces an amnesty granted by Queen Victoria on the occasion of her coronation. Regarded conventionally, Louis XIV stands as the primary emblem of a rational order in *Tartuffe*, while Queen Victoria symbolizes an equally irrational order in *The Threepenny Opera*; yet neither of these offstage characters should be treated merely as symbolic ornaments just because they fail to make an entrance. Since each wields power that realises itself mimetically in terms of action, each is fully potent as an *actor*; and cognizance of this fact will considerably enlarge our view of the protagonist's units of both comedies.

Absentee type 2 (the convenient death) is so ubiquitous a pattern that a single illustration should here suffice. In Farquhar's *The Beaux' Stratagem* Aimwell impersonates his elder brother, Lord Viscount Aimwell, for the purpose of wooing a fortune; but upon securing the affection of the heiress, Dorinda, his conscience forces him to confess the imposture. At this embarrassing juncture Sir Charles Freeman enters to announce that the offstage brother has died, and that Aimwell is now indeed the lord he counterfeited. While all present wish him joy of the occasion, Aimwell exclaims, "Thanks to the pregnant stars that formed this accident!" Farquhar is, of course, using the convenient death convention in an ironic manner to underscore the social satire at the root of his comedy. Yet the offstage elder brother is something more than a joke. In fact, he is the principal antagonist of the piece; and our recognition that the first Lord Viscount Aimwell and the system of primogeniture he represents are among the real villains of *The Beaux' Stratagem* permits us to see much more clearly the structural analogue between the professional highwaymen of the sub-plot and the "gentlemen" highwaymen of the main action.

One of the largest and most potent groups of hidden players is comprised of offstage divinities, who frequently operate as motives for the mortal figures onstage. The behind-the-scenes influence of gods in plays of religious ethos creates a situation under which mortal characters may suffer worldly defeat or even death and still be counted victorious, so long as their deeds accord with the express or implied divine will. Thus, Sophocles' Antigone remains a protagonist throughout the drama's action, even though her fate is entirely tragic in the secular sense of that term. Antigone belongs in the dominant unit because her struggle to give proper ritual burial to Polyneices' corpse is expressly motivated by reverence for the gods of the nether world who require such rites. The heroine's acts are in express or oblique accord with all the major chthonic deities: Hades, king of the underworld; Persephone, his queen; Demeter, protector of law, order, and marriage; Dike or "Justice," who dwells with the gods below; Thanatos, governor of law for all the dead; and the Furies, who punish violators of the laws of kinship. With such an awesome array of barely concealed powers motivating it, Antigone's self-sacrifice must be counted not only as a moral victory but as an earthly triumph of divine law.

Christian drama of the Middle Ages presents little difficulty with regard to hidden divinities, for the priestly authors of the great Corpus Christi cycles had no qualms about direct mimetic representation of the Father and Son, or of their adversary, Satan, onstage. With the advent of the Protestant Reformation, however, and the enactment of iconoclastic laws prohibiting the depiction of deities, playwrights were forced to develop oblique methods of expounding the truths of moral theology. Although their works consequently assumed a superficially secular focus, Elizabethan and Jacobean dramatists by no means entirely abandoned the religious preoccupations of their times. If obliged to retire God and Satan from the physical stage, they still often allow them to operate behind the scenes as motives for other characters' actions, and therefore as full members of the cast. Iago's open espousal of villainy is directly linked with satanic motives, while Desdemona's fidelity, innocence, and willingness to forgive exemplify cardinal Christian virtues; Macbeth expounds at length upon the "deep damnation" awaiting the murderer of a virtuous king, and after the horrible deed Banquo and Macduff place their hopes "in the great hand of God"; Hamlet wonders whether his father's ghost brings with it "airs from heaven or blasts from hell." All such allusions to the Christian duality or to Church doctrine should incline one to suspect the presence of a larger conflict whose major adversaries are God and Satan, and whose implications are therefore conventionally moral.

The soundness of positing God and Satan as the chief offstage combatants of any classical or modern drama will ultimately be verified at the second and third levels of analysis; for if a play's ethos is indeed Christian, conventional iconography referring to godly or demonic attributes will be opposed in the dialectic of imagery, while such antonyms as "salvation" and "damnation," "grace" and "despair," along with the cardinal moral virtues and deadly sins, will be required, at the third stage, to describe the opposing functional units. When, on the contrary, a purely secular ethos informs the action, as it does in the Roman plays of Shakespeare and Jonson, it will be impossible to posit specifically godly or satanic motives for any of the characters' deeds; neither will the imagery include compelling religious symbols, nor the qualitative reduction of the colliding forces require terms denoting Christian virtues or their opposing vices.

Whether mortal or divine, living or dead, offstage characters play a role whose importance must never be underestimated; for without taking them into account as primary constituents of action and counteraction, the drama's binary structure is bound to remain obscure. Indeed, it is nearly impossible to apprehend the dialectical character of dramatic fantasy without understanding this principle of occultation, which expands our vision of the drama's events to a frame much wider than the stage proscenium or the margins of the *dramatis personae* page. That conventional literary criticism has tended to regard hidden players (when it has regarded them at all) as mere auxiliary symbols rather than as active members of the cast, has prevented it from perceiving them to be substantive elements of a larger binary system.

THEOREM 5
MISDIRECTION

A drama's binary form will be obscured whenever its author directs most of his attention to one side of the argument, to only a few characters among the fantasy's active participants, or to arresting internal conflicts within a single camp. In order to avoid being diverted by such oblique strategies of representation, it is necessary to exercise special vigilance in accounting for characters who operate in relative shadow, away from the spotlighted action.

Rationale. Dramatic fantasy objectifies an internal argument that is essentially two-sided. Unlike the lyric poem, which may eschew conflict altogether by describing a simple, uncomplicated affective state, the drama must express a fundamental dichotomy in terms of action and counteraction, whether that opposition assume a form grossly physical or almost purely conversational. Thus, every play or screenplay will begin to develop, usually within its first few scenes, a radical collision that determines the course of all that is to follow. Nevertheless, for sundry reasons ranging from artistic economy and finesse to opportunism and obfuscation, dramatists often direct the spotlight of their (and our) attention onto but a few elements of the larger binary structure, illuminating only a portion of their argument while relegating other dialectically capital elements to relative shadow. Such chiaroscuro effects as these tend to create the impression that the drama's truly significant activities take place only in its more brightly lit corners; and as a consequence the spectator or reader may be distracted from perceiving the argument as a whole in its actual binary shape.

This sort of dramaturgical "misdirection" generally employs three main techniques, either singly or in concert: (1) relegation of one entire functional unit to an offstage role; (2) intense concentration (in terms of character development, amount of dialogue, and emotional intensity) on one side of the conflict, while leaving the other side relatively undeveloped; and (3) the creation of diverting internecine conflicts within one or both of the major warring camps. The first and most radical of these oblique strategies I have already discussed in the previous section on "Hidden Players." The remaining two types of misdirected focus are shown below in schematics which represent the spotlighted characters as empty circles, the shadowed ones as blackened circles:

(1) Concentration on a single functional unit:

(2) Internal conflicts within one of the functional units:

In both of these diagrams I have intentionally shown the spotlighted events to occur in the antagonists' units, for the great majority of such chiaroscuro effects do in fact highlight the recessive function while leaving its opposed dominant function in relative obscurity. This seemingly illogical strategy is much favored by writers of irony, who thereby avoid direct articulation of the guilt-arousing wish by concentrating instead on the drama of its obverse fear. However, ironists may also use this technique to enhance the awesomeness of their malign victors by leaving much that is partially hidden to the auditor's fertile imagination. In tragedy and satirical comedy a similarly intense focus on the antagonists often results from the richer dramatic possibilities afforded by the depiction of evil, as well as from the frequent presence in the dominant unit of offstage divinities and their sometimes lackluster mortal representatives onstage.

Despite the natural tendency to concentrate on developing the easy histrionic possibilities of the negative pole of action, playwrights nevertheless occasionally reverse this strategy in order to give high definition to the heroic victors, while at the same time casting symbolic shadows on their benighted opponents. Consequently, it is always well to anticipate both types of misdirected focus by paying close attention to so-called "recessive characters" on either side of the argument, as well as to events whose low emotional charge might permit them to escape memory's grasp.

One of the most persistent obstacles to correct structural definition of a drama's radical conflict is the distracting presence of secondary, internal collisions within one or both of the major warring camps. These internecine struggles frequently receive so much of the dramatist's attention that they can be easily mistaken for the play's central conflict. Instead of being placed, as it were, on a promontory from which they can view the whole mêlée, the spectators are often set down in some corner of the battlefield where, if they do not seek better vantage-ground, they will witness only a power struggle among members of the same army. As a result of this skewed perspective, they are likely to mistake a mere mutiny for the entire war.

Jonson's *Volpone* provides an excellent case in point; for the antagonists of this comedy are not only more numerous and intrinsically interesting than the protagonists, they are also engaged in a rivalry so complicated and vociferous as to suggest to the unwary the presence of a radical collision. Indeed, a casual reading of this play might tempt one to view its main plot as essentially a struggle between the fox and the birds of prey, that is, between the seeming-rich Volpone and the three old fortune hunters, Voltore, Corbaccio, and Corvino. Further reflection, however, might lead one to conclude that the ultimate conflict is rather between servant and master, for at the end Mosca attempts to out-swindle Volpone himself. Yet a more careful reading of the action, taking every character into full account, reveals that Volpone, his parasite, and the three old men all belong in the antagonists' column for the critical reason that they fail utterly, not only in their attempts to exploit each other, but also in their schemes to abuse the dramatically pallid protagonists, Bonario and Celia. Jonson thus creates a common but analytically confusing situation in which one side of the dialectic utterly dominates the stage with its hilarious internal squabbling throughout most of the action. This internecine conflict between the play's antagonists may be represented diagrammatically as a vertical column:

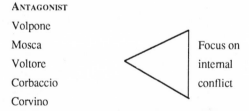

ANTAGONIST
Volpone
Mosca   Focus on
Voltore   internal
Corbaccio   conflict
Corvino

Although each of these characters is at war with each of the others, they all in common oppose Bonario and Celia, all share the vice of greed, bear type-names signifying scavenging animals, and, most important, ultimately fall to defeat. Bonario and Celia, on the other hand, begin as innocent victims of these predators, share an attitude of Christian charity, bear adjectival names indicating moral probity, and emerge triumphant at the play's conclusion. The trouble is that the final victory of Bonario and Celia is as lackluster as their characters; it almost appears to have been tacked on in order to provide a morally acceptable excuse for all the wicked fun that has gone before in the antagonists' camp. The internecine struggle among demi-devils is simply much more engrossing than the general war between them and the demi-angels, and as a consequence the latter may be easily forgotten after the curtain falls. Yet this would be to ignore the comedy's radical collision, whose primary opponents include two most potent hidden players—the superhuman instigators of the terrestrial struggle onstage. The true binary form of this morality comedy may therefore be schematized as a horizontal row comprising two vertical columns:

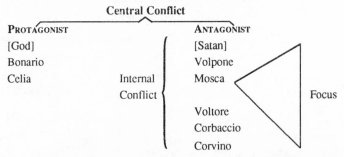

It should be stressed that this sort of misdirected focus is not confined to Jacobean moral allegory. On the contrary, similar internal conflicts abound in the drama of all ages and schools, and are to be found as readily in contemporary cinema as in ancient Greek tragedy. Moreover, these internecine struggles may occur at a single pole of action, as in *Volpone*, or in both of a drama's warring camps simultaneously—thus compounding the potential for confusion between purely secondary arguments and the radical collision itself. This is not to say, however, that all works for stage or screen contain such internal conflicts; indeed, many are content to develop their arguments using a clear antiphony that gives nearly equal weight to both choruses, without distracting dissonances on either side. Yet whenever a multiplicity of arguments tends to obscure the issue, we can be certain that all of these quarrels are purely internal save one.

The principal defense against any sort of misdirection consists, as I have indicated, in a special scrupulosity in accounting for each and every character of the drama, however apparently minor or pallid by comparison to other members of the cast. For only when all of the belligerents have been reviewed will we begin to perceive the general war in its entirety, undistracted by mutinies within a single camp, or by authorial refusal to give equal coverage to both sides of the conflict. Only when the entire cast is clearly in the mind's eye may we begin with confidence to engage the other principles of dialectical analysis in the task of defining the drama's controlling binary opposition.

Theorem 6
Unidirectionality

The alignment of forces at a drama's conclusion can only be determined after accounting for any and all characters who, owing to changes of allegiance or fortune, shift between dialectical poles during the course of action. Calculation of such movement in plays that contain multiple apostasies reveals that, no matter how many characters move, their shifts are invariably unidirectional, always ending at the same point, whether positive, negative, or neutral. Never do the characters of a drama move in opposed courses. The presence or absence of movement, and the particular direction of that movement, when it occurs, constitute the fantasy's most critical dynamic characteristic, its kinetic signature. Moreover, a strictly limited number of movement possibilities within the drama's essentially binary system permits the development of structural models that will serve as patterns for the recognition and analysis of all dynamic types.

Rationale. Theorem 2 proposes that a drama's dialectical meaning hangs on its final alignment of forces at the primary level of action, that the wishful and fearful motives objectified in the fantasy's conflict can only be determined by analysis of its ultimate stasis. But because a play's descriptive meaning does not become manifest until the action achieves closure, we cannot accurately derive the opposing systems represented by the protagonists' and antagonists' units without taking into account those characters who are made to switch allegiance or otherwise undergo radical changes of fortune during the progress of the argument. For if these apostates are negligently left in the camp they have abandoned (or been expelled from), our later descriptive reduction of the members of that camp to their essential common characteristics will be obstructed by the presence of the dialectically misplaced, while abstraction of the opposing unit will suffer equally from our failure to include their eventual membership. It is therefore vital to note any difference between the opening and closing alignment of forces resulting from changes of allegiance or condition at any points during the course of action.

Shifting characters, as I shall call them, execute the dialectical leap whenever they are represented as moving from a state of freedom and happiness to one of bondage and unhappiness, or vice versa. And although certain dramas render this distinction less than obvious by forcing us to determine protagonist and antagonist in the most niggardly sense of "one up" and "one down," yet in all cases the dialectical shift is precipitated by a permanent reversal in the character's ability to achieve his overriding wish.

In the course of graphing the dynamics of these shifting characters through the analysis of numerous plays and screenplays varying widely in style and date, I have noted with some fascination the emergence of a heretofore unremarked pattern: *dramatic apostasy is always unidirectional.* Whether characters move toward the protagonists in certain plays, toward the antagonists in certain others, or toward a dialectically disengaged "neutral" position in yet others, such shifts are never multidirectional in the same work. No matter how many characters change allegiance or experience reversals of fortune during the course of any particular drama, the curious and compelling fact is that they always move in a parallel course to the same goal. Their shifts may occur at different moments during the action, but never in different directions.

As mysterious as it may at first seem, the phenomenon of unidirectional movement is comprehensible, I believe, from at least three different perspectives: aesthetic, modal, and psychological.

From the aesthetic point of view unidirectional movement obviates the mental squint that would result from focusing on two or more characters whose destinies are moving them in opposite directions—much as would happen in a tennis game in which both players served balls simultaneously. The governing principles here would be those of unity and clarity: the spectator (or for that mater, the author) can only concentrate on one radical alteration of fortune at a time; and the focus is further resolved by pointing any other transformations in the same direction, that is, by organizing them according to the same teleological principle. Moreover, because the fantasy's purport depends upon its final stasis(Theorem 2), the impetus to closure that effects such stasis seems to require the full force of a movement that is not vitiated by tendencies in other directions. This argument receives support from the modal perspective, in which, for instance, a character's movement from unhappiness to happiness has quite the opposite emotional effect from his movement in the reverse direction. Simultaneous shifts from misery to bliss and from bliss to misery would send contradictory or self-cancelling messages and, at the very least, prevent the emotional release of unalloyed joy or sorrow. Indeed, as we shall see in Part Two, a drama's whole tone, and sometimes even its purport, depend to a large degree upon the direction in which its characters move; hence, even works that fall into such ambivalent modal categories as irony or so-called black comedy will be seen to conform to unidirectional rather than multidirectional patterns.

A psychological explanation for unidirectionality might run somewhat as follows: We are dealing with a binary system in which the positive pole of action objectifies the superior function of the authorial personality, while the negative pole speaks for the inferior side (Theorem 1). The primary work of the fantasy is to bolster the superior function and allow it symbolic gratification of its desires; but in order to do this it must re-establish the complete separation of opposites, thus assuring the integrity of both dominant and recessive functions. A dialectically misplaced character represents the contamination of one function by its opposite, and such contamination is an irritant that prevents the whole system from operating normally. In order for the dominant function to retain its position of superiority and achieve its overriding wish it must expel any foreign elements, any uncharacteristic tendencies, as it were, and relegate them to the value system of the opposite, shadow side. The same is true, in reverse, for the inferior function, from which discordant elements will eventually escape, propelled as much by their repulsion from the values of the inferior function as by their attraction to those of the superior one.

But why cannot both types of catharsis—expulsion from positive to negative and from negative to positive—occur together in the same fantasy? The answer would seem to be that contaminating elements on both sides would tend to negate each other, rather like subatomic particles and antiparticles annihilating each other upon colli- sion, thus leaving the system in its usual state of delicate equilibrium. The superior function would then still remain in control, with no immediate need for symbolic reinforcement and no necessity for decontamination. Therefore, the urge for catharsis would usually arise only when a *single function* were contaminated, and the resulting expulsion of foreign elements from one side of the system to the other would then produce the phenomenon of unidirectional movement.

Whatever the precise mechanisms governing the principle of unidirectionality, the discovery of this inherent characteristic of dramatic fantasy opens up a rich field, for it makes possible the development of a limited number of structural models adequate for the description of all movement possibilities within the drama's binary system. Familiarity with these underlying dynamic patterns, and with certain mythical and modal tendencies of each, places us in an advantageous posture to recognize the dynamic class of any particular drama, and thus to sort out its controlling opposition of forces. Part Two of this study deals at length with each of these dynamic classes. For the present, however, it will be helpful to expand on the principle of unidirectionality by providing a few guidelines for charting shifting characters, who oftentimes can be rather elusive.

Our first general observation has already been set down: the mobile characters of any particular play or screenplay always travel in the same direction, whether from the antagonist to the protagonist, or vice versa (Part Two, Models 2–3). At other times the shifting characters will move from an initially disengaged apex position to the protagonist, as occurs in love triangles of the standard comedic variety; or else from the same "neutral" position to the antagonist, as we find in the less common negative love triangle (Part Two, Models 4–5). Occasionally characters will move instead from one or both of the primary camps to the position of a dialectically disengaged moderating character who himself becomes the ultimate protagonist (Part Two, Models 6–7). Whatever the particular direction of movement in a play under consideration, *discovery of one clear, indisputable dialectical movement indicates that any further shifts will be in the same direction.* Characters may sometimes give the impression of moving in opposite courses; but this impression is invariably an illusion resulting from an error either in determining the work's radical polarity or in charting an apostasy where it does not in fact occur. Several potential complexities may cause one to plot nonexistent dialectical shifts, or to overlook shifts that really do occur.

At the outset it must be emphasized that one structural class is defined by the fact that it contains no shifting characters whatever (Part Two, Model 1). Although such "static" actions are in the minority, they nevertheless constitute one of several ever-present dynamic possibilities, none of which should be ruled out at the commencement of textual analysis. When, therefore, examination of each and every member of the cast fails to uncover a single radical change of allegiance or reversal of fortune, when we can demonstrate that the final alignment of forces remains exactly as it stood at the beginning, then we must conclude that the action is static. Yet it is well to recall that the odds are fairly high against the occurrence of this rigidly bi-polar structure: the majority of dramas do in fact depict the apostasy of one or more characters from the functional unit in which they began.

When dialectical movement does occur, its presence and singleness of direction are usually obvious—so long as we have correctly assessed the drama's radical conflict by rigorously engaging theorems 1 through 5. Nevertheless, certain works complicate this job by creating the illusion of characters' brushing past one another in opposite directions. When, for example, Macbeth's fall from power coincides with Macduff's release from the usurper's yoke, these two figures would seem to execute a dialectical countercross, one taking a positive and the other a negative course. But this does not accurately describe the drama's dynamics, for in actuality Macduff is never in a position to move positively because he and all the other victors are situated in the dominant unit from beginning to end. Whatever sufferings they are forced to endure, the tragedy's protagonists remain steadfast in their loyalty to the institution of the monarchy, to legitimate royal succession, and to the Divinity who assures that right of succession. "In the great hand of God I stand, and thence / Against the undivulged pretence I fight / Of treasonous malice," cries Banquo, speaking for all those, including Macduff, whose overriding motive corresponds with the Divine will and thus qualifies them as protagonists no matter how grievous their earthly burdens. The illusion of the countercross is further dispelled once the "hidden players" theorem is engaged to reveal the overriding cosmic opposition which separates the faithful from the despairing, the loyal from the disloyal. Consequently, the drama's only dialectical shift occurs when Macbeth's violation of the Divine Right of Kings propels him from the camp of the faithful to that of the Ultimate Rebel. The drama's action therefore conforms to a dynamic pattern that is strictly unidirectional, despite the appearance of cross-directional movement.

Such examples could be multiplied indefinitely. The impression of characters' moving past each other in opposite directions is often especially pronounced in populous dramas of intrigue, where wavering loyalties make it hard to keep track of each character's initial and final stance (Theorem 2). Yet attractive as it may appear as a descriptive possibility, the countercross does not correspond to the realities of dramatic plotting; it is a chimera that usually arises from an analytical error in regard to the dialectical placement of one or more of the apparently mobile characters. Careful review of the drama's action from the standpoint of the first five theorems will eventually correct the error and reveal a single vector for all apostates. In fact, the only correct dynamic possibilities for cross-dialectical motion are the unidirectional shift of all mobile characters from the negative to the positive poles of action (Figure 1), and from the positive to the negative poles (Figure 2).

FIGURE 1: Correct model,showing unidirectional movement for all mobile characters from negative to positive poles of action:

PROTAGONIST   ANTAGONIST

  W   X

  Y ◄————————————————— (Y)

  Z ◄————————————————— (Z)

FIGURE 2: Correct model,showing unidirectional movement of all mobile characters from positive to negative poles of action:

PROTAGONIST   ANTAGONIST

  W   X

  (Y) —————————————————► Y

  (Z) —————————————————► Z

FIGURE 3: Incorrect model,showing illusory countercross in opposite directions:

PROTAGONIST   ANTAGONIST

  W   X

  (Y) —————————————————► Y

  Z ◄————————————————— (Z)

The principle of unidirectionality holds not only for dramas containing full cross-dialectical movement but also for those "triangular" works in which the contested characters eventually shift from an initially disengaged apex position to one of the primary poles of action. The principal belligerents of such comedies remain dialectically immobile because *movement from the contested apex position automatically precludes movement to or from any other point of the triangle.* Thus, the only shifts in love triangles are executed by the contested figures, who eventually move from their initial position of technical neutrality to the side of the protagonists.

But if this is true, what is one to make of the fact that many comedies depict the fall from power of "blocking characters" and the concomitant rise of the hero and heroine from a state of distress to one of joyous triumph? This would seem to constitute a cross-dialectical countercross in addition to the heroine's movement from the apex. In fact, however, such multidirectional patterns are obviated by two general features of comedic love intrigues, the first being that the hero's fate is held in only the mildest suspense because the genre leads us to anticipate his eventual success at winning his prize; the second, that the hero's rival and the parental blocking figures who support him are always dysfunctional "humour" types—oily manipulators, braggart warriors, or concupiscent old misers backed by an assortment of social-climbing guardians, cast mistresses, over-eager matchmakers, and jealous superannuateds. Thus crippled by their own character aberrations, the hero's opponents are incapacitated for realizing their primary wish and therefore must be counted as losers from beginning to end. The protagonist's initial frustration at securing the object of his desire only sweetens the anticipation of victory; rarely is there any serious doubt of his eventually securing his prize, to the chagrin of the antagonists, whose maneuvers on their own behalf have been self-defeating. As the result of their primal right-way/wrong-way mythos, love-triangles never contain cross-dialectical movements between the radical poles of action: the principal belligerents remain fixed in their opposition, thus making way for the heroine's movement from the apex of the triangle to the side of the protagonist.

Molière's *The School for Wives* provides a capital instance both of the comedic love triangle and also of the principle of unidirectionality. To the unwary it might appear that this comedy's protagonist and antagonist switch positions in a teeter-totter action that depicts the blocking character, old Arnolphe, in an apparently superior stance during the opening acts, only to be toppled at the dénouement by the hero, Horace. However, any countercross between these primary combatants must be ruled out. The result of their contest for the hand of Agnès is a foregone conclusion because Arnolphe, by insisting on a minimal, cloistered education for his ward, has rendered her entirely innocent of the way of the world, and therefore a perfectly guileless and guiltless accomplice to her young suitor. Although she occupies a technically neutral position throughout most of the action because she has neither the desire to marry her guardian nor yet the freedom to run off with Horace, Agnés quite innocently encourages the latter's blandishments and thus poises for her leap to the protagonist's side—a movement held in mild suspense until the end, when the question of how (not whether) Horace will win her is answered. Consequently, the protagonist and antagonist of this triangle remain fixed in opposition, with the only shifting character being the contested female. Had there been other mobile figures in *The School for Wives*, they also would have moved from the same apex position to the protagonist— never to the antagonist.

Thus, the single invariable pattern of comedic love triangles is the unidirectional shift of all mobile characters from the apex to the protagonists' unit (Figure 4). Three tempting but always incorrect paradigms of such works are the bi-directional shift of the mobile characters from the apex to both the protagonists' and antagonists' units (Figure 5); the cross-dialectical shift plus the shift from the apex to the protagonists' unit (Figure 6); and, lastly, the dialectical countercross plus the shift from the apex to the protagonists' unit (Figure 7).

FIGURE 4: Correct model, showing unidirectional shifts of all the mobile characters from the apex to the protagonists' unit:

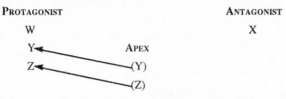

FIGURE 5: Incorrect model, showing bi-directional shifts of the mobile characters from the apex to both primary poles:

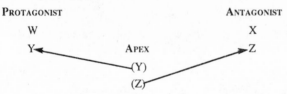

FIGURE 6: Incorrect model, showing the cross-dialectical shift plus the shift from the apex to the protagonists' unit:

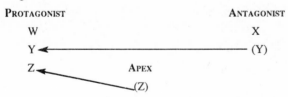

FIGURE 7: Incorrect model, showing the dialectical countercross plus the shift from the apex to the protagonists' unit by the various apparently mobile characters:

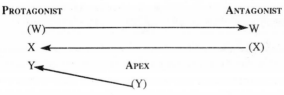

The illusion of bi-directional movement can also be generated by another mirage, namely, the impression that some characters change allegiance more than once during the course of action, thus executing a "double-cross" between the drama's primary poles. This descriptive trap is especially hazardous in dramas of dynastic struggle, in which betrayal and the guilt attendant upon it, closet wars, skullduggery and conniving to stay on the winning side—all complicate the work's middle episodes, often obscuring perception of the true differences between its opening and closing alignment of forces.

Strictly observed, however, characters who appear to shift several times will be seen to move only once, or not at all. The latter instance—the appearance of movement where none actually occurs—is well illustrated in *Julius Caesar* by the action of the populace, that "many-headed monster" which operates functionally as a single character. Expository dialogue reveals that the Roman citizenry have already betrayed the memory of their erstwhile hero, the fallen Pompey, by turning their affections to his conqueror, Caesar. Then, following Caesar's murder, they briefly applaud Brutus' defense of the coup. But finally, the crowd swings just as abruptly away from Brutus to Antony and furiously demands death for the conspirators. Despite all this turning back and forth, however, the citizenry merely pivots, as it were, on the same piece of ground—that dominated first by Caesar and later by his loyal Antony: their brief approval of Brutus is expressed in mere words that lead to no actual change of allegiance. Although *Julius Caesar* does represent the dialectical shift of Brutus' friend, Massala, and his slave, Strato, from the camp of the antagonists to that of the protagonists, the mob itself does not participate in this positive movement, but remains a part of the play's dominant function from beginning to end despite the appearance of multiple crosses.

Two strictures will be helpful in all such cases: first, that the effect of a double-cross is commonly an illusion created more by what a character says than what he does (Theorem 3); and second, that even a genuine apostasy followed by a backsliding has absolutely no dialectical significance because a play's dynamic pattern can only be ascertained by comparing the *initial* and *final* commitments of each character relative to the conflict's bi-polarity (Theorem 2). In emphasizing this second point one can do no better than to adopt the maxim formulated by G. Spencer-Brown in his *The Laws of Form*: "To cross again is not to cross." Graphically, this principle reveals that the apparently double-crossing character has in fact either remained immobile throughout the action (Figure 8), or has moved cross-dialectically only once (Figure 9). The always inaccurate description of a double-cross is represented in Figure 10.

FIGURE 8: Correct model: Possibility #1, showing character Z, the ostensibly mobile character, to have remained immobile in the protagonists' unit:

PROTAGONIST   ANTAGONIST

    X   Y

    Z

FIGURE 9: Correct model: Possibility #2, showing the mobile character Z to have made a single dialectical shift from antagonist to protagonist:

PROTAGONIST   ANTAGONIST

    X   Y

    Z ◄—————————————————— (Z)

FIGURE 10: Incorrect model, showing an apparent double-cross from protagonist to antagonist and back again:

PROTAGONIST   ANTAGONIST

    X   Y

   (Z^1) ——————————————► (Z^2)

   Z^3 ◄——

To recapitulate, shifting characters are forced to move because at the outset they are dialectically misplaced; the argument forming in the author's mind can attain closure only after the opposites have been thoroughly segregated within the fantasy's binary system, positive with positive, negative with negative. The dominant function cannot achieve symbolic gratification while it contains intrusive fragments from the recessive system, nor yet while the latter harbors forces either necessary to swing the balance of power or sensed in some manner as congenial to the dominant function and therefore as signal accompaniments of its triumph. Only when this process of separation has been completed in fancy's alembic can the dominant unit, now purged or augmented, realize its wish and thereby permit the solution to rest. Either subsystem may require purging, but never both systems in the same fantasy; consequently, the characters of any particular drama always move to the same point, whether positive, negative, or neutral. Dynamically speaking, these shifts of characters between the functional units constitute the most critical moments in the argument's search for resolution, and thus for realization of its meaning.

DIALECTIC OF IMAGERY

Theorem 7
Figurative Opposition

The drama's bipolarity at the primary level of action is augmented at the secondary level of imagery by a corresponding figurative opposition. This rhetorical clash provides emotional heightening and definition for the struggle between the dominant and recessive camps of belligerents. Consequently, the play's images divide into a binary system of complementary tropes in which one constellation qualifies the action's protagonists, and the other dialectically opposed constellation qualifies the antagonists.

Example 1. The Mozart-da Ponte opera *The Magic Flute* supplies a clear instance, in the romance mode, of the clash between two radically opposed figurative constellations which mirror (and greatly augment) the conflict between the drama's protagonists and antagonists. Thus, the spiritual kingdom of the all-wise Zarastro is filled with the radiant light of day and images of the sun-disk emblem of the god Osiris, while the opposed realm of spiritual ignorance exists in a literal darkness ruled over by The Queen of the Night. This visual contrast is reinforced in Mozart's score by the opposition between solemn, slow tempi, sustained chords, and low tonalities for the priesthood of Zarastro on the one hand, and agitated rhythms, rapid tempi, and strident, high pitches for the Queen of the Night and her minions on the other. The triad of slow, rising chords serving as a noble leitmotif for Zarastro is provided with an exact counterpart in the rapid, dotted triad sung by the Queen of the Night's ladies-in-waiting. Zarastro's sublime aria, "In these holy halls," which was judged by Bernard Shaw to be the only opera solo fit to issue from the mouth of God, receives its counterpart in the Queen of the Night's ranting coloratura set-piece, whose blatant melodrama annoyed the composer Hector Berlioz to such a degree that, misunderstanding its purpose, he judged it a grave lapse of taste. These visual and auditory oppositions in *The Magic Flute* are enhanced by the contrast between the thunder and lightning dominating the wild landscape ruled over by the Queen of the Night and the ordered architecture and protective walls surrounding Zarastros' city of enlightenment. All of these figurative oppositions are parts of a general scheme designed to highlight the spiritual conflict between the opera's belligerents and thus reinforce its polarization of forces at the level of action.

Example 2. Realistic dramas usually develop more subtle but nonetheless equally pervasive figurative oppositions. In Ibsen's *John Gabriel Borkman*, for instance, the hero, Erhart, is torn between his sense of duty to his guilt-ridden family and his attraction to a liberated divorcee named Fanny Wilton. Ibsen orchestrates these two extremes (between which his hero must choose) with a rich series of contrasting figures. Thus, the natural warmth and charm of Fanny Wilton is played off against the mother's constant chilliness and need for overheated rooms; the sunny south of France, to which Fanny and Erhart wish to travel, against the bleak winter of icy Norway; the gaily lit ballroom where the lovers meet against the gloom of the Borkman home; the sound of the silver sleigh bells of Fanny's coach against Saint-Saens' "The Dance of Death," which Erhart's father insists on having played for him repeatedly; the fresh air of the out-of-doors against the father's voluntary confinement to his stuffy room for eight years; and, finally, the features of youth and beauty against those of old age and death. These are but a few of the drama's more obvious figurative oppositions, which, together with other contrastive groupings, compose two larger constellations qualifying and lending emotional definition to the collision at the primary level of action in Ibsen's drama.

THEOREM 8
FUNCTIONAL UNITS

Just as the individual characters of the drama operate as fragments of a single oppositional unit, so also do their qualifying images and symbols function as component elements of a larger rhetorical system, either dominant or recessive. Each separate trope thus resonates in harmony with the choir to which it contributes but a single voice, and in discord with the opposed choir of images. Although dominating metaphors or groups of closely related figures often form distinct and important subsections within a functional unit, these sections contribute only a single line to the overall texture of the choir to which they belong.

Example 1. Eliot's *Murder in the Cathedral* employs the metaphor of the wheel as a major device by which to epitomize the difference between salvation and damnation, grace and despair. The unmoving hub ("the still center") of the turning wheel becomes an emblem of spiritual beatitude, and more specifically of Archbishop Becket's serenity and unflinching courage in the certainty that God's will and King Henry's will cannot be reconciled. The outside of the wheel, its revolving rim, comes to symbolize the shifting, uncertain, and ultimately satanical nature of man's temporal ambitions in general, and those of Henry in particular. Yet, despite their metaphorical importance in encompassing both sides of the play's dialectic within a single image, the two parts of the wheel are in fact but leading elements of two greater figurative constellations. Thus, Becket's hub is directly related to all the conventional iconography and paraphernalia of the Church of England, while King Henry's rim corresponds to the trappings of the world, its dirt and blood, its soldiers and instruments of death, together with the many bestial figures which populate the antagonists' unit. These two image-systems form a larger binary opposition which corresponds to the cosmic war between God and Satan being fought out on the stage by their mortal representatives.

Example 2. The title of Williams' *The Glass Menagerie* announces the symbol that will dominate the play's figurative scheme. For Laura's beloved collection of crystal animal figures provides an ideal metaphor for its possessor's own fragility, shyness, introversion, and loneliness. Moreover, the breaking of Laura's most beloved piece, the unicorn, by her awkward "gentleman caller" becomes the symbolic trigger for her permanent and tragic retreat into the regressive world of unfulfilled dreams and passivity she shares with her mother—and with her lifeless animals. But, however commanding as a metaphor, Laura's glass menagerie is nevertheless only a single member of a much larger body of imagery qualifying the girl and her mother, who together constitute the play's antagonists. Figures correlating with the menagerie include Laura's frail beauty, her physical disability and leg-brace, as well as her playing hooky from school and hiding in the museum. To these must be added a long string of equally fragile and pathetic things associated with the girl's mother, Amanda: the old faded dresses, the unplayed classical records, the unpaid light bills, and the obsessive memories of a more genteel past. In clear opposition to these figures, the protagonists of this ironic tragedy generate a constellation redolent of vigor, optimism, adventurousness, and social adjustment: athletics and dancing, school dramatics, speech classes, changing jobs, traveling to exotic locales, and mobility in general. Thus, any small group of closely related images, however important in themselves, will be found to have clear associative links with a larger system, which, in turn, faces off against an antithetical system carrying emotionally opposite resonance.

THEOREM 9
EQUALITY OF IMAGE AND SYMBOL

For analytical purposes there is little need to draw a fine distinction between the conventional symbol and the contextual image, except to acknowledge that the affective resonance of the former is largely predetermined by culture, while that of the latter is almost wholly determined by the value assigned to it by the author. Hence, the Leviathan and the common trout, the Wheel of Fortune and the humble bicycle tire may all function together as separate monads carrying potentially equal weight within the figurative opposition of the drama as a whole.

Example. The conflict in Shaw's *Caesar and Cleopatra* between Rome and Ptolemaic Egypt is orchestrated, as one might expect, by the clash of numerous conventional symbols associated with those two ancient cultures: the Imperial eagle against the images of the Sphinx and the god Ra, the austere armor of the Roman soldiers opposed to the diaphanous and outlandish costumes of Cleopatra's court, and the Roman horses set off against the crocodile of the riverbank and the black cat of the luxurious palace. As important as these historically "assigned" symbols are in establishing the vast cultural difference between the vigorous young empire on the move and the decadent kingdom of the Nile, Shaw also employs many other figures of a more purely contextual nature which are equally weighty in establishing an emotional counterpoint for the drama's conflict. Thus, the Roman soldiers devour greasy roast boar while their counterparts in Cleopatra's palace sup upon peacock's brains; so, also, the contrast between the Roman sword thrust to the chest and the

Egyptian knife in the back or slit throat, the Roman operations during the light of day and the Egyptian machinations in the deep of night, the exterior scenes of action for Caesar's legions and the dimly lit interiors for Cleopatra's courtiers. Indeed, the separate tropes of each opposed cluster are so inextricably intertwined that any distinction of rank between conventional symbol and contextual image becomes purely academic. Our dialectical chart of these figures must therefore list them quite democratically as equally vital members of the body dramatic.

THEOREM 10
SHIFTING IMAGES

Characters who during the course of action shift from one dialectical unit to another usually carry with them certain critical images. These shifting images resonate dissonantly with the figurative constellation in which they begin, but harmoniously with the opposed cluster which they eventually join. In so doing they prefigure the character's eventual movement by underscoring his essential foreignness to the camp in which he begins, and his spiritual affinity with the camp to which he is finally drawn.

Example 1. When, in Shakespeare's *Richard II*, the most prominent nobles transfer their loyalty from the ineffectual king to the usurper, Bolingbroke, they permit the simultaneous transfer of the realm's most important symbol—the crown of England. Shakespeare makes much of this figurative shift in the famous scene where the defeated Richard formally relinquishes the crown to his conqueror with studied theatricalism, keeping his grasp on the object's rim even as he hands it over to Bolingbroke, and delaying its release while he delivers a self-serving peroration on the Divine Right of Kings calculated to make the ceremony as embarrassing as possible. At the end of his speech, however, Richard releases the crown, and the actual transfer of power is thus accompanied by the literal shift of its principal symbol. In fact, both the nobility and the crown they support are dialectically misplaced at the beginning of action because Richard is incompetent to rule; the parallel shift of both characters and image to the capable Bolingbroke is therefore represented as a positive movement to a new era of vigorous and wholesome dynastic rule.

Example 2. In comedic love triangles the mobile characters (usually female) move to the side of the protagonists from an initially disengaged position between the two dialectical poles (Part Two, Model 4). When these contested figures at last make the leap to the men of their choice in the dominant unit, their movement is often accompanied by the simultaneous shift of certain other attractive properties. From the mere ten groats that Lucrezia brings to Callimaco in Machiavelli's *The Mandrake* to "the great bag of money" Hoyden promises Young Fashion in Vanbrugh's *The Relapse,* to the cool millions Kitty will bring Jack in Thomas' *Charley's Aunt,* the contested ladies' charm and beauty are thus happily augmented by the means to facilitate elopement at least, and a luxurious married establishment at the optimum. When the contested females assume more archetypal proportions, as they do for instance in Shaw's *Heartbreak House,* their bewitching charms may comprehend a "booty" as large as the material and spiritual wealth of the entire nation.

THEOREM 11
MIRROR IMAGES

Specific images qualifying one side of a drama's collision will frequently have obvious counterparts on the opposing side, as if the two were mirror reversals of one another. Such figurative isomorphs epitomize the larger rhetorical conflict by reducing it to a head-on clash between discrete monads, rendered the more visible by their obvious complementarity.

Examples. Pirandello's obsession with the tenuous distinction between reality and illusion inclines him to the heavy tactical use of isomorphic images, mirror reversals intended to heighten the confusion between substance and form, face and mask. Thus, in *Henry IV,* the two worlds of the Marquis di Nolli—his "normal" life as a contemporary aristocrat and his retreat (advance?) into total identification with a long dead monarch—are everywhere contrasted through figurative reversals. The three-dimensional "statues" of the *tableau vivant* thus have their direct counterparts in the two-dimensional portraits of historical figures; real faces masking falsehood are contrasted to faces in theatrical make-up reflecting the truth. And so on, through such contrastive pairings as the clock (and pulse) beating and stopped, the automobile and the horse, modern dress and historical costume, electric lights and oil lamp. These figurative antitheses are not intended to be subtle, merely disturbing; for Pirandello operates with a high degree of philosophical awareness as to the nature of the conflict he is dramatizing. Other playwrights use such isomorphs more sparingly, and sometimes, one senses, less advertently. Whenever they appear, however, these dialectical "pairs" serve as pointers to a much more general figurative opposition, and ultimately as paradigms for the drama's argument as a whole. One has only to recall the poignant sound of the axe against the tree in Chekhov's *Cherry Orchard* to grasp how such figurative oppositions may in a single stroke not only epitomize the central conflict itself but also clearly indicate who ultimately dominates in that collision.

THEOREM 12
IMAGE AS A CHECK ON ACTION

Sometimes during the process of analysis an image or group of images will appear to be uncomfortably out of harmony with the functional unit to which it has been assigned. This often indicates that an error has been committed during the primary stage of action-analysis, resulting in the dialectical misplacement of the character to whom the imagery in question belongs. In such cases the reinstatement of the character to his rightful camp will bring the associated images back into proper alignment, and the correction will be seen at once to have sorted out a confusion of polarities at both the primary and secondary levels. If such an adjustment fails to clarify matters, this is a sign that a more serious error has been made at the level of action, possibly a wholly incorrect assessment of the radical conflict itself.

Example. On first approach to O'Neill's *Long Day's Journey Into Night*, I mistakenly placed James Tyrone's dead father among the drama's protagonists, probably because he was, like them, an offstage figure (having died before the commencement of dramatic time proper), and also because the few facts provided about his existence seemed to have little bearing on his son's life as an American matinee idol. Upon proceeding to draw up a chart of the play's imagery, however, I was immediately struck by the jarring contrast between the images connected with Tyrone's late father and those of the protagonists with whom I had placed him; for while the latter were all associated with profitable businesses and the trappings of material success, the former painted the very picture of squalor and defeat: Irish bogs, dirt, broken files in the machine shop, pigs drowned in the duck pond, and, finally, suicide by rat poison. It immediately became clear that the father's imagery corresponded rather with that of his son and the other antagonists—with their foggy beaches, dim light, cheap hotels, watered whisky, and, most importantly, their slow suicide by alcohol and morphine. The repositioning of Tyrone's father in the antagonists' column not only brought his associated images into correct alignment, it also pointed up the essential connection between him and his descendants. For it was the old man's abject poverty that had filled his son, James, with such horror that he gave up his dream to be a great actor in order to make money playing only a single popular role; it also produced in him the compulsion to buy the overpriced land that contributes to the insecurity and depression of his wife and sons. In this way a figurative disharmony within a single functional unit led to the repositioning of a dialectically misplaced character, and at the same time to a fuller understanding of the spiritual connection between this figure and his descendants in the recessive unit.

Had this repositioning of Tyrone's father *not* brought his associated imagery into harmony with that of the antagonists, or had there remained other figurative discords within both functional units despite such adjustment, this would have indicated that the initial stage of analysis had gone more gravely astray, either misplacing several characters or, at worst, misapprehending the nature of the central conflict itself. In this way, the dialectic of imagery serves as a check upon the dialectic of action, warning us that figurative dissociations in either functional unit are symptoms of something gone wrong at the initial and most critical stage of analysis.

IMPLICATIONAL DIALECTIC

THEOREM 13
DESCRIPTIVE ABSTRACTION

The third stage of analysis consists of the descriptive reduction of the protago- nists' and antagonists' units as they have been derived at the first two stages of action and imagery. This procedure entails finding appropriate one-word abstractions to epitomize the essential common characteristics of the individual functional units, carefully examining each for salient qualities shared by all of its members, as revealed both in their actions and in the figurative orchestration that accompanies those actions (see Theorems 14–16). Every commonly shared attribute—whether physical, social, psychological, economic, moral, aesthetic, or any other trait from the lexicon of human values—should be set down under the unit exhibiting this characteristic, with applicable terms being added to each column until the descrip- tive possibilities appear to be exhausted. Even somewhat redundant terms are desirable if they discriminate between slightly different but nonetheless distinct aspects of the same unit. The resulting two columns of abstractions will constitute a qualitative description of the drama's action and counteraction—its implicational dialectic.

THEOREM 14
QUALITATIVE OPPOSITION

The third-level descriptive abstractions always function antithetically, reflecting the oppositional character of dramatic action and counteraction in general. Consequently, if a certain qualitative term (say, "salvation") applies to the protagonists' unit, then its dialectical opposite ("damnation") must necessarily apply to the antagonists' unit. For the truly essential attributes of one side of the argument will always find their antithetical qualities on the opposed side. If, however, the antonym of a seemingly appropriate abstraction for one unit does not apply with equal justice to the opposing unit, then both terms must be rejected as irrelevant to the fantasy's argument; and, in fact, it will usually be seen in such cases that either the original choice of abstraction was infelicitous, or else an inaccurate term had been selected to stand as its antonym. An apposite pair of antonyms constitutes a single, irreducible descriptive unit of the fantasy's implicational dialectic.

THEOREM 15
TERMS EXTRAORDINARY

Common abstract nouns together with their most appropriate antonyms will suffice in most cases to describe single qualitative aspects of the drama's bipolarity. Occasionally, however, it will be necessary to invent brief phrase-antinomies to render certain unusual qualitative oppositions for which the language possesses no convenient terms. Thus, our descriptive reduction of Sophocles' **Oedipus the King** *(Part Two, Model 2) renders a central aspect of that drama's religious fatalism with the improvised phrase-antinomy "Acceptance of Destiny/Rejection of Destiny." The briefer "Acceptance/Rejection" will not do because it omits the critical concept of "destiny," while the more modern opposition of "Predestination/Free Will" cannot be used because the second term of the set is utterly foreign to the tragedy's ethos. Even contemporary dramas may require such improvisation when unusual qualitative oppositions are present. Similarly, it may occasionally be convenient to restore certain archaic abstractions—such as Shakespeare's well-known "Being/Seeming" dichotomy—whenever they convey an important feature of the drama's bipolarity with particular felicity.*

THEOREM 16
VERIFICATION OF ACTION & IMAGE

The abstract terms employed to describe a particular functional unit must be appropriate to each and every character in that unit. If, however, they accurately describe all the characters save only one or two, it is probable that the exceptional characters have been dialectically misplaced and belong in the opposing camp. When such errors of placement have not already been detected at the previous stage of imagery-analysis (Theorem 12), they will usually become quite obvious at the stage of descriptive abstraction; for while the abstract terms describing the unit in which a character has been misplaced will seem highly inappropriate to him, the antithetical terms qualifying the opposing unit will apply to him with equally great propriety. If not, a more serious error has probably been committed at the initial stage of analysis, and there are grounds for suspicion that the central conflict itself has been wrongly anatomized.

THEOREM 17
SUB-PLOTS

Most sub-plots are structurally and conceptually parallel to the main plots upon which they hang; as a result, the two can usually be treated together as a single action assuming the same dynamic pattern and generating but one set of implicational dichotomies. Secondary actions are therefore usually analogs to the main actions. However, in certain rare cases—some British Restoration dramas, for instance—the "upper" and "under" plots are not parallel, and thus require analysis as separate actions conforming to different dynamic models and generating two different sets of descriptive abstractions.

THEOREM 18
IMPLICATIONAL "DEPTH"

The relative implicational complexity of a particular drama can be measured by the total number of descriptive antinomies necessary to describe its collision at the levels of action and imagery. Thus, an exceedingly rich drama may demand thirty or more descriptive pairs to abstract its argument, an average work from eleven to twenty pairs, and a particularly thin piece no more than five to ten. Yet complexity in this sense has no necessary bearing on dramatic impact, which depends primarily upon the artistry with which the motives are objectified, secondarily upon their particular combination, and, finally, upon the auditor's subjective reaction to that combination (Theorem 21). Hence, some justly celebrated dramas require only a moderate number of descriptive pairs; some, indeed, only a few.

THEOREM 19
DOMINANT/RECESSIVE AS WISH/FEAR

The dominant and recessive voices of a drama's argument constitute an oppositional system for which modern analytical psychologies have provided several useful paradigms. But whether the dominant voice of this argument be regarded in terms of the Freudian "ego ideal" or the Jungian "Imago" matters little, so long as it is understood that the victorious protagonists objectify the authorial ideal of self at the time of composition. Conversely, the recessive unit of the antagonists projects the feared antithetical self, whether the latter be understood in terms of "repressed impulses" or the "shadow" side of the personality. Our descriptive reduction of the text's argument therefore constitutes an abstraction of the authorial self and "anti-self," the wished-for and dreaded attributes, as these interior adversaries have become reified in the fantasy's action and counteraction.

THEOREM 20
IRONY AS CONTAMINATED DOMINANT FUNCTION

From a structural point of view, irony occurs whenever the protagonists' unit requires descriptive terms that are conventionally negative in character. The depth of a drama's irony can therefore be reckoned by the ratio of negative to positive terms required by the dominant unit, with gentle irony producing but few negatives, moderate irony a nearly equal admixture of negative and positive, & deep irony a preponderance of negatives. Because the dominant unit objectifies the fantasy's wishful function, heavily ironic dramas may be said to constitute a negative wish, a concession to impulses felt to be degrading or dysfunctional but nevertheless imperious. In psychological terms, irony may be understood as a contamination of the "self" by the "shadow."

IDEOLOGICAL DIALECTIC

THEOREM 21
DRAMA/AUDITOR DIALECTIC

The confrontation between drama and spectator engages two otherwise separate diadic systems: the superior and inferior functions of the drama on the one hand, and those of the auditor on the other. The agreement or divergence of motives resulting from the interface of these oppositional systems must therefore be suspected as major sources of aesthetic pleasure or displeasure. The range of possible experience, from enchantment through indifference to revulsion, from emotional catharsis to frustration, will thus vary with the amount of overlap between the auditor's own superior and inferior value systems and those objectified in the dominant/recessive functions of the drama. Knowledge of the drama's motivational oppositions—obtained by rigorous engagement of the preceding theorems—will assist auditors to intellectually comprehend their instinctive responses to that fantasy, and thus to gain clarity with respect to their own prevailing values as they either harmonize or clash with those of the text.

Part II

The Seven Structural Models

. . . . evolution is neither a free-for-all, nor the execution of a rigidly predetermined computer programme. It could be compared to a musical composition whose possibilities are limited by the rules of harmony and the structure of diatonic scales—which, however, permit an inexhaustible number of original creations. Or it could be compared to a game of chess obeying fixed rules but with equally inexhaustible variations. Lastly, the vast number of existing animal species (about one million) and the small number of major classes (about fifty) and of major phyla (about ten), could be compared with the vast number of works of literature and the small number of basic themes or plots. All works of literature are variations of a limited number of *leitmotifs*, derived from man's archetypal experiences and conflicts, but adapted each time to a new environment—the costumes, conventions and language of the period. Not even Shakespeare could invent an original plot. Goethe quoted with approval the Italian dramatist Carlo Gozzi, according to whom there are only thirty-six tragic situations. Goethe himself thought that there were probably even less; but their exact number is a well-kept secret among writers of fiction. A work of literature is constructed out of thematic holons—which, like the homologue organs, need not even have a common ancestor.

Arthur Koestler, The Ghost in the Machine

INTRODUCTION

The postulates set forth in Part One of this study suggest a strictly limited number of dynamic possibilities for the playing-out of dramatic fantasy. I shall argue that there are in fact but seven basic movement-patterns, and that every dramatic conflict will conform to the dynamic tendencies of one or another of these seven classes. At first glance, however, the number of patterns would appear to be even smaller. For if plays and screenplays are essentially binary and oppositional in structure (Theorem 1), and if the movement of characters between negative and positive poles of action is always unidirectional (Theorem 6), then there would seem to be just three dynamic patterns implicit within the system: (1) no movement at all, (2) movement from positive to negative poles of action, and (3) movement from negative to positive. These three kinetic possibilities may be represented by the following schematics, in which the letter-symbols stand for any number of characters, and the arrows indicate the direction of motion, if any:

(1) No movement:

PROTAGONIST	ANTAGONIST
W	X
Y	Z

(2) Movement from negative to positive:

PROTAGONIST	ANTAGONIST
X	Y
Z ◄——————————————— (Z)	

(3) Movement from positive to negative:

Aside from these three patterns obviously implicit within the binary system, there are, as I have indicated, four other possibilities. Two of these additional movement-patterns often appear when characters adopt at the outset a position of neutrality or dialectical disengagement between the major poles of action. Dramatists employ this sort of "triangulation" whenever they represent certain characters to be the objects at issue in the struggle between the primary contestants, as occurs in the standard boy-meets-girl-and-defeats-rival situation, popularly (and rightly) known as the "comedic love triangle." Less well understood is what I call the "negative love triangle," in which the contested apex character is eventually captured by the antagonist and as a result comes to a bad end. In either case, the apex figure eventually moves from his (or her) initially disengaged position to one of the triangle's primary poles of action. Thus, in addition to the first three dynamic patterns clearly implicit in any binary opposition, these two initially triangular situations provide fourth and fifth possibilities:

(4) Movement from apex to positive:

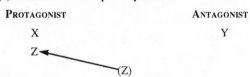

(5) Movement from apex to negative:

The potential for dialectical disengagement between the major camps also opens up two further dynamic possibilities, this time involving movement away from the primary poles and towards the apex of the triangle. These "synthetic" situations occur whenever both thesis and antithesis are represented to be equally invalid, that is to say, whenever the motives of both protagonist and antagonist appear to be morally and rationally unacceptable. In such instances a dialectically disengaged character will be strategically placed at the apex of the triangle, from which position he will argue for a rational and humane alternative to the ugly battle between the primary opponents. The first variant of this pattern permits at least one of the initial belligerents to be won over by the arguments of the apex character and thus to move to his side, from which augmented "synthetic" position the remaining primary belligerent will be easily defeated. The second variant does not give such power to the apex character, but instead merely "plants" him as a visible rational alternative to an otherwise stale-mated war between clearly unacceptable opponents; here the author refuses to engineer the synthetic resolution that is so strongly implied by his apex character, rather leaving it for the audience to make the only sensible inference. These two synthetic dynamics may be represented schematically as follows:

(6) Movement from primary pole to apex:

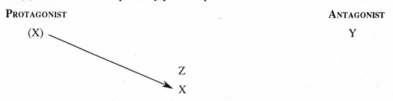

(7) Implied movement from primary poles to apex:

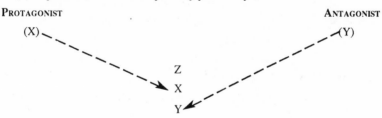

These seven dynamic patterns exhaust the possibilities of movement within the drama's system of binary opposition. For in such a system characters can only be located at either the positive or negative poles, or else in a dialectically disengaged position at the apex. Any movement among these three positions is thus limited to two types each: (1) cross-dialectical, positive or negative; (2) from the apex, positive or negative; or (3) towards the apex, from positive or negative. Taking into account the single structure that permits no kinesis whatever, we have thus found that the potentials for movement, or non-movement, in dramatic fantasy are limited to these seven. Using the biological metaphor, one might therefore say that the realm of dramatic fantasy is composed of a single phylum (the principle of wishful binary opposition), seven classes (the dynamic possibilities within that system), and innumerable species (the individual dramatic works themselves).

It should be confessed at once that the seven classes of movement outlined here were not primarily deduced from general principles, but rather inferred by induction from the analysis of many dramatic works over a period of years. The only general principle on which I relied from the outset was the hypothesis that dramatic structure is inherently binary in character (Theorem 1). It was through the attempt to work out the implications of this hypothesis in the texts of specific dramas that the other principles—most especially those of unidirectional movement (Theorem 6), hidden players (Theorem 4), and misdirection (Theorem 5)—began to fall into place as natural extensions of the original hypothesis. Once these and other corollary principles were formulated, it was only a matter of time until the strictly limited number of dynamic possibilities became evident; for, in practical fact, every drama to which the theorems were applied conformed to one of these seven patterns. Nevertheless, a natural skepticism led me to spend much effort in the attempt to discover other kinetic potentialities within this system, and even to disprove the validity of the original hypothesis itself. But the longer I searched for alternative or even completely random patterns, the more I became convinced that I had stumbled upon what appeared to be the basic moves in the chess game of drama—that these seven dynamic classes constituted the fundamental strategies for the imaginative resolution of all internal conflicts objectified in dramatic form. In the realm of the drama, at least, these patterns appeared to be none other than the elusive "thematic holons" which Arthur Koestler, in his *The Ghost in the Machine*, had posited as basic skeletal structures underlying the myriad individual species of the form.

One of the most intriguing aspects of these seven dynamic patterns is that, although infinite variations can be played on any one of them, all such variations share certain mythical and modal characteristics in common. Moreover, works conforming to the two "synthetic" dynamics even share a large number of identical motives, implications which are inherent in the very nature of these two structures, and which therefore reappear again and again, whether the specific incarnation come from ancient Greece, Elizabethan England, or French New Wave cinema. Knowledge of the peculiarities of plot, tone, and sometimes motive of each dynamic class will therefore greatly assist in the work of identifying the structure of any particular drama. And once the critical task of determining the play's action-structure has been accomplished, it will then be possible, following the other theorems set forth in Part One, to elucidate its dialectics of imagery and symbolism (Theorems 7–12), and to proceed from there to a descriptive reduction of the work's implicational dialectic—an abstraction of the wishful and fearful motives objectified at the previous levels of action and imagery (Theorems 13–20).

In the pages that follow I shall devote a separate chapter to each of the seven dynamic classes, defining them at greater length, surveying in a general way the mythical, modal, and characterological tendencies of each, and also giving examples of the types of plays, screenplays, and opera libretti that assume the various patterns. The final, and largest section of each chapter will consist of a complete dialectical analysis of a noteworthy and typical instance of the dynamic class in question. The purpose of these analyses is threefold: to offer the reader a detailed picture of how the individual play or screenplay conforms to the structural model defined in the chapter, to demonstrate in practice the methodological principles set forth in Part One, and to elucidate the individual drama according to these lights.

Because I shall be drawing not only on pieces written in English but also in ancient Greek as well as modern Russian, Italian, French, and German, it will be necessary to work (as our theatre has long been obliged to do) with reputable English translations of these foreign classics. Inevitably, therefore, some distortion, particularly at the level of imagery, will be carried over into my discussions; however, so long as the translation does not diverge from the general content and order of the speeches, or in any way alter the drama's basic events at the most critical level of action, then it should suffice for my purposes. In every case, I have attempted to draw upon translations by recognized specialists. Where particularly sensitive decisions have hinged on the precise interpretation of specific locutions, I have consulted the original texts and, where necessary, rendered those locutions in the original or in Roman transliteration.

Owing to limitations of space, I have chosen not to offer my own ideological reaction to the plays in question (Theorem 21), but have instead restricted my concluding comments on each work to a few general remarks about certain tendencies and peculiarities revealed in its implicational dialectic. I have left it for the reader to engage his or her own ideological dialectic with the motives revealed in these plays.

FIRST MODEL
STATIC

Definition. The static structure allows of no dialectical movement or apostasy from one functional unit to another. In this it is unique among the dynamic classes; for here the polarization of forces is absolute, and dissension within the ranks of either camp never leads to outright secession *. Consequently, both functional units retain the integrity of their original make-up throughout. Static actions are so contrived that the protagonists' unit achieves its victory neither through defections from the antagonists' unit nor through the expulsion of contaminating elements from its own ranks, but rather by simple main force. Hence, plays of this structure can be likened to artillery duels across a great canyon: the army with the largest guns and most ammunition will eventually silence its opponent. To say that a drama is static, however, does not mean that its argument is stalemated, but rather that, though one camp always emerges victorious, the final alignment of forces remains exactly the same as it was at the beginning. In Hegel's vocabulary this situation represents the most blatant form of "cancellation" of the unacceptable force; for in the static structure no accommodation is possible between protagonist and antagonist, and the former's ultimate dominance is seen in retrospect as inevitable.*

Schematic. The following chart represents the dialectical position of various characters (indicated by letter-symbols) throughout the entire course of a hypothetical drama. Because the action of this drama is static there is no need to employ arrows graphing movement between dialectical poles: all of the characters who begin in the protagonists' unit remain in that dominant position until the end; likewise, those who begin in the antagonists' unit remain condemned to their recessive role:

PROTAGONIST	ANTAGONIST
W	X
Y	Z

General. The static structure presents an argument so clear-cut and extreme, so obviously dialectical, that its tone is invariably tense and melodramatic. This accounts for the almost exclusive appearance of this form in the modal phases of romance and its counterpart, irony. For whether the action depicts a struggle between good and evil (as in romance) or between two mutually exclusive evils (as in much irony), the utterly irreconcilable nature of the argument arouses a deep sense of division and frustration.

Romance dramatists who favor the static structure employ the tactical approach of simple denial, always permitting the side of righteousness to emerge victorious, yet at the same time refusing to concede the dialectical interdependence of the opposing force. The apostasy of characters from one unit to another would constitute a tacit admission of the potential for both good and evil in the same agent; however, the radical dualism of the static structure cannot accommodate such moral flexibility, and as a consequence romances which take this form give the impression of näivety.

Shakespeare's *Pericles*, with its simple moral allegory and self-conscious archaism, provides an exemplary picture of static drama in the mode of romance; for the separation of forces in this play is radical and permanent. On the victorious side, Neptune, a thinly disguised Christian God, enables the noble Pericles to survive a series of unlikely misadventures, including the "resurrection" of his wife from the dead and the rescue of his daughter from a brothel, her virginity intact. Of the two pairs of villains, the incestuous Antiochus and his daughter are summarily dispatched by a bolt of lightning, while Cleon and his scheming wife are burned at the stake by the outraged citizens of Tarsus—such strict poetic justice casting a tendentious glow of the hell-fires awaiting the agents of Satan. *Pericles* depicts neither conversions nor backslidings, for in representing spirit and flesh, innocence and knowledge to be absolutely inimical this drama also carves out an impassable chasm between salvation and damnation: where there are no degrees of guilt and no hope of redemption from sin, neither is there freedom of will. Apostasy or conversion, represented dramatically as cross-dialectical movement, therefore become impossible. In this respect *Pericles* resembles Eliot's *Murder in the Cathedral*, which also assumes the static form and therefore necessarily opens the same unbridgeable gap between salvation and damnation, faith and despair.

The disadvantages of the static structure for exhortatory purposes can be illustrated by comparing *Pericles* with Betti's *The Queen and the Rebels* whose more fluid, "apostatic" structure (Model 2) permits us to witness the heroine's spiritual regeneration. For Argia's self-sacrificing act of atonement allows her to move from the fraternity of the damned to a state of grace—dialectically, from the camp of the rebellious and despairing to that of the (offstage) Protagonist of all Christian dramas. Such movement implies a freedom of will, a drawbridge always ready to come down across the moat separating Babylon from the City of God. However, this traffic is not possible in static dramas such as *Pericles*, where the opposing functional units are divided by an insuperable barrier.

Molière's *Don Juan* provides another instance of a dialectically static drama in the mode of romance, for this work also creates a rigid separation of forces that permits no crossing of ideological lines. Unlike the later Mozart-daPonte version of the legend, in which the Don's servant, Leporello, finally refuses to obey his earthly lord's commands and thus moves to the bosom of the godly, in Molière's treatment Sganarelle stays by his master's side to the end of his blasphemous career. Don Juan claims to be a rationalist, but under pressure lets slip that he has faith in at least one supernatural agent: the Devil. Thus, as in Shakespeare's *Pericles*, the chief offstage combatants of *Don Juan* reveal themselves to be God and Satan, under one or the other of whose banners each character begins, and remains, throughout the drama's action (Theorem 4). Whatever Molière's private thoughts about the legend's hellfire and brimstone morality, the play's anti-Enlightenment sentiment manifests itself in a radical polarization of forces that prevents the transformation of evil into righteousness.

Irony, as Frye has pointed out, constitutes an inversion of romance; for here the gods (if indeed they are still seen to exist) appear in their malign aspect, while the hero possesses less than average human power rather than more. Yet despite, or perhaps because of, its inverse relationship to romance, irony often favors the static structure. Like romance, irony offers small hope for reconciliation between the colliding forces at its heart; but the picture now becomes bleaker, for neither protagonist nor antagonist appears to be morally or psychologically acceptable. Instead of an irreconcilable war between good and evil, we are here presented with an equally unaccommodating struggle between bad and worse, with the latter force often emerging triumphant (Theorem 20).

Although a highly developed sense of moral vertigo among twentieth-century dramatists often inclines them to favor the static structure in its ironic phase, this modal variant has antecedents that go back to ancient Greece. Indeed, the earliest examples of this form, with its terrible lop-sidedness and tension, come from Euripides, who in three of his most famous dramas pits weak and benighted mortals against the all-powerful but malicious gods. Neither *Hippolytus*, *The Trojan Women*, nor *The Bacchae* represents the movement of characters from one camp to another, for the perception of a great void between the pitiful desires of mere humans and the unfathomable will of the capricious Olympians prohibits any true communion between the two realms. Each of these dramas represents the conflict between the mortal characters onstage as a purely internal struggle incited by the irrational and sadistic machinations of their immortal puppet-masters. Yet this radical polarity is occulted in both *Hipploytus* and *The Trojan Woman*, where the spotlight plays almost entirely upon the internecine conflicts and resulting *pathos* of the victims: their persecutors either remain offstage (Theorem 4) or appear only in brief but ominous prologues (Theorem 5). But if the purport of such withering irony was apparent to Euripides' original audiences (who awarded him but few prizes), it is less obvious to moderns owing to the dramatist's use of misdirected focus. Only in *The Bacchae* does the major protagonist, Dionysus, repeatedly appear onstage as a constant reminder of who is responsible for the unspeakable sufferings wrought upon the god's detractors and devotees alike.

These works of Euripides establish the static form's penchant for protagonists who have all the cards stacked in their favor from the beginning. And if the ultimate victory of such all-powerful figures seems inevitable only in retrospect, this is both because we are led to empathize with the beleaguered victims, and also because the playwright must hold the outcome in temporary suspense if he is to develop any dramatic tension worth mentioning. Of course, the outcome of many a drama seems inevitable in retrospect; but the static structure creates an especially strong sense of fatality (and thus futility) owing to the extremely lop-sided character of the battle. It is almost as if the practitioners of this form derived a certain sadistic pleasure in toying with the antagonist, reveling in his frustration, and demonstrating at leisure how easy it is to polish off an animal who is already trapped. Thus, in Green's famous screenplay *Odd Man Out*, all escape routes are cut off for Johnny, the IRA man on the run; and the utter hopelessness of his plight is epitomized in the amazing scene in which an alcoholic artist insists on painting his portrait in order to capture the expression of a man who is bleeding to death!

The adjectives "schizoid" and "autistic" have been applied with some justice to dramatists such as Pirandello, Beckett, and Ionesco; for the conflicting impulses objectified in many of their plays admit of no accord, except the agreement to disagree to the bitter end in duels where words have lost meaning and fantasy assumes the character of an oppressive reality. The vestiges of romance can still be traced, however, in the domination of God figures now rendered nearly devoid of moral substance, the suffocating triumph of social conventions and taboos depicted as malign, or (as in the case of Pirandello) an assertion of the superiority of poetic illusion over logic and workaday experience. Apostasy is less common in the works of these dramatists because compromise becomes impossible where the conflicting motives are represented as absolutely and eternally inimical. Thus, both Pirandello's *Right You Are (If You Think So)* and Ionesco's *The Bald Soprano* develop actions which, at the implicational level, present "either-or/both-and" dichotomies, with the scales heavily weighted in favor of the dissociative and imperative "either/or."

When dramas of the static structure assume the mode of ironic tragedy, their central characters are still portrayed as victims—though less of malign adversaries than of their own character deficiencies, which condemn them to failure from the outset. O'Neill's James Tyrone and Miller's Willie Loman are both temperamentally incapable of emulating the successful types they so envy, and their oblique recognition of this incapacity forces them to withdraw from the race—the former retreating into alcoholic self-justification, the latter seeking the peace of self-inflicted death. Similarly incapacitated by temperament for life in the household of her vulgar sister and brother-in-law, Williams' Blanche DuBois eventually withdraws into psychosis. Much the same situation obtains in Truffaut's screenplay *The Story of Adelle H.*, which depicts the anatomy of a passion so obsessive and unrealistic as to lead the heroine to madness; for Adelle's self-consuming and maniacal worship of the social-climbing Lieutenant Pinson creates between her and "normal" bourgeois society a psychological barrier so formidable as to render her dream a lost cause from the beginning. A less melodramatic version of this same incapacity to meet society on its own terms is to be seen in the film *Stevie* (based on the life of the poetess Stevie Smith), in which the central character's unhappiness and death are predicated on her morbid fear of adult sexuality and of the outside world in general. Each of these static dramas erects an impenetrable wall between ordinary social commerce on the one side, and the essentially introverted and maladaptive fantasies of the lonely antagonists on the other.

Surprisingly enough, the true protagonists (victors) of these ironic tragedies will for the most part require conventionally positive qualities to describe their motives, while the self-defeating antagonists (however one may pity them) will generate negative terms. Thus, Willie Loman and James Tyrone are both impelled by a concatenation of clearly dysfunctional motives, as are Blanche DuBois and Adelle H. What is sometimes difficult to perceive in such cases—because events are viewed, as it were, largely through the victim's eyes—is that the seemingly callous protagonists objectify values that are largely normative and life-affirming. Therefore, however ironic in tone, tragedies assuming the static form are rarely ironic in the structural sense of requiring negative descriptive terms to qualify their protagonists.

The contrary is often true, however, when static dramas leave the mode of ironic tragedy and enter that of irony proper. In this even darker mode they usually also become fully ironic in the structural sense of permitting the victory of characters whose motives range from the merely perverse to the obviously malign—from the deeply secretive and schizoid "heroes" of Pirandello to the irrational and sadistic Olympians of Euripides. The protagonists of such works will therefore require, at the third, implicational stage of analysis, descriptive terms that are predominantly or partially negative in any conventional accounting (Theorem 20).

When static dramas move into the phase of ironic comedy—most notably in the sunnier works of Pirandello—they may or may not become ironic in the structural sense; that is to say, their protagonists may objectify either largely negative or largely positive attributes, depending on the whim of the author. Thus, the dominant characters of Pirandello's *Right You Are* are motivated by a constellation of ominous qualities that can only be epitomized as anti-social; yet the protagonists of Nabokov's *The Waltz Invention*, which is also static in structure, require conventionally positive abstractions to characterize them.

In general, however, it is fair to say that, outside the modes of romance and tragedy, the static structure inclines more to negative protagonists than any other dynamic class. For this is the preferred form for dramatists who wish to indulge the shadow side of their personality.

Owing to its extreme dissociation of forces, static drama tends to contain a large number of dialectically paired images, figures which are clearly antithetical, often even mirror reversals of each other (Theorem 11). Thus, of the two opposed households in Pirandello's *Right You Are*, the first Ponza establishment contains a wall-mirror that reflects images in the normal fashion, while the second home contains a mirror that reflects no images whatever. Williams' *Streetcar Named Desire* epitomizes the extreme contrast between the worlds of Stanley Kowalsky and Blanche DuBois in the figurative opposition between the glare of bare light bulbs and the soft light of bulbs covered with Chinese paper lamp shades. Similarly, in *The Dance of Death*, Strindberg places the offstage Colonel's home on the mainland with its convenient telephone system, while banishing the onstage antagonists to a remote island whose only means of communication with the outside is by telegraph. Such obvious figurative isomorphs serve to emphasize not only the extreme psychological contrast between the belligerents but also the grave imbalance of forces in favor of the protagonist.

As we have seen, the static structure is unique among the seven dynamic classes in that neither of its functional units is contaminated by intrusive elements from the opposed function; consequently, the urge for decontamination (catharsis) cannot be imputed here as a motivating factor in the fantasy. With the opposites neatly separated and the protagonists' unit clearly in control from the outset, these dramas nevertheless insist on playing themselves out, on reasserting, as it were, the dominance of a superior function whose control is never seriously threatened in the first place. Yet if all other forms express the urge for decontamination by forcing characters to shift positions (Theorem 6), what then does the static structure express in the absence of such requirement? I would suggest that the underlying motive here is precautionary, based on the fear that chaos might ensue if the rigid segregation between "self" and "shadow" were ever to break down. This may explain why static dramas tend to create a high degree of anxiety, even in the romance mode, and further, why they always have about them a frustratingly preordained quality. For these are pre-emptive wars, initiated in fear, which is often masked by an arrogant assertion of the right. Either that, or impotent indictments of an (internal) order perceived to be malign but nevertheless inescapable (Theorem 20).

In dealing with static drama of any era or mode, we should therefore expect to encounter a collision between mutually exclusive absolutes, one of which the playwright usually demands that we accept at the implicit risk of incurring either divine wrath or authorial derision. Nor are the characters permitted a "choice," a change of conscience that would alter the overwhelming and permanent imbalance of forces inherent in this structure, of which I shall now examine in detail one capital example.

ANALYSIS
Luigi Pirandello, *Six Characters in Search of an Author*[1]

(1) *Dialectic of Action*

The opposition of forces in Pirandello's most celebrated play can be summed up in three words: characters against actors. For the central conflict of this work derives from the family of characters, whose offstage author has left their story unfinished, "independently" imposing their will and asserting the superiority of their tragic and immortal "reality" over that of the mere mortals who earn their daily bread in the theatre by representing characters and stories other than their own. However complicated by amusing philosophical ambiguities and illusion-breaking jokes, *Six Characters in Search of an Author* leaves no room for doubt about the nature of its radical collision, thus obviating confusion between purely internecine fracases (of which there are many on the protagonists' side) and the drama's central conflict (Theorem 5). Therefore, our main task at the opening stage of analysis is to verify the apparently obvious victory of the characters over the actors. This precaution is necessary in order to make certain that we do not mistakenly reverse the dominant and recessive poles of action.

The play offers some temptation to such an error, particularly at the outset, because the characters enter as suppliants pathetically eager to dramatize the melodramatic story, which their author has refused to commit to paper, or even to complete in his imagination. Naturally, the Producer and his company at first resent this intrusion on their rehearsal of Pirandello's *Rules of the Game*. Later, however, the troupe's vexation turns to curiosity and pity as the apparently demented family begins to

---

[1]Luigi Pirandello, *Six Characters in Search of an Author*, translated by Felicity Firth, in *Luigi Pirandello Collected Plays*, vol. 2, edited by Robert Rietty (London: John Calder. New York: Riverrun Press, 1988). All page references are to this text.

unfold its tale of woe and mutual recrimination. Indeed, the characters' lurid story begins to look like a "natural" for theatrical exploitation. How, then, can these miserable six "unfinished" suppliants possibly dominate the action when they place themselves at the mercy of the opportunistic Producer and his company?

Yet dominate they do, and from the very outset when their unexpected entrance completely disrupts the rehearsal of a scheduled play. Adamant that their story be finished, the characters override the Producer's curt order to throw them out, while Father and Step-daughter, the most loquacious of the six, begin an alternately pathetic and acrimonious diatribe on the family's bizarre history. With growing fascination the actors learn of the Father who throws his simple-minded wife into the arms of an employee, with whom she runs away and conceives three illegitimate children; of this same Father who abandons his legitimate Son to the charity of a humble family of farmers, while himself succumbing in his loneliness to a shameful attraction to juvenile prostitutes. They hear also of the Mother who drags her eldest daughter to work at Madam Pace's hat shop, which turns out to be the front for a brothel; of the Father's shocking chance encounter with his own Step-daughter in this very establishment; and of the Son's disgust at the unexpected arrival of his Mother, the Step-daughter, the little Boy, and baby Girl as suppliants at his doorstep. These recollections, narrated with great emotion, urgency, and no little disagreement, bring the rehearsal to a complete halt.

So absorbed, in fact, do the members of the troupe become that they abandon their plan to stage Pirandello's *Rules of the Game* and decide instead to create a scenario based on the story of the six characters. But even in this project they are at first unnerved and in the end utterly frustrated by the phantom family. Real trouble begins when the company attempts to rehearse the piquant scene between Father and Step-daughter in Madam Pace's hat shop. To the great annoyance of the Producer and his principal actors, the scene's original participants alternately express anguish and amused disgust at being represented by outsiders. They constantly interrupt, demanding absolute verisimilitude; for them nothing extraneous, neither actors, costumes, nor cut-out scenery, can adequately express their true and only "reality" (43–53).

The squabbling rehearsal of the first two scenes (there are no formal act or scene divisions, merely intervals which are supposed to represent actual breaks in the rehearsal) leads to a philosophical debate in the third section when the Father attempts to prove not only that he and the other five characters are "real," but also that the Producer and his company are merely "illusions":

> FATHER: . . . I just wanted to show you that if we (*he refers to himself and the other CHARACTERS*) have no other reality outside illusion, then perhaps you ought not to place too much faith in your reality, either, the solid flesh and blood you have today—on the grounds that like yesterday's reality, today's too will surely turn out to be illusion by tomorrow.
>
> PRODUCER (*determined to make light of all this*): That's good! Now tell me that you and this play of yours are more real and true than I am!
>
> FATHER (*with the greatest seriousness*): But of course; without doubt!
> (57).

The crux of the Father's argument is that the "immutable reality" of dramatic characters renders them ontologically superior to mere mortals with their constantly changing temporal illusions.

From the characters' point of view, however, one grave obstruction has so far rendered their "eternal moment," their otherwise "fixed reality" somewhat less than absolute; for, as much as they have tried to tempt him, their author has stubbornly persisted in his refusal to complete their story, thus abandoning them to the shadowy realm of the rejected fantasy (58–9). Because the author might die and leave them incomplete forever, the characters must intrude on the present fantasy in a desperate effort to secure immortality. This they accomplish in a properly catastrophic manner. For when they approach the most shocking scene of all—the one the playwright has refused to commit to paper—the mesmerized company watches the characters succeed in overwhelming both stage illusion and authorial rejection. As the Mother describes going to the Son's room to plead with him for acceptance of her illegitimate family, the little Girl acts out her drowning in the garden fountain, while her terrified and despairing brother (the Boy) puts a pistol to his head and fires (62–7). The company's astonishment and confusion at this *coup de théâtre* results in a brief argument as to whether the suicide is genuine or not:

> LEADING ACTRESS: . . . He's dead! Poor boy! Oh, how ghastly!
>
> LEADING ACTOR: . . . Some corpse! He's pretending! It's a fake! Don't believe it!
>
> OTHER ACTORS: . . . It's not a fake! It's true! He's really dead!
>
> OTHER ACTORS: . . . Rubbish! It's a fake! He's pretending!

Above this tumult rises a single voice:

> FATHER (*standing up and shouting them all down*):
>> There's no pretence! It's the truth; it's real!
>> That, ladies and gentlemen, is reality! (67–8).

Believing the Father to have spoken the truth, the actors and technicians rush in panic from the theatre—as the six characters remain behind in solemn and triumphant tableau (68). For with the acting-out of this, their final scene, the fictional beings have proven their superiority over mere actors, while at the same time concluding their drama against the wishes of the author, whom they have forced by the strength of their fantastical reality to grant them the immortality they so desperately sought. As the Father had pronounced at the outset, ". . . a character really does have a life of his own, stamped with his own characteristics which ensure that he is always who he is. While a man . . . can very easily be 'no one'" (56).

The six characters, then, constitute the protagonists of this ironic melodrama; the members of the theatrical troupe make up its antagonists. Before constructing an action-chart, however, it will be prudent to account for any characters who might be lurking offstage; and, indeed, hidden players are to be found in both functional units (Theorem 4). On the protagonists' side, for instance, belongs the Mother's lover who dies before the commencement of action, together with the beneficent family of farmers (not further described) who raise the abandoned Son. However obliquely, these offstage characters form links in the phantom family's story, and thus earn for themselves the immortality that only fictional beings can attain.

By far the most important hidden player is to be found in the drama's recessive unit. For with characteristic irony, Pirandello has cast himself in the offstage role of principal antagonist—the actual author of *Rules of the Game*, whose rehearsal comes to a stop when the six characters enter, and also (as only the audience knows) the unnamed playwright who loses his struggle to suppress the family's drama. Through the voice of the Father, the author confesses his helplessness in the grip of a fantasy that obsesses him:

> . . . . on the whole authors keep quiet about the birthpangs they endure producing their creations. Once an author's characters come to life and stand before him as living beings, they decide what to say and do, and he simply follows their suggestions. If he doesn't like the way they are, that's just too bad! (58).

Pirandello's admission of powerlessness in the mysterious presence of his six characters thus situates the author himself as a hidden player at the head of the recessive unit, that is, among the ranks of those mere mortals who are used as instruments for conferring immortality upon fictional beings. That he and the members of the theatrical company also achieve literary immortality through their involvement in the character's drama is a logical conundrum that Pirandello has slyly avoided, even as he has suppressed the ontological difference between himself as actual author and the players as virtual players.

With the addition of these offstage figures, it is now possible to construct a complete action-chart of *Six Characters in Search of an Author*. Hidden players' names are enclosed in brackets, while characters who die during or prior to dramatic time are distinguished by an "X" mark. The absence from this chart of arrows indicating the apostasy of characters from one camp to another constitutes the hallmark of the static action:

ACTION-CHART: Pirandello, *Six Characters in Search of an Author*:

PROTAGONIST	ANTAGONIST
Father	[Author]
Mother	Producer-Director
x [Mother's Lover]	Leading Actress
Stepdaughter	Leading Actor
x Boy (non-speaking)	Second Actress
x Little Girl (non-speaking)	Young Actress
Son	Young Actor
[Family of Farmers]	Actors & Actresses
Madam Pace	Stage Manager
	Prompter
	Property Man
	Chief Stage-Hand
	Producer's Secretary
	Commissionaire
	Stage Hands & Staff

Having derived an action-chart for the drama, our next task consists of gathering and assessing the various images adhering to the opposed functional units. For if our first step has taken the right direction, the rhetorical figures gathered under the heads of

"Protagonist" and "Antagonist" should verify this fact by evincing an obvious dialectical opposition to each other (Theorems 7–12).

(2) *Dialectic of Imagery*:

In his opening stage directions to *Six Characters in Search of An Author* Pirandello insists that the radical ontological difference between the characters and actors be augmented by all physical means possible:

> Any stage production of the play must make absolutely clear the fundamental distinction between the SIX CHARACTERS and the ACTORS of the Company. The physical separation of the two groups, recommended in the stage directions once both are on the stage, should certainly help to make the distinction clear. Different coloured lighting could also be used to reinforce it. But the most effective and opposite means I can suggest would be the use of special masks for the CHAR- ACTERS. . . . The masks will help convey the idea that these figures are the products of art, their faces immutably fixed so that each one expresses its basic motivation . . . (8).

This thoroughgoing physical segregation of the two sets of beings is further enhanced by the fact that the characters bring with them over twice as many images as their opponents. This situation befits a static drama in which nearly all of the protagonists appear on stage, thus reinforcing their overwhelming dominance at the primary level of action with a comparable figurative imbalance.

The running images in the protagonists' unit of *Six Characters* assume an obvi- ously funereal tone whose "tragic solemnity" foreshadows the death of the two children and provides dark orchestration for their elders' shame and grief (11). This lugubrious figuration also serves as a major device with which to emphasize the family's fixity in time as dramatic characters, who, however superior as immortals, cannot but repeat the same woeful tale over and over again for all literary eternity. Thus, both Mother and Step-daughter appear in black mourning dress. The Boy, who will commit suicide before the action's end, also wears a suit of mourning; his doomed little sister a white dress, but with a black sash. And although neither Father nor Son appears in mourning, both are nevertheless attired conservatively. The overall effect of these somber costumes is enhanced by the tragic expression on the wearer's faces (or masks), which they repeatedly lower and cover with their hands, often making it necessary for one character to lift up another's head in order to communicate (11, 15).

These images of sorrow receive support from related figures of silence and hiding. Thus, except when in the throes of violent grief or anger, the characters speak softly, often inaudibly; indeed, the doomed Boy and Girl remain mute throughout the action. This low tonality consorts with the shadows out of which the family first appears and to which its members allude so often, as well as with the mysterious green light that bathes them as they are last seen staring fixedly at the panicked Producer—and at the audience. Pirandello augments the muted tonality by placing a transparent screen, or "scrim," in front of the family as it forms the final tableau. This cognate screen motif heightens the impression of things hidden and shameful; for it is also behind a screen in Madam Pace's bedroom that the Step-daughter disrobes during her encounter with the Father, and from his hiding-place behind a cypress tree that the Boy witnesses his sister's death (68, 49, 64).

Superficially at variance with this dark figuration qualifying the protagonists is the repeated evocation, always in the past tense, of flowers. Madam Pace's bedroom had flowered wallpaper (37), while the "famous couch" itself had a yellow plush upholstery decorated with a floral pattern (32); the Father bought the Step-daughter a big straw hat "with little rosebuds round the brim" (23); the little Girl picked small bouquets for her elder sister in the garden where the final calamity occurs (60). Aside from its incidental association with funerals, this floral motif links with the other running images by reason of its invariable connection with shameful deeds whose recollection expresses itself in darkness, sobbing, mourning dress, and the like (32, 60).

Undoubtedly the single most potent image associated with the six characters is that of immobility, a figure which reappears with variations throughout the drama. Thus, while asserting his superiority as an "immortal," the Father several times employs vivid metaphors to express the awesomeness of permanency. His constant sense of shame makes him feel as if he were "dangling from a hook" (52). That stiff thing, dignity, he likens to "a tombstone over a grave. That way we don't have to look at our shame; we have hidden and buried all trace of it and can forget it" (24). When the mortified Son turns to leave the stage "*he is held back as if by some mysterious force*," at which the haughty Step-daughter triumphantly exclaims, "He can't get away!. ... He is tied and chained by a bond that's quite indissoluble" (62). These variations on the immobility theme receive their most eloquent summation by the Father in a solemn declaration to the Producer explaining why the Step-daughter insists on re-enacting the scene of his greatest humiliation:

> The eternal moment! I told you about it. She's here to catch me, to string
> me up before the public, fixed, hooked, chained for ever to the pillory of
> that one shaming moment of my life. It is what she has to do. And you,
> sir, cannot really let me off it (52).

Thus, the immutable plot which binds the characters together for all eternity also ties
them to shameful deeds—abandonment, adultery, criminal neglect, pandering,
whoring, and (averted) incest. Immobility therefore correlates with fixation to the
past and the constant recollection of guilt, a key implicational term that will engage
our attention at the next stage of analysis.

Vividly contrasting with figures of gloom, silence, and fixity qualifying the
victorious characters, three of the four running images generated by their adversaries
are those of light, noise, and activity. Even before the action begins, the audience
faces the unconventional spectacle of a empty stage that is "almost dark"; then the
Producer enters with the command to "Get us a bit of light," whereupon the stage
becomes flooded with the full battery of theatrical illumination (3, 5). As rehearsal
time approaches and the members of the troupe begin to assemble, the stage-direction
informs us that

> ACTORS and ACTRESSES should be dressed in cheerful clothes, light
> in tone, and this first impovised scene should be very lively . . ."(4).

At the conclusion of the first session of the rehearsal the curtain is again left open,
this time with the stage lights remaining at full intensity in order to create the
impression that the company has merely taken a short break from an actual rehearsal
(31). Following a twenty minute interval, the second session proceeds until it reaches
a crescendo with the lurid Madam Pace episode (designated in the text as "The
Scene"), at the end of which the Director excitedly shouts, "Yes, we'll cut it right
there! Curtain! Curtain!"—indicating that the action should stop precisely at that
dramatic moment. However, the confused Stage Manager mistakes this for a
command, thus stranding the Father and Producer out on the apron of the stage in the
darkness of the auditorium (53). This variation of the screen motif provides a striking
visual intimation of the ultimate ascendancy of the characters' darkness over the
actors' light.

Amid the hubbub following the Boy's suicide in the garden, the shaken Producer
cries, "Lights! Lights! Lights!" A last blaze of electricity illuminates the frightened
actors as they hastily leave the theatre; then darkness again prevails as the Producer.

cursing the loss of a whole day's rehearsal, orders the lights turned off—only to find himself unable to see his way out. An angry request for at least some illumination results in the accidental turning up of eerie green lights behind the back cloth—upon which are now projected giant shadows of the characters! Seeing this, the Producer runs panic-stricken from the theatre. At last the front of the stage is bathed in moonlight blue as the characters, "like figures in a trance," emerge from behind the back cloth to form their final tableau vivant (68).

Images of noise and activity are generated by the theatrical company throughout the action, particularly during the opening scene before rehearsal of *Rules of the Game* commences. As stagehands hammer away, the arriving members of the acting troupe variously chat, smoke, play the piano, run through dance steps, or read aloud from trade journals (4). Start of the rehearsal is announced by the Producer's clapping his hands for attention and the Second Stage Manager's shouting, "Right! That's enough now! Come on! The Producer's here!" Animated arguments immediately arise: the presence of the Leading Lady's lap dog irritates the Producer, and the Leading Man doesn't want to wear the chef's hat required for the opening scene of *Rules of the Game* (5–7). Even after the ghostly family interrupts the scheduled rehearsal to plead for the enactment of their own story, the company members continue to react audibly with grumbles, laughter, applause, and arguments in response to the new and highly unusual situation (9–11). Once the Producer decides to dramatize the family's tale, stage hands and electricians are put to work noisily improvising new settings and lighting (31–33).

But just as the intensity of light begins to diminish with the growing dominance of the characters, so the volume of noise subsides as the spectral figures start to enact their melodrama in the low tones of actual speech. Unable to understand what the characters are saying, the actors become restive, shouting, "I can't hear a word!" and "Speak up! Speak up!" (40). The Producer finally interrupts to explain to the Step-daughter the necessity for vocal projection:

> My dear child, in the theatre you have to make yourself heard. Do you
> realise we can't hear you even up here on this stage? What the devil's it
> going to be like when there's an audience? And anyway you can perfectly
> well speak out loud to each other; we shan't *be* here when the time comes
> (40).

Ironically, however, the loudest single noise of the action comes not from the actors or stagehands but from the report of the Boy's pistol. This startling sound, signalizing an even more shocking event, reduces the theatrical company to dazed murmuring: all of its previous hubbub has been "upstaged" by a solitary auditory image associated with the characters and linked most directly to the other funereal images surrounding them (67).

A fourth major trope in the antagonists' unit—that of writing—also contrasts dialectically with the figurative constellation emanating from the victorious characters. For the latter come to present their drama in a legitimate theatre without a script! (13). When the Producer points out this obvious and apparently insurmountable problem, the Father suggests that the Producer himself act as playwright, adding, "There's nothing to it! Look at all the people who do! And your job is made that much easier for having us all here alive in front of you!" (30). But once caught up in the character's story, the company is nevertheless obliged to improvise a script—at first a scene-by-scene outline of the action, then a shorthand transcript of the speeches to be distributed later in separate longhand parts (30, 33). This process of theatrical transmutation profoundly disturbs the Father, who cannot comprehend the necessity for a script or actors when the "real" living characters are there in person. His fears of mimetic betrayal are construed by the Producer as a mad desire to usurp authority and abuse theatrical custom:

> PRODUCER: Bloody marvellous! You're proposing to do the whole
> thing on your own, then! Be your own actors, your own producers,
> everything!
>
> FATHER: Of course, just as we are.
>
> PRODUCER: Well, my word, that would be some show, I can tell you!
> (34).

Yet without either written script or actors to impersonate them, the characters manage to bring off their "show," just as they succeed in breaking away from their offstage author, who believes that without a finished script their story will remain untold. The Step-Daughter portrays the author's refusal in a single vivid description:

> I used to go, to tempt him, time after time . . . in that cheerless study where
> he did his writing, just as it was getting dark. He would be sitting there,
> sunk in his armchair, not even bothering to turn on the light. The room
> would get darker and darker and the darkness would be teeming with our
> presence. We went there to tempt him (58).

From this point on the various figurative strands woven by the six characters compose a single fabric of size and texture sufficient to obscure their adversaries. Shadows, silence, immobility, and absence of script completely dominate the company's light, noise, movement, and need for written text—just as the characters themselves have, despite all opposition, and apparently all logic, successfully outmaneuvered Producer, actors, and offstage author in order to play out their lurid story to its grim conclusion.

The following image-chart provides a reasonably exhaustive list of rhetorical and scenic figures orchestrating both camps of *Six Characters in Search of An Author*. The necessarily longer list in the "Protagonist" column has been broken down by individual character for easier identification, but without the least intent to suggest that these separate personages, or the images they carry with them, form anything more than fragments of a single economic unit. Dialectically opposed "pairs" of images have been keyed numerically for cross-reference.

Scanning the separate units first downwards, and then across, will reveal the obviously antithetical impact of the two separate figurative constellations:

IMAGE-CHART: Pirandello, *Six Characters in Search of an Author:*

PROTAGONIST

FATHER: Sobbing (1); Large, sensuous mouth with mustache; "quicksilver quality"; lowered eyes; Pale visage; Hiding face in hands; Speaking softly (2); Mourning dress (3); Insinuating tone; Shadow behind backdrop; Green light; Pale blue envelope with money; Paper bag in hand; Fact = empty sack; Lifting Stepdaughter's head; Removing Step-daughter's hat; Looking at Stepdaughter's flowered panties; Caressing Stepdaughter; Pushing Stepdaughter; Flesh alive with desire; Young prostitutes; Wrestling with Son; Straw hat with flowers; Bodies & faces (4); "Monster"; Sancho Panza & Three Muscateers (= "immortals"); Fly caught between window & screen; Caught by giant hook & frozen in time; Dignity like a gravestone hiding shame; No script (5).

STEPDAUGHTER: Sobbing; Speaking softly; Hiding face in hands; Lowered eyes; Lowered head; Black dress; Insinuating tone; Green light; Alone in shadows; Shadow behind backdrop; Reaching out to illuminate shadows; Tempting the Author at twilight (6); Sleeping in same bed with Girl & Boy in squalid room; Beautiful face; Contaminated body; Braids to shoulders; Provocative poses; Trembling in anguish; Vein pulsing in arm; Loud, cynical laughter; Crocodile tears; Suggestive French love song; Short skirt; Flowered panties; Straw hat with flowers; Head sinking on Father's chest; Taking off dress (7); Unbuttoning brassiere; Nearly naked; Eyes closed; Walking in garden; Nausea; Placing Girl in fountain basin; Real garden (8); Real fountain (9); Holding flowers.

ANTAGONIST

DIRECTOR, COMPANY AND AUTHOR: The stage; Open curtain; Prompter's box; Footlights; House lights up; "Lights up"; "Lights! Lights!!!"; Blaze of light; Flood of blue light (15); Light colored, gay clothing (3); Plain white backdrop; Playing piano; Dancing; Reading aloud; Gossiping; Laughing (1); Speaking loudly ("projecting") (2); Small dog; Clapping hands; Barking commands; Screaming; Excited whispering; Smoking; Hammering & sawing; Carpenter's tools; Lumber; Dropping curtain by accident; Turning lights out by accident; Dropping curtain by accident; Moving scenery; Looking confused; Busy movements about stage; Following the characters around the stage; Pocket watch; Call bell; Chef's hat; Beating eggs; "Book" (script); Author's unfinished script; Script for Pirandello's *Rules of the Game* (5); Script of Characters' story; Clip-board with paper; Writing in shorthand. Author sitting at desk, dozing (6); Battered, soiled props; Two-dimensional cut-out cypress trees lowered from flies (14); Artificial garden setting (8); Cut-out fountain (9); Garden, but no bedroom; Iron bed (12); Plain, green bedspread (13); Small gilt table (14); Striped wallpaper (11); Refusal to take off dress (7); Costume & makeup (4); Name for character (10); Leaving theatre in panic.

IMAGE-CHART: Pirandello, *Six Characters in Search of an Author* (cont.):

PROTAGONIST	ANTAGONIST

MOTHER: Real name (Amelia) (10); Sobbing; Hiding hands in face; Chalk white, waxen face; Eyes downcast; Widow's veil; Holding veil down; Moaning; Screaming; Mysterious tone of voice; Secretive smile; "Mental deafness"; Fainting; "Old widow"; Wandering like a lost animal; Tearing off Madam Pace's wig; Following Son into garden; Shadow behind backdrop; Green light; Drawing Son as if by invisible string.

MADAM PACE: Fat & ugly; Dignified, self-important manner; Carrot-colored wig; Long silk gown; Cigarette in long holder; Heavy Spanish accent; "Witch," "Devil"; Hats on display; White, flowered wallpaper (11); The celebrated wooden bed (12); Yellow bedspread with large floral pattern (13); Mahogany table (14); Mirror; Screen; Clothes hangers; Hand under Stepdaughter's chin; Rouged & powdered.

SON: Shadow behind backdrop; Green light; Coldness; Knocking Father down; Inability to leave the stage ("chained"); Running away from Mother; Crossing garden; Hiding in room.

BOY: Mute (silent); Mysterious green light; Crying; Hiding in corners; Clinging to Mother; Hands in pockets; Eyes of a madman; Head falling forward; Wasting away; Project growing in eyes; Hiding behind real trees; Final cry of horror; Revolver; Sound of shot.

GIRL: Mute (silent); Playing in garden sun (real light) (15); Showing small flowers to Stepdaughter; Real fountain with ducks (9); Trying to catch ducks; Real trees (14); Casting shadows; Drowning.

Two salient features of the preceding chart warrant brief comment: first, that it contains no shifting images, and, second, that it includes a relatively large number of dialectically paired figures. Shifting images, such as one often encounters in plays conforming to other dynamic types, simply do not occur in static actions because the movement of images between dialectical poles is always contingent upon the simultaneous movement of characters (Theorem 10). Obviously opposed dialectical pairs, or mirror-images, can and do appear in all structural types (Theorem 11), yet nowhere more frequently than in static actions, where the colliding forces are represented as utterly inimical.

(3) *Implicational Dialectic*:

Having completed the first two stages of structural analysis, we are now in a position to begin the third and perhaps most interesting step, namely, qualitative reduction of the separate economic units of *Six Characters* to their essential common characteristics. Following the general ground rules elaborated in Part One (Theorems 13–20), this next task involves searching out the most appropriate antinomies to describe the play's dominant and recessive poles, its wishful and fearful motives. I shall list these dialectical pairs numerically, including with each set of terms a brief rationale for my choice:

1. *Illusion as Absolute/Illusion as Relative.* Pirandello's manifest subject concerns the alleged superiority of poetic illusion over mundane reality. But because the word "reality," as Nabokov justly observes, is probably the one term in any language always requiring quotation marks, we stand in need of a more precise set of antonyms to distinguish between two separate *kinds* of "reality"—that of the characters and that of the actors. For the characters, one single illusion is the "only reality"; and that illusion is all-absorbing and absolute. The Father insists that "we, the six of us . . . have no other reality; that we don't exist outside this illusion!" (55). To the actors, on the other hand, theatrical illusion consists of contingent "realities," of various dramas and sundry characters portrayed in full consciousness of their mimetic nature and with entire complacency as to relative verisimilitude. Total withdrawal into fantasy, here associated with the dominant function, is an autistic trait often apparent in static drama assuming the ironic mode.

2. *Abstraction/Concreteness.* The characters are represented as the abstract creatures of fantasy, conceived but not fully realized in the mind of an author who finds their story distasteful. Paradoxically, the actors appear as "real" troupers concerned

with the concrete (if mundane) details of their profession and their daily lives. The figurative opposition of shadow to light enhances this distinction between the incorporeal and the solid.

3. *Irrationality/Rationality.* As poetic abstractions rather than flesh-and-blood mortals, the protagonists arise from that shadowy realm of the mind least associated with logic and rationality. Moreover, their story is one of unremitting obsession and emotionalism. By contrast, the "mortals" comprising the acting company, while occasionally appearing confused or obtuse, concern themselves in a fundamentally practical and rational way with the business of producing plays.

4. *Bondage/Freedom.* Forever chained to each other by an immutable plot, the protagonists live in bondage to the past, compelled forever to repeat the same story without the slightest alteration. The reverse is true of the antagonists, who can and do exercise relative freedom of choice—in the case of the players, freedom to choose which drama they would rather perform, and, in the case of the author, which fantasy he will accept or reject.

5. *Inflexibility/Flexibility.* The characters refuse to accept the fate of all dramatic personages, namely, to be represented by actors. Nor do they easily tolerate such relatively minor theatrical adjustments as the substitution of one kind of furniture or wallpaper pattern for another, a simulated garden for a "real" one, etc. This naturally annoys the Producer, who pleads for more "flexibility" on the part of the characters. One is reminded of Ibsen and O'Neill, neither of whom could easily suffer the alteration of their fantasies by representation in the theatre. Ibsen once bellowed at a famous actor rehearsing the title-role of one of his late plays, "John Gabriel Borkman does not wear yellow spats!"

6. *Immortality/Mortality.* The Father makes several impassioned speeches asserting the ontological superiority of dramatic characters over mere mortals, an ironic proposition which is allowed to prove itself "beyond doubt" during the course of the play. This philosophical notion hinges on the fact that fictional characters are immortal and without contingent "realities." Pirandello's refusal to position his offstage author, a mere mortal, in the victor's column adds a disingenuous touch to this idea, especially from a playwright obsessed, as he was, with the prospect of literary immortality. Thus, it is only through his characters that an author lives forever.

7. *Remembrance /Forgetfulness.* Although the single-minded characters can

forget neither the guilty actions which bind them together nor the purpose of their quest for immortality, the theatrical troupe constantly makes absent-minded gaffes: dropping the curtain at the wrong time, putting on or off the wrong lights, lowering the wrong backdrop. Moreover, the actors need written parts as memory aids, for to them the characters' story is just another "script," something to be learned and then forgotten once the performance is over—just as they forget all about Pirandello's *Rules of the Game* when a more exciting drama presents itself. "The neurotic suffers from memory," opined Freud. Indeed, there is a strong sense in this drama of fixation to memories from the past that cannot be repressed.

8. *Obsession/Obliviousness*. The protagonists not only remember their traumatic past, they are positively obsessed with every detail of that in which their entire being resides. Not so the actors, whose attention to any particular drama derives solely from motives of theatrical exploitation, and whose fleeting lives are connected only by way of their common profession.

9. *Impracticality/Practicality*. The characters' demands for absolute verisimilitude cannot be accommodated in a theatrical milieu dedicated to the mere illusion of reality. Thus, when they succeed in breaking free of both actors and author, the characters finish their story without benefit of the "real" scene of action—a practical difficulty which even Pirandello could not overcome, any more than he could avoid permitting actors to play both actors and "characters."

10. *Perversity/Normality*. These highly volatile antonyms are entirely justified implicational derivations, for they apply to the opposite camps at almost all levels of meaning—legal, psychological, and moral. A look at the play's imagery alone creates, on the protagonists' side, an overwhelming impression of things dark, hidden, sleazy, and unnatural, while the antagonists' unit bustles with commonplace objects and activities. Turning to action, one encounters, as in several other works by Pirandello, the dominant motif of incest (unwitting, as in Oedipus' case). Yet although the Producer and his company occasionally seem befuddled, they do nothing more extraordinary than to show an interest in the bizarre.

11. *Dishonor/Honor*. This set of terms scarcely requires elaboration, except perhaps in regard to the antagonists, whose behavior may seem honorable only by contrast to that of their adversaries. One must not forget, however, the offstage author who rejects the characters' story precisely because it offends him, nor the Producer who wishes to add a few humorous touches in order to "lighten the crudity a bit" (41).

Nor, finally, the theatrical company's genuine shock and sorrow at the Boy's death.

12. *Impropriety/Propriety*. This pair overlaps with the previous set, while adding quality not yet precisely defined. The Leading Lady, for instance, refuses to appear nearly naked as the Step-daughter had done at Madam Pace's. More importantly, the company attempts to behave with kindness and understanding for the suppliant family, but is treated in return with rudeness, open scorn, and contempt for the proprieties of theatrical convention.

14. *Formality/Informality*. Despite their radically unconventional nature, the six characters exhibit a conservatism in dress and pomposity of manner that cause them to appear extremely formal by contrast to the casual, easy-going actors. Even the outrageously painted and bewigged Madam Pace assumes "an air of great importance" (41). Images of immobility versus activity enhance this contrast between the formal and informal.

15. *Seriousness/Humor*. Laughing only in derision or hysteria, the protagonists exhibit no real sense of humor whatever; for the sordid past with which they are totally absorbed does not provide a fit subject of merriment. The Producer, as we have seen, hopes that Madam Pace's heavy accent will provide some comic relief for the characters' tale of woe (41), while the actors constantly chatter, joke, applaud, and emit noises of approval—at least until the melodrama they are adapting takes its final, grim turn.

16. *Guilt/Innocence*. Each adult member of the spectral family, together with the Mother's deceased lover and the seventh onstage character, Madam Pace, stands guilty of immoral behavior, either in the court of his or her own judgment or in that of another character. Even the offstage family of farmers is guilty after the fact in the Father's abandonment of his Son. But what of the Boy and his little sister? In order to qualify as a necessary implicational derivation, the term "guilt" must apply to all members of the protagonists' unit (Theorem 16); and in an odd but compelling way it does. For the mute Boy and Girl are the illegitimate products of an adulterous union—silent emblems of everyone else's misconduct, the sources of mutual recrimination, who in death magnify and indeed put the seal on the other characters' eternal shame. Without their death, paradoxically, the family's tale would never have survived; for it was the children's dreadful fate that caused their author to reject the whole story, thus forcing the family to assert its independent "reality" in order to conclude their drama. By contrast, the theatrical troupe entertains the idea of staging

the characters' story totally innocent of its bloody catastrophe, which, when it occurs, causes them immense shock.

17. *Secrecy/Candor.* "We all carry round inside us a world made up of things as we see them; each one of us a whole world of his own! . . . We think we understand each other. In fact we never do" (19). With this general truth the Father sums up a trait most especially evident in the protagonists of *Six Characters*: an alienated, secret self which can never adequately be comprehended by another human being, and which, moreover, does not wish to be comprehended. This secret self generates what the Father, in reference to the Mother, describes as "mental deafness," an inability to see anything from another's point of view (20). Hence, the family's constant mutual recriminations and disagreements as to the relative burden of guilt. On the other side, the Producer and his company are eager to hear the characters out, to learn their conflicting versions of the story, while at the same time freely admitting the limitations of their own profession.

18. *Obscurity/Clarity.* In order to get the characters' story straight, the Producer specifically requests that everything be explained "clearly"—a task the protagonists find impossible owing to the "mental deafness" with which not just the Mother but all of them are afflicted. Thus, the actors obtain a montage of overlapping images, of subjective "truths," from which they are nevertheless able to construct a relatively clear composite picture.

19. *Suffering/Happiness.* The protagonists' whole tale, indeed their entire fictive existence, is compounded of resentment and grief, which cause them to moan, sob uncontrollably, hide their faces, engage in unseemly physical combat, or scream in anguish. Such activities are entirely foreign to the antagonists, who register painful emotion only in response to the final, bloody turn of events.

20. *Passion/Action.* "This isn't fiction! This is life! This is passion!" The Father's equation of life with passion runs counter to the experience of the Producer, who responds tartly, "That's as may be. It will never do on the stage" (23). For if the character's intense recollections cannot be translated into concrete action, they are not suitable for theatrical representation. Once again, the many contrasting figures of immobility and activity enhance this classic dichotomy.

21. *Emotionalism/Calmness.* We are told that the offstage author objected to, among other things, the Step-daughter's "over-emotionalism"—a term that applies with equal justice to all the protagonists. However, aside from expressing occasional

annoyance or impatience, the antagonists preserve an attentive and business-like calm.

22. *Romanticism/Realism*. If the essence of romanticism is self-absorption, then the characters are archetypal romantics, totally oblivious of anything unrelated to their own melodrama, from which they seek immortality. The actors, on the other hand, make a profession of submerging their own personality beneath various roles in order to entertain audiences; their life is thus fundamentally practical and other-directed, despite the occasional gaffes and hurt egos of imperfect mortals.

23. *Competition/Cooperation*. Throughout the action the protagonists constantly engage in internecine conflict with their fellows, while at the same time moving remorselessly toward the conclusion of their drama against the wishes of their author and to the utter horror of the acting troupe; in fact, their whole fictive existence is based upon disagreement and conflict. Not so the actors, whose profession is one of the world's most cooperative and tolerant, and whose occasional disagreements are skillfully mediated by the Producer in the general interest.

24. *Contradiction/Agreement*. Overlapping with the previous set, these antonyms describe a further dimension of the drama's basic opposition—on the protagonists' side a constant and passionate difference of opinion as to where the guilt really lies; on the antagonists' side an acceptance of such disagreement as part and parcel of any truly dramatic situation.

25. *Implacability/Compromise*. The characters will permit no one, not even their own creator, to halt the inexorable course of their story, which they insist be performed as they see fit. In the face of these overbearing demands, the actors exercise extraordinary patience, merely pointing out the necessity for that compromise with "reality" imposed upon them by the inherent limitations of the theatre. As the Producer reminds the impatient Father, "You've got to consider the requirements of the medium!"(40).

26. *Superiority/Inferiority*. When the formerly offstage Madam Pace suddenly enters in person to play her big scene, the acting company wonders how she got there, and whether her presence is necessary. To which the Father responds, "You're destroying the miracle, for that's what it is! Reality itself kindled into life, conjured up, brought into being by this scene and drawn towards it, with more right to life in this place than you have. She has more truth than you have!" (39). As self-proclaimed beings of a mysterious and yet more "real" order, the characters are made to appear ontologically superior to the bewildered "mortals" who attempt, without success, to

make sense of the intruders' peculiar demands. This set quite literally illustrates our thesis that a drama's dominant characters are products of the superior function of the authorial mind at the time of composition (Theorem 1).

27. *Complexity/Simplicity*. Both because they are representatives of a higher order and because of their "complicated spiritual agonisings," the fictional characters seem much more profound and intricate than their "mortal" counterparts (23). Indeed, the actors, and even the author, are made to appear impotent bumpkins in the presence of the shadowy intruders.

28. *Misanthropy/Sociability*. The members of the phantom family are not only filled with animosity towards each other, they also repeatedly express imperious contempt for all humans, whose reality of today, according to the Father, "will surely turn out be illusion tomorrow" (57). Indeed, if the visitors to the artist's chamber of fantasy are the only beings whose reality is true and absolute, then the spurious reality of mere humans renders them contemptible from every point of view. As the passive instruments, one might even say the creations, of a superior and quite independent order of beings, even artists have no truly creative function: their "inspiration" and their "will" are wholly subservient to the demands of their visitors—as the offstage author discovers to his chagrin.

With these twenty-eight antinomies qualifying the opposed functions of *Six Characters in Search of An Author*, the possibilities of descriptive abstraction seem about exhausted. Perhaps another pair or two could be added, or a few overlapping sets of terms conflated; but, in general, this moderately long list appears adequately to abstract the drama's argument.

We are now in a position to gain a broader overview of that argument by constructing an implicational chart which will list the opposed sets of terms in two columns. Scansion of each column downwards will provide a more instantaneous impression of the play's dominant and recessive functions, the wishful and fearful impulses for which its action and imagery stand as objective correlatives:

IMPLICATIONAL CHART: Pirandello, *Six Characters in Search of an Author*:

Dominant Function	Recessive Function
Illusion as Absolute	Illusion as Relative
Abstraction	Concreteness
Irrationality	Rationality
Bondage	Freedom

Inflexibility	Flexibility
Immortality	Mortality
Remembrance	Forgetfulness
Obsession	Obliviousness
Impracticality	Practicality
Perversity	Normality
Dishonor	Honor
Impropriety	Propriety
Unconventionality	Conventionality
Formality	Informality
Seriousness	Humor
Guilt	Innocence
Secrecy	Candor
Obscurity	Clarity
Suffering	Happiness
Passion	Action
Emotionalism	Calmness
Romanticism	Realism
Competition	Cooperation
Contradiction	Agreement
Implacability	Compromise
Superiority	Inferiority
Complexity	Simplicity
Misanthropy	Sociability

This overview of the implicational dialectic makes clear the drama's highly ironic character; for, taken as a whole, its dominant (wishful) function presents a generally negative, indeed somewhat repugnant list of attributes (Theorem 20). No great psychological acumen is required to see that dark, obsessive, and fundamentally painful impulses here dominate the fantasy, and that these motives are countered, though ineffectively, by thoroughly sunny, peaceful, bourgeois instincts.

That Pirandello had long been aware of this dichotomy in his spiritual make-up, and cognizant also of the wide gulf separating the dominant and recessive sides of this fracture, we learn from a letter he wrote to his bride-to-be twenty-eight years before he penned *Six Characters*. To Antonietta he explained,

> It's almost as if there are two people in me. You know one of them, but
> even I hardly know the other. I mean that I consist of a big self and a little
> self: these two gentlemen are constantly fighting each other; one of them
> is often extremely uncongenial to the other. The first is taciturn and
> continually absorbed in thought, the second talks with facility, jokes, and
> even laughs and makes people laugh. When the latter says something
> rather stupid the former goes to the mirror and kisses him. I am constantly
> divided between these two people. Sometimes one of them predomi-
> nates, sometimes the other. I naturally prefer the first, I mean my big self.
> I adapt myself to and pity the second, who is basically a being like all
> others, with their virtues and their defects.[2]

The "big self" to which Pirandello alludes, the self continually absorbed in thought, taciturn, dour, and filled with a sense of its own dignity—the side favored by its host—corresponds with startling exactitude to the function that dominates the argument of *Six Characters in Search of An Author*. The "little self," the side inclined to chatter, joke, and laugh, the perfectly ordinary and essentially pathetic being, resembles in an equally clear manner the drama's recessive function, objectified by the theatrical company. That this same internal conflict should seek poetic expression nearly three decades after Pirandello described it to his fiancée bears witness both to its chronic nature and also to its recurring oppugnancy as a motive for the dramatist's creative activity. Rarely has an author described the *bellum intestinum* at the core of his personality—and his art—with greater candor (Theorem 1).

Reflecting on others of Pirandello's works for the stage in light of his statement about the alternating predominance of "these two gentlemen" within him, it is noteworthy that the ironic and melodramatic *Henry IV* requires implicational deri-vations almost identical to those of *Six Characters in Search of an Author*, while comedic pieces such as *Rules of the Game* (here an actual image in the recessive unit) tend either to reverse the implicational poles or to mix up the antinomies in a happier manner, with more conventionally positive qualities generated by the dominant unit. From this, one is able to confirm the playwright's admission to possessing a highly mercurial temper: the canon of many another dramatist exhibits greater consistency in the relation of dominant to recessive motives.

---

[2] Luigi Pirandello, quoted in Gaspare Guidice, *Pirandello. A Biography*, translated by Alastair Hamilton (London: Oxford University Press, 1975), p. 63.

In general, *Six Characters in Search of an Author* provides a highly typical instance of static drama in its ironic phase. The claustrophobic atmosphere, the insuperable barrier between the contending parties, the inexorable triumph of a "superior" but essentially inhuman and morally suspect force, the lack of cathartic release at the denouement—these are constants of the present dynamic class in the mode of irony, whether the specific manifestation come from the pen of a Pirandello or that of a Büchner, Rice, Beckett, or Ionesco. Most importantly, the "extremely uncongenial" relationship between the two sides of the argument allows of no apostasy from one camp to another, none of that movement between dialectical poles which characterizes all other structural types—as we shall see in the following chapters.

SECOND MODEL
APOSTATIC-POSITIVE

Definition. *The apostatic-positive structure is distinguished by the movement of one or more characters from the recessive unit of the antagonist to the dominant unit of the protagonist. No matter how many characters shift, their course is always unidirectional, from negative to positive. Mobile figures may here include central, supporting, or minor characters, whether singly or in combination. However, at least one important personage will always remain behind in the antagonists' unit throughout the action, while his (her) counterpart will also be positioned in the protagonists' unit from the start; for dialectical collapse occurs only in certain "synthetic" structures. In all other forms, including the apostatic-positive, dialectical tension is always maintained by the permanent opposition of at least two characters, whether they appear on stage or operate from the wings as "hidden players."*

Except in its ironic mode, the apostatic-positive dynamic represents the escape of the mobile character from a state of moral or psychological bondage to a new life of spiritual freedom; and this release from mental constraint often coincides with an escape from some form of physical confinement, whether involuntary or self-imposed. The manifest intent of most dramas of this class being clearly exhortatory, their major concern is to depict the re-education or conversion of the shifting character and, thus, by a sort of mimetic induction, to re-orient the audience or to reinforce its presumably shared beliefs.

Schematic. Graphic representation of the apostatic-positive structure shows the shifting character "Z" enclosed in parentheses to indicate his (her/their) initial position, an arrow to show his movement to the protagonists' unit, and the same letter-symbol without parentheses to represent his final position in the action. "X" and "Y" stand for any number of immobile characters:

PROTAGONIST	ANTAGONIST
X	Y
Z ⟵—————————	(Z)

General. By far the most common of dramatic structures, the apostatic-positive tends to appear in five related mythical guises: (1) tragedy or melodrama in which the central character is plainly villainous, and from whom other characters flee in order to restore a just moral order; (2) religious plays representing the central character's conversion to the true faith; (3) romance or rite of passage dramas in which the major figure escapes from mental or physical bondage in order to claim a birthright; (4) *Lehrstück* or propaganda pieces which represent the hero's conversion to philosophical or political causes represented as superior modes of action and perception; and (5) ironic dramas which work variations on the first four themes, but which arouse moderate to high degrees of ambivalence about the moral or psychological soundness of the apostate's movement from weakness to power. Yet even in its ironic mode the apostatic-positive structure retains its central mythos: the passage from bondage to freedom, impotence to control.

Schiller's *Wallenstein's Death* and Pushkin's *Boris Godunov* provide capital examples of tragedy whose central figure is tainted, for in both of these plays the title-characters find themselves progressively deserted by their noble cohorts as the heinousness of their deeds becomes ever more apparent. Wallenstein's growing madness and eventual treason against the Emperor Ferdinand cause him to be abandoned by the legions of supporters he had once commanded, and ultimately assassinated by his last follower. Likewise, Boris Godunov, murderer of the Tsarevich Dimitry and usurper of the throne, watches with a growing sense of his own guilt as the Russian nobility and peasantry alike welcome the armies of the "False Dimitry." Both plays represent the wholesale apostasy of characters from the dysfunctional antagonist to the more powerful if romantically less interesting protagonist. Yet, although mass defections are common to apostatic-positive drama, the movement of but one or two characters is sufficient to establish this morphological type. Thus, the defection of Brutus' friend Messala and his slave Stato to Marc Antony in *Julius Caesar*, or Leporello's abandonment of his master in *Don Giovanni*, both fulfill the minimum requirement for this structure.

In speaking of the "hero's fall," the conventional literary vocabulary implies a type of movement that does not reflect the dynamic of this subspecies of apostatic-positive drama, about which it would be more appropriate to speak of the apostates' rise—an ascent from out of the morass in which the central character begins and ends his losing struggle. The movement of secondary characters away from the primary antagonist thus serves to stress the dysfunctional nature of the "hero," whose often attractive qualities such as bravery, intellectual cunning, or rhetorical bravura might otherwise tempt an audience to persist in its empathy with a figure pursuing an ignorant course of action. A list of such tainted "heroes" could be expanded to include not only outright villains like Richard III but also such lesser sinners as Edward II, Richard II, and the later Antony, all of whose crimes, though perhaps venial, arise from faults grave enough to justify the punishment of isolation that abandonment provides. The archetype of such often initially attractive antagonists is Oedipus, of whom I shall have more to say later in this chapter.

Showing as it does the movement of characters from bondage to freedom, the apostatic-positive dynamic is particularly congenial for dramas devoted to religious or political evangelism. In the religious sub-species the shifting characters flee a pagan or satanically ordered society, thus moving from a state of spiritual emptiness to one of fulfillment; and here the protagonists' unit is always headed either by an offstage deity (Theorem 4) or by an allegorical "divinity" on stage, to whom the shifting characters move, often at the cost of their lives but to the infinitely more important salvation of their souls. In *King Lear*, for instance, the title-character heads a list of apostates including Albany, the Servant to Cornwall, Gloucester, and even the latter's bastard son, Edmund, all of whom begin under Nature's (Satan's) influence, but at last, through spontaneous acts of contrition, repentance, and atonement, move to the ranks of the godly. Among Neo-classical dramas of this sub-species the most notable instance is Corneille's *Polyeucte*, which depicts the title-character's conversion to Christianity from the polytheistic beliefs of ancient Rome. Anouilh's *Becket, or The Honor of God*, a well-known modern instance of this type, recounts Thomas' appointment as Archbishop of Canterbury and his gradual spiritual awakening— an experience that forces him to stake his life defending the Church against the will of his erstwhile bosom friend, the worldly Henry II. Aside from Shakespeare's Albany and Edmund, all of the shifting characters mentioned above suffer martyrdom of various sorts; and in this we see the tendency of the apostatic-positive structure in general to stress the ordeal that must be undergone as a result of the passage from benightedness to a new, superior mode of belief and action.

Perhaps the most radical of these rite of passage transformations finds embodiment in Calderon's Sigismundo, who experiences shock of unspeakable intensity as he finds himself suddenly metamorphosed from a wild man chained in a cave into the King of Poland leading victorious armies. Here, as in all romance drama that obeys the apostatic-positive dynamic, the birthright regained through ordeal provides the central motif, however otherwise varied the philosophical implications from play to play. Behind this theme undoubtedly lies a puberty ritual whose outlines are apparent even in such modern films as McCullers' *Member of the Wedding*, wherein Frankie Addams provides an unpretentious example of the positively shifting character as she is propelled from the world of the back porch—with its asexual games, its dependence upon the black nanny, its infantile fear of things that go flop in the night—into the adult world of sexuality, conventionality, and self-confidence.

Dramas carrying political messages also find the movement from negative to positive a most congenial dynamic for showing conversions from social ignorance to enlightenment. Thus, although several of Brecht's more complex plays of the Marxist period take other forms, his least ambiguous full-length drama, *The Mother*, assumes the apostatic-positive dynamic. Pelagea Vlassova's conversion by her son to the cause of the revolutionary workers, her subsequent advancement of the struggle by distributing political leaflets, and, more importantly, her winning over of two other characters (the Butcher and the Housemaid) provide a most obvious picture of this structure in the service of propagandistic ends. A more widely known and crudely powerful use of this dynamic for purposes of political suasion is Eisenstein's film *Potemkin*. This free rendering of events during the 1905 Russian Revolution depicts the naval mutiny and Odessa uprising in a sequence of five clear dialectical movements: the sailor Valkunichuk exhorting the ship's crew to rebel, the subsequent mutiny of the Potemkin's crew, the disastrous sympathy protest by the citizens of Odessa, and finally the mutiny of the entire naval squadron. This portrayal of numerous separate apostasies as parts of a larger rebellion lays great stress on the concepts of brotherhood, solidarity, and socialism at the heart of this film's implicational dialectic. As in most other political dramas assuming this structure, we again witness the agony and frequent death of characters who strike out against a weakening but still dangerous antagonist. Indeed, in the Trumbo/Kubrick film *Spartacus* the title-character and his whole army of slaves suffer crucifixion as the result of their rebellion against their Roman masters. Nevertheless, because such risks are represented as willingly undertaken as part of the characters' overriding wish, such martyred apostates must be accounted dialectical victors, whether or not one personally shares their religious or political aspirations.

In its ironic phase apostatic-positive drama creates a chilling effect by showing the movement of characters to a powerful but malign protagonist. This discomfiting situation is not especially alleviated by regular portrayal of the deserted antagonist variously as a bumbling idealist, an unsuspecting "patsy," or a person guilty of misdeeds long past and scarce remembered. Apostasy away from the antagonist therefore assumes the character of a betrayal—a movement from the lesser to the greater evil. This diabolical pattern is evident in Dürrenmatt's *The Old Woman's Visit*, where Claire Zachanassian achieves retribution out of all proportion to the original crime committed against her by her first lover. Jilted many years ago by Ill, the immensely rich Claire contrives his death by literally buying the small town in which he lives, causing there a severe economic depression, and then offering a stupendous bribe to the poverty-stricken citizens for their complicity in his murder. Even more cynical in tone, Genet's *The Balcony* depicts the revolutionary leader, Roger, eventually succumbing to secret lusts for sex and power which cause him to abandon his comrades in arms in order to play out his fantasy of being the Chief of Police—thus permitting the *ancient regime* to retain its hold on the popular imagination.

Caution should always be exercised in approaching plays that appear to be ironic versions of the apostatic-positive: most dramatists baulk at delineating movement from the lesser to the greater evil, and many works which at first appear to follow this pattern will on closer inspection reveal themselves to adopt the reverse course of the apostatic-*negative* dynamic (Model 3). The presence, for example, of a strongly implied social or religious teleology—as occurs in such works as Ibsen's *An Enemy of the People* or Barnes' *The Ruling Class*—may often turn what appears to be an ominous positive movement into a cleansing negative one, as we shall see in the following chapter.

Whatever its mythical or modal variants, the apostatic-positive dynamic seeks to bolster the dominant function with reinforcements drawn from the competing, recessive system. Employment of this mimetic strategy apparently serves to decrease the power of the "shadow," while at the same time reasserting the integrity of the "self." Presumably the reader or spectator will experience a similar cleansing and strengthening, so long as his own prevailing values sufficiently overlap with those of the author. In the case of irony, however, where the play's dominant function conflicts with prevailing values, the majority response will be one of heightened anxiety, varying in range from nervous laughter to outright revulsion.

ANALYSIS
Sophocles, *Oedipus the King*[1]

(1) *Dialectic of Action*:

The Occident's most famous drama provides a capital instance of our first subspecies of the apostatic-positive structure: tragedy of the unwittingly tainted hero, whom other characters abandon in order to redress the moral imbalance wrought by his misdeeds. This description may seem surprising considering Oedipus' apparent change of fortune from good to bad, a dramatic reversal impressed upon us by Aristotle's famous comments on the play in his *Poetics*. Although consistent in his general argument, Aristotle has nevertheless initiated the tendency to view Oedipus' case wrongly as a prime example of what has come to be known as the "tragic fall," a movement of the hero from power to weakness, or, dialectically, from positive to negative poles of action.

That Oedipus never moves at all, but instead remains fixed in the antagonists' column from beginning to end, can be adduced from his unfulfilled overriding wish, which is to escape Apollo's prophesy that he will murder his father and also be the cause of his mother's death (995–9). His other explicit wish to discover the murderer of Laius and thus rid Thebes of the devastating plague constitutes a secondary motive that unwittingly runs directly counter to the primary one, for his discovery that he himself is the murderer of Laius proves with shattering irony that Oedipus has never been able to avoid the Oracle's prediction.

---

[1] Sophocles, *Oedipus the King*, translated by David Grene, in *The Complete Greek Tragedies*, edited by David Grene and Richmond Lattimore (University of Chicago, 1958), vol. 2. All line references are to this edition.

Dialectically speaking, therefore, Oedipus does not "fall"; rather his subjects abandon him when, after the peripety or reversal, the unspeakable nature of his crime against Apollo reveals itself. Hence, the drama's only mobile characters are Creon and the citizens of Thebes, who shift from the recessive to the dominant pole of action once the source of pollution has been driven from their midst (Theorem 6).

It is not necessary to dwell upon Oedipus' crimes of patricide and incest, which, though shocking in themselves, are represented as having been committed in ignorance, and therefore without attaching to themselves the full stigma of ritual impurity (*miaron*)[2]. To Sophocles—and this is a critical point of dogma that the rationalistic Aristotle seems to have overlooked—the hero's deepest sin, his unforgivable act of hubris, consists precisely in his overriding motive: the utterly blasphemous attempt to avoid destiny.[3] Indeed, the depth of Sophocles' religious fatalism in *Oedipus the King* can only be fathomed when one realizes that the title-character's opponents include no fewer than eleven offstage deities (Theorem 4). Heading this list is Moira, or Fate, the awesome goddess who spins the thread of man's life from beginning to end, determining that course from which he cannot stray. Echoing an ambiguity in the theology of his time, Sophocles seems unconcerned as to whether Moira is prior in authority to Zeus or is instead his subordinate instrument for executing the Olympian decree; nonetheless, the collaboration, if not entire conflation, of Zeus with Fate can hardly be questioned. In its second ode, following Jocasta's blasphemy against Apollo's oracle, the Chorus clearly associates Moira with divine ordinance in general:

> May destiny [*moira*] ever find me
> pious in word and deed
> prescribed by the laws that live on high;
> laws begotten in the clear air of heaven,
> whose only father is Olympus;
> no mortal nature brought them to birth,
> no forgetfulness shall lull them to sleep;
> for God is great in them and grows not old (351–8).

---

[2]Gerald F. Else, *Aristotle's Poetics: The Argument* (Cambridge: Harvard University Press, 1967), pp. 368, 422–43ff.

[3]Else, pp. 351–2.

Elsewhere our text renders Moira's function variously as "fate," "fortune," or as "Time who sees all" (376–7, 470–4, 1213, 1457). Whatever the rendering, however, such repetitions create the unavoidable impression that by attempting to escape the Oracle's prediction Oedipus not only violates the irrevocable command of Moira but also simultaneously provokes the wrath of Zeus, of his spokesman Apollo, and also of Zeus' daughter Dike, goddess of Justice:

> If a man walks with haughtiness
> of hand or word and gives no heed
> to Justice and the shrines of the Gods
> despises—may an evil doom
> smite him for his ill-starred pride of heart! (884–8).

The "doom" that befalls those who disregard Justice comes in the triple form of the Erinyes, or Furies, who punish violations of the laws of kinship; and with them stalks Nemesis, "she whom none can escape," punisher of excessive arrogance and trespasses against the normal order of things (792–4).[4]

To this already formidable group of deities arrayed against Oedipus must be added three as yet unmentioned Olympians: Athene, Artemis, and Dionysus. The two goddesses, along with Apollo, are collectively supplicated by the Chorus of elders to drive the pestilence out of Thebes. Finally, as a gesture to the native god of Thebes (and god of tragedy, upon whose sacred precinct at Athens the drama is enacted), the Chorus appeals to Dionysus to "combat the god who burns us" (190–1).

Here, in the Parados, we have our first explicit reference to an offstage antagonist of superhuman power, namely, Ares, whom the Chorus repeatedly identifies as the "God of War" and as "a god unhonored among the other gods" (151–215). According to Seyffert, Ares is indeed hateful to all the other Olympians, especially to Athena, goddess of ordered battalions, who can always defeat him despite his strength because he fights without wisdom.[5] One of the War God's principal symbols is the burning torch, which the Chorus specifically identifies with the plague's fever. At the third, implicational stage of analysis we shall encounter many negative qualities which the young king of Thebes shares with the rash and cruel Ares, but for the present

---

[4]Oscar Seyffert, *Dictionary of Classical Antiquities* revised and edited by Henry Nettleship and J. E. Sandys (Cleveland and New York: World Publishing Co., 1967), pp. 224–5, 414.

[5.] Seyffert, p. 60

it is sufficient simply to note that the major offstage antagonist of *Oedipus the King* is the God of War, brother of Eris (strife), father of Phobos (fear) and Deimos (fright).

Fittingly, the first onstage character to seek help from the gods, and also from Thebes' riddle-solving king, is the Priest of Zeus, who learns that Oedipus had already dispatched Creon to the Priestess of Apollo at Delphi in order to ascertain the cause of the city's blight. However, neither the Priest nor Creon can as yet be placed in the protagonists' unit; for, like Oedipus and all those who inhabit the city, they initially suffer the same distress. Therefore the confrontation between Oedipus and Creon (Episode II), wherein the king unjustly accuses Creon of plotting to usurp the throne, must be interpreted as an internal conflict—one which nevertheless foreshadows a more radical break to come. The same does not hold, however, for the previous confrontation between Oedipus and the blind seer, Teiresias, who is summoned from without the city's precinct to tell what he knows of the plague's cause. His reticence on the ground that Fate will reveal all things in due course ("Of themselves things will come, although I hide them and breathe no word of them.") (340–1) provokes Oedipus to a rage whose cruel pitch of invective finally moves Teiresias to reveal the truth: Oedipus is the source of pollution. Here, then, in the first Episode, occurs the initial collision of a radical nature: by rejecting the seer's powers of prophecy the king again challenges Apollo, whose spokesman reluctantly speaks of unspeakable deeds committed by Oedipus as a direct result of his lifelong flight in defiance of the god's oracle (300–461).

Like Teiresias, the two remaining onstage protagonists also dwell outside the contaminated walls of Thebes, and the information they bear confirms beyond any doubt that by attempting to avoid his destiny Oedipus has run directly into its web. The first of these personages is the Messenger from Corinth who comes to Thebes with the news that Oedipus' putative father, King Polybus, has died, thus apparently clearing the hero of the crime of patricide. But Oedipus' relief at this news turns again to alarm when the Messenger assures him that he need not fear the old oracle in regard to Queen Merope either, because he was adopted as an infant by the rulers of Corinth! The Messenger claims that he himself received the baby from the arms of a shepherd in the employ of King Laius. Oedipus at once summons the old Herdsman to the city and threatens him with torture until he reluctantly confesses that he took pity on the infant left to die upon the mountainside by order of Laius and Jocasta (925–1185). But although this stunning episode brings about the drama's peripety, it constitutes a change of fortune for Oedipus only in his own eyes; for his destiny had ever been what the Oracle predicted it would be. The simultaneous *anagnorisis* or recognition of the truth therefore assumes greater importance than any so-called reversal of fortune: the truth is that Oedipus' fortune was always a misfortune.

Just as the shepherds serve unwittingly as instruments of Fate, so also do the offstage Polybus and Merope, whose childlessness inclined them to adopt the infant Oedipus as their son. For although the royal couple and the common herdsmen occupy positions far removed in the social pyramid, their mutual complicity as kindly instruments of Olympian will and their residence away from Thebes link them in an essentially dramatic way to the play's other protagonists, whether divine or mortal, powerful or weak. And although Polybus dies offstage during the action, neither sin nor plague destroys him—merely ripe old age (Theorem 2).

At this point it will be helpful to make a list of the initial protagonists, both onstage and off, taking into account deities directly invoked by other characters and also those contextually implied by their functional standing within the Greek theogeny. Opposite them appears Oedipus and, above him, the (offstage) primary antagonist:

Protagonist	Antagonist
[Moira (Fate)]	[Ares]
[The Erinyes (Furies)]	Oedipus
[Nemesis]	
[Zeus]	
[Apollo]	
[Dike (Justice)]	
[Athene]	
[Artemis]	
[Dionysus]	
[Pythian Priestess]	
[Polybus]	
[Merope]	
Teiresias & Boy	
[First Messenger]	
Herdsman	

A glance at this list reaffirms graphically the tremendous weight of forces, particulrly hidden supernatural ones, which Sophocles has aligned in the dominant unit. But why should Ares stand at the head of the opposed, recessive unit? And why should the playwright choose to implicate this god in the crimes of Oedipus?

It has already been noted that Ares is a god hated by the other Olympians, even by Zeus, his father. Yet the major gods' opposition to Oedipus would not in itself provide sufficient cause for linking him with the War God. Sophocles seems to have had another reason for such grouping, namely, an ancient and intimate association between Ares and the house of Cadmus, founder of Thebes.

According to the myth, Cadmus slew a dragon which guarded the local source of water. This serpent was the offspring of Ares; and when, at Athena's command, Cadmus sowed the teeth of the dead monster they grew from the earth as armed men who immediately fought and killed each other. At last only five warriors remained alive, and these *spartoi* (Sown Ones) helped Cadmus build Thebes' first fortress and found the city's aristocracy. Cadmus subsequently took to wife Harmonia, daughter of Ares and Aphrodite. The great-great grandson of this union (through Polydorus, Labdacus, and Laius) is Oedipus, who therefore descends from the Wrathful God. Indeed, the king seems to touch obliquely upon this hereditary taint when he asks whether his afflictions were not "sent by some malignant God" (828–9). Oedipus' blood, like that of the previous rulers of Thebes, is infused with the living spirit of Ares, who continues to curse the descendants of Cadmus with the blight of his rage— the same intemperance of spirit that possessed both Oedipus and Laius when, like true *spartoi*, they fought at the crossroads.[6]

Aside from Ares, one other supernatural but not immortal agent belongs in the antagonists' column: the Sphinx, whose terrifying presence, according to Creon, caused the people of Thebes to neglect inquiring into the murder of Laius (130–3). Sent to punish Laius for an unspecified crime, she poised on a rock outside the city and devoured all passers-by who could not answer her riddle. According to one version of the myth it was not Hera who sent her to Thebes but Ares, and this variant would seem to correspond to the Sophoclean treatment in which the blood of the War God continues to plague the descendents of Cadmus from generation to generation.[7] Thus, Laius was driven to Delphi to discover why the "dark-singing" beast-woman

---

[6.] Seyffert, pp. 106, 828-9, 341-2, 501.

[7.] Seyffert, p. 601.

haunted his city, only to meet his death at the hands of Oedipus. The latter then journeyed to Thebes where he drove the Sphinx to suicide by solving her riddle, and in so doing became at once the city's king and his mother's consort. Occurring prior to dramatic time proper, these events link Laius and his son with the randomly murderous Sphinx as self-destructive agents of the Wrathful God.

Although our text of *Oedipus the King* refers in passing to Cadmus and his grandson, Labdacus, as Oedipus' ancestors, none of the former kings except Laius seems to warrant dialectical placement as a hidden antagonist; for Sophocles focuses relentlessly on the blasphemous maneuvers of Laius, Jocasta, and Oedipus to circumvent the oracle—attempts which in each case lead to the commission of further crimes and ultimately to death or mutilation for the perpetrators. The conscious effort of Laius and Jocasta to thwart Apollo's prediction by exposing their child to die upon Mount Cithaeron constitutes prolicide, a practice condoned by the *spartoi* only in the case of physically defective infants; hence, the royal couple's act bears the stigma of child-murder, if not of literal blood-guilt within the family (for no blood was actually shed). And although Oedipus' own crimes of patricide and incest apparently do not entail the same degree of "uncleanliness" because committed in ignorance, they nevertheless spring from the same blasphemous motive. Indeed, the speeches of Jocasta and Oedipus are riddled with contumely directed at Destiny and her agents. Upon receiving the news of Polybus' death, Jocasta exults, "O oracles of the Gods, where are you now?" And Oedipus goes on to enlarge the blasphemy:

> Ha! Ha! O Jocasta, why should one
> look to the Pythian hearth? Why should one look
> to the birds overhead? They prophesied
> that I should kill my father! But he's dead,
> and hidden deep in earth, and I stand here
> who never laid a hand on spear against him,—
> Unless perhaps he died of longing for me,
> and thus I am his murderer. But they,
> the oracles, as they stand—he's taken them
> away with him, they're as dead as he himself is,
> and worthless (945–71).*

---

*Similar blasphemies, or accusations of blasphemy, occur in the following passages: 398–9, 430, 555–62, 707–25, 796–7, 856–8, 900–10, 977–80, 1329–35, 1424–9, 1444–5, 1476–9, 1515–20.

Such constant derision of the gods' oracles repeatedly underscores deeper sins: acts against Destiny committed in fear or wrath by Laius, Jocasta, and Oedipus. Laius has already paid Fate by fated death at his son's hands; and following the peripety Jocasta settles her own unholy debt by hanging herself—just before the frenzied Oedipus calls for a sword and rushes to the palace ("As he raved / some god showed him the way—none of us there") (1258–9). Oedipus' own self-inflicted punishment may evoke sympathy, and also, as Else interprets Aristotle, cleanse the title-character of unwitting blood pollution; however, the Chorus of elders views the matter otherwise:

> I cannot say your remedy was good;
> you would be better dead than blind and living (1367–9).

Fate has other things in store for Oedipus: together with his sister-daughters, Antigone and Ismene, he must yet suffer a long, peripatetic exile.

With the addition of the Sphinx, Laius, and Jocasta to the list which also includes Ares and Oedipus, we have almost completed our placement of those antagonists who remain in the recessive unit from beginning to end. The unfortunate Antigone and Ismene also belong here; yet, having no direct bearing on the play's action except as mute sufferers of Ares' infection in the blood of Cadmus, they must be listed in triangular brackets as walking symbols rather than as true players.

Still, one easily forgotten offstage character remains to complete the list of antagonists: the drunken man who at Polybus' table accuses Oedipus of being a bastard (776–800). This cruel charge understandably upsets King Polybus and Queen Merope, but it provokes Oedipus to a silent fury that drives him in haste to Delphi where he hears the oracle concerning himself and as a consequence makes the blasphemous decision to prove Apollo a liar. Like all other hidden players in the tragedy, whether protagonist or antagonist, the unnamed inebriate also functions as a critical agent in the chain of events leading to the drama's catastrophe (Theorem 4). Yet, unlike the play's mortal victors, who uniformly hesitate to question the divine order of things or to reveal that which will bring pain to another, the drunken guest betrays a rash and impious disregard both for the laws of hospitality and for secrets better left unspoken. The accusation that starts Oedipus on his blasphemous journey clearly places the callous speaker in the camp of the brutal and ignorant Ares.

Our list of permanent antagonists complete, we must now account for those characters who, following the tragedy's peripety, shift as a group from the recessive to the dominant functional unit. Foremost among these is the Chorus of Theban elders, whose wailings, lamentations, and prayers speak in token for the city's whole offstage population. In more individualized form appear the Priest of Zeus with the mute children who at the central altar implore the gods to save them from the plague; Creon, Jocasta's brother, who upon return from the Delphic Oracle finds himself accused of palace treason; and, finally, the Second Messenger who brings word of Oedipus' attempt to murder Jocasta, and of the latter's suicide. Dynamically speaking, all of these characters begin in the antagonists' column as innocent victims of the plague brought by Oedipus, then shift to the protagonists' unit once the source of pollution is discovered and removed from sight. This apostatic-positive movement occurs simultaneously and well after the peripety; for even following his terrible discovery, Oedipus continues to remain in the light of Thebes' sun. As Creon warns, this constitutes an offense to Apollo:

> But if you still
> are without shame before the face of men
> reverence at least the flame that gives us all life,
> our Lord the Sun, and do not show unveiled
> to him pollution such that neither land
> nor holy rain nor light of day can welcome (1422–7).

Despite this pious warning Oedipus continues to remain in the sunlight of Thebes' *agora*, bemoaning his fate, attempting to give orders regarding his future, and still blaspheming even as he "blesses" Creon for his mercy:

> . . . may God guard you better on your road
> than he did me! (1478–9).

Only with Oedipus' final exit, prior to the Chorus' last cautionary ode that concludes the tragedy, is the defilement lifted from the city and the apostatic-positive movement effected.

The following chart indicates those characters who shift dialectically, the positive direction of their movement, and the drama's final stasis:

ACTION CHART: Sophocles, *Oedipus the King*

PROTAGONIST	ANTAGONIST
[Moira (Fate)]	[Ares]
[The Erinyes (Furies)]	x [The Sphinx]
[Nemesis]	[Drunken Man]
[Zeus]	x [Laius]

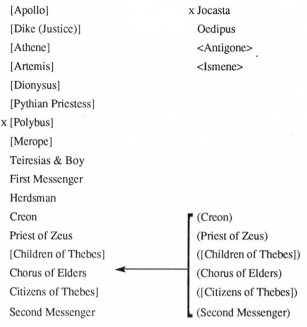

[Apollo]	x Jocasta
[Dike (Justice)]	Oedipus
[Athene]	<Antigone>
[Artemis]	<Ismene>
[Dionysus]	
[Pythian Priestess]	
x [Polybus]	
[Merope]	
Teiresias & Boy	
First Messenger	
Herdsman	
Creon	(Creon)
Priest of Zeus	(Priest of Zeus)
[Children of Thebes]	([Children of Thebes])
Chorus of Elders	(Chorus of Elders)
Citizens of Thebes]	([Citizens of Thebes])
Second Messenger	(Second Messenger)

(2) *Dialectic of Imagery*

Unlike Neo-classical drama, which largely eschews figurative in favor of abstract language, most classical Greek plays vie with those of the Elizabethans in weight of imagery. *Oedipus the King* is no exception; and although the bulk of its tropes predictably appear in the choral odes, many rhetorical figures also color its dialogue and monologue. Examination of this imagery in translation leads to a sense that our primary dialectic of action has been properly derived; for, after the play's positive apostasy has occurred, the rhetorical figures clothing protagonists and antagonists at the ultimate stasis exhibit an obvious, indeed resounding opposition to one another. Moreover, the shifting images carried along by the mobile characters consort most harmoniously with those of the initial protagonists to whom they move (Theorem 10).

Much rhetorical analysis of *Oedipus the King* has dwelt upon the tragedy's famed dialectic of sight versus blindness. Yet these opposed figures comprise but parts of a larger dialectical cluster which might be abbreviated as "light-gold-sight" versus "darkness-dirt-blindness" (Theorem 8). Furthermore, Sophocles employs the initial image of this threefold antinomy (light) to qualify *both* sides of the conflict, but with quite contrary affective results. Thus, the protagonists' light is represented as a controlled and stabilizing force within the natural and moral orders: the illumination of Apollo's prophetic vision coupled with the god's second aspect as Helios, giver of all life; the lightning bolts of Zeus which strike those who violate moral law; the gleaming torches with which Artemis scours the Lycean hills in search of trespassers against the same law. By contrast, the antagonists' light is an unnatural and immoral fire: the flame of pitch emanating from Ares' searing torches, here equated with the plague's contagion afflicting human, animal, and vegetable life; the night sky's stars by which Oedipus measures his distance from Corinth, and, as he believes, from Fate. This opposition of light in its moral and immoral aspects the Chorus makes explicit when, in the Parados, the city's elders supplicate Zeus to use his thunderbolt and Dionysus his torch of pine to combat the War God who burns them (197–200). Thus, the drama's opening figurative motif pits fire against fire, the cleansing heat of justice against the corrupting heat of injustice.

This complicated opposition of light against light in two separate aspects quickly modulates, however, to the simpler figurative counterpoint of light versus darkness. The clarity of Apollo's vision; the holy rain and light of day to which the offenders must eventually be exposed to shame; heaven's clear air, through which career birds used for divining truth; Parnassus' bright heights, sacred to Apollo; Mount Olympus, from which the gods see all; the wind flushed face of Dionysus; Athene's throne of fame sitting in the center of the marketplace; the flocks peacefully grazing on the slopes of Mount Cithaeron—these and related images create for the protagonists an aura of things bright, fresh, clean, elevated, and open for all to see. Quite at variance with this luminous orchestration for the tragedy's pious victors, a dark, heavy pedalpoint underscores the plight of the doomed antagonists: the plague's black death; the dark singing Sphinx of obscure speech; Pythia's warning that the unheeded thing escapes; the dark riddles, old and dim oracles which Oedipus cannot divine; the murderer envisioned as lurking in savage forests and caverns; men lying with their mothers in the dreams of night; the night long past which bred the murderer; the twisting thickets in which the infant Oedipus was found; the western shores of sunset where the death god waits for those afflicted by the plague.

The second cluster of this major figurative triad pits gold against dirt and blood. In its opening prayers the Chorus supplicates "Pytho rich in gold"; Apollo, "child of the golden hope," whose arrow shafts are "winged by the golden corded bow;" and, finally, Dionysus, "with the turban of gold" (151–215). Complementing the dominant image of luminosity, such references to the metal symbolizing perfection stand as emblems both of the material and spiritual wealth of the gods and their shrines. Nor does the fact that Oedipus blinds himself with Jocasta's gold chased brooches seem fortuitous, but rather a further reminder of the gods' role as vigilant punishers of those guilty of hubris. But gold in its negative aspect is mere dirt, the drinker of man's blood and tomb of his corruption. Thus, for the tragedy's antagonists all is dust: the unlucky place where the three roads met, the narrow way that drank Laius' blood; Jocasta's lying dead upon the palace floor; Oedipus' swollen feet, which have carried him far from the golden navel of the earth at Delphi, and upon which he will again be forced to wander, this time tapping his way with a stick; the furrows plowed by both father and son; the child cast upon a pathless hillside; the black rain and bloody hail streaming down from Oedipus' sightless eyes; the house which rivers cannot purge of pollution.

These contrasts between "light-gold" and "darkness-dirt" assume completed form in the last and most famous element of the figurative triad: the opposition of "sight" and "blindness." Teiresias, though physically blind, sees with the inner light bestowed by Apollo, while Oedipus, though sighted, remains blind to his sins against Destiny. Yet when the king finally discovers the truth, he no longer wishes to look upon the world he has been unable to master. Little need be added here to the commentaries of others on this ironic contrast, except to reiterate its intimate symbolic connection with the first two dialectical pairs of the triad, which also pit images suggesting holiness and wisdom against others implying moral pollution and benightedness.

Oedipus the King contains several other figurative clusters of less weight than those just summarized; for instance, the opposition of traditional religious symbols to blasphemous words, of silence to noise, and of wings to feet. However, the play's most elaborate single conceit, running from the Prologue through to the Exodos, lies in the antagonists' column, while its dialectical opposite is merely implied in the protagonists' unit. This prolonged metaphor envisions the stricken Thebes as a ship foundering through a violent storm and Oedipus as the frightened pilot unable to find a safe anchorage. The city reels like a wreck, all its timbers rotten, scarcely able to lift its prow above the bloody surf. For after his first "lucky" voyage (destroying the Sphinx), Oedipus finds in Jocasta a "haven no haven." Following the peripety Oedipus himself pleads to be thrown into the sea, while in its final ode the Chorus puts a period to the conceit by chanting "the breakers of misfortune have swallowed him!" (23–5, 100–4, 169, 121–4, 1412, 1527). By implication the safe haven lies in the sacred places of the gods and in an unquestioning acceptance of Destiny. Sophocles did not feel obliged to delineate this quiet anchorage because of its obviousness within the religious ethos of the drama as a whole; the very reticence of the gods and their oracles produces an effect of serenity that those who defy the inevitable will never find.

As commonly occurs in apostatic-positive actions, the shifting characters carry with them certain key images which in their initial position create a dissonance presaging their eventual movement, but which in their final stasis add to the harmony of the dominant cluster they have joined (Theorem 10). Among such figures in *Oedipus the King* are the suppliant crowns adorning the children at the central altar, and similar garlands worn by offstage citizens in the Theban marketplace at the double shrine of Athene (14–223). Intertwining with these symbols of piety are the "sprigs of holy laurel" crowning Creon's head as he returns from Apollo's oracle at Delphi. Strategically embedded in the drama's Prologue, such religious emblems foreshadow the ultimate removal of pollution from Thebes and the movement of its citizens to the safe harbor of the gods.

The shift of these images from negative to positive poles of action will be represented at the top of our image-chart both because they appear early in the text and also because of their importance as elements of the play's apostatic-positive dynamic. The remaining figures, including one late shifting image, will be listed simply in aproximate order of their appearance in the text. Again, dialectically opposed pairs (Theorem 11) are pointed up by number-keying.

IMAGE-CHART: Sophocles, *Oedipus the King*:

PROTAGONIST		ANTAGONIST
Creon's laurel crown from Delphi	————	(Creon's laurel crown from Delphi)
Children with suppliant crowns	————	(Children with suppliant crowns)
Citizens with suppliant crowns	————	(Citizens with suppliant crowns)
Double shrine of Athene	————	(Double shrine of Athene)
Hymns and incense	————	(Hymns and incense)
Central alter	————	(Central altar)

PROTAGONIST: Silent children; Priest of Zeus; Light from Apollo; Pytho rich in gold; Apollo, child of golden hope; Artemis' throne of fame in market place; Artemis, earth upholder; Birds swift on the wing (1); Athene, golden daughter of Zeus; Escaping the night; Light of day; Zeus, lord of lightning (2); Apollo's arrows winged by golden corded bow; Gleaming torches of Artemis scouring the Lycean hills; Bacchus with the turban of gold & wind flushed face; Bacchus' torch of pine; Silence (3) Apollo's sight; Teiresias led by mute boy: No eyes (inner sight) (4); Oracles of birds (5); Delphi's prophetic rock; Apollo's fire & lightning bolt (2); Fates close on Oedipus' heels; Voice flashing from Parnassus; Holding one's tongue (3); Sleep untroubled; Laws that live on high; Clear air of heaven; Olympus; Shafts of the God; Dancing in honor of the gods; Olympia, navel of the earth; Birds screaming overhead; Unbinding fettered feet (6); Cythaeron by the limitless sky; Dancing & singing to Apollo; Dionysus' nymphs; Grassy slopes; Old Cythaeron; Time who sees all; Evils brought to light;

ANTAGONIST: City reeling like wreck, scarcely lifting prow; Bloody surf; Blight on plants & animals (1); Women infertile; Pestilence; Black Death; The cruel, dark singing Sphinx; Empty towers & ship; Tears; Bloodshed; Destroying storm; Pollution; Ares' torches of fire (the plague); "The thing unheeded escapes"; Destruction's flames; Ship's timbers rotten; Fire unmastered; Fire smitten by Zeus' lightning (2); Dead, naked children; Moaning & wailing; Cries of men; Ares, the god who burns (2); Speech (3); Neither greeting nor offering to gods, nor water to wash hands; Land destroyed & blighted; Bed & wife; No crops, No children; Fortune leaped upon Laius' head; Disease; Waves of sea where there is no safe anchorage; Pain; Oedipus provoked like a stone; Sight without seeing (4); Blind in mind, ears, & eyes; No knowledge from birds (5); City's destroying storm; Deadly footed double striking curse; Enemy to kin beneath the earth; Darkness on eyes; Cythaeron ringing with cries; Jocasta, haven no haven; Dark riddles; Blindness for sight (4); Tapping way with stick through foreign country; Sower in father's bed;

IMAGE-CHART: Sophocles, *Oedipus the King* (cont.):

PROTAGONIST

Thebes' sacred places; The flame that gives all life; Our Lord the Sun; Holy rain & light of day.

ANTAGONIST

Bloody handed murderer; Lurking in savage forests & caverns like mountain bull; Feet far from navel of the earth; Eyes not straight in head; Wasting country; Place where three roads meet (bad omen); Pierced ankles (6); Cast forth on pathless hillside; Laius' grizzled hair; Laius' carriage & two-pointed goad; Lying with mother; Showing to daylight a race accursed; Measuring distance from Corinth by stars at night; Laius thrusting Oedipus out of the road by force; Striking; Pushing; Laius falling backward from car, killing Laius' guards; Traveling alone; Falling from roof-top to where feet are of no service; Glutted by surfeit; Walking with haughtiness; Fingers itching for untouchable things; Old & dim oracles; Ship's pilot frightened; Jocasta's incense offerings for escape from the curse (blasphemy); Mother's bed; Men lying with their mother in dreams; Oedipus found on Cythaeron's slopes in twisting thickets; "Oedipus" = "Swell-foot" (by transference "Swell-head"); Rushing in wild grief; Twisting shepherd's arm behind him; Seeing the light of a match accursed; Shooting bolt beyond others to win prize; Hooked taloned maid of riddling speech; Standing a tower against death for Thebes in past; Jocasta as Oedipus' great haven; Born by furrows plowed by father and son; Weeping & crying in dirge of lamentation; Streams cannot purge the house; A bitter groaning's worth; Jocasta raging & tearing her hair; Night long past which bred a child; Groaning & cursing the bed; Infamous double bond;

IMAGE-CHART: Sophocles, *Oedipus the King* (cont.):

PROTAGONIST

Chorus hiding eyes from Oedipus ◄------------

ANTAGONIST

Mother making children with her son; Oedipus bursting doors; Yelling for sword to rip open womb of double sowing; Bellowing; Wrenching bolts out of sockets Oedipus bursting open doors; Twisted rope around Jocasta's neck; Cutting the noose; Jocasta lying on ground; Deadly-footed, double striking curse; Tearing gold chased brooches from Jocasta's robe & eyes; Bleeding eyeballs gushing; Stained beard; Black rain & bloody hail; Shouting for door to be unbolted; Bolts opening.

(Chorus hiding eyes from Oedipus)

Voice borne on wind to and fro; Terrible place whereof men's ears may not hear or eyes behold; Darkness; Nothing sweet to see; Ears untouched by joyful greeting; Begetter in same seed from which he sprung; Dirge of lamentation; No sight of children or city; Father's old house; Crossroads, hidden glade & narrow way that drank father's blood; "Throw me into the sea;" No sound of human voice; Two accursed daughters whose table never stood apart from their father's; Oedipus touching Antigone & Ismene ; Sobbing; Weeping; Tears; Touching Creon's hand; Being sent inside away from light of sun; "Breakers of misfortune swallow him."

(3) *Implicational Dialectic*:

Here, as in the previous chapter, I shall render into abstract terms those antinomies which most accurately describe the essential common characteristics of the opposing functional units of *Oedipus the King*, attempting to lay bare the drama's dominant and recessive functions so far as modern language can accommodate ancient concepts and beliefs (Theorems 13, 14, 17):

1. *Acceptance of Destiny/Rejection of Destiny*. This set of antinomies together with the very last of our derivations (Happiness/Unhappiness) represent the alpha and omega of the tragedy's implicational dialectic. For as Sophocles treats the myth of Oedipus, the hero's sorrows derive wholly from his impious attempts to flee that which the gods have ordained for him. The quibble that under no circumstances could Oedipus have avoided his misery because it was preordained only adds weight to the drama's overpoweringly fatalistic ethos. All the Olympians, save one, demand human compliance; only Ares, whose hot blood infects Oedipus, is foolish enough to defy the other gods and cause his mortal descendants to make war upon themselves by doing likewise. Oedipus, Laius, and Jocasta are crushed by the gods because the race of Cadmus bears the curse of the dragon's tooth: they fight without wisdom, and in the very face of destiny.

2. *Purification/Pollution (katharós/miaron)*. Until Creon orders Oedipus inside the palace and out of the holy light of the sun, Thebes suffers from a plague whose cause is the presence of one "polluted" or "unclean" (*miaron*). The pollution derives not so much from Oedipus' unwitting crimes of patricide and incest as from a literal uncleanliness in his royal blood, through which courses the fire of Ares, hated of gods. From this hereditary taint Oedipus acquires his intemperance of spirit, a rashness that provokes him to commit the ultimate blasphemy of defying Fate. Removal of Oedipus from sight in anticipation of his banishment fulfills the requirement for Thebes' purification (*katharós*).

3. *Piety/Blasphemy*. In its opening prayer the Chorus invokes nearly all the major Olympians; and though later in the action some doubt of Apollo's oracle creeps into its collective voice (Ode II), the Chorus reacts to Oedipus' eventual exposure by "shuddering" as at one "unclean" (1300–6). Reverence for the gods is objectified more directly in the Priest of Zeus, the seer Teiresias, and the offstage Pythian Priestess, as well as by the simple goodness of Polybus and Merope, the old Herdsman, and the Corinthian Messenger. In striking contrast, Laius and Jocasta have previously transgressed against the gods' decree by attempting to murder their infant

son in order to avoid the oracle's prediction, while Oedipus and Jocasta repeatedly revile the gods throughout the action. Even Jocasta's single prayer to Apollo (Episode III) amounts to blasphemy because her only request is to escape the "curse" (i.e., Fate).

4. *Innocence/Guilt.* "Now I am found to be/ a sinner and a son of sinners" (1397–8). With this admission Oedipus acknowledges his own guilt as well as that of Laius and Jocasta, and also, by implication, the guilt of all the Cadmean descendants of Ares. Comparison of the play's ultimate protagonists and antagonists makes further commentary on this set of antinomies scarcely necessary—except to point out that the shifting characters, though initially afflicted by the plague, are innocent of its cause, which, when discovered, they reject as "unclean."

5. *Kindliness/Cruelty.* The second term of this pair claims special attention because cruelty is the principal attribute of Ares and also a major component of Oedipus' character—though the latter fact has received insufficient critical emphasis. Yet sympathy for the title-character tends to dwindle when his inhumanities are reviewed: (1) Abandonment of his adoptive parents even before seeking advice from a seer on the meaning of the oracle; (2) Killing an old man and his servants when they demand right-of-way at a narrow crossroads; (3) Taunting Teiresias for his blindness and mocking his powers as a seer; (4) Unjustly and publicly accusing Creon of palace treason; (5) Torturing and threatening to execute an old shepherd for attempting to withhold information; (6) Intending, under the assumption that she is still alive, to rip open Jocasta's womb; (7) Remaining in the light of day and thus prolonging the plague after realizing that his presence is the cause of the city's affliction. Contextually, neither Fate nor the major Olympians so closely identified with the general concept of destiny can be accused of cruelty, for their workings are represented as all-wise, if sometimes inscrutable.

6. *Tranquility/Strife.* Those who revere the gods and humbly submit to the divine will, as do the mortal protagonists of *Oedipus the King*, will be favored with tranquility of mind; but not those who, like the play's antagonists, struggle against the inevitable. Eris (strife) is the sister of Ares, whose blood pollutes the *spartoi*; and conflict has plagued the Theban aristocracy since its beginning, when the wedding gifts of the gods to Cadmus and Ares' daughter, Harmonia, "had everywhere the fatal property of stirring up strife and bloodshed."[8]

---

[8]Seyffert, p. 269.

7. *Courage/Fear*. Honor of the gods permits one to accept one's fate with humility and courage. But the descendants of Cadmus are afflicted by Ares' son Phobos (fear), who strikes them with terror in the face of that which is to come. Such terror leads to elaborate avoidance behavior, which, because of its irrational (blasphemous) nature, tends to create (fulfill) precisely those situations (prophecies) that are most feared.

8. *Trust/Suspicion*. He who possesses courage is also capable of trust. However, Oedipus trusts no one when fear strikes him. Once Teiresias has singled him out as Laius' murderer, the king rashly accuses Creon of conspiring with the old seer in order to usurp the throne. Likewise, Jocasta repeatedly warns Oedipus against putting his trust in the oracles of the gods.

9. *Sanity/Madness*.

>Poor wretch, what madness came upon you!
>What evil spirit leaped upon your life
>to your ill-luck—a leap beyond man's strength! (1300–2).

Thus, in the great *kommos* of Ode V, the Chorus of elders addresses the broken and self-blinded Oedipus. The "evil spirit" that has afflicted the king's life is here specifically identified as "madness" or *mania*. Sophocles apparently assumed, in a way difficult for the modern mind to apprehend, that the assertion of free-will represented the most grievous form of madness.

10. *Humility /Pride*. The tragedy's ultimate protagonists address the problem of ending Thebes' plague with humble piety, offering prayers and libations to the various gods, journeying to Delphi to seek the Oracle's advice, and supplicating their young king to save the city as he had done once before. Yet Oedipus' first response to these requests clearly betrays a self-aggrandizing streak which subsequent revelations will fully expose to be an "ill-starred pride of heart." The Grene translation of this monologue, whose ostensible substance is the king's compassion for his subjects, opens with the personal pronoun "I" and repeats that pronoun, with its variants "me" and "myself," no fewer than eighteen times within nineteen lines (58–77). The entirely reflexive, self-referring tenor of this speech vitiates its content and apprises us in a none too subtle way of Oedipus' tendency toward what is commonly rendered directly from the Greek as "hubris."

11. *Wisdom/Ignorance*. Within the ethos of this tragedy wisdom consists in piety, whose highest expression is the ability to accept the inevitable with good grace. Laius, Jocasta, and Oedipus are entirely incapable of assuming this attitude. In the excess of

their pride they behave much like the cruel Sphinx who committed suicide the first time someone succeeded in divining her riddle.

12. *Justice/Injustice* (*dike/adikia*). Dike, daughter of Zeus, personifies the concept of justice, which, like that of wisdom, is here clearly subsumed under the head of piety; for, as the Chorus reminds us, the laws that live on high were brought to birth by no mortal nature (865-70). Hence, Sophocles offers a theological rather than a secular idea of the right, according to which Oedipus' offenses against justice must be viewed as the direct consequences of his defiance of Zeus (Fate).

13. *Courtesy/Insolence*. A natural offspring of justice, courtesy is another attribute of those who, whether king or common herdsman, revere the gods. But, as the Chorus warns in its second ode, "Insolence breeds the tyrant" and also brings him down "to the ruin that must be" (874-9).

14. *Decency/Indecency*.

> O Polybus and Corinth and the house,
> the old house that I used to call my father's—
> what fairness you were nurse to, and what foulness
> festered beneath! (1394-7).

Like the other protagonists of *Oedipus the King*, Polybus and Queen Merope are characterized as behaving towards others with fairness and decency—qualities which Oedipus belatedly recognizes in the adoptive parents he has abandoned, and which he simultaneously disclaims in himself. His use of the past tense hints at a "foulness" in his nature prior even to the commission of patricide and incest, thus reminding us of the taint of Ares in the blood of Cadmus.

15. *Moderation/Excess*. The unseemly pride that leads to thirst for excessive power also breeds rashness, a characteristic of nearly all Oedipus' actions both during and anterior to dramatic time proper. The same holds for Laius, and even for Jocasta, whose several ineffectual attempts to stop Oedipus from pursuing the investigation are couched in terms blasphemously contemptuous of the gods' oracles. Cautious ones, like Teiresias and Creon, do not tempt destiny by deprecating its auguries.

17. *Honor/Shame*. Those who honor the gods' decrees are themselves honored by the very exercise. But Oedipus honors none above himself—except perhaps inadvertently the outcast among gods from whom he descends.

18. *Compliance/Obstinacy*.

> If you think obstinacy without wisdom
> a valuable possession, you are wrong (549-50).

By the way in which he frames this assertion to the king, Creon implies that stubbornness can be a valuable attribute, but only tempered with wisdom. Yet, as we have already seen, wisdom is here universally equated with compliance to the will of the gods.

19. *Nobility/Ignobility*. After the peripety Oedipus concedes that Creon has acted with a noble spirit toward one who used him vilely (1432–4). The overreaching monarch's ignoble conduct, like that of the other antagonists, is represented as a natural consequence of impiety.

20. *Normality/Perversion*. These terms apply not so much in their current vague psychological sense as they do in a more specific sense of moral rectitude. For, although shocking in itself, Oedipus' unwitting commission of incest is not the play's central dramatic "issue," which consists rather in a distinction between those who accept Fortune with dignity and those who attempt to disturb its course and tamper with its rhythm. To do the latter is represented as perverse by definition, and the cause of further perversion in the more common meaning of that term.

21. *Health/Sickness*.

> . . . there is not one of you, sick though you are,
>
> that is as sick as I myself (60-1).

The famous Sophoclean *double entendre* is here stunningly employed to remind us at the outset of the true cause of Thebes' plague, and further, that the sickness is a moral one, of which the "pollution grown ingrained within the land" forms a symbolic extension. Fulfillment of the "healing god's" command that the source of pollution be driven out of the city restores Thebes' citizens to a state both of physical and moral well-being.

22. *Fertility/Barrenness*. Overlapping with the previous terms, these derivations must also be interpreted in a moral as well as literal sense. For just as Apollo the Healer alleviates the plague, so in various ways the other gods confer the blessings of fertility upon the land—but only on that land where the laws conferred from on high are obeyed. Like most of the tragedy's other implications, these are also directly linked to piety or impiety, acceptance or rejection of Destiny.

23. *Inclusion/Exclusion*. Oedipus' deposition as king and removal from sight not only restore the city to health and moral equilibrium but also return to its citizens the benefits of their collective ancestral worship, from which the presence of one "unclean" had deprived them.

24. *Blessedness /Accursedness.*

> Take me away, my friends, the greatly miserable
> the most accursed, whom God too hates
> above all men on earth! (1341–4).

Though many years later in *Oedipus at Colonus* Sophocles will provide a mystical redemption for the aged title-character, the present work concentrates relentlessly upon the young Oedipus' crimes, chief among which is defiance of the gods. For this blasphemy, and the other misdeeds that issue from it, Oedipus is indeed accursed among men—just as his divine ancestor is hated among gods.

25. *Happiness /Unhappiness.*

> You that live in my ancestral Thebes, behold this Oedipus,—him who
> knew the famous riddles and was a man most masterful; not a citizen who
> did not look with envy on his lot—see him now and see the breakers of
> misfortune swallow him! Look upon the last day always. Count no mortal
> happy till he has passed the final limit of his life secure from pain.

In the drama's famous concluding lines the Chorus warns against those who, like Oedipus, presumptuously attempt to master rather than humbly accept their personal destiny, no matter how bitter. The blame lies not with the gods for their sternness but with the individual whose pride causes him to hold in contempt the laws that live on high.

With this last set of antinomies we appear to have completed the derivations required by the protocol for descriptive abstraction. As in the previous chapter, many of the terms used to qualify the drama's motivational opposition necessarily overlap because the work advances an extremely well articulated conception of piety based on religious fatalism. The depth and particular quality of the Sophoclean ideal (and its cautionary opposite) will be apprehended by scanning downwards the separate units of the following implicational chart:

IMPLICATIONAL CHART: Sophocles, *Oedipus the King*

DOMINANT FUNCTION	RECESSIVE FUNCTION
Acceptance of Destiny	Rejection of Destiny
Purification	Pollution
Piety	Blasphemy
Innocence	Guilt
Kindliness	Cruelty
Tranquility	Strife
Courage	Fear

Trust	Suspicion
Sanity	Madness
Humility	Pride
Wisdom	Ignorance
Justice	Injustice
Courtesy	Insolence
Decency	Indecency
Moderation	Excess
Caution	Rashness
Honor	Shame
Compliance	Obstinacy
Nobility	Ignobility
Normality	Perversion
Health	Sickness
Fertility	Barrenness
Inclusion	Exclusion
Blessedness	Accursedness
Happiness	Unhappiness

Re-examination of the tragedy's conceptual duality confirms that its dramatic fulcrum, its pivotal thought content, consists in a complex and mystical religious attitude according to which man's nobility of character lies in humble submission to the will of the gods and acceptance of the inevitable with stoical grace. Objectified most intensely in its title-character, the drama's recessive function provides a frightening cautionary example of what befalls those who decline to observe these pieties. Nor does Sophocles in any way compromise this deep fatalism: the curse on Oedipus seems insufferable, yet his denial of its reality is shown to be the very means by which the oracle fulfills itself. The dramatist was possibly counting on his audience's knowledge of the outcome of the Oedipus myth—of the mystical blessing in death conferred on the hero after long years of learning how to bear his sufferings, and his end, as all men must.

Dynamically speaking, *Oedipus the King* provides a somewhat uncommon picture of the apostatic-positive structure because its shifting characters (the Theban citizenry) move from negative to positive poles simultaneously and near the very end of action. It is therefore prudent to reiterate that numerous other plays of this dynamic represent their characters' shifts separately and often at widely spaced intervals. But whenever and however they occur, these dialectical movements from negative to positive comprise the major pulse beats of the drama, disrupting the action's initial alignment of forces and leading to the final stasis which represents the fulfillment of the authorial wish.

THIRD MODEL
APOSTATIC-NEGATIVE

Definition. *The apostatic-negative structure reverses the dynamic pattern of the apostatic-positive by depicting the movement of one or more characters from the dominant to the recessive pole of action. Although it may represent the shift of several figures, the apostatic-negative variant commonly focuses upon the lone apostasy of an attractive central character who makes a calamitous choice that results in his moving from a state of power, happiness, and grace to one of helplessness, sorrow, and damnation. The downfall of this personage usually proceeds from some moral or psychological impediment, a "tragic flaw," whether of naivety or ambition, that confounds his better judgment and undermines his loyalty to higher principles. His (rarely her) expulsion from the protagonists' unit is therefore represented as a necessary punishment for the willful contravention of divine or natural law. Such betrayal of principle is the common failing of all mobile characters of this dynamic, including subordinate figures who sometimes accompany the leading character in his downfall, as well as secondary personages who occasionally constitute the only shifting characters of the plays in which they appear.*

Depicting the moment of choice that leads from happiness to unhappiness, the apostatic-negative dynamic is ideally suited to the dramatization of cautionary homilies stressing the principle of free will. Consequently, dramas of this structure tend to outright moral or religious allegory, demonstrating the awful consequences of yielding to temptation.

Schematic. The shifting character (Z) is shown in parentheses to indicate his (her/their) initial position in the protagonists' unit. An arrow plots his negative apostasy to the antagonists' unit, and the same letter-symbol without parentheses represents his final position in the action:

General.

> Had I as many souls as there be stars
> I'd give them all for Mephistophilis.
>
> Marlowe, *Doctor Faustus*

Most plays conforming to the apostatic-negative model are dominated by the mythos of the Faustian bargain, whereby a character sells his eternal soul to the Devil in return for unlimited power and pleasure during his earthly life. From *Doctor Faustus* and *Macbeth* to the *The Godfather, Part One,* dramas of this class depict a fatal moral choice's being made before the very eyes of the audience. Whether it be Macbeth's yielding to vaulting ambition despite the promptings of his better conscience, or the young Michael Corleone's reluctantly assuming leadership of the bloody family business, the audience is given to witness the chilling spectacle of an otherwise good person consciously abandoning his moral scruples to adopt a course of action that is plainly evil. Macbeth speaks openly of the "deep damnation" awaiting the murderer of good King Duncan, just as Corleone stands before the priest and falsely forswears Satan at the very moment his first gangland executions are being carried out. Both of these negative apostates are therefore conscious sinners, fully aware of their free choice in the matter, and also of its inevitable consequences. At their moment of apostasy they, and all figures like them, might well echo Marlowe's self-doomed hero: "Now, Faustus, must thou needs be damn'd, cans't thou not be saved!"

Works obeying the apostatic-negative dynamic fall into the modal phases of tragedy or irony—never that of comedy. For these are blood-and-thunder melodramas, often preoccupied with religious eschatology and therefore obsessed with death and (most especially) damnation. Redolent of sulphur and gore, their antagonists' units regularly teem with assassins, furies, and witches, while behind these deformed figures lurks Old Nick himself in one or another conventional or private incarnation.

The stage lighting here is all *chiaroscuro*, with the steady radiance of the morally undefiled protagonists played off against the moist, flickering shadows of the antagonists; for this is a war between good and evil, whether its principal (offstage) adversaries be God and Satan or the mythically decomposed figures of a purely secular morality projected against the cosmos. During the course of this struggle someone will pass from light into darkness, salvation to damnation, thereby serving as a cautionary example of moral transgression. "Murder will out" provides the motto here; or, if not murder, then some other grave moral lapse predicated upon the gravest sins of betrayal and despair. Consequently, although some modern instance of the apostatic-negative assume an ironic tone, such dramas are never truly ironic in the structural sense of permitting negative motives to contaminate the dominant unit of the protagonists; for such a mixture of good and evil would be quite contrary to the purpose of the moral allegory upon which this dynamic thrives.

Especially suited for depicting the fall from grace that proceeds from yielding to temptation, the apostatic-negative is a most congenial pattern for many dramas of Christian ethos. Elizabethan and Jacobean dramatists are especially fond of showing through this dynamic the reversals of fortune attendant upon succumbing to various of the mortal sins, whether they be Satanism and pursuit of the black arts (*Doctor Faustus*), thirst for vengeance (*The Revenger's Tragedy*), the sin of pride and lust for power (*Macbeth*), proscribed sexuality (*'Tis Pity She's a Whore*), or weakness of faith (*Othello*) . In each of these works the principal offstage adversaries are God and Satan, whose cosmic opposition motivates the human struggle onstage, and between whose camps the mobile characters shift to their souls' peril during the course of action. This is not to say, however, that all or even most dramas of Christian ethos assume the apostatic-negative structure: the majority in fact obey other models. Yet whenever a dramatist wishes to focus on the moment of choice that leads to the commission of a mortal sin, he will usually gravitate to this dynamic, which is tailor-made for his purpose.

Even in its modern incarnations the apostatic-negative form often harbors a religious eschatology, which it sometimes attempts to soft-pedal by avoiding all but the most oblique references to sacred symbolism or moral theology. Thus, Ionesco's *Macbett,* though in many ways a parody of its Shakespearean namesake, nevertheless retains God and Satan as its principal offstage belligerents, while at the same time carefully avoiding any overt references to Catholic theology. In a more forthright manner, Shafer's *Amadeus* incorporates (even into its title) the old God–Satan dialectic of the revenge tragedies. For when Antonio Salieri vows to seek Mozart's ruin, his choice is represented as an open act of defiance against God for permitting Mozart to serve as an instrument of His sublimity while denying that gift to Salieri:

> *Dio injuisto*—You are the Enemy! I name thee now—*Nemico Eterno!*
> And this I swear: To my last breath I shall *block* You on earth, as far as
> I am able! (*He glares up at God. To the audience*) What use, after all is
> man, if not to teach God his lesson? (I, xii)

If Shafer's drama quite openly reveals its major protagonist to be an offstage deity, John Huston's ironic screenplay *The Treasure of the Sierra Madre* is more reticent about such higher powers; yet even this apostatic-negative morality drama of temptation and betrayal hints at a cosmic justice in the workings of its action, as the old prospector, Howard, affirms in the last scene:

> Laugh, Curtin, old boy, it's a great joke played on us by the Lord or fate
> or nature—whichever you prefer, but whoever or whatever played it,
> certainly has a sense of humor. The gold has gone back to where we got
> it. Laugh, my boy, laugh. It's worth the months of labor and suffering—
> this joke is.

Although not clearly identified in a sectarian manner, the invisible force that plays this cosmic joke is nonetheless represented to be the prime mover of the film's dominant unit, just as its dialectically implicit counterpart is the power that draws Fred C. Dobbs to his destruction in the benighted search for earthly riches at the cost of betraying friends. In light of the quietly Catholic ethos of other Huston films, it is probably safe to identify the primary combatants of *The Treasure of the Sierra Madre* as God and Satan, even though the novel from which the film was adapted came from the pen of a Marxist.

Whenever dramas of this structure are not informed by a religious ethos, Christian or otherwise, they nevertheless tend to incorporate some other sort of programmatic dualism according to which the shifting character's apostasy must be seen as a violation of the laws of history, a betrayal entailing some form of eternal shame—at least in the eyes of posterity. Ibsen's *An Enemy of the People* thus propounds a secular idealism which, by demanding the voluntary sacrifice of self-interest to the general weal, cannot but represent the abandonment of that ideal by the "solid majority" as the betrayal of the human spirit, and therefore also as a negative dialectical movement. In a more systematic fashion, Brecht incorporates into his *Life of Galileo* a

Hegelian/Marxist teleology from whose vantage point Galileo's recantation and grudging return to the fold of the church must be viewed not only as an act of personal cowardice, but also as an (ultimately futile) betrayal of the historical process itself.

Although the negative apostate of this structure is usually also the drama's principal character, occasionally the dialectically mobile figures will be drawn instead exclusively from the ranks of the supporting players. In such instances the central character will be a saintly or heroic figure who remains dialectically immobile in the dominant unit, while other, weaker souls slide down from his lofty and dangerous perch atop the moral mountain. This variant pattern occurs in Bolt's *A Man for All Seasons*, whose focal character, Sir Thomas More, staunchly refuses to compromise his faith, and as a result finds himself abandoned and eventually betrayed by his former devoted friends, Norfolk and Rich. The exclusive movement of secondary figures also occurs in Ibsen's *An Enemy of the People*, wherein the crusading Dr. Stockman is deserted first by his former allies in the press and then by nearly everyone in town, once the economic implications of his discovery of contamination of the local spa waters are clearly perceived. In all such cases the heinousness of the shifting characters' disloyalty is played off against the principal figure's steadfastness in the faith, whether religious or secular. And if the negative apostates appear to be guided by the calloused hand of conventional wisdom, their faint-heartedness must nevertheless be viewed as a defeat of the human spirit and a betrayal of future generations, though not always as the cause of actual damnation in a world to come.

Somewhat more common than dramas depicting the negative apostasy of secondary figures exclusively are those in which the central character drags one or more of the supporting cast along with him on his downward career. Emphasizing the socially demoralizing nature of the focal character's change of heart, this variation especially suits plays such as Brecht's *Galileo,* in which the characters of Federzoni and The Little Monk are driven to despairing renunciation of their own scientific work as a result of their master's public abjuration of his belief in the heliocentric universe. Similarly, Ionesco's *Macbett* adds a dynamic twist to its namesake by making Banco (Banquo) a companion to Macbett in his journey down the primrose path to the everlasting bonfire.

In most dramas of this structure a single image of great metaphorical weight, though of superficially trifling proportion, often accompanies the shifting character on his road to ruin, serving as a symbolic pointer to the hero's fatal character flaw and, more materially, as the proximate cause of his downfall. Paradigmatic of such shifting images (Theorem 10) is the magical heirloom handkerchief which Othello presents as a wedding gift to Desdemona, and which, when misappropriated by Iago, leads the Moor to suspect his wife's honor. Fashioned by an Egyptian sorceress and given to Othello by his mother as a charm against marital infidelity, this apparently harmless object becomes a sign of the general's pagan background and his superstitious credulity—the fatal chinks in his armor of Christian faith and trust. Similarly, in Brecht's *Life of Galileo*, such apparently innocuous trifles as gifts of goat cheese and geese serve as reminders of the relish of creature comforts that was a critical factor in the great physicist's moral collapse when faced with threats of torture and privation; for these delicacies that he overvalued in freedom provide but meagre solace to him in a shameful captivity, of which they have become the emblems. Other downhill pointers likewise cast their shadows across many cinematic versions of the apostatic-negative dynamic: the winning lottery ticket #13 that launches Fred C. Dobbs on his fatal prospecting career into the Sierra Madre, or the provocative photograph of Lola that serves as a catalyst for the prudish Professor Rath's moral collapse in von Sternberg's *The Blue Angel,* to mention but two. Occasionally these negatively shifting images are less tangible than purely symbolic entities, as in Barnes' *The Ruling Class*, where the schizophrenic Fourteenth Earl of Gurney's identification with God eventually makes possible his "rehabilitation" from "Jesus Mark II" to reactionary "Lord" by day, and Jack the Ripper by night—his madness in both incarnations hinging on the conviction of omnipotence. All such negatively pointing images and symbols serve as metaphors for the flaws of character that precipitate the mobile figures in their fall from grace.

At the third, descriptive stage of analysis, dramas of the apostatic-negative class exhibit a fair degree of implicational variation one from another, though indeed somewhat less than those of the apostatic-positive or several other structures. The reason for this slightly more constricted motivational range is to be found in the moral preoccupation of the form, with its clear-cut good/evil, right-way/wrong-way dialectic and its consequent structural inability to permit ironic admixtures of positive and negative qualities within the same functional unit. Moreover, when plays of this type are informed by a Christian ethos, they will regularly demand descriptive terms appropriate to an opposition between the theological or moral virtues and vices. Hence, the common necessity for such antonyms as "grace/despair," "pride/humility," and the like (Theorem 14). Yet even if the drama in question fails to yield these particular oppositions, it will nonetheless require at least one invariable set of antonyms, namely, "loyalty/betrayal," or its variant "fidelity/infidelity." For the shifting characters of this structure are always renegades, apostates from the true faith (however the author defines that faith) and consequently traitors to the protagonists' unit which they eventually abandon. Indeed, so ubiquitous is the "loyalty/betrayal" dichotomy in this structure, that the form could well be named "The Drama of Betrayal."

Although the mythos of this dynamic—the story of an otherwise good man moving from happiness to unhappiness as the result of a grave error—neatly conforms to Aristotle's definition of the best and most tragic of all plots, it is curious that no surviving Greek tragedies appear to adopt the apostatic-negative structure. Aside from the fact that the vast majority of Hellenic and Hellenistic plays have been lost to posterity, and with them possibly some instance of this type, there are other reasons why the apostatic-negative model might not have been congenial to the ancient temper. For one thing, Aristotle's ideal tragic situation can also be accommodated by the apostatic-positive dynamic (Model 2) whenever it reveals the central character's initial transgression to have taken place before the commencement of dramatic time proper—as it does in *Oedipus the King*. This technique avoids direct representation of the fatal choice itself, instead placing the emphasis where Aristotle suggested it ought to be: upon the character's (and spectator's) recognition of the former misdeed, and upon the terror and pity that such recognition elicits. In a way perhaps inconceivable to the fatalistic temper of the ancients, modern dramatists, on the contrary, often choose to focus upon the initial error itself in order to stress the character's knowing complicity, his freedom of choice in that as in all other moral matters. Hence, instead of depicting characters moving in a positive direction away from a central figure who is unwittingly tainted from the beginning, later dramatists often prefer to show the negative apostasy of a hero who quite freely conspires in his own downfall. Unlike ourselves, the ancients apparently did not find edifying the spectacle of an otherwise good man consciously choosing an evil course of action.

ANALYSIS
Shakespeare, *Othello, The Moor of Venice*[1]

(1) *Dialectic of Action*:

Perhaps no celebrated drama better exemplifies the apostatic-negative structure than Shakespeare's *Othello*, which chronicles in the clearest possible manner its central character's radical descent from an initial state of honor, happiness, and grace to an ultimate condition of shame, misery, and despair. At the commencement of action the Moor stands thrice blessed as a convert to Christianity and willing defender of the faith against the Moslem infidel, a general honored above all others in the service of his adopted republic, and the successful suitor to the fairest and most virtuous lady of the city; at the close he lies stripped of command and under arrest for the murder of his beloved—a fall from grace to which he responds with the ultimate despairing act of suicide.

Othello's tragic decline plays itself out against a panoramic background of the defense of Christian Europe against the onslaughts of the Ottoman Empire— specifically the threatened Turkish attack upon the Venetian-held island of Cyprus around the year 1508. This larger military struggle is the nearest thing to a sub-plot that the drama contains; and, like most other secondary actions in Shakespeare, it serves the functions of analogue and key to the main plot (Theorem 17). It is therefore not gratuitous that Othello's temptation and fall occur within the context of a war between Christian and infidel, Christ and Anti-Christ. This cosmic dialectic is foreshadowed in the play's sub-title *The Moor of Venice*, a jarring phrase that at once raises the question of what a heathen from North Africa might have to do with the City of Saint Mark, self-styled "Bastion of the Faith." Like Shakespeare's *The Merchant of Venice,* which treats of a similar opposition between Christian and infidel Jew, *Othello* is set in that dangerously independent and tolerant place where occident and orient met as often on terms of friendly commerce as those of war, a city ambivalently regarded by Northern Europeans of the time as a symbol both of freedom and of grave temptation. The forward Mediterranean garrison of Christendom against the Moslem invaders, Venice was also feared at times to be a weak plate in the armor of faith by reason of her long association with the schismatic Byzantine Church as well as her

---

[1]Shakespeare, William. *The Tragedy of Othello The Moor of Venice*. Edited by Tucker Brooke and Lawrence Mason. New Haven and London (Yale University Press, 1965). All line references are to this text.

close trading relations with Islam, Jewry, and the Far East. When, therefore, it is revealed at the opening of *Othello* that the "Serene Republic" has entrusted the defense of Cyprus to a Moor, this is a circumstance calculated to suggest peril to an Elizabethan audience. Nor is the sense of danger lightened by the information that one of the Moor's discontented officers has hatched against him a plot that results in his being accused of employing witchcraft to seduce a senator's daughter. The implicit overriding dramatic question at once concerns the quality of this "convertite" general's faith, and whether it will be firm enough to withstand simultaneous onslaughts form the misbelievers without and the misbeliever within. Typical of early seventeenth-century dramas obeying the apostatic-negative pattern, *Othello* therefore announces itself as a symbolic war between the agents of God and Satan for the soul of its hero and, by extension, for the spiritual well-being of Christendom in general.

If the drama's background conflict fixes upon the offstage "heathen" invaders as the principal representatives of Satan, its foreground action confers that terrible distinction upon the person of Iago, a Venetian officer whose philosophy is summed up in the belief that virtue is worth but a fig, and that the passion of love is "merely a lust of the blood and a permission of the will" (1.3.320, 335–6). A canonical descendant of Richard III and cousin-german of *King Lear's* Edmund, Iago is a self-proclaimed "seemer" or hypocrite, a "Natural Man" who obeys the Machiavellian ethic of pure self-interest and openly professes himself to be one of those

> Who, trimmed in forms and visages of duty,
> Yet keep their hearts attending upon themselves;
> And, throwing but shows of service upon their lords,
> Do well thrive by them; and, when they've lined their coats,
> Do themselves homage (1.1.50–4).

Frustrated in his ambition for rapid advancement in the army owing to Othello's promotion of the less experienced Michael Cassio to the lieutenancy before him, Iago seeks revenge in "double-knavery" upon both the Moor and the handsome young officer, thereby revealing his motives to be compounded of the capital sins of pride, covetousness, envy, and wrath. Sexual jealousy, a bedfellow of envy and pride, also plays its unseemly role, in close embrace with the theological sin of injustice:

> I hate the Moor;
> And it is thought, that twixt my sheets

> He's done my office. I know not if't be true;
>
> Yet I, for mere suspicion in that kind,
>
> Will do as if for surety (1.3.385–9).

Iago's forthright association with the Devil has not escaped the notice even of scholars chary of the play's religious ethos. Indeed, so monstrous is his character that he is qualified among the *dramatic personae* of the First Folio simply as "villain." Lodovico makes the association explicit by calling him a "hellish villain," while Othello dubs him a "demi-devil" (5.2.357, 3.300). Iago himself makes the identification with Satan unquestionable:

> Divinity of hell!
>
> When devils will the blackest sins put on,
>
> They do suggest at first with heavenly shows,
>
> As I do now . . . (2.3.351–4).

The repeated association of Iago with Satan reaches its most elaborate development near the end, when the ruined Othello faces his tormentor and almost expects to see him walking on the Devil's cloven hoof: "I look down towards his feet: but that's a fable." Suddenly a demented rationalization for vengeance occurs to the Moor: "If that thou be'st a devil, I cannot kill thee"—whereupon he lunges and wounds Iago, who hisses back with chilling defiance, "I bleed, sir, but not killed" (5.2.286). The association could hardly be more explicit, and yet a few lines later the link is forged of still another metal when Cassio learns of Iago's plan to murder him and exclaims, "Most heathenish and most gross!" (5.2.313). This line is cited by the *Oxford English Dictionary* as an early use of "heathenish" to denote behavior "unworthy of a Christian." In context, the term also supplies a neatly pointed analogy between Iago's diabolical sins and the threats to Christendom from the Ottomites. The "heathen" Turks' incursions into Christian Europe and Iago's "heathenish" trespasses against Christian morality are thus both characterized as the work of the Anti-Christ, the earthly manifestations of Satan.

As a creature of the Devil, Iago cannot be killed; yet neither does he succeed in accomplishing his overriding intent, which is to execute his revenge upon Othello and Cassio without being detected. Although his dissimulation of the blackest sins behind heavenly shows prospers so far as to convince Othello of his wife's infidelity with Cassio, Iago's plans nevertheless ultimately miscarry—as do those of the would-be invaders of Cyprus. For just as the Turks had not expected an act of God in the form of a tempest to destroy their invasion fleet, so Iago never suspects that his formerly meek and slavish wife will rebel against him, driven to disobedience through compassion for the martyred Desdemona and belated insight into her husband's duplicity. Heralded by the exclamation of "O God! O Heavenly God!" Emelia's sudden defiance of Iago results in his complete exposure to all assembled; and the naked "demi-devil" instantly confirms the truth of his wife's charges by killing her in their presence (5.2.221).

If Iago objectifies all that is diabolical, his true antithesis among the drama's principal figures is not the Moor whom he eventually drags down into the abyss with him, but rather the Moor's bride, the "divine Desdemona." Indeed, Shakespeare traces so many lines of divinity in Desdemona's features and grace in her actions that some commentators have justly complained that the portrait is something less than human. Before even the second act has run its course, this noble lady has been characterized by the general voice—swelled inadvertently by her angry father and even the spiteful Iago—as a paragon of virtue, a woman "full of the most blessed condition" (2.1.251). She is variously qualified, nay, over-qualified, as divine, exquisite, fair, fresh, tender, and gentle; as serene, modest, compassionate, dutiful, and courageous. Metaphorically, Desdemona becomes a "jewel," a "pearl," and a "fair warrior." "She is indeed perfection," affirms Cassio, who welcomes her to Cyprus with a fervor bordering on religious awe:

> Ye men of Cyprus, let her have your knees,
> Hail to thee, lady! and the grace of heaven,
> Before thee, behind thee, and on every hand,
> Enwheel thee round! (2.1.84–7).

This divine pneuma which envelops Desdemona might be understood as mere hyperbole, the poetic reflection of her charm in the eyes of courtiers, were it not more than born out by the subsequent testimony of her gracious deeds. At the very outset Desdemona shows tenderness for both husband and father when she asks to accompany Othello on his campaign rather than stay behind to put her angry sire "in impatient thoughts" by remaining in his sight (1.3.241). Later she demonstrates Christian charity, justice, and no small amount of courage by continuing to plead for the re-enstatement of the falsely discredited Cassio in the face of her husband's jealous displeasure (3.3). Moreover, her loyalty and innocence shine forth as she responds to Othello's increasingly suspicious and fell temper with loving forbearance, meeting his most cruel accusations of infidelity with simple, repeated appeals to faith:

>OTHELLO. Impudent strumpet!
>
>DESDEMONA. By heaven, you do me wrong.
>
>OTHELLO. Are you not a strumpet?
>
>DESDEMONA. No, as I am a Christian.
>
>>If to preserve this vessel for my lord
>>
>>From any other foul unlawful touch
>>
>>Be not a strumpet, I am none.
>
>OTHELLO. What, not a whore?
>
>DESDEMONA. No, as I shall be saved.
>
>OTHELLO. Is't possible?
>
>DESDEMONA. O, heaven forgive us! (4.2.81–8).

And never does the grace of heaven envelop Desdemona more completely than in her last moments, when, knowing she is to die by her husband's hand, she protests that her only sins are the loves she bears him, and that "That death's unnatural that kills for loving" (5.2.42). Othello is merciless: "Thou art to die." "Then have mercy on me!" she cries, adding,

>And have you mercy too! I never did
>
>Offend you in my life; never loved Cassio
>
>But with such general warranty of heaven
>
>As I might love (5.2.58–61).

The Moor remains unmoved, denying even her plea for time to say one final prayer. But as he begins to stifle her, Desdemona manages to gasp out three times, "O Lord, Lord, Lord!" (1st 4 to). Nor is this an end; for in a most curious piece of dramaturgy by naturalistic standards, Shakespeare causes the apparently lifeless Desdemona to revive a few moments later, as if by effort of will, and to spend her last breath attempting to shield her husband by refusing to name him as her murderer:

>EMELIA. O, who hath done this deed?
>
>DESDEMONA. Nobody: I myself. Farewell!
>
>>Commend me to my kind lord. *She dies* (5.2.123–4).

Strangely suspended almost beyond time, this moment calls attention by its very unexpectedness to the extreme importance attached to Desdemona's last, loving gesture. She has died not only guiltless and with the Lord's name on her lips, but also in effect granting Christian forgiveness to her persecutor. Within the religious ethos governing the drama, Desdemona's worldly defeat must therefore be counted a victory both spiritual and also dialectical; for in the extremity of her final moments she has achieved her overriding motive of remaining faithful to the Lord's most difficult injunction: to return love for hatred. Her martyrdom in this life assures her eternal reward in the life to come, because the end of action for every personage in the Christian drama occurs not in this world the but at the Last Judgment when the blessed shall be separated from the damned.

The radical moral contrast between Desdemona and her murderer is underscored in this same scene when the crazed Othello responds to his wife's telling Emelia that she has taken her own life by roaring out "She's a liar gone to burning hell / Twas I that killed her." To which the horrified Emelia retorts,

> O, the more angel she,
> And you the blacker devil! (5.2.129–30).

Othello has indeed become an instrument of Satan during the course of action. His rejection of the truth proclaimed by his "divine" bride and his acceptance of the "hellish" Iago's lies precipitate the Moor's negative movement between these ultimately cosmic polarities. Although at the beginning Othello is regarded by the Venetian senate as a "noble and valiant general" (2.3.1), and even by the sneering Iago as of a "constant, noble, loving, nature" (2.1.291), the Moor is not without impediment of character, as commentators have long pointed out. Iago's early observations that the general is proud and willful ("loving his own pride and purpose"), and that his language is stuffed with "bombast circumstance" (1.1, 12), are borne out to a large degree by Othello's defense of himself against Brabantio's charge of witchcraft. For though substantially honest, his speech to the senate contains an uncomfortable mixture of braggadocio and self-pity (1.3.76ff). Othello's primary weakness is thus shown to be the sin of pride, in combination with a quality that would by itself constitute a moral virtue: innocence. It is the Moor's näivete that inclines him to trust the seemingly plain-spoken Iago, and his vanity that is too suddenly and deeply stung by the merest false hint that Desdemona has played the strumpet with Cassio.

Yet Othello is subject to another, less-remarked weakness of character—the convert's insecurity of faith. Although a baptised Christian with "All the seals and symbols of redeemed sin" (2.3.344), one who goes to confession and receives the Sacrament (1.3.122), the Moor nevertheless retains disturbing vestiges of a pagan mentality. His firm belief in the supernatural properties of the Egyptian handkerchief would not have been lost on an Elizabethan audience:

> There's magic in the web of it:
> A sybyl, that had numbered in the world
> The sun to course two hundred compasses,
> In her prophetic fury sewed the work;
> The worms were hallowed that did breed the silk;
> And it was dyed in mummy which the skillful
> Conserved of maiden's hearts (3.4.69–75).

At a time when those suspected of heterodox belief or practice were subject to arrest, examination under torture, and death at the stake if judged guilty, Othello's obvious faith in the efficacy of a pagan "charm" steeped in the blood of ritual human sacrifice would have afforded the clearest possible evidence of heresy—perhaps sadly to be expected of a convert so fond of boasting of his youthful exploits in non-Christian lands. That he should present this handkerchief to his bride as a charm against infidelity bespeaks his distrust of her plighted troth in marriage. It is therefore most appropriate that this relic of pagan superstition should serve as the engine by which Iago pulls Othello to his ruin, inducing his wife to steal it from her mistress and then "planting" it on Cassio to provide the ocular proof of infidelity that the Moor demands.

Othello's actual moment of apostasy, his dialectical shift from the side of Desdemona to that of Iago (and therefore also from the standard of God to that of Satan), can be pinpointed with precision. The fatal move occurs in Act III, scene 3. Until this moment the Moor, though easily provoked to jealous incoherence by Iago's insinuations, has nonetheless continued to demand hard evidence of his wife's infidelity. But since ocular proof of the non-existent is difficult to obtain, Iago hits upon the ruse of the handkerchief, which at least is something tangible. However circumstantial, this piece of "evidence" works easily upon the Moor precisely because of his unquestioning belief in its magical properties. The instant he learns that the handkerchief is in Cassio's possession, Othello is hooked:

> Now do I see 'tis true. Look here, Iago;
> All my fond love thus do I blow to heaven.
>
> *(Hisses contemptuously.)*
>
> 'Tis gone.
> Arise, black vengeance, from thy hollow cell!

> Yield up, O love, thy crown and hearted throne
>
> To tyrannous hate (3.3.444–9).

A moment later Othello and Iago are kneeling down together, assailing heaven with oaths of vengeance most bloody. As they arise, the Moor commands, "Within these three days let me hear thee say / That Cassio's not alive" (3.3.474). With this order the dialectical shift has been made; from this moment onward Othello will function as an agent of Iago, and thus of Satan. The attempt on Cassio's life and the murder of Desdemona are but logical consequences of Othello's yielding up of love to tyrannous hate. Thus, the drama's apostatic-negative dynamic fulfills itself as the title-character's mortal sin propels him headlong from the dominant unit, governed by the unseen Protagonist of all Christian allegory, and into the abyss of the recessive unit, misgoverned by God's fallen angel.

Yet even at the end, when the Moor learns to his horror of Iago's treachery, and of the innocence of the martyred Desdemona and the maimed Cassio, he still has at his disposal the opportunities that every Christian may take to redeem himself: contrition, repentance, and atonement. And for a moment it appears as if he will indeed seek God's mercy, first asking his mortal judges to look at the facts unblinkingly:

> I pray you, in your letters,
>
> When you shall these unlucky deeds relate,
>
> Speak of them as they are. Nothing extenuate,
>
> Nor set down aught in malice. Then you must speak
>
> Of one that lov'd not wisely but too well;
>
> Of one not easily jealous, but, being wrought,
>
> Perplex'd in the extreme; of one whose hand
>
> (Like the base Indian*) threw a pearl away
>
> Richer than all his tribe. . . . (5.2.340–8).

But just as it appears that Othello may begin to redeem himself in the eyes of man and God, his speech takes a sudden turn that reveals his ever imperfect idea of Christian conduct, and ends with the ultimate gesture of despair:

> And say besides, that in Aleppo once,

---

*Contextually, the Folio spelling of "Iudean" seems preferable, in reference to the biblical "jewel of great price."

> Where a malignant and turban'd Turk
> Beat a Venetian and traduc'd the state,
> I took by the throat the circumcised dog,
> And smote him thus. *He stabs himself* (5.2.352–6).

The Moor's damnation is complete. As Gratiano exclaims, "All that's spoke is marr'd" (5.2.357).

As with so many other dramas of this class, the central character of *Othello* is the action's solitary apostate. All the other figures, onstage and off, remain dialectically immobile from start to finish, and are clearly segregated according to their fealty either to God or to Satan.

The moral symmetry that so obviously balances the principal characters of *Othello* also carries over to the drama's secondary personages, most of whom are rather neatly counterpoised against their spiritual opposites. For just as Iago functions as a moral reversal of Desdemona, the depraved Roderigo serves as a counterweight to the loyal Cassio—and is wounded by the latter's sword while attempting to murder him at Iago's instigation. Indeed, Roderigo and Cassio provide somewhat more "human" instances of moral strength and weakness, for each bears within him just a trace of his opposite number. Thus Cassio, though an officer of great probity, becomes in his cups a brawler (significantly, with Roderigo), and also frequents the bed of a woman whose dubious reputation he has no intention of rehabilitating with an offer of marriage (2.3.145ff; 4.1.120ff). Likewise, Roderigo, though a fool and a knave, at least has the instinct to desire as his mistress none other than Desdemona, and the sense occasionally to doubt the good intentions of Iago (1.3; 4.2.174ff). Yet Cassio's sins are as negligible as Roderigo's virtues; neither the essential goodness of the one nor the depravity of the other is seriously impaired by these occasional lapses. Poetical justice eventually segregates the two characters forever, as Roderigo, wounded in the commission of a mortal sin, receives the *coup de grace* from his erstwhile "friend" Iago, while Cassio goes on to replace the Moor as military commander of Cyprus (5.1.61ff; 5.2.332).

When hidden players are taken into account (Theorem 5), the same moral symmetry will be seen to extend to virtually all the remaining figures of the drama. Thus, the offstage Egyptian Sorceress, who originally gave the charmed handkerchief to Othello's mother, provides a counterweight to Emelia, who innocently conveys this same object to Iago, and who later dies by her husband's hand for courageously exposing his duplicity in the matter. Such antithetical pairings serve to contrast two radically different kinds of affection: a self-sacrificing Christian love and a jealous possessiveness that relies upon witchcraft, dishonesty, or violence to secure the fidelity of others. Ultimately resolving itself into a dialectic of faith and superstition, belief and disbelief, this opposition is most generally objectified in the war between the offstage Ottomites and the onstage representatives of the City of Saint Mark—the Duke and Senators of Venice, the Governor of Cyprus, together with Desdemona's noble kinsmen, Lodovico and Gratiano ("Gracious"). These symmetries are too neat to be fortuitous, nor are they surprising considering the drama's clearly allegorical scheme.

Despite its generally pointed counterbalancing of forces, *Othello* nevertheless contains several characters whose dialectical status appears to be somewhat problematical. The first of these is Desdemona's father, Brabantio, a senator so highly respected that his counsel carries authority almost equal to that of the Duke himself (1.2.12). Yet this worthy stands up against the Duke and the entire senate of Venice in seeking an annulment of the secret marriage of his daughter to Othello. Brabantio simply cannot believe that Desdemona—courted by all the "wealthy curled darlings" of the Republic—could have fallen in love with the "sooty bosom" of this convert general, unless the latter had "practic'd upon her with foul charms" (1.2.63). Brabantio's fulminations against the Moor reveal that the grounds of his disapproval are compounded of racial, social, and religious objections. The charge of witchcraft, however, gives priority to the religious issue. For if, as Brabantio believes, the Moor has bound Desdemona in chains of pagan magic, then he is guilty of the capital crime of heresy, is in fact "an abuser of the world, a practiser / of arts inhibited and out of warrant" (1.2.72–81).

Brabantio's accusation is, of course, without foundation: the far more natural charms of admiration, pity, and love freely given have bound Desdemona to the general (1.3.145ff). Moreover, the Duke is eager to have Brabantio drop the charge, partly because he believes the lovers' story, but equally because he urgently requires Othello's services against the Ottomites (1.2.171, 199, 220). Brabantio relents under pressure, but with a bad grace; and his parting shot as he leaves the council chamber is a warning, ironically, to Othello:

> Look to her, Moor, if thou hast eyes to see:
> She has deceiv'd her father, and may thee (1.3.292–3).

With these, his final words of the drama, Brabantio may be said to have planted in Othello's mind the very first seed of suspicion, a seed which does not germinate, however, until tenderly cultivated by Iago.

Although Brabantio disappears from the stage in Act One, we learn that he lives on for a while in Venice, a broken old man whose death mercifully occurs before the murder of his daughter. This important information as to the character's ultimate end (Theorem 2) is revealed by his brother, Gratiano, as he addresses Desdemona's lifeless body:

> Poor Desdemona, I am glad thy father's dead.
> Thy match was mortal to him, and pure grief
> Shore his old thread a-twain. Did he live now,
> This sight would make him do a desperate turn,
> Yea, curse his better angel from his side,
> And fall to reprobation (5.2.203–8).

Brabantio thus dies of grief, pure and simple, not despair—although his brother fears it might have turned to despair had the old man lived to hear the ghastly outcome of his daughter's marriage. However, this late reference to Brabantio serves another purpose beyond the mere heightening of pathos: it reminds us that the senator's original reasons for objecting to the match were much closer to the mark than anyone cared to believe. For although Othello did not employ witchcraft to attract Desdemona, he did in fact rely on the black arts in a totally unnecessary attempt to assure her fidelity. Indeed, the whole calamity has hinged upon this vestige of pagan superstition, thereby proving that the Moor's profession of faith was as shaky and contaminated as his reluctant father-in-law had originally suspected! Brabantio's doubts have been vindicated in substance, if not in the particulars. By obediently submitting to the Duke on the matter of annulment, the crusty old man has lain himself open to the grief that soon destroys him; torn between the shrewd instincts of his faith and his loyalty to the senate, he, too, dies a martyr's death. Brabantio must therefore be described as a protagonist from beginning to end.

By far the most ambiguous figure of the drama (at least by modern standards) is Bianca, Cassio's mistress—or, as Iago would have it, his "whore" (4.1.177). Bianca belongs to that relatively small tribe of minor characters who are difficult to place within the oppositional structure of the drama, usually because their creators employ them as devices for engineering some turn of plot and then neglect them once they have served their limited purpose. Such figures do not alter the basic dynamic of the drama's action; but because the information about them is scanty, and sometimes contradictory, their dialectical positioning becomes a delicate matter. The best procedure in these cases is simply to weigh all the limited evidence carefully and see which way the scale tips—as tip it usually will.

In Shakespeare's plot source for *Othello*, Cinthio's *Hecatommithi* (*The Hundred Fables*), Bianca is simply a nameless "courtesan" from whose house the Captain (Cassio) is returning when the Ensign (Iago) attacks and wounds him. The Captain also has a wife, to whom he gives the handkerchief that has been dropped in his apartment by the Ensign. Shakespeare chooses to conflate Cassio's wife and mistress into a single personage, and therein perhaps lies the ambiguity at the root of Bianca's character. The cast list of the first Folio describes her simply as a "courtesan." Indeed, Cassio refers to her as a perfumed "fitchew" (polecat; i.e., prostitute) and treats her in a manner so cavalier as to suggest that this appellation is correct. The problem is that Bianca does not actually appear to *do* anything (at least by today's standards) that would place her in the same sinister league with Iago and the other antagonists of the drama. In fact, her worst of sins seems to be a constant, doting, and ultimately hopeless love for Cassio. Nor is Bianca included in the general meting-out of punishment reserved in this drama for the more obvious of Satan's agents. Shakespeare apparently did not wish to add further dark touches to Cassio's character by giving him a mistress who was an egregious villain.

The cynical and disparaging Iago describes Bianca as "A housewife that by selling her desires / Brings herself bread and clothes" (4.1.94–6). Elsewhere Cassio's enemy writes her off as "a notable strumpet," nothing more than common "trash" whose desperate love for Cassio is but a hazard of her profession: ". . .'tis the strumpet's plague / To beguile many and be beguil'd by one" (4.1.78, 85). Although Iago is far from the ideal character witness, his low opinion of Bianca is reinforced, as we have seen, by Cassio himself, who frequents her bed but does not otherwise take her seriously. Indeed, the lieutenant breaks into fits of laughter whenever his affair with Bianca is mentioned—a fact which Iago counts on when he places the Moor in a position to overhear a conversation which the latter thinks concerns Desdemona but really is about Bianca (4.1.99ff). With Othello listening from the wings, Iago approaches Cassio and teases him with the rumor that he has asked Bianca's hand in marriage, to which Cassio responds,

I marry her! what? a customer? [whore] I prithee,

bear some charity to my wit; do not think it so

unwholesome. Ha, ha, ha! , . . . This is the monkey's

own giving out, She is persuaded I will marry her,

out of her own love and flattery, not out of my promise . . . (4.2.120–30).

Bianca clearly dotes upon Cassio, to his public chagrin. Indeed, she cannot bear his absence; and when Cassio avoids her for a week (sunk in "leaden thoughts" about his dismissal for brawling), she goes to seek him out and tax him for his neglect (3.4.170ff). Cassio makes a brief excuse and then peremptorily asks her to copy the embroidery of the handkerchief he has found in his apartment, whereupon she becomes irrationally jealous:

> BIANCA. O Cassio! whence came this?
>
> > This is some token from a newer friend;
> >
> > To the felt absence now I feel a cause;
> >
> > Is't come to this?
>
> CASSIO. Go to Woman!
>
> > Throw you vile guesses in the devil's teeth,
> >
> > From whence you have them. You are jealous now
> >
> > That this is from some mistress, some remembrance.
> >
> > No, by my faith, Bianca (3.4.178–85).

Her quickness to suspicion and jealousy links Bianca with Othello, a connection which Cassio here underscores by pointing out the diabolical origin of this character flaw. Yet Bianca dotes upon Cassio, following him about in the streets, complaining of his absences, and constantly inviting him to "sup" with her at her lodging—which he does, frequently (3.4.167–9; 4.1.158–65). In fact, Cassio is wounded by Roderigo as he leaves the house of Bianca, who hears the sounds of the scuffle and rushes out to her wounded lover's side, crying, "O my dear Cassio! My sweet Cassio! Cassio! Cassio!" (5.1.76). Iago attempts to take advantage of the situation by drawing suspicion for the crime onto Bianca, whose pale (painted?) visage he cites as evidence of her guilt:

> IAGO. This is the fruit of whoring. Pray, Emelia,
>
> > Go know of Cassio where he supp'd to-night.—
> >
> > What! do you shake at that?
>
> BIANCA. He supp'd at my house, but I therefore shake not.
>
> IAGO. O, did he so? I charge you, go with me.

> EMELIA. Fie, fie upon thee, strumpet!
> BIANCA. I am no strumpet, but of life
>   as honest as you that thus abuse me (5.2.116–23).

This plea of innocence cuts both ways; for although her claim to being honest does not compare in villainy with Iago's seeming so for his own "peculiar end," yet Bianca also finds herself caught up in a lie: she is a courtesan, but would seem otherwise. Indeed, her whole profession consists of feigning love for gain, just as Iago's life-project consists of simulating "forms and visages of duty" in order to put money in his pocket. That Bianca has indeed fallen hopelessly in love with Cassio is at once her misfortune and an entirely justified punishment for one whose life is supported by sin. The play's religious ethos requires that we condemn her in this light, just as we must (despite our somewhat more even-handed views of these matters) forgive the otherwise noble Cassio for his cavalier involvement with this fallen woman.

Before drawing up an action-chart of *Othello* it will be helpful to look a bit more closely at one other character, whose doings might possibly be construed as a violation of the apostatic-negative dynamic itself. The character in question is Iago's wife, Emelia; and the issue she raises is whether her initial obedience to her husband and her later exposure of his villainy cause her to shift dialectically. For if Emelia did shift, her trajectory would have to be from the antagonists to the protagonists; and such a positive movement would then form a counter-cross to Othello's negative shift, thereby confuting the principle of unidirectionality (Theorem 6). This question is quickly resolved, however, when we recall that Emelia only carries out her husband's orders so long as she takes them to be innocent; for, like everyone else in the drama, she believes Iago's lies implicitly until the evidence against him becomes overwhelming. But when, after the murder, Othello reveals that it was Iago who told him of Desdemona's supposed infidelity, Emelia's response is blunt and forceful: "If he say so, may his pernicious soul / Rot half a grain a day! He lies to the heart" (5.2.154–5). A moment later Iago enters, and his wife demands that he refute the Moor's charge:

> EMELIA. Disprove this villain if thou be'st a man:
>   He says thou told'st him that his wife was false.
>   I know thou didst not. Thou'rt not such a villain.
>   Speak, for my heart is full.
> IAGO. I told him what I thought, and told no more

> Than what he found himself was apt and true.
>
> EMELIA. But did you ever tell him she was false?
>
> IAGO. I did.
>
> EMELIA. You told a lie, an odious damned lie;
>
> Upon my soul, a lie, a wicked lie.
>
> She false with Cassio! Did you say with Cassio?
>
> IAGO. With Cassio, mistress. Go to, charm your tongue.
>
> EMELIA. I will not charm my tongue; I am bound to speak.
>
> IAGO. What! are you mad? I charge you, get you home.
>
> EMELIA. Good gentlemen, let me have leave to speak.
>
> 'Tis proper I obey him, but not now.
>
> Perchance, Iago, I will ne'er go home
>
> (5.2.171–96).

When, in his desperation, Othello clutches at the fact of having seen Desdemona's handkerchief in Cassio's possession, Emelia's suspicions of her husband are confirmed beyond doubt. Over Iago's shouts of "Villainous whore!" and "Filth, thou liest!" she tells of his having asked her to steal the fatal object for him. The frenzied Iago can take no more, and in effect confesses his villainy by stabbing his wife in front of everyone. As she slumps to the floor, Emelia gasps out her last request: "O lay me by my mistress' side" (5.2.223, 236). Thus, although Desdemona's loyal serving woman dies a martyr for the truth which she had failed to see before, her final act, as we have indicated, does not qualify as a dialectical shift for the critical reason that she would have never supported her husband in the first place had she known that he was lying. Emelia's former cooperation with Iago was therefore morally innocent—a fact which places her in the protagonists' unit from the start, and which is emphasized by her heroic resistance at the last.

With all characters, onstage and off, accounted for in terms of their loyalty to either victors or vanquished, and the drama's single change of allegiance duly noted (Theorems 1–6), it is now possible to draw up a dialectical chart of action. This schematic is composed of two columns, the one on the left listing the protagonists, and the opposed, right-hand column the antagonists. As usual, hidden players are enclosed in brackets, while characters who die during the course of action are designated by an "X":

ACTION-CHART: Shakespeare, *Othello, The Moor of Venice*:

Protagonist	Antagonist
[God]	[Satan]
Venetian Senators	x [Ottoman Army]
[Venetian Army]	[Egyptian Sorceress]
Gratiano ("Gracious")	[Othello's Father]
Montano	[Othello's Mother]
Lodovico	Iago
x Brabantio	x Roderigo
x Emelia	Bianca
x Desdemona	
Clown	
Musicians	
(Othello) ⎯⎯⎯⎯⎯⎯⟶	x Othello

The title-character's solitary dialectical shift will be seen to constitute the most salient dynamic feature of an action in which all the other characters remain fixed in opposition from beginning to end. Othello's movement from the dominant to the recessive unit therefore qualifies the drama as conforming to the apostatic-negative model; for, as we have seen, the indisputable shift of but a single figure is sufficient to determine a play's dynamic class (Theorem 6). That this work adheres to the apostatic-negative model in other ways as well becomes apparent when we turn to its structures of imagery and symbolism.

(3) *Dialectic of Imagery*:

Despite its almost neo-classical leanness of action, *Othello* remains thoroughly Jacobean in sheer bulk and texture of figurative detail. Not surprisingly, the great preponderance of this imagery is employed to qualify the drama's antagonists; for in a morality play such as this, the features of evil are at once more tangible and more inherently dramatic than those of goodness. As a consequence, the deeds of the godly protagonists are left to speak for themselves largely at the primary level of action, with rhetorical highlighting supplied less by concrete evocations of the sublunary world than by abstractions indicative of moral and theological virtues. The sins of the antagonists, on the contrary, are everywhere associated with the earth's slime and gore, its more repellent fauna, and its outright monstrosities.

The celebrated bestial imagery of *Othello* forms but the leading strand of a broader fabric clothing a moral regression which can be abstracted as "Passion, Lust, Bestiality, Monstrosity." For Iago's open espousal of villainy and Othello's fatal weakness of faith are both represented as perversions of reason caused by ungoverned passions—whether for advancement, monetary gain, sexual control, or jealous revenge. The inability to restrain these passions leads to violation of both the natural and moral orders, which are seen as inseparable; and such trespasses therefore give birth to deformed, indeed, monstrous offspring. Appropriately, this chilling image of the misbegotten creature of passion makes its first entrance the moment Iago conceives of his plan for revenge:

> I have it! it is engender'd. Hell and night
> Must bring this monstrous birth to the world's light (1.3.402–3).

The same figure is repeated when Othello notices that Iago is behaving "As if there were some monster in his thought / Too hideous to be shown" (3.3.107–8). Iago cynically tosses it back in his famous warning to the Moor to beware of jealousy: "It is the green-eyed monster which doth mock / The meat it feeds on" (3.3.166–7). And as Othello succumbs to the beast, his tormentor cooly varies the figure by remarking, "I see, sir, you are eaten up with passion" (3.3.391). Indeed, the man so devoured turns into the very thing that consumes him; for, as Othello expresses it in his anguish, "A horned man's a monster and a beast" (4.1.63).

The declension from bestiality to monstrosity seems to run as follows: when man permits his reason to be overruled by his passion, he becomes a beast; and for a human to behave like an animal is monstrous, against nature, and therefore in opposition to God's will. Othello senses this process's occurring in himself when, early in the action, his anger rises at the sight of Cassio and Roderigo brawling:

> Now, by heaven
> My blood begins my safer guides to rule,
> And passion, having my best judgment collied,
> Assays to lead the way. (2.3.205–8).

The cause of Othello's rage is Cassio, who, having become drunk at Iago's instigation, falls a victim of his own baser passions. This officer also picks up the bestial figure when, shamefaced and repentant, he berates himself for his condition: "To be now a sensible man, by and by a fool, and presently a beast! . . . Every inordinate cup is unblessed and the ingredience is a devil" (2.3.306–9). Nor is it without significance that Cassio should see Satan as the active agent of this degrading elixir.

The bestiary becomes both more specific and more populous as the action progresses. Thus, when Othello demands ocular proof of his wife's supposed infidelity, Iago suggests that it would be unendurable for him to see her in bed with Cassio:

> Where's satisfaction?
> It is impossible you should see this,
> Were they as prime as goats, as hot as monkeys,
> As salt as wolves in pride, and fools as gross
> As ignorance made drunk (3.3.401–5).

These images stick in the Moor's mind to return at inopportune moments—as when he offers formal welcome to Lodovico, the senate's messenger to Cyprus, and then, to the utter bewilderment of all assembled, suddenly blurts out, "Goats and monkeys!" (4.1.261).

Desdemona's protests of innocence are to no avail, for, to Othello, women's tears are merely "crocodile" (4.1.243). The bestiary expands when Iago's ineffectual henchman, Roderigo, compares himself to a dog that follows in the chase, "not like a hound that hunts, but one that fills up the cry" (2.3.364–5). And later, as he lies dying, Roderigo repeats the canine figure in cursing his murderer: "O damn'd Iago. O inhuman dog!"—an epithet which Lodovico seconds at the play's conclusion with "O Spartan dog!" and to which he adds the symbolically weightier epithet of "viper" (5.1.60; 5.2.36, 285).

The ultimately diabolical nature of this beastliness, real or imagined, is pointed up as Othello seizes Desdemona's hand and finds it "hot, hot, and moist . . . For here's a young and sweating devil here / That commonly rebels" (3.4.39). And when the Moor's bride later earnestly hopes that her husband esteems her honest, the latter growls back, "O, ay. As summer flies are in the shambles, / That quicken even with blowing" (4.2.65–6). In his jealous anguish, Othello claims

> I had rather be a toad,
> And live upon the vapor of a dungeon,
> Than keep a corner of the thing I love
> For others' uses (3.3.270–3).

To his imagination Desdemona, the fountain of his love, has degenerated into "a cistern for foul toads / To knot and gender in!" (4.2.60–1). In a similar vein, though for apparently justified reasons, Cassio refers to the courtesan, Bianca, both as a "monkey" and as a "fitchew" (polecat) (4.1.128, 145).

The monstrous birth engendered by Iago with his original plan for revenge is eventually seconded by a malformed brother in the soul of the Moor, who, as he prepares to murder his innocent bride, recapitulates the figure of the misbegotten creature of passion gone awry:

> . . . confess thee freely of thy sin;
> For to deny each article with oath
> Cannot remove or choke the strong conception
> That I do groan withal. Thou art to die (5.2.53–6).

Like all the siblings of Iago's initial conception, Othello's spiritual deformity—born in the sweating agony of chewed lips, rolling eyes, and epileptic seizures—turns murderous the moment it sees the light. And if its victim is innocence itself in the person of Desdemona, this beast of misspent passion can be none other than Satan, the snarling voice of worldly experience and tireless predator of the Shepherd's flock.

Of those consumed by jealousy, Emelia explains to her mistress,

> They are not ever jealous for the cause,
> But jealous for they are jealous.' Tis a monster
> Begot upon itself, born on itself (3.4.158–60).

To which Desdemona responds, "Heaven keep that monster from Othello's mind!" And Emelia concludes, "Lady, amen" (3.4.161). Such appeals for heaven's protection against irrational passion provide the principal symbolic counterweights to the great number of bestial (and ultimately diabolical) figures generated by the antagonists. As the somewhat perplexed Iago says of his wife's simple faith in God,

> This is a subtle whore,
> A closet lock and key of villainous secrets;
> And yet she'll kneel and pray. I have seen her do't (4.2.20–2).

As for the innocence and piety of Desdemona, even her suspicious husband feels bound to say that "If she be false, O then heaven mocks itself" (3.3.278). Indeed, Iago himself describes her sarcastically, yet with perfect accuracy, as "of so free, so kind, so apt, so blessed a disposition, that she holds it a vice in her goodness not to do more than she is requested" (2.3.320–2). That this goodness extends so far as loving those who hate her, we see as Desdemona, with instinctive forebodings of calamity, prepares for what is to be her final night with Othello and sings the famous "Willow

Song," which not only gives voice to her sorrow but also anticipates her ultimate action of Christian charity in forgiving her murderer:

> *Sing all a green willow must be my garland.*
> *Let nobody blame him, his scorn I approve,—*
>
> (4.3.5–2).

If Desdemona provides the drama's sovereign exemplar of Christian virtue, the other protagonists also share, to varying degrees, her essential piety and spirituality. The antagonism between the spirit, which sublimates man towards the divine, and the body, which degrades him to the gross and merely animal, thus becomes the drama's principal symbolic cleavage. This dichotomy receives no more succinct expression than in Cassio's lament at having sullied his good name in a drunken brawl: "I have lost my reputation. I have lost the immortal part of myself, and what remains is bestial" (2.3.264–5).

The division between the immortal soul and a body subject to corruption both physical and moral ultimately proceeds from the universal struggle between God and Satan. That this battle is indeed cosmic, and not merely psychological, the dramatist reinforces with a steady counterpoint between the protagonists' constant supplications to heaven and the antagonists' many curses and blasphemies. Iago's oxymoron "Divinity of hell! " sets the tone for his other outrageous impieties of speech, as when he asserts, "Heaven is my judge, not I for love and duty, / But seeming so for my peculiar end" (1.1.59–60). Or when he goads Roderigo, "Zounds, sir, you are one of those that will not serve God if the devil bid you:" (1.1.108–9). "Zounds" (God's wounds), "Sblood" (God's Blood), "By Janus" (the Roman two-faced deity), "*Diablo*, ho!" and "Divinity of hell!" drop from his lips as readily as his blasphemous vow to the Moor, "Witness, you ever-burning lights above! /. . . Let him command, / And to obey shall be in me remorse, / What bloody work soever" (3.3.463–9). And at his moment of apostasy, Othello, too, begins to blaspheme in the same style, prefacing his order for Cassio's murder with the oath,

> Now, by yonder marble heaven,
> In due reverence of a sacred vow
> I here engage my words (3.3.460–2).

From this point on, Othello's cursing of Desdemona grows both loud and deep: "Damn her, lewd minx! O, damn her!" (3.3.475). Punctuating his speech with such oaths as "uds death" (God's death), the Moor repeatedly calls his wife a "devil" and commits her soul to hell (3.3.478; 4.1.181, 242; 4.2.36; 5.2.69). Indeed, he eventually begins to identify her with Satan's dwelling itself:

> You, mistress,
>> That have the office opposite to Saint Peter,
>> And keep the gate of hell! (4.2.90–2).

But although he resolves to "Abandon all remorse" and "Do deeds to make heaven weep" (3.3.369–71), even the Moor recognizes that, if his suspicions are false, then he, not his victim, is beyond redemption:

> O I were damned beneath all depth in hell
> But that I did proceed upon just grounds
> To this extremity (5.2.136–8).

In utter contrast to the many and shocking blasphemies of the antagonists, the drama's victors constantly implore heaven's aid and mercy in their battle against the agents of Satan. "So help me every spirit sanctified," is Desdemona's plea when she begins to notice the strangely altered behavior of her spouse (3.4.124). And as the drama progresses, the "divine" Desdemona begins to supplicate heaven more often and with greater urgency, employing such pious oaths as "by my life and soul," "as I am a Christian," "pray heaven," "would to God," "by this light of heaven," "as I shall be saved," "heaven doth know," "heaven pardon him," and, finally, as Othello begins to smother her, "O Lord, Lord, Lord!" The frequency and urgency of these appeals to God elevate them beyond the merely conventional figure of speech, to the point where they become crucial symbolic foils to the egregious impieties of Iago and his minions. Nor is Desdemona the only protagonist to whom such pious phrases come naturally; for Emelia, Montano, and Cassio also call upon heaven in their moments of extremity. Thus, even when drunk and disjointed of tongue, Cassio manages to convey his simple faith in the providential ordering of the universe:

> Well, God's above all; and there be souls must be
> saved, and there be souls must not be saved. . . . God forgive us our sins!
> (2.3.102–3, 111–12).

In a similar vein, Emelia makes the distinction between Othello and his murdered bride with a characteristically pious comparison:

> This deed of thine is no more worthy heaven
> Than thou wast worthy her (5.2.159–60).

The contrapuntal alternation between figures spiritual and bestial, prayerful and blasphemous, is swelled throughout by a nearly related opposition between things Christian and those specifically heathen, infidel. Thus, the problematical nature of Othello's status as a Christian convert is rendered the more disturbing by his boasting of exploits in North Africa, where there are "Cannibals that each other eat," not to speak of "men whose heads / Do grow beneath their shoulders" (1.3.143–5). When Brabantio learns of the Moor's secret marriage to Desdemona, the exasperated old man opines that "if such actions may have passage free, / Bondslaves and pagans shall our statesmen be" (1.2.98–9). And after the Duke urges him to withdraw his opposition to the union and to accept the inevitable with good grace, Brabantio relents with the sarcasm, "So let the Turk of Cyprus us beguile, / We lose it not so long as we can smile" (1.3.210–11). This symbolic connection between Othello's elopement with Desdemona and the attack upon Cyprus by "the general enemy Ottoman" seems outrageous at first blush, but in retrospect it appears no more preposterous than Brabantio's charge that the Moor is capable of using witchcraft to possess his love.

At the outset Othello himself is of mind sound enough to draw a sort of distinction between pagan and Christian behavior, as when he halts the scuffle between Roderigo and Cassio; but even at this early stage the contrast is somewhat equivocal:

> Are we turn'd Turks, and to ourselves do that
> Which heaven has forbid the Ottomites?
> For Christian shame put by this barbarous brawl
> (2.3.171–3).

Yet the Moor finally jettisons all Christian principles, descending to Iago's depth of betrayals so foul and unspeakable that the best to be said of them is, "Most heathenish and most gross!" (5.2.313). And, as we have seen, Othello prefaces his suicide by announcing that the punishment he deserves is the same impulsive one he inflicted on a Turk for beating a Venetian and traducing the state—death by stabbing (5.2.352–6). Thus, the general's ultimate act of despair is strategically accompanied by an allusion to his own, and another's, barbarism. Remarking that "These Moors are changeable in their wills," Iago at the outset dismisses Othello as a mere "erring barbarian"; by the final curtain we know that the villain's instinct, in this matter at least, is quite unerring (1.3.347–8, 357).

Othello's fall from grace is prefigured, as we have also seen, by the negative movement of an image that is specifically pagan in character: the celebrated magical handkerchief, soaked in the blood of human sacrifice by an Egyptian sorceress, and given by Othello to Desdemona as a "charm" to prevent her from committing adultery. A symbol of the Moor's questionable faith both in his innocent wife and in his adopted religion, this repellent object is clearly misplaced on the undefiled person of Desdemona. It is therefore not merely symbolically appropriate but also dialectically necessary that the bewitched handkerchief be transferred into Iago's sullied hands, and that, thus restored to its native surroundings among things un-Christian, this symbol of infidelity should become the very instrument which shakes the Moor's faith in the honesty of his innocent bride. The dialectical shift of the charmed handkerchief therefore presages, and indeed precipitates, the negative apostasy of the one personage who believes in its magic—a parallel movement of kindred image and character that is especially noticeable in dramas of the apostatic-negative class (Theorem 10).

Shakespeare develops several other major figurative contrasts in *Othello*—as, for example, the oppositions of music to noise, beauty to ugliness, cleanliness to filth, peaceful life to violent death, and giving to taking. Although space does not permit a detailed excursion into these tropical contrarieties, it will be helpful to dilate upon one other figurative opposition, both because of its importance in the play's symbolic action and its frequency among dramas of this dynamic type, namely, the primal contrast between light and darkness.

Blood-and-thunder moralities supremely confident of their distinction between good and evil, metastatic-negative dramas tend naturally to a view the universe in terms of black and white—a metaphorical contrast they often literally reproduce through the painterly technique of *chiaroscuro*. Such melodramatic counterplay of intense light and darkness is everywhere present in *Othello*. Indeed, this drama opens at the "odd-even and dull watch o' th' night" (midnight) with Iago and Roderigo busy hatching their plot of revenge (1.1.123). But as the first act progresses the uneasy obscurity of the night is gradually penetrated by small and then greater lights, beginning when the roused Brabantio calls for tapers to guide him to his daughter (1.1.160-166), increasing as Cassio and the Officers arrive bearing torches and the news that messengers have come from the Venetian fleet (1.2.28, 34, 40), and culminating at the Doge's Palace where the guardians of the City of Saint Mark—the Duke and Senators—appear in council seated around "*a table with lights and Attendants*" (1.3.1). Yet the act concludes with a return to that darkness befitting the conception of Iago's villainous scheme, in whose behalf he invokes all the powers of "Hell and night" (1.3.402).

All of Iago's principal stratagems are, in fact, night-hatched. Thus, the drunken brawl that he incites between Roderigo and Cassio occurs after dark (2.3.1), just as the subsequent attempt on Cassio's life is carefully planned to take place "between twelve and one" in the morning so that the cover of darkness will permit the cowardly Roderigo to surprise his victim with a sudden sword thrust (4.2.237–8). This failing, Iago steals up and wounds Cassio from behind, whereupon the innocent victim calls for help—and light (5.1.27). And, at the drama's climax, the murder of Desdemona occurs in the couple's bedchamber after nightfall.

This same *chiaroscuro* technique serves to heighten the extreme moral contrast between Iago and his victims. For Iago knows full well, indeed boasts, that he has put on the devils' "blackest sins" when he hits upon the idea of discrediting Desdemona in her husband's eyes:

> So will I turn her virtue into pitch,
> And out of her goodness make the net
> That shall enmesh them all (2.3.361–3).

And once enmeshed, the Moor picks up the same figure:

> Her name, that was as fresh
> As Dian's visage, is now begrim'd and black
> As mine own face (3.3.386–8).

This struggle between luminosity and gloom reaches its climax during the murder scene, as Othello enters the sleeping Desdemona's darkened bedchamber carrying a burning taper:

> Put out the light, and then put out the light.
> If I quench thee, thou flaming minister,
> I can again thy former light restore,
> Should I repent me; but once put out thy light,
> Thou cunning'st pattern of excelling nature,
> I know not what Promethean heat
> That can thy light relume (5.2.7–13).

Contemplating the apparently lifeless Desdemona moments later, and struck by the enormity of his deed, the Moor vents his despair by invoking a general darkness upon the world:

> Methinks it should be now a huge eclipse
> Of sun and moon, and that the affrighted globe
> Should yawn at alteration (5.2.99–101).

That this dialectical opposition of light and darkness is meant to be understood primarily in moral and theological terms we are reminded by Emelia's response to Othello's confession of the murder: "O the more angel she, / And you the blacker devil" (5.2.129–30). Still, in the end it is impossible to avoid the implication, so distasteful to modern sensibilities, that the Moor's "sooty" complexion itself is employed as a symbol of things un-Christian, and therefore diabolical—that, Iago's cynicism notwithstanding, the "black ram" and the "white ewe" are in fact emblems of moral incompatability. "If virtue no delighted beauty lack," the Duke reassures Brabantio, "Your son-in-law is far more fair than black" (1.3.289–90). However, in response to Iago's insinuations, the Moorish general's moral complexion also turns from fair to black, thus moving into symbolic conformity with his physical appearance. Hence, although the light/darkness distinction is primarily moral and religious rather than racial, Shakespeare does not hesitate to evoke Othello's swarthy features both as a reminder of his Islamic origins and as a precursor of his relapse into the benightedness of disbelief—and finally into the utter darkness of despair.

The following image-chart provides an overview of the major figurative constellations in *Othello*, with abstract headings distinguishing the several principal groups, an approximate count of individual tropes in each cluster indicating its relative weight, and one or two quotations offering typical instances of the figurative type in question. The numerical tabulation of separate images can be approximate at best; for many passages comprehend several figures in close proximity, rendering highly subjective the decision as to whether each image should regarded separately or collectively as part of a larger discrete unit. Because of this textual intimacy, several of the categories discussed above have also been collapsed into larger units. Nonetheless, such tabulation does offer a fairly accurate picture of the comparative size and importance of the various categories. Moreover, the single shifting image (Theorem 10) will be seen to move from a position in which it is clearly misplaced to one in which it is figuratively most congenial:

IMAGE-CHART: Shakespeare, *Othello*:

1. CHRISTIANITY. *Approx. count*: 6 images.

Example: OTHELLO. (a) For Christian shame put by this barbarous brawl (2.3.173).

(b) . . . as truly as to heaven / I do confess the vices of my blood (1.3.122–3).

(The Handkerchief ——————→

("There's magic in the web of it")

1. PAGANISM. *Approx. count*: 41 images.

Example: (a) 3 GENT. The desperate tempest hath banged the Turks/That their designment halts (2.1.21–2). (b) BRABANTIO. So let the Turk of Cyprus us beguile / We lose it not so long as we can smile. (1.3.210-11).

The Handkerchief

("There's magic in the web of it") (3.6.69)

2. HEAVEN/SALVATION/SPIRITUALITY.
Approx. count: 52 images.

Example: (a) CASSIO. Hail to thee, lady! and the grace of heaven, / Before, behind thee, and on every hand / Enwheel thee round! (2.1.85–7). (b) CASSIO. Tempests themselves. . . . do omit / Their mortal natures, letting go safely by / The divine Desdemona (2.1.68–73). (c) DESDEMONA. God me such usage send, / Not to pick bad from bad, but by bad mend (4.3.105–6).

2. HELL/DAMNATION/BESTIALITY.
Approx. count: 50 images.

Example: (a) BIANCA. Let the devil and his dam haunt you (4.1.147). (b) EMELIA. If any wretch have put this into your head / Let heaven requite it with the serpent's curse! (4.2.14–15). (c) IAGO. Divinity of hell! (2.3.351). (d) IAGO. 'Zounds, sir, you are one of those that will not serve God if the devil bid you (1.1.108–9).

3. HONESTY ("BEING"). *Approx. count*: 11 images.

Example: (a) OTHELLO. Swear thou art honest/DESDEMONA. Heaven doth truly know it (4.2.36–37). (b) EMELIA. I durst, my lord, to wager her honest /Lay down my soul at stake (4.2.11-12).

3. DISHONESTY ("SEEMING"). *Approx. count*: 43 images.

Example: OTHELLO. If thou dost slander her and torture me, / Never pray more. Abandon all remorse; / On horror's head horrors accumulate; / Do deeds that make heaven weep; all earth amaz'd; / For nothing cans't thou to damnation add / Greater than that (3.3.368–73).

4. LIGHT. *Approx. count*: 22 images.

Example: OTHELLO. . . . but once put out thy light, / Thou cunning'st pattern of excelling nature, / I know not where is the

4. DARKNESS. *Approx. count*: 28 images.

Example: OTHELLO. Arise, black vengeance, from thy hollow cell! / Yield up, O love, thy crown and hearted throne / To

IMAGE CHART: Shakespeare, *Othello* (cont.):

Promethian heat /That can thy light relume (5.2.10–13).

5. GENTLENESS. *Approx. count:* 16 images.

OTHELLO. I have a pain upon my forehead here.

DESDEMONA. Faith, that's with watching; 'twill away again / Let me but bind your head; within this hour / It will be well (3.3.284–7).

tyrannous hate (3.1.447–8).

5. VIOLENCE. *Approx. count:* 47 images.

(a) OTHELLO. I will chop her into messes. Cuckold me— (4.1.200). (b) OTHELLO. I would have him nine years a-killing (4.1.178).

(3) *Implicational Dialectic*:

In proceeding from the drama's dialectic of action to its dialectic of imagery, we have advanced in levels of generalization from the concrete to the more abstract, from the physical conflict itself to the symbolic orchestration of that conflict. In turning now to implicational dialectic of *Othello*, we move to an even greater degree of generalization, at which it becomes possible to survey the first two stages of the collision and to reduce them to the opposed values for which they serve as metaphors (Theorems 13–20). As in the previous chapters, our qualitative abstraction involves developing a series of dialectical "sets," in which the first term of each set qualifies the dominant unit of the protagonists, while the second, opposed term characterizes the recessive unit of the antagonists:

1. *Grace/Despair*. In its archaic sense as the undeserved mercy of God leading to eternal salvation, "grace" is the quintessential attribute of the drama's victors—chiefest of whom is the invisible dispenser of grace Himself. Among the mortal recipients of this largess, Desdemona stands at once as principal beneficiary and sovereign exemplar—she who in Cassio's blessing is enwheeled round by "the grace of heaven" (2.1.84–7), and who even in Iago's envious but discerning eyes is of "so free, so kind, so apt, so blessed a disposition" (2.3.320–1). Her "parts and graces" are so manifold that she "is indeed perfection" (2.3.28). Nor is it without significance that her uncle bears the name of Gratiano ("Gracious"), or that her father is described as "much belov'd" and of moral authority equal to "his grace" the Duke (1.2.12–14). The theological opposite of grace is the sin of despair, a state of disbelief in the very possibility of salvation. Iago glorifies this state when he dismisses virtue as "a fig," claiming that man fashions his destiny not by obeying God's will but by exercising his own (1.3.320ff); Roderigo gives voice to the same spiritual condition when he claims that "it is silliness to live when life is a torment" (1.3.308); and Othello at last succumbs to despair when, consumed by remorse without repentance, he confesses that "in my sense 'tis happiness to die," an assertion he ratifies by taking his own life (5.2.290).

2. *Faith/Superstition*. Grace has long been defined as the gift of faith—a gift with which the drama's protagonists are all blessed, and upon which their ultimate triumph, whether in life or in death, is predicated. This unshakable faith reveals itself not only in their many vocal expressions of belief, but especially in their tenacious adherence to their "divine part" even in extremis. Iago, on the contrary, is proud that

his beliefs do not center outside himself, while Othello's weak bond to the Christian faith is sundered the moment the "charmed" handkerchief in which he so superstitiously believes turns up in the hands of Cassio.

3. *Christianity/Paganism*. As we have seen, the fundamentally religious character of the drama's symbolic action reveals itself most clearly in the attack of "the general enemy Ottoman" upon Christendom's outpost island of Cyprus, and in the parallel between this incursion and Iago's "heathenish" attack on the very foundations of Christian morality. Both attempts are foiled—the first by a direct act of God, the second by Emelia's act of moral courage. The symbolic connection between Iago's self-styled paganism and the Ottomites' official brand is underscored in the play's only comic scene, wherein the ancient castigates the female sex and Desdemona accuses him of slander, to which he rejoins, "Nay, it is true, or else I am a Turk" (2.1.114).

4. *Spirituality/Bestiality*. Without his "immortal part," as Cassio phrases it, man becomes a mere beast. It is therefore only appropriate that one who, like Iago, denies any spiritual regulatory principle beyond his own will should begin to conceive of thoughts "monstrous." For to rely solely upon one's own instincts is to become a mere animal, a condition which the text equates with monstrosity because it violates God's will for the being fashioned in His image, and is therefore out of the normal order of creation. In choosing to follow Iago, the Moor himself retreats from his newly acquired spirituality, descending into a sub-human state of pure corporality and passion; and, as he does so, his thoughts and acts turn towards matters bestial. In early seventeenth-century iconography, as in the medieval, Satan's agents are depicted as monstrous beasts.

5. *Piety/Blasphemy*. A natural extension of the previous set, this dichotomy most particularly expresses the contrast between the protagonists' repeated appeals to Christian morality and faith and the antagonists' equally numerous vocal assaults on heaven—the antipodes of Desdemona's "So help me every spirit sanctified" and Iago's "Divinity of hell". Or the Moor's assurance that the charmed handkerchief was "dy'd in mummy which the skilful / Conserv'd of maidens' hearts," and Desdemona's response, "Then would to God that I had never seen it!" (3.4.74–7).

6. *Humility/Pride*. The cause of Lucifer's fall, and the gravest of the Seven Deadly Sins, pride is also the mainspring of this drama's tragic action. For it is Iago's suspicion that both Othello and Cassio have slept with his wife that induces him to

plot their destruction, and Othello's readiness to believe himself dishonored by his bride that permits him to justify killing her. "What shall be said of thee?" demands Lodovico of the once boastful Moor, who responds characteristically,

> Why, anything:
> An honorable murderer, if you will;
> For nought I did in hate, but all in honor (5.2.293–5).

In an entirely different vein, Cassio laments his drunken conduct by exclaiming "One imperfection shows me another, to make me frankly despise myself" (2.3.298–9), while the "modest" Desdemona taxes herself as an "unhandsome warrior" for arraigning Othello's unkindness in her soul (3.4.149).

7. *Obedience/Rebellion*. Pride caused Lucifer to rebel against God, and this act of disobedience had the immense consequence of morally bifurcating the universe. Reflecting that primordial split, the separation of forces in this play also hinges on the distinction between those who obey God's moral injunctions and those who do not. In a more limited sense, obedience to the lawful will of superiors in the social heirarchy is also an important parallel issue here. Thus, while Othello lures Desdemona into a secret marriage against her father's wishes, Brabantio nevertheless defers to the senate in withdrawing his charge of witchcraft against the Moor. Iago induces Cassio to disobey military orders by brawling with a superior; Desdemona remains obedient to Othello at the cost of her life; Emelia also meekly defers to Iago, until she realizes that his commands are wicked; and Othello rebels against the most fundamental tenets of his adopted faith when he chooses to believe Iago's lies. True disobedience is equated in every case with faithlessness and moral turpitude, while rebellion against unjust authority (as in Emelia's case) is seen to be a superior form of moral obedience.

8. *"Foolishness" (Innocence)/"Cunning" (Experience)*.

> Nay, lay thee down and roar,
> For thou hast kill'd the sweetest innocent
> That e'er did lift up eye (5.2.197–9).

Emelia's rebuke to the killer of her mistress evokes the image of the predatory beast and its victim, or, more specifically, the lion of experience and the lamb of innocence. This clear allusion to a traditional icon representing the eternal war between good and evil, Christ and Satan, is anticipated in the maidservant's earlier contrast, "O the more angel she, / And you the blacker devil" (5.2.129–30). Iago's catchphrase, "Put money in thy purse," might provide the motto on the coat of arms of experience. It is at once ironic and dialectically inevitable that the moral quality of innocence—so prized in the Christian lexicon, and often revered in the Jacobean idiom as "foolishness," a sort of holy idiocy—should be the attribute most vulnerable to the machinations of the unscrupulous.

9. *"Being" (Honesty)/ "Seeming" (Hypocrisy)*. Intimately connected with the previous set, this antinomy is pithily evoked in Iago's epigram,

> Men should be what they seem;
> Or those that be not, would they might seem none!
> (3.3.126-7).

The ancient's disingenuous plea for moral transparency reflects an existential dilemma with which the dramatist and his age were obsessed: the fact that it is possible for evil men to feign virtue and thus to victimize the truly good. Though one might assume that, in a universe ordered by God, people and things would actually be as they appear, one has only to recall that the introduction of evil into the world was brought about by the rebellion of God's most beautiful angel. This mythical explanation for the attractiveness of sin is reflected in the old adage, "The Devil is a gentleman." Just such a one is the smooth, charming Iago (i.e., "Jack," an old nickname for Old Nick). "An honest man he is," claims the hoodwinked Moor, "and hates the slime / That sticks on filthy deeds" (5.2.147–8).

10. *Love/Lust (Hatred)*. Iago makes no distinction whatever between love and lust. As he tells Roderigo, "we have reason to cool our raging motions, our carnal stings, our unbitted lusts, whereof I take this that you call love to be a sect or scion" (1.3.331). He dismisses love as "merely a lust of the blood and a permission of the will"— something that can be harnessed by reason (cunning) and worked for personal gain; intelligent people therefore use their powers of attraction as means for putting money in their purse (1.3.335; 340ff; 2.3.349). Beyond this limited goal, however, Iago also employs his personal magnetism as an instrument of his openly avowed hatred for Othello and Cassio, and in so doing he accomplishes the ultimate perversion of Christian love (charity). This other, diametrically opposed sort of love is exemplified in the person, the words, and most especially the deeds of Othello's bride, who when commanded by the Moor to think on her sins, replies, "They are the loves I bear to you" (5.2.40), and who, at the end, even attempts to protect her beloved murderer from discovery (5.2.122–4).

11. *Loyalty/Betrayal*. "If I do vow a friendship, I'll Perform it / To the last article." Thus does Desdemona reassure Cassio that his cause is her own, and that she would "rather die" than give it up (3.3.20–2). These words are no mere hyperbole, for her tenacity in advancing Cassio's suit to the jealous Moor is the indirect cause of her death. And even on the threshold of death she takes the dangerously honest tack of reassuring Othello that she "never lov'd Cassio / But with such general warranty of heaven / As I might love" (5.2.58–61). Similarly, Emelia lays down her life in defense of her dead mistress' honor, just as Brabantio relinquishes his suit against the Moor out of loyalty to the senate, and dies of grief as a result. The only major protagonist who does not suffer the ultimate test of allegiance is Cassio, who nevertheless receives a crippling wound at Iago's hand. On the antagonists' side, however, the watchword is betrayal, as Roderigo seeks to cuckold Othello, Bianca makes a profession of infidelity, and Iago stands as the very figure of treachery to wife, friend, and superior. As we have seen, the loyalty/betrayal dichotomy is the single implicational constant of the apostatic-negative dynamic.

12. *Trust/Suspicion (Jealousy)*. In an effort to give the appearance of honesty, Iago admits to at least one indubitable weakness of character—his tendency to be "vicious" in his judgment of people:

> . . . As, I confess, it is my nature's plague
> To spy into abuses, and oft my jealousy
> Shapes faults that are not . . . (3.3.145-8).

As a consequence he wrongly suspects Othello and Cassio of having made love to his wife, and therefore formulates the project of engendering suspicion in the mind of Othello about his own wife's relationship with Cassio. Roderigo is also jealous of Othello and, though a stupid scoundrel, has enough perspicacity to suspect Iago of using him for ulterior reasons. And the courtesan, Bianca, immediately assumes that Cassio has been unfaithful the minute he shows her the embroidered lady's handkerchief. Among the protagonists, however, only Brabantio evinces seemingly unwarranted suspicions; yet, despite these doubts, he is willing, in the name of Venetian security, to yield to the senate in the matter of the marriage and to interfere no more— at the expense of his peace of mind, and ultimately of his health. Emelia and Desdemona both trust their husbands implicitly, until it is too late to save their own lives.

13. *Liberality/Greed (Envy)*. Othello's bride is the very model of liberality, for, as Iago remarks,

> 'tis most easy
> Th' inclining Desdemona to subdue
> In any honest suit; she's framed as fruitful
> As the free elements (2.3.240–3).

Indeed, at every turn this "bounteous" lady sacrifices her own comfort and safety in the interest of others, whether by accompanying her husband to the threatened garrison of Cyprus, advancing Cassio's suit to her jealous mate, or attempting, even in her dying breath, to shield the Moor from a charge of murder. The projects of Desdemona's counterpart, however, are everywhere motivated by selfishness and a sense of insufficiency; for Iago's plot of revenge is based upon his envy of Cassio, his association with Roderigo upon avarice ("Thus do I ever make my fool my purse"), and his relationship with his wife upon the principle of slavery. His oft repeated motto, "Put money in thy purse," finds its moral complement in Desdemona's declaration that, instead of losing the handkerchief the Moor gave her as a wedding present, "I had rather have lost my purse / Full of cruzadoes" (1.3.340ff; 3.4.25–6).

14. *Temperance/Intemperance.* "O thou invisible spirit of wine! if thou hast no name to be known by, let us call thee devil!" Thus does Cassio, lured by Iago into drinking and then into fighting, berate the immediate cause of his dishonor (2.3.282–4). But his tempter defends the elixir: "Come, come; good wine is a good familiar creature if it be well used. Exclaim no more against it" (2.3.310–12). For Iago's method is to divine and exploit a person's principal shortcoming, or "weak function," as he terms it (2.3.349). If Cassio's major defect is his inability to hold his liquor, Othello's failing is his besottedness with his beautiful wife, and his insecurity about his age and appearance in her eyes. Both victims are therefore assailed at the vulnerable point where appetite most readily overrules reason and moderation.

15. *Kindness/Unkindness.* Shakespeare and his contemporaries often punned on the word "unkind," drawing upon its now obsolete sense of "untrue to one's kind or species, and therefore unnatural." Since man is the being endowed by God with moral choice, and enjoined by Him to do the good and charitable thing, any falling away from this course constitutes an act of unkindness, of inhumanity. This is the sense in which Desdemona laments that there has been an "unkind breach" between Othello and Cassio (4.1.224–5), and it is also the subtext of her vow to love the Moor no matter what he does to her:

> Unkindness may do much;
> And his unkindness may defeat my life,
> But never taint my love (4.2.160–2).

16. *Justice/Injustice.* When Iago proposes that Desdemona be strangled in the very bed she has supposedly "contaminated," Othello rejoins, "Good, good. The justice of it pleases. Very good" (4.1.207–10). And when, with murderous intent, the Moor later approaches his bride's sleeping figure, he exclaims,

> O balmy breath, that doth almost persuade
> Justice to break her sword! (5.2.16–17).

Even after the deed is completed the shaken felon hangs onto this defense: "O I were damn'd beneath all depth in hell / But that I did proceed upon just grounds / To this extremity" (5.2.136–8). Iago and Othello thus pervert the theological virtue of justice into its opposite.

17. *Forgiveness/Vengeance.* "Vengeance is mine, saith the Lord." But Iago arrogates to himself the divine option when he reveals that he has a double motive for hating the Moor: first because he himself loves Desdemona, and secondly because he suspects that Othello has done his office with Emelia:

> And nothing can or shall content my soul,
> Till I am even'd with him, wife for wife,—
> Or failing so, yet that I put the Moor
> At least into a jealousy so strong
> That judgment cannot cure (2.3.301–5).

Once his reason is destroyed, Othello, too, begins to pursue the same program of vendetta. The moral counterweight to this perversion of justice is his victim's Christian act of forgiving her murderer.

18. *Courage/Cowardice.* Never does the vindictiveness of Iago and Roderigo manifest itself in direct and open acts of raw animal courage; rather it seeks its target circuitously and safely, by stealth, insinuation, and ambush. The formerly warlike Moor eventually stoops to these same cowardly stratagems, as he seeks to have his "rival" murdered by another's hand, reserving his own valor for the slaughter of his wife, and, finally, for his own despairing escape from the responsibility of his deeds. The cardinal virtue of courage is to be found neither in the famous general nor in his standard bearer but rather in the moral fortitude and loyalty of their trusting victims.

19. *Forbearance/Rashness.* Neither Desdemona, Cassio, nor Emelia suspect the worst until the worst is upon them. In part this bespeaks the secure trust which a natural charity leads them to place in others, in part the hope that is said to be the essence of grace. As a consequence, these characters exhibit extraordinary patience,

self-control, and long-suffering in the face of injustice. Even Brabantio, who suspects the worst at first, exercises great forbearance when he submits to the senate on the matter of his daughter's marriage. The antagonists, however, are not only quick to suspect injustice but also desperately rash in seeking to punish it.

20. *Gratitude/Ingratitude*. One cannot read Shakespeare for long without becoming aware that his bête noir is ingratitude—a subject which reaches its fullest development in *King Lear*. Although not the principal leitmotif in *Othello*, the theme of ingratitude nevertheless provides a somber companion to that of betrayal; for Iago's whole project is founded upon his inability to feel the slightest obligation to anyone but himself. "I never knew a man who knew how to love himself," he tells the despairing Roderigo, adding, "Ere I would say I would drown myself for the love of a guinea-hen, I would change my humanity with a baboon" (1.3.314–17). Moreover, as Iago rightly suspects, the Moor is so enthralled by Desdemona's beauty that she could, if she wished, cause him "to renounce his baptism, / All seals and symbols of redeemed sin" (2.3.344–8). Although Iago, not Desdemona, acts as Othello's tempter, the Moor's apostasy from the principles of his adopted faith on such slight provocation as a handkerchief constitutes the last word in ingratitude.

21. *Gentleness/Violence*. If Iago's projects are savage, so are the images which clot his speech. As he jokingly tells Desdemona, "my invention comes from my pate as birdlime does from frieze. It plucks out brains and all" (2.1.125–7). He itches to "poison" Brabantio's delight, to "plague him with flies," and even fantasizes having stabbed the old man under the ribs (1.1.68; 1.2.4–5). Figures of torture, murder, poison, dismemberment, and violent illness swell the antagonists' language, as first Iago and then Othello become obsessed with barbarous solutions to imaginary affronts. "I'll tear her all to pieces!" cries the Moor, "I will chop her into messes," "Get me some poison, Iago, this night" (3.3.431; 4.1.200, 204). At the peak of his jealousy Othello trembles violently, and then, with the exclamation of "Noses, ears, and lips," falls into an epileptic trance (4.1.42–3; 51–2). His "bloody passion" later leads him, gnawing his lower lip and rolling his eyes with a "fatal" wildness, into his lady's chamber for the crowning act of savagery (5.2.37–8; 43–4).

22. *Beauty/Ugliness*.

> If Cassio do remain,
> He has a daily beauty in his life
> That makes me ugly (5.1.18–20).

Thus Iago, who also notes that the lieutenant "is handsome, young and hath all those requisites in him that folly and green minds look after"; in short, that he's "a proper man" (2.1.246–8; 2.1.391–7). As to Desdemona's beauty, both physical and moral, everyone is in agreement. Even her suspicious mate remarks in her defense,

... my wife is fair, feeds well, loves company,
Is free of speech, sings, plays, and dances well.
Where virtue is these are more virtuous (3.3.184–6).

But Iago doubts that such a paragon could long find the Moor physically attractive: "Her eye must be fed; and what delight shall she have to look on the devil?" (2.1.226–7). The Jacobean tendency to equate physical beauty with goodness, and ungainliness with evil, is further elaborated here through the figurative oppositions of music to discord, and silence to noise.

23. *Penitence/Impenitence.* When Cassio berates himself for having become a drunk and disorderly "beast," his tempter, Iago, demurs, "Come, you are too severe a moraler," adding "You or any man living may be drunk at some time" (2.3.300; 314–15). This transaction epitomizes the radical disparity between those whose moral bearing is fixed to the divine pole star, and those others who take their headings solely from the internal lights generated by impulse and self-interest. Because they are utterly self-justifying, Iago's motives are not subject to the workings of conscience, and his behavior is therefore "pernicious." Moreover, since he personifies the principle of evil, he cannot be killed, a fact which leaves torture as the only appropriate punishment. Nor, after his downfall, is Othello capable of genuine repentance either, but only of a self-justifying remorse that seeks to avoid atonement through suicide.

24. *Contentment/Discontent.*

If it were now to die,
'Twere now to be most happy, for I fear
My soul hath her content so absolute
That not another comfort like to this
Succeeds in unknown fate (2.1.189–93).

With these fair words Othello voices his joy in rejoining Desdemona after his safe passage across a stormy sea, and also in knowing that the same tempest has destroyed the Turkish invasion fleet. But his expression of almost unspeakable happiness sits ill with the envious Iago, who hisses in an aside,

> O! you are well tun'd now,
>
> But I'll set down the pegs that make this music,
>
> As honest as I am (2.1.200–3).

25. *Nobility/Baseness.* Iago fears that the Moor is an unlikely candidate for cuckoldom because his "constant, noble, loving nature" will make him a "most dear husband" to Desdemona (2.1.291–95). Since it will therefore be impossible to discredit Othello in her eyes, Iago must try instead to shake the husband's faith in his wife. And once that trust is destroyed, the Moor's behavior turns as vicious as that of his tempter. By his own admission he becomes

> . . . one whose hand
>
> (Like the base Indian) threw a pearl away
>
> Richer than all his tribe . . . (5.2.346–8).

It is difficult not to interpret this process of moral degeneration allegorically, viewing the "bride" and the "pearl" as code words for religious "faith."

26. *Honor/Dishonor.* The *dramatis personae* page of the first Folio describes Cassio as "*an honorable Lieutenant*" and Iago bluntly as "*a villain.*" This contrast suggests that honor is to be understood in terms of inherent moral rectitude rather than as the mere reputation for it; or, rather, that reputation itself, as Cassio affirms, is inseparable from man's "immortal part." Iago naturally disputes the moral basis of honor, claiming that "You have lost no reputation at all, unless you repute yourself such a loser" (2.3.263ff). The connection between honor and true virtue is reaffirmed in the drama's final scene when Othello, having been placed under arrest and disarmed by Montano, descants,

> I am not valiant neither,
>
> But every puny whipster gets my sword.
>
> But why should honor outlive honesty?
>
> Let it go all (5.2.242–5).

27. *Reason/Passion.* As we have seen, the Moor provides a hint of the extremes of passion to which he is susceptible when he vents his anger at Cassio and Montano for brawling:

> Now, by heaven,
>
> My blood begins my safer guides to rule,
>
> And passion, having my best judgment collied,
>
> Assays to lead the way. Zounds! If I stir,

> Or do but lift this arm, the best of you
>
> Shall sink in my rebuke (2.3.–205–10).

Significantly, this passage begins with the mild oath of "by heaven" and builds to the blasphemous contraction "Zounds!" (God's wounds), thereby linking inordinate passion with a diminution of faith. On the other hand, it was formerly believed that reason (the Right Reason of medieval scholasticism) was man's safest spiritual guide.

28. *Sanity/Madness.* When Othello falls into his second epileptic "trance" in as many days, Iago warns Cassio not to disturb the unconscious figure:

> The lethargy must have his quiet course.
>
> If not he foams at the mouth, and by and by
>
> Breaks out to savage madness (4.1.54–6).

It is this violently irrational state that Iago seeks to induce by deceiving the Moor as to the real reasons for Cassio's laughter, for "As he shall smile, Othello shall go mad" (4.1.101). And that is precisely what happens when the general overhears his lieutenant making sexual innuendoes about some unnamed woman: he waits until Cassio makes his exit and then rushes in to ask breathlessly, "How shall I murder him, Iago?" (4.1.170). Later in the same scene, when Desdemona dares to suggest a reconciliation between her husband and Cassio because of the love she bears for the latter, Othello suddenly strikes her. The company is flabbergasted, and once the unhappy pair have left the stage Lodovico breaks the silence by inquiring, "Are his wits safe? is he not light of brain?" (4.1.267). Evil is thus seen to be a form of insanity induced by inordinate passion, which rears its head when one's "weak function" is sorely beset.

29. *Wisdom/Ignorance.* In the drama's single comic scene Desdemona sets Iago to extemporizing couplets on various sorts of women, and when she asks him what he can say about the ones who are "foul (i.e., ugly) and foolish" he responds cynically,

> There's none so foul and foolish thereunto
>
> But does foul pranks which fair and wise ones do.

To which Desdemona rejoins, "O heavy ignorance that praises the worst best!" (2.1.139–43). Iago's obtuseness lies in his refusal to make any moral distinction between the wise and the foolish because, to him, both are essentially corrupt. But if the ancient is unable to distinguish good from evil, Othello instead confuses the two, trusting the lies of his standard bearer and disbelieving the truth of his bride—for which Emelia berates him as a moral imbecile: "O thou dull Moor!" "O gull! O dolt! / As ignorant as dirt!" (5.2.162–3, 223–4).

30. *Order/Chaos.*

>   Perdition catch my soul
>   But I do love thee! and when I love thee not,
>   Chaos is come again (3.3.90–2).

This equation of love with order, and the cessation (or negation) of love with chaos, derives from the Christian veneration of *agape* as the primary attribute of God—and therefore also of God's universal order. Any gross betrayal of Christian charity thus constitutes a monstrous violation of nature, an intimation of the radical disorder implicit in Lucifer's rebellion, and a cause, moreover, of "perdition" in the life to come.

31. *Salvation/Damnation.*

>   Moor, she was chaste. She lov'd thee, cruel Moor.
>   So come my soul to bliss as I speak true
>   (5.2.249–50).
>   O ill-starr'd wench!
>   Pale as thy smock! When we shall meet at compt,
>   This look of thine will hurl my soul from heaven,
>   And fiends will snatch at it (5.2.272–5).

The preceeding thirty-one derivations abstract in a reasonably exhaustive manner the antithetical values which operate as mainsprings for the colliding forces in *Othello*. In many of these sets both terms appear repeatedly as manifest issues of the dialogue; in others only one of the two terms crops up in the text, while its complementary opposite is implicit not only by dialectical inference but also by clear dramatic necessity; in still others, neither quality is an overt subject of dialogue, yet both nonetheless accurately sum up the qualities reflected in the drama's surges of action and counteraction. It will be helpful in summation to provide a "print-out" of these antithetical value-terms by themselves so that we may quickly scan the two columns in order to gain a more immediate grasp of the drama's dominant and recessive motives, its internal argument:

IMPLICATIONAL CHART: Shakespeare, *Othello, The Moor of Venice*:

DOMINANT FUNCTION	RECESSIVE FUNCTION
Grace	Despair
Faith	Superstition
Christianity	Paganism

Spirituality	Bestiality
Piety	Blasphemy
Humility	Pride
Obedience	Rebellion
"Foolishness" (Innocence)	"Cunning" (Experience)
"Being" (Honesty)	"Seeming" (Hypocrisy)
Love	Lust (Hatred)
Loyalty	Betrayal
Trust	Suspicion (Jealousy)
Liberality	Greed (Envy)
Temperance	Intemperance
Kindness	Unkindness
Justice	Injustice
Forgiveness	Vengeance
Courage	Cowardice
Forbearance	Rashness
Gratitude	Ingratitude
Gentleness	Violence
Beauty	Ugliness
Penitence	Impenitence
Contentment	Discontent
Nobility	Baseness
Honor	Dishonor
Reason	Passion
Sanity	Madness
Wisdom	Ignorance
Order	Chaos
Salvation	Damnation

Scansion of the dominant and recessive derivations for *Othello* reveals the drama's deeply religious cast in the many requisite antinomies conforming to the dialectic of Christian theology, not least among them the comprehensive opposition of "Christianity" to "paganism" in general. It is therefore only natural that the capital terms of "grace" and "despair" should confront each other at the head of the two columns as the essential conditions for either "salvation" or "damnation," which face off at the bottom; for these two sets of antitheses constitute the alpha and omega of Christian morality, as they do also of the play's wishful and fearful motives. Moreover, the drama's villains are impelled by no fewer than six of the Seven Deadly Sins, namely, pride, envy, lust, greed, gluttony ("intemperance"), and wrath ("violence," "unkindness," "hatred"), the only sin eluding them in their vigorous course of evil being sloth. The protagonists, on the other hand, not only possess all of the corresponding moral virtues, they also exhibit the four cardinal virtues of wisdom, temperance, justice, and courage. Even more important, the dominant characters exemplify the theological virtues of faith, hope (here subsumed under "grace" and "trust"), and charity ("love"), while their opposite numbers objectify the negations of these qualities: superstition, despair, and hatred. Taken together, these assorted virtues and failings represent all of the most fundamental contrarieties of Christian morality.

The immanence of these moral and theological values in the symbolic action of *Othello* provides confirmation for the opinion of G. Wilson Knight and others, who contend that the drama must be understood primarily as a religious allegory. At the same time the dominating presence of these specifically Christian values stands as a caution to interpreters who would see the work largely as an expression of psychological concerns, many of a suspiciously modern cast. Indeed, even those derivations which are not exclusive parts of the religious vocabulary of the time produce, as a group, a somewhat archaic and conventional resonance; nor does their number include any of the more intimate and biographically suggestive antinomies that frequently crop up in Shakespeare's comedies or "problem plays," and, indeed, occasionally in his other tragedies. In the case of *Othello*, at least, it would appear that many of the "issues" which have beguiled modern interpreters—as for instance that of latent homosexuality—simply do not arise as necessary implications of the drama's oppositional structure.

As an ideological representative of its dynamic type, *Othello* is highly typical. For, like most other apostatic-negative dramas, it preserves a severely moralistic tone throughout, permitting no ironic mingling of positive with negative values in the same functional units. This rigid segregation of conventional opposites, producing a black and white view of the moral universe, is what lies beneath the highly melodramatic cast of this and other dramas of the same class. So is the programmatic dualism which enforces this separation, and which here takes the conventional form of Christian moral doctrine as it stood at the beginning of the seventeenth century, with theological, cardinal, and moral virtues played off against their opposed vices.

Most typical of all is its hero's betrayal of the central positive injunctions of this doctrine and his consequent fall from grace into despair and eternal shame; for, whatever the doctrine, betrayal of faith is the central mythos of the apostatic-negative dynamic.

FOURTH MODEL
METASTATIC-POSITIVE

Definition. *Long known in its most common form as the "love triangle," the metastatic-positive structure is characterized by a struggle between protagonist and antagonist for control of a contested third party who at the outset is either unwilling or unable to commit to the more attractive rival. Eventually, however, the contested figure moves from an initially disengaged "apex" position to the protagonists' unit. And when, as often happens, the apex unit contains several contested figures, the latter all eventually shift to the dominant column, thus leaving the drama in a bipolar configuration at its final stasis.*

The metastatic-positive structure best describes most comedic and ironic love intrigues in which two or more men vie for the affection of varying numbers of women. Occasionally, however, this situation may be reversed to depict the primary belligerents as female, and the contested figure as male. Nor are the major poles of action always populated by characters of the same sex: occasional figures of opposite gender may be present in both the protagonists' and antagonists' units, usually as confidantes or go-betweens for the principal rivals. And although its predominant mythos is the love intrigue, this initially triangular dynamic also comprehends tragi-comedies containing no love interest whatever. In such cases, instead of the stock beautiful young heiress and restless wife, the metastatic characters may also include the suppliant, the wayfarer, the lost soul, and the purely symbolic prize for victory. Consequently, the quintessential motif of this dynamic class is not love intrigue (which may be found in all other structures) but rather a fight to enjoy the benefits, of whatever nature, attendant upon possession of the apex character, a figure who may be said to embody the fantasy's motivating desire. The personal attributes of the protagonist are proven to be those requisite for the attainment of such a dream, while the characteristics of the antagonist are represented as least suitable for its fulfillment.

Schematic. The contested character "Z" is shown enclosed in parentheses to indicate her (his/their) initially disengaged position between the major warring camps. An arrow traces the metastatic shift to the protagonists' unit, and the letter-symbol without parentheses represents the apex character's position at the drama's ultimate stasis:

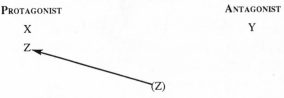

PROTAGONIST   ANTAGONIST

X   Y

Z

(Z)

General. Because the great majority of metastatic-positive dramas develop comedic love triangles, it will perhaps be prudent at the outset to discuss works of four other types that also occasionally assume this structure: (1) commedia or tragi-comedy in which a suppliant faces the threat of death, or even succumbs to death, but either is rescued or achieves apotheosis through the intervention of the protagonist; (2) irony or satire focusing on a misfit or mental runaway whose ultimate possession by the protagonist brings economic or sexual advantage to the latter but often confers a dubious blessing on the contested figure; (3) satire or romance in which an apex character (often mute) is awarded to the victor as a symbolic prize; and (4) the tragic love triangle, in which two characters come together despite insuperable odds; and though they perish as a result, their union is represented as a triumph of eros and/or *agape.*

Among the commedia of our first subspecies undoubtedly the most distinguished is Sophocles' *Oedipus at Colonus.* Although they are not the principal combatants in this work, Oedipus and his daughters nevertheless constitute the source of conflict between Theseus and Creon, Attica and Thebes; for the oracle has promised to confer a great blessing on the city that will offer the old man sanctuary during his last years, and honorable burial in death. But the goal cannot be attained without difficulty. Though an exile from the Thebes he despises, Oedipus meets with resistance from the citizens of the Attic deme of Colonus both because of his terrifying history and also because he has unwittingly trespassed upon the sacred precinct of the Eumenedies (Furies). Moreover, having heard of the new oracle concerning Oedipus, Creon and Polybus attempt to wrest the old man back to Thebes, first by force and then by persuasion. Only when King Theseus intervenes with his Colonian subjects on behalf of Oedipus is the title-character at last assured the benefit of sanctuary required for his death and apotheosis, as well as for Attica's glory. Through these events one can trace the basic pattern of all metastatic-positive drama of whatever subspecies: a contested figure who is the cause of the central conflict and whose ultimate alliance with the protagonist confers a reward upon the latter while leaving the antagonist in discomfiture and disgrace. The same pattern, also bearing the motifs of reprieve or apotheosis, governs such otherwise diverse works as Aeschylus' *The Suppliants*, Euripides', *Alcestis*, Shakespeare's *Measure for Measure*, and the Mozart-da Ponte opera *The Magic Flute*. Yet it is well to recall that this mythos may also assume other dynamic patterns, as it does, for instance, in Shakespeare's *The Winter's Tale* (See Model 6); consequently, presence of the suppliant motif does not always guarantee that the drama in question belongs to the metastatic-positive class.

Like their ancient counterparts, modern dramas containing the suppliant motif and assuming the metastatic-positive structure are comparatively rare; moreover, they usually appear in "mythically decomposed" form, commonly portraying the contested figure as a mental runaway and those who "succor" him as malign forces playing upon his personal failings. Thus, in Dürrenmatt's *The Physicists* the central character, Möbius, commits himself to an insane asylum in order to avoid revealing the formula for a doomsday bomb—only to discover that his congenial fellow inmates are spies for foreign powers, and the sanatorium's owner and chief psychiatrist, Fraulein Dr. von Zahnd, heads an international cartel which also seeks, and eventually gets, his secret for the ultimate weapon. If this sort of crushing irony usually eschews the metastatic-positive structure, it is because positive movement from the apex naturally lends itself to happier results; and it therefore comes as no surprise that most triangles of this grim character in fact obey the metastatic-*negative* dynamic (See Model 5).

The third subspecies of metastatic-positive drama consists of occasional plays in which a passive and mute apex character is formally conferred upon the protagonist as a token of victory and symbol of his overriding wish. Aristophanes provides a deliciously ironic instance of this pattern in *The Birds*, where the enterprising Pisthetarios, chief engineer of Cloudcuckooland's victory over both men and gods, extorts from the latter the symbol of their power, "Miss Dominion," to whom he is married at the play's conclusion. Brecht's *Caucasian Chalk Circle* also employs the same ancient pattern for entirely different reasons when Judge Azdak, following the wisdom of Solomon, awards the infant Michael to the woman who can best care for him—just as in the play's framing scenes the land has been taken away from its original owners and given over to those who prove able to cultivate it most productively. Irony and romance of this sort could be easily described by the static structure (Model 1) rather than the metastatic-positive were it not for the presence of these contested figures, who, though silent and without will of their own, carry tremendous symbolic weight as emblems of victory. Furthermore, the metastatic shift at the conclusion of such plays aids in preserving a lighter, more comedic tone than that possible in static actions.

In rare instances of the metastatic-positive love triangle the contested figure's eventual movement to the protagonist will result not in happy marriage but rather in destruction for one or both of the lovers. Yet in order to sustain their positive dynamic such "tragic" actions must invariably represent the eventual union of the lovers in death as a higher good, as the ultimate self-sacrificing fulfillment of their overriding desire, and therefore a triumph of eros against all odds. Consequently, despite their tragic tone, plays of this subspecies are, strictly speaking, commedia—as befits the general character of the positive triangle. Senta's fatal leap to save the soul of the doomed sea captain in Wagner's *The Flying Dutchman* is thus represented as a positive action, at once the absolute proof of her selfless devotion and the cause of the Dutchman's release from bondage to the Devil. As in other dramas of this type, the offstage opposition of God and Satan creates an eschatological vision that prevents the lovers' death from being a mere tragic surcease and makes it rather an apotheosis; hence, the final scene of Wagner's opera depicts Senta and the sea captain literally ascending together into heaven. But, to repeat, such situations are comparatively uncommon; the great majority of love-death triangles lack such spiritual vistas and consequently fall not into the metastatic-positive but into the metastatic-negative dynamic, which will be described at length in the following chapter.

Finally, we come to the most common of all metastatic-positive subspecies: the ubiquitous comedic (or ironic) love triangle. And here it is necessary to dilate on several structural principles mentioned earlier, as well as to introduce certain other features peculiar to this sort of love intrigue in general.

It is important at the outset to realize that the principle of unidirectionality holds for every dynamic model including the metastatic-positive, which represents the movement of all contested figures from the same initial apex position to the protagonists' unit—never to *both* winner and loser. Nor do metastatic actions contain simultaneous shifts from the apex and cross-dialectical movements between the major poles of action (Theorem 6). Hence, the losers in love triangles may concede defeat gracefully or otherwise, but they never actively change positions to cooperate with the victors. If a so-called blocking character reverses course in order to assist the protagonist, reassessment of the action will reveal that the character in question belonged in the protagonists' unit from the beginning (Theorems 2, 3). Such is the case in Congreve's *The Double Dealer*, where Lord Touchwood opposes the match between Cynthia and Melefont only until Lady Touchwood's lies have been exposed; however, his approval of the marriage, once he is disabused, cannot be taken as a dialectical shift because his wife's secret perfidy had from outset placed him in unwitting opposition to her and therefore in the protagonists' column from the very start. Conversely, the presence in any play of an indisputable cross-dialectical shift indicates that the work under consideration does not conform to the metastatic-positive dynamic, even though its plot contains some sort of love intrigue.

A second and most important characteristic of love triangles: victory is not necessarily predicated upon actual physical possession of the contested female; the mere securing of her affection and/or cooperation often constitutes a sufficient basis for placing her in the apex unit which will eventually be incorporated into the dominant unit of the protagonist. To draw again upon Congreve for an instance of the situation in question, we find in his *The Way of the World* that all of the female characters, even the maid servants and coffee house wench, evince an affection for Mirabell that allows him or his surrogates in the protagonists' camp to force compliance to their will. The ladies' rivalry for Mirabell's attentions constitutes merely an internal conflict among those whose overriding wish is in fact identical (Theorem 5); and even spiteful characters such as Mrs. Fainall must be placed in the apex unit if their actions are clearly motivated, like hers, by frustrated love for the protagonist. Appreciation of this situation blows much of the plot-fog away from a comedy notorious for its novelistic complexity of action; indeed, the determination of victory on the basis of affection or cooperation, as well as that of actual possession, provides a simple and elegant means of unravelling many another maddeningly tangled love intrigue.

It cannot be sufficiently emphasized that, from an economic viewpoint, metastatic actions consist initially of only three "characters," with all figures comprising the apex unit moving to the protagonist *en bloc* as objectifications of a particular attitude toward women (or men) in general. When, for instance, in Beaumarchais' *The Marriage of Figaro* Susanne and the Countess exchange clothes (and rank) in a variation of the old "bed trick" for the purpose of foiling the Count's design upon Figaro's intended, we are offered a most striking glimpse of the interchangeability of the play's females—as if the dramatist were here intent upon pointing up this doubling, of which audiences are usually only subliminally aware.

Nevertheless, as we have seen, the essential likeness of all the characters comprising the metastatic group may often be obscured by internal conflicts within that unit. These struggles frequently take the form of a sometimes unwitting rivalry between two or more females for the chief protagonist's affections, an internal contest that eventually leads to disappointment for all but a single candidate, thereby creating the apparent anomaly of losers in a camp that shifts to the positive pole of action. Why, for example, should Lady Loveit and Bellinda be counted among the metastatic females of Ethredge's *The Man of Mode* when the cavalier hero, Dorimant, betrays them both to marry the wealthy Harriet? Because, simply put, they have given their affection as well as their persons to Dorimant.   Moreover, neither Loveit nor Bellinda can function as blocking characters in the antagonists' unit because they know nothing of their faithless gallant's plans to wed another, and are therefore powerless to prevent them. As for the much acclaimed difference in kind between Harriet and these "fallen women," few commentators have noted that Harriet alone possesses sufficient fortune to hold out for marriage. Apart from this single distinction, Etheredge offers nothing by way of action to suggest that any woman can long resist Dorimant's charms—even the "modest" Emelia, who repeatedly praises the hero's parts, and whose marriage to Young Bellair Dorimant encourages in the belief that "nothing can corrupt her but a husband" (I, i). The author's cynical attitude toward feminine virtue is thus reflected in the essential tractability of the play's mobile characters—a fact easily overlooked owing to purely superficial dissimilarities created by the internal conflict between Dorimant's feminine admirers.

Such internecine conflicts may sometimes occur in all three of a metastatic comedy's initial units, thus further complicating the job of determining the work's radical cleavage, its true protagonists and antagonists. Nor is this task simplified by large cast plays containing several parallel triangles with hidden players at one or more corner, or by comedies featuring those mistaken identities and "cross-wooings" for which Marivaux's *False Confessions* and *The Game of Love and Chance* are notorious. But although such complicated love triangles abound, they represent but a minority when compared to those in which every Jack gets his Jill, where parallel triangles are clearly so, and where in fact the victorious males and contested females often collaborate to defeat those who would block their romantic inclinations.

In stressing the essential similarity of the apex females of metastatic-positive comedy, I may have created the impression that only males are to be found at the two other corners of such triangles, that is, in the protagonists' and antagonists' units. Although this is indeed commonly the case, female characters do nevertheless occasionally appear as protagonists and especially as antagonists in love intrigues. Lady Touchwood has already been mentioned as a principal blocking character in *The Double Dealer*. Like her, such females are typically older women, frequently guardians of the contested female, whom they seek to keep out of the hero's reach by various stratagems including advancing the suit of a wealthy rival. Machiavelli's *The Mandrake* furnishes an early example of this type in Sostrata, whose foolish collaboration with her daughter's senile husband contributes to the latter's being crowned with cuckold's horns. When, as rarely occurs in love triangles, a female appears in the protagonists' camp, she will usually fill the role of confidante to one of the victorious males but exercise little if any real influence on the action's outcome. Molière's *The Miser* contains two such characters: the husband-hunting Foisine and Anselm's offstage wife, both of whom play minimal roles in the protagonists' struggle against the avaricious Harpagon. Yet whether protagonist or antagonist, passive or active, such females share one characteristic by which they can usually be recognized: there is little or no contention between the major warring camps to secure their cooperation because they are dialectically engaged from the outset.

In its ironic mode the metastatic-positive love intrigue does not differ structurally from the normal comedic triangle. Only the tone is altered, for here the author expresses ambivalence if not outright distaste for those characters who nonetheless emerge as dominant elements of his fantasy (Theorem 19). In a certain figurative sense, however, the ironic triangle frequently reverses the purely comedic situation by representing the victory of age over youth, experience over innocence, realism over idealism. The Oedipal motif common to so many ironic triangles finds expression in the betrayal of weak and impotent antagonists by fickle women, who in turn are often betrayed or abused by the paternal figures who win their affection or control their actions. Turgenev's *A Month in the Country*, Chekhov's *The Seagull*, and Shaw's *Heartbreak House* all work variations on the triumph of wealthy, realistic males whose very indifference to their rivals constitutes one of the decisive factors in their victory. For the contested females, disappointment or neglect is the common result of their movement to the dominant unit; for the antagonists, suicide or banishment often ends the struggle. This mythos receives perhaps its most brutally frank treatment in Kurosawa's screenplay *Rashomon*, which depicts—depending on point of view—the rape (or seduction) of a gentlewoman before the eyes of her samurai husband, who is subsequently killed in a duel with (or executed by) his wife's bandit attacker. The extremely oblique unfolding of this story through the eyes of the living witnesses points up the ambivalence usually evident in metastatic-positive drama when it assumes the ironic mode.

Such ambivalence consistently leads to the employment of secretive dramaturgical techniques: hidden players in one or more of the functional units (thus obscuring triangular relationships), self-contradiction and denial on the part of the contested females, disagreements about events that have occurred prior to dramatic time proper, and the apparent disinterest of the victorious males, to list but a few. Because all of these oblique strategies are employed by Chekhov in *The Three Sisters*, dialectical analysis of this work should provide an example sufficiently complex as to render the anatomy of most other metastatic-positive dramas relatively simple to graph.

ANALYSIS
Anton Chekhov, *The Three Sisters*[1]

(1) *Dialectic of Action*:

To assert that *The Three Sisters* can best be described as an ironic love triangle, whose female characters all belong in the initial apex unit, may alarm those

---

[1] Anton Chekkhov, *Chekhov: The Major Plays*. Translated by Ann Dunnigan. Foreword by Robert Brustein (New York and Toronto: New American Library Signet Classics, 1964). All page references are to this text.

accustomed to viewing the play's action largely in terms of a class conflict between the weary, hypersensitive Prozorov sisters and the social climbing Natasha. Indeed, there is a certain justification for much of what has been said about the apparent difference in kind between Natasha and the other women in the cast; for Chekhov employs an internal conflict between the apex females as a screen with which to divert attention from the authentic structure of his work, and thus away from its motivating thought content. Not alone among ironists who are attracted to the metastatic-positive dynamic, Chekhov prefers his auditors to occupy themselves with vague social and philosophical issues rather than directly confront the highly sensitive and personal confession at the heart of his drama. For the internal argument objectified here does not so much concern historical change or class conflict as it does an idiosyncratic attitude toward love between the sexes and a self-deprecating opinion about those male attributes most, and least, likely to attract women or radically influence their destinies. Examination of the drama's several triangles will enable us to define more specifically the character of this attitude, and to apprehend the special quality of its irony.

The first triangular situation in *The Three Sisters* is doubly obscure by reason of its having taken place prior to dramatic time proper and also because two of its principals are no longer living: Chebutykin, the old army doctor and lifelong friend of the Prozorovs, reveals that he was "madly in love" with their mother even after she married General Prozorov. When Masha asks the physician whether her mother ever returned his love, Chebutykin claims that he can no longer remember (242, 299). Were this all the information provided on the subject, it would be impossible to determine the intrigue's protagonist and antagonist. However, as though inadvertently, Chebutykin reveals that his languishing passion for Madam Prozorov kept him from ever marrying another woman, that his disappointment in love was the cause of his chronic loneliness and also, by clear inference, the origin of his nihilism, which expresses itself in a constant "It doesn't matter" response to any crisis (275). This confession permits us to see the triangle in its true form, with the inept, alcoholic physician as sole survivor of an oblique contest in which he was the antagonist, General Prozorov the protagonist, and Madam Prozorov the contested female. That Chebutykin remains a friend to the Prozorovs, and after their death preserves a strong sentimental attachment to their children, bespeaks a resignation and constancy in defeat characteristic of all the play's antagonists. Of Madam Prozorov we learn only that she died in Moscow before her children were grown up. However, the fleeting glimpses of her military husband, Sergei, permit us to anticipate certain attributes of the drama's other victors. We learn, for instance, that his children have come to regard his death with equanimity, although he died only one year to the day of the play's beginning, and on his younger daughter's nameday; that, though a brigade commander in charge of a thousand men, few people followed his coffin to its grave; that he forced his son, Andrei, to prepare for an academic career to which the young man was ill-suited; and that, in fact, he "oppressed" his children with education, requiring them to learn foreign languages which they considered a "needless luxury" in a provincial setting (235, 246, 248–9). These bits of information do not complete the mosaic, but they provide enough pieces to reveal the features of a commander unpopular among his subordinates, an overbearing father, insensitive to his children's feelings, and a man with pretensions to culture.

The play's second love intrigue has the advantage of taking place during dramatic time proper, yet it too receives oblique treatment because the triangle's protagonist never appears on stage. This hidden player is Protopopov, suitor to Natasha before she marries Andrei Prozorov, and her lover subsequent to the unhappy union. Head of the District Council on which Andrei serves as a subordinate member, Protopopov has the cool effrontery to drive his troika up to the Prozorov house and wait outside for an evening tryst with Natasha, who slips out to join him while her husband reads in his study and her sisters-in-law sit languidly in the drawing room. Almost everyone in the household seems to ignore what is going on behind Andrei's back while he variously plays the violin, peruses old university lecture notes, or spends evenings with Chebutykin at the club losing thousands of rubles at cards. Andrei himself appears largely unconcerned when, later in the action, Protopopov becomes a regular guest in the drawing room of the house now mortgaged to pay off his gaming debts. Yet even the absent-minded would-be professor eventually admits his awareness and grudging acceptance of the situation, for his diatribe against the degrading effects of provincial life contains the revealing assertion that, in order to relieve their boredom, "the wives deceive their husbands, while the husbands pretend not to see or hear anything, and an overwhelmingly vulgar influence weighs on the children" (305). Indeed, we last view Andrei wheeling his son about in a perambulator, while District Councilor Protopopov sits inside the house with Natasha's second child—the presumptive offspring of their illicit union (310–11).

Despite the apparent difference in sensibility between the vulgar, social-climbing Natasha and her over-refined sisters-in-law—a difference generally supposed to express the play's radical conflict—one cannot fail to note the startling similarity between Natasha's situation and that of Masha. For, like Andrei's wife, Masha despises her school teacher husband, Kulygin, and conducts a love affair with the town's dashing new battery commander, Lieutenant Colonel Vershinin. The analogues between this triangle and the former two are manifold. Like the dead General Prozorov and the offstage Protopopov, Vershinin holds a high post of authority in the town; and his power over women is underscored by the fact that his wife (another hidden player in the apex unit) continues to love him despite his infidelities and seeks to keep his attention at home by repeated yet unsuccessful attempts at suicide. On his part, Masha's sad, pedantic spouse finds himself in exactly the same position as Andrei, for both tolerate without direct reproach their wives' open infidelities—just as Chebutykin had endured visiting in the house of a married woman who did not return his adoration. When the affair between Masha and Vershinin is abruptly terminated after the battery receives its marching orders, Kulygin publicly pleads for Masha to return home and promises that he will never mention the affair (309). The likenesses among Kulygin, Chebutykin, and Andrei are heightened by the fact that all have been largely incapable of putting their formal education to good use: they are either intellectual incompetents or pedants. Chebutykin confesses that he hasn't read a medical book for twenty-five years; Andrei laments never having taught at the university in Moscow, and that now the most he can aspire to is mere board membership on the District Council; while Kulygin's only literary effort is a history of his high school, written because he had "nothing better to do" (239, 250–1, 259, 283).

A fourth love-triangle in *The Three Sisters* involves the youngest Prozorov daughter, Irina, who, in despair of ever finding a true romantic passion, allows herself to become affianced to Baron Tutzenbach, a man she does not love. Her engagement provokes the wrath of the strange and frightening Captain Solyony, whose abrupt and unsuccessful bid to woo Irina is followed by the promise that if he cannot have her, neither will anyone else. Solyony keeps his word, killing the Baron in a duel. Although the Captain gives nothing to Irina except sorrow, he nevertheless emerges as the protagonist of this peculiar triangle for the critical reason that by his single act of violence he exerts a compelling influence on the young woman's destiny, causing her to follow her sister Olga into the unromantic profession of teaching high school. In order to test our protocol here, we must again search for analogues between the members of this triangle and their counterparts; nor, indeed, are the parallels difficult to find. Like the other antagonists, Tutzenbach loves a woman who does not return his affection, offering to marry her in full awareness of this impediment. And despite his high social position, the baron of German extraction shares the awkwardness,. pessimism, and physical unattractiveness of the other losers. As protagonist, Solyony presents a somewhat more difficult case because his peculiarly repulsive mannerisms would seem to exclude him from placement with, say, the relatively attractive Vershinin. On closer inspection, however, Solyony can be seen to possess all the critical attributes of the drama's other protagonists. He, too, holds an official position of command; and though socially ill-at-ease, his vague physical resemblance to the poet Lermontov (with whom he identifies) invests him with an aura of brooding romanticism. Nor are his unpleasant mannerisms foreign to the other victors, for it must be recalled that Vershinin's callous neglect of his wife and children, not to mention Masha's honor, assumes a character as boorish as Protopopov's open affair with Natasha and his encroachment upon the household. It seems just, therefore, to say that Solyony's barbarous conduct represents merely a more pronounced aspect of the callousness exhibited by all of the protagonists—including the late but not much lamented General Prozorov.

Thus far the placement of Chekhov's characters in a triangular configuration, with the apex females dominated by the male protagonists, seems to fulfill the qualifications of a metastatic-positive action. But what, then, of the eldest sister, Olga, for whose affection nobody appears to compete? If the drama's action is truly metastatic, we should also expect Olga to function as part of the contested unit and to be drawn with her sisters into the protagonists' camp. This, however, would require the existence of a protagonist to whom she moves, as well as that of an antagonist whom she abandons. And, indeed, if we discount the love motif common but not essential to positive triangles, we shall see that Olga too shifts from a disengaged apex position to the protagonists' unit— in this case to the offstage director of the high school at which she teaches. For it is this official who pressures her to accept a promotion to the job of headmistress, a position that takes both her and the old family nurse, Anfisa, away to live in government housing, thus leaving her brother Andrei alone to cope with his unfaithful wife. Olga's move from the family home constitutes a loss not only for Andrei but also for Chebutykin, who has depended upon the three sisters' companionship, as well as for Kulygin, who reveals that he would have liked to marry Olga had it not been for Masha (282).

Also a loser by reason of the compassionate Olga's removal from the premises is old Ferapont, the decrepit family butler and porter for the District Council, who remains behind to bear the brunt of Andrei's frustration at having to sign official papers when his mind is preoccupied with other sorrows. Deaf and in his second childhood, addicted to trivial stories culled from newspapers, Ferapont epitomizes the impotence characteristic of the other antagonists.

The remaining two characters to be considered in an action-dialectic of *The Three Sisters* are Lieutenants Fedotik and Roday, who, though they do not affect the action in any critical manner, nevertheless help to round out the collective image of the protagonists. Their martial aspect, their overbearing cordiality, and the almost rude nonchalance with which they take leave of the family whose hospitality they have accepted so complacently, add to the impression of assurance and callousness generated by those other characters who manage to obtain their desires in this drama's rather secretive argument. The emblematic significance of such minor figures is often ignored because of their relative unimportance to the plot, yet their mannerisms often succinctly abstract the chief attributes of the camps to which they belong. Thus, though they function rather more as images than as actors, Fedotik and Roday, like their opposite number, Ferapont, provide important signposts to a qualitative description of the drama's major colliding forces.

A schematic representation of these forces in *The Three Sisters* will now permit us to observe the metastatic-positive description to which our protocols have led, revealing five parallel triangles. Again, brackets enclose the names of hidden players, while an "X" denotes characters who die before or after the commencement of dramatic time proper:

ACTION-CHART: Anton Chekhov, *The Three Sisters*

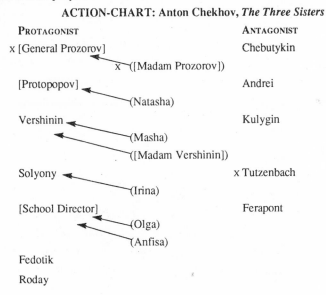

PROTAGONIST	ANTAGONIST
x [General Prozorov]	Chebutykin
x ([Madam Prozorov])	
[Protopopov]	Andrei
(Natasha)	
Vershinin	Kulygin
(Masha)	
([Madam Vershinin])	
Solyony	x Tutzenbach
(Irina)	
[School Director]	Ferapont
(Olga)	
(Anfisa)	
Fedotik	
Roday	

Having thus described the action of *The Three Sisters* in terms of the metastatic-positive dynamic, with all female characters including Natasha occupying the mobile apex unit, we are now obliged to examine the drama's imagery in order to test whether our conclusions at the primary level are validated by figurative consonances within the individual functional units, and also by obvious dissonances between the primary poles of action (Theorem 12).

(2) *Dialectic of Imagery*:

Consisting initially of three functional units, the metastatic-positive structure also develops three discrete clusters of imagery. The additional cluster lending emotional resonance to the apex unit is usually less elaborate than those formed around the dialectically opposed camps, and it often contains several prominent images either duplicating or in clear symbiosis with their partners in the protagonists' unit. Such images connecting the contested figures with those who eventually possess or control them may assume forms as uncomplicated as youthful appearance, physical beauty, and mutual expressions of merriment; however, the more guarded ironic triangle often develops around its apex characters a larger image-cluster whose rhetorical harmonies with the protagonists are less apparent. *The Three Sisters* falls into the latter category, with scores of figures, both scenic and verbal, surrounding its seven apex females, as well as a correspondingly large body of imagery qualifying and setting apart the victors from the vanquished. In discussing these figures, I shall deal first with the dialectically opposed camps, then with the apex unit and its special symbolic linkage to the protagonists.

The most pronounced figurative distinction which Chekhov draws between the contending male characters in *The Three Sisters* are those of relative physical appearance and vitality; for on the dominant side of the conflict the author creates portraits of fitness and vigor, while on the recessive side he limns the features of flaccidity and lassitude. At the head of the protagonists' unit, General Prozorov had commanded a thousand men, maintained for many years a large household in the absence of his wife, and, with martial discipline, trained his children to arise promptly at seven in the morning and to apply themselves diligently to their studies (238). The offstage Protopopov (the "Pro-ov" ablaut connects him with the general) conducts the business of the district as Chairman of the Local Board, sending official papers for Andrei to sign, while using his spare evenings to collect Natasha in his troika. Battery Commander Vershinin, though older looking than when he used to visit the Prozorov house in Moscow (where he was known as "the lovelorn major"), is still attractive enough to engage Masha's sensuality and at the same time retain his wife's desperate love. When fire breaks out in the town, Vershinin rushes to save his children and home from the flames. Returning in muddy uniform to the sleepy Prozorov house, he praises the army's part in putting out the fire:

> If it weren't for the soldiers, the whole town would have burnt down.
> Brave boys. *Rubs his hands with pleasure* Salt of the earth! Ah what a fine
> lot! (283).

Vershinin's enthusiasm for philosophical conversation, the countryside, the beautiful Prozorov home, and especially for Masha, defines a vital, passionate nature, exuding charm.

"Charm" is not quite the correct word for Vershinin's comrade in arms, Staff Captain Solyony, whose boorish, non-sequitur remarks frighten Irina and cause embarrassing conversational pauses; yet, for all his talk about the table wine's being made of cockroaches, there is something oddly romantic about this figure who claims to possess the looks and temperament of the poet Lermontov, and who splashes cologne on his hands because, like King Lear, he senses that they smell of mortality (271, 302). Solyony lifts weights, has fought two duels, and says that he is awkward in company only because he prefers to converse tête-à-tête—an assertion he proves in a startling manner during his first moment alone with Irina, to whom he apologizes for his unrestrained comments earlier, then suddenly and passionately declares his infinite love. After Irina's cold rebuff, Solyony concedes that "love cannot be forced," yet swears that "there must be no happy rivals"—an oath he keeps by shooting Baron Tutzenbach (271, 275–6). Solyony's last line in the play, a quotation from Lermontov, sums up his restive nature:

> And he, rebellious, seeks the storm,
> As if in storms lay peace (302).

The restlessness and vitality of the major protagonists are epitomized in the lesser figures of Lieutenants Fedotik and Roday. Bubbling with enthusiasm, these two chatter loudly, sing and play the guitar for the company's enjoyment, and bustle around taking photographs of their hosts. Fedotik, who volunteers time from his military duties in order to teach gymnastics at the local high school, also takes an almost fatherly interest in Irina, to whom he brings flowers, crayons, a penknife, and, at parting, a notebook and pencil.

In contrast to such images of robust health and activity, the overwhelming impression created by the drama's antagonists is one of unprepossessing appearance and helpless passivity. Thus, Chebutykin, sixty years old and entering a premature second childhood, looks forward to retiring from the army within a year and returning to live again near the three sisters. A boarder in the Prozorov house, he has not paid his rent for eight months—though he joins his seemingly unconcerned landlord, Andrei, for the occasional night of gaming at the club. For the rest, Chebutykin spends his time cutting trivial stories from newspapers, napping, sitting in the garden easy chair, and combing his beard. During the town's fire he is too drunk to attend the victims; instead he laments his ignorance of medicine and general failure in life:

> Last Wednesday I treated a woman in Zasyp—she died, and it's my fault
> she died. Yes . . . I used to know a thing or two twenty-five years ago,
> and now I remember nothing. Nothing. Maybe I'm not even a man, and
> am just pretending I have arms, legs, and a head; maybe I don't even exist,
> and only imagine I'm walking about, eating, sleeping. [*Weeps*] Oh, if only
> I didn't exist! (282).

Shortly after this maudlin speech Chebutykin drops and smashes a clock that belonged to Madam Prozorov, the only woman he ever loved.

Broken hopes and an almost masochistic acceptance of failure also plague Andrei Prozorov, the general's son who once dreamt of being a university professor in Moscow and scholar of national repute. But within a year of his father's death Andrei (like Hamlet) has grown stout and short-winded, and has taken to reading until four in the morning. During the days he potters around making small picture frames and other wooden knick-knacks; when not reading nights, he passes his time at the club amassing gambling debts that eventually climb to 35,000 rubles. Although Irina blames her brother's marriage to Natasha for having caused him to grow shallow, dull, and prematurely old, nothing he does in Act One (before his marriage) suggests that Andrei required any particular assistance in developing these attributes. The fact is that he allows life to live him, passively tolerating both his wife's high-handed management of the household and her affair with Protopopov, just as he comes to believe that serving under this same Protopopov on the District Board is a task "as high and as sacred as serving science" (293). Observing Andrei wheeling the baby carriage in the garden, Masha strikes a bathetic note:

> Look at Andrei, our little brother . . . All our hopes vanished. Thousands
> of people raised the bell, a great deal of money and effort were expended,

and suddenly it fell and was shattered. All at once, without rhyme or
reason. That's how it was with Andrei . . . (300).

Yet Masha has failed to observe that Andrei's downfall was neither sudden nor
without reason: laziness and timidity of spirit have rendered him a complacent victim
of fate's vagaries, a person who plays the fiddle in his bedroom while the town burns.

Resignation and passivity are also the keynotes of Irina's ill-fated admirer and
eventual fiancé, Baron Tutzenbach-Krone-Altshauser. Born in "cold, idle Petersburg" where he was shielded from work and had a footman to pull off his boots,
Tutzenbach nevertheless lauds the virtues of hard work and envies common laborers
because they must be able to fall exhausted into bed and sleep soundly. Resigning his
army commission in order to live near Irina and wait for ten or twenty years if
necessary for her to marry him, he dreams of working in some unspecified capacity
at a brick factory, an occupation he claims will make them both rich and happy. Yet
despite his apparently sanguine hopes, the baron is at bottom a pessimist who asserts
that life will never change for the better, and who, when asked by Masha if there is
some meaning to life, responds, "A meaning . . . Look, it's snowing. What meaning
has that?" (266). Embarrassed as much by his German ancestry as by his homely
appearance (especially in his latterly acquired civilian clothes), Tutzenbach yet
laments that he cannot discover the key to the "locked piano" of Irina's soul—an echo
of Andrei's having lost his keys to the drawing room liquor cupboard, and a clear
allusion of both men's failure in love. Like Andrei, the baron possesses some musical
talent and fancies arranging a benefit concert for the victims of the fire, but we do not
learn whether it is ever presented. Before his fatal duel with Solyony, Tutzenbach
anticipates his ultimate passivity in a curious observation to Irina: "There's a tree
that's dead, but it goes on swaying in the wind with the others. So it seems to me that
if I die, I'll still have a part in life, one way or another" (304).

The homeliness, passivity, and self-abnegation of the drama's antagonists are
summed up with embarrassing candor in Chekhov's portrait of Masha's husband,
Fyodor Kulygin, who describes himself as "a plain, honest man . . . *Omnia mea mecum
porto* [What I have I carry with me]"—a reference to the book learning of which he
is excessively vain. Indeed, his whole life centers around two things: his high school
teaching career and his unfaithful wife. For when not occupied with faculty meetings,
organized walks for teachers and their families, or evenings at the home of the School
Director (whom he mentions on every possible occasion), Kulygin runs to the

Prozorov house in craven attempts to draw Masha back to home and hearth. Never missing an opportunity to lavish questionable praise upon his adored spouse, he exclaims for everyone to hear that with Masha he is "content, content, content!" To which she responds, "Bored, bored, bored," and then sends him home alone (288). But Masha's scorn seems lost on this self-complacent mediocrity, and in the last act we see the cuckold pedagogue proudly wearing his Order of Stanislaus, second degree, for services rendered to education, openly praising his own cleverness, and looking especially ugly without the mustache he has shaved off, "*modus vivendi*," in imitation of the School Director—"Nobody likes it, but I don't care. I am content. With a mustache or without a mustache, I am equally content . . ." (297).

Turning from the major competitors to the apex females of *The Three Sisters*, we are confronted once again with an almost Byzantine profusion of figurative detail, and a mosaic in which certain elements appear at first glance to set Andrei's wife at some distance from her sisters-in-law. Natasha's unfashionable, gaudy clothes, including the pink dress with the green sash that so shocks Olga; her officious management of a household otherwise dedicated to genteel aimlessness; her annoying solicitude for the comfort of little Bobik and Sofochka; her impatience with the decrepit nurse, Anfisa; her awkward attempts to put on aristocratic airs; and her apparent lack of interest in the cultural attractions of Moscow—these and other touches of portraiture lend some credence to Andrei's description of his spouse as "a small, blind, sort of thick-skinned animal" (301). Yet if Natasha truly belongs in the play's metastatic unit, we should nevertheless be able to detect more consonance than discord between her features and those of the other females in the cast, just as we should expect Andrei's highly unflattering description of her to apply in some inadvertent way to Masha, Olga, and Irina as well. Indeed, a most complicated network of images—including the town, countryside, house, garden, and especially the fire—links Natasha most firmly to the other women, whose fate, happy or otherwise, so largely depends upon the whims and desires of men in whom the capacity for action has been inhibited neither by the workings of conscience nor the yearning for domestic security.

As in so many other love triangles, whether comedic or ironic, the contested females of *The Three Sisters* are symbolically equated with property—above all with the lovely Prozorov house, its flower bedecked drawing room, and its sunny garden giving onto the river, beyond which lies the crown forest. One way or another the drama's protagonists take possession of this estate, using or abusing its comforts as cavalierly as they accept the favors of its female inhabitants. The ancient allegory of the lady of the castle and garden here receives an ironic twist, for the fortress of virtue now easily yields to the siege, inviting its ramparts to be stormed and its flowers crushed—the latter quite literally mowed down by the phallic fire engines that must cross the garden in order to pump water from the river. The knight charged with defending the castle has instead mortgaged it, while his comrades hasten to exchange battle dress for civilian clothes. "Our garden's like a public thoroughfare," observes Irina, "People keep walking and driving through it" (306).

The emotional malaise that renders vulnerable not only the three Prozorov sisters but also Natasha and Madam Vershinin is shown most clearly to have its origin in sexual hysteria—a state most appropriately symbolized by the fire which erupts in the third act, and which brings all the play's living females together under the same roof to join their laments with the other, unseen victims of the conflagration. The cries of "To Moscow," the complaints about boredom, the alternate fits of weeping and laughter, the rude barking at the old nursemaid and angry shouting downstairs, the romantic expressions of longing for a more perfect world and meaningful work, the intimations of madness and threats of suicide—all these various signs of frustrated sensuality Chekhov delineates with his physician's eye for such matters, employing the most common symbol of passion as an enveloping metaphor. For it is in Olga's and Irina's bedroom, warmed by the lurid glow of the conflagration outside, that the sexual issues left largely unspoken in the first two acts flare up as if by spontaneous combustion. The drunken Chebutykin blurts out what everyone has been elaborately ignoring, namely, that Natasha is conducting an affair with Protopopov; Irina admits that she became engaged to the baron only after having given up all hope of finding a "true love" in Moscow; Olga quietly reveals that she would marry any decent man who asked her, even if he were old; Masha at last confesses her love for Vershinin, much to Olga's distress; and the offstage Madam Vershinin is suddenly heard downstairs yelling furiously at her wayward husband (285, 290–1).

In the midst of these revelations and recriminations Natasha silently crosses the bedroom carrying a lighted candle—just as she had done in Act Two on the night of her tryst with Protopopov. "She goes around looking as if it were she who started the fire," observes the startled Masha, expressing a truth almost more literal than figurative (290). For it is Natasha who kindles the flame that eventually spreads to consume, in varying degrees, the drama's other apex figures; she who sets the example for Masha's infidelity (the "Masha–Natasha" ablaut cannot be ignored here, any more than Natasha's entirely inappropriate "Maiden's Prayer" song and Masha's transformation of Pushkin's evocative "A green oak by a curved seashore" into "A green cat . . ."). In a less direct way Natasha also causes Irina to place Baron Tutzenbach in mortal danger, for the neglected Andrei's increasing need for the consolations of cards and drink forces his sister to despair of the family's ever getting to Moscow where she might meet the man of her dreams. Finally, it is Natasha who, through Protopopov, induces the School Director to draw the practical Olga away, leaving Andrei to shift distractedly for himself (281).

Yet those commentators who see Natasha as the principal engineer of the Prozorovs' so-called downfall neglect several critical facts, foremost among them the fickleness and vulnerability of all the drama's females, whose fates are uniformly dominated by self-seeking men. Moreover, the internal conflict between Natasha and Andrei's three sisters—a struggle based less upon deeds than upon secondary differences of class and sensibility (Theorems 3, 5)—serves to disguise the essentially selfish nature of the Prozorov women themselves. For the fire with which they burn is also that of the flesh, not the spirit. Class snobbery aside, little moral distinction can be drawn between the infidelities of Natasha and Masha, except that the latter conducts her affair with a man who is married. Or between Natasha's selfishness and Irina's shocking disregard both for Tutzenbach's feelings and his physical safety. Or, for that matter, between Natasha's officious practicality and Olga's abandonment of the household for a government appointment once it becomes apparent to her that none of its military guests will pay her court.

The essential similarity of the play's apex females receives imagistic emphasis through the repetition, in different keys, of several parallel thematic strands: (1) Like their brother, Andrei, both Irina and Masha displace their frustration by snapping angrily at the nursemaid, Anfisa; yet when Natasha yells at the old woman and threatens to sack her, Olga protests that she cannot bear such insensitivity. (2) In Act One Olga rudely crcizes the bright green sash worn by Natasha, although the latter's hurt reply reveals that she is probably color–blind; however, in Act Four Natasha just as rudely tells Irina that her sash is in poor taste because its color is too dull. (3) While the Prozorov sisters take somewhat ambivalent pride in their knowledge of foreign languages, Natasha employs a liberal sprinkling of French when scolding Andrei—an echo of Masha's conjugating the Latin verb "to love" in irritable response to her husband's protestations of devotion. (4) Both Natasha and Masha play the piano; Irina's soul is compared to a locked piano. (5) Natasha's constant fretting about the health of her two children finds its counterpart in the offstage Madam Vershinin's worry about her two sickly daughters. (6) Kulygin observes that Irina has come to resemble Masha physically, wearing the same pensive expression. (7) At the end of the play Natasha threatens to cut down the avenue of fir trees leading to the garden and to replace them everywhere with fragrant flowers—a motif hearkening back to Act One and the drawing room bedecked with cut flowers in honor of Irina's nameday. Examples of such figurative linkages could be easily expanded; however, my task is now to show, briefly, the metastatic connection between these images, taken as a rhetorical unit, and those qualifying the drama's protagonists.

The figurative consonance between the apex females of *The Three Sisters* and the play's victors is nowhere as direct and apparent as that found in most purely comedic love triangles. In fact, at first glance Chekhov's women here seem to exhibit more rhetorical affinity with the rather feminized males whom they betray or otherwise disappoint than with the cavalier "heroes" who take advantage of their vulnerability. Yet it is this very vulnerability of the apex figures—their childishness and irritability, their longing for romance and sexual fulfillment, for more "civilized" surroundings, for a diversion from the routine of provincial life, for a sense of purpose that has previously evaded them—that makes these women easy prey for males of energetic, passionate, and unprincipled disposition. This situation provides the drama's major rhetorical irony; for it is the figurative disassociation, the difference in romantic sensibility between the apex characters and the protagonists, that permits the latter to storm the fortress of dullness to which the women have been consigned. The entrance of this leitmotif occurs when the wind wails drearily in the chimney, reminding the sisters of their dead but not much-lamented father, and of their short-lived mother. As in so many other ironic love triangles, the Oedipal motif of ambivalence towards the attractive but at the same time threatening father, the abused mother, and the impotent son here receives characteristic elaboration at the levels both of action and imagery.

Our image-chart—this time containing an extra, central column for the apex females—will provide a more immediate glimpse of the consonance within each functional unit, the rhetorical opposition between the major poles of action, and also the ironic relation by disrelationship, the vacuum that draws the apex unit into that of the protagonists. Once again, the separate images are listed character by character, and mirror images in the primary camps (Theorem 11) are number-keyed for quick cross-reference.

IMAGE CHART: Chekhov, *The Three Sisters:*

PROTAGONIST

[GENERAL PROZOROV]: Clock striking when he died; Wind wailing in chimney at death; Few people walking behind coffin in rain & snow; Old Basmanaya St. in Moscow; Salute fired at cemetery; Regimental commander; Trained children to rise at 7.00 am; Made them study foreign languages, and "oppressed" them with education.

[PROTOPOPOV]: Cake as present for Irina; Chairman of District Council; Collecting Natasha in troika at night; Sitting in drawing room of Prozorov house (unseen from outside); Sending official papers for Andrei to sign (1); Attending to little Sofia inside house (2).

VERSHININ: Recalls General Prozorov's face as plain as life; Studied in Moscow for a long time; Visited the Prozorov house in Moscow; "The love-lorn major" (3); Looks much older now; Also lived in Old Basmanaya St. in Moscow; Krasny Bar-

→ **APEX**

The town; the woods; the Crown Forest; the river; The Prozorov House; Drawing room with flowers; Garden with avenue of fir trees; Reception room; The fire in the town.

[MADAM PROZOROV]: Buried in Moscow; Died when the children were very young.

NATASHA: Out of style, "gaudy" clothes; Pink dress with green sash; Adjusting dress; Color blind; Crying; Wearing dressing gown; Carrying candle on night of tryst with Protopopov; Worrying about little Bobik's fever;

"Good morning, Bobik"; French phrases; Bobik looking ill; Bobik smiling; Sending guests away from party; Bobik & Sofia fast asleep; Afraid of influenza; Di-

ANTAGONIST

CHEBUTYKIN: Old army doctor; Reading newspapers; Napthelene as cure for falling hair; Silver samovar as present to Irina; Combing beard; Gambling at the club with Andrei; Rent unpaid for 8 months; French phrase; Balzac married in Berdichev; Making notes; Smallpox in Tsitsikar; "Like a little boy, always pratling nonsense"; Violin music offstage; "Chekhartma" (a lamb dish)

(6); Song & dances; "Little latticewood porch;" Terribly drunk during fire; Washing hands; His fault a woman patient died; Weeping; Shakespeare & Voltaire as subjects of ignorant chatter; Feeling crooked in soul; Dropping & smashing clock belonging to Madam Prozorov; "May I offer you a fig?" (song); "It doesn't matter" (constant refrain); Old-fashioned striking watch; Knocking on floor as signal; Sitting in garden easy chair; Military cap & stick; Attending at fatal duel; Forgetting to say good-bye to soldiers; Sound of harp & violin; "We merely

IMAGE CHART: Chekhov, *The Three Sisters* (cont.):

PROTAGONIST

racks by gloomy bridge with roaring water bench (Moscow); Knew Madam Prozorov; Rank of Battery Commander (Lt. Col.); Living in small apartments; Needs flowers in his life; Rubbing hands; Rushing to put out fire near his house; Drinking dark vodka (4); Thirst for tea; Hunger; Slamming door & leaving wife & children; Kissing Masha's hand; Didn't go to Academy; Read a great deal; "Work, work, work," if only for remote descendents; Life ever-changing; Prisoner noticing birds, but when released not noticing them (like Moscow); House nearly burned down; "If it weren't for the soldiers the whole town would have burned down"; Covered with dirt from putting out fire; Laughing & singing; "To love at every age we yield" (song); "Tram-tam-tam"; Thinks it odd that railway station is 10 versts away from town; Looking at watch; Looking around garden; Laughing; Lack of war has left great gap in life with nothing

APEX →

shevelled appearance; Gaining weight; Yelling at Anfisa; Moving Irina to Olga's room; Kissing Olga; Taking charge of the housekeeping & expenses; Stamping foot; Carrying lighted candle during fire in the town "as if she set the fire"; Looking to see if there is a fire in the house; "Maiden's Prayer"; "Small, blind animal"; Yelling at Andrei from window; Plans to cut down fir trees & plant flowers; Every morning in Olga's room.

MASHA: Black dress; Whistling tune softly; "A green oak by a curved seashore...upon that oak by a golden chain;"Humming; Laughing through tears; Knowledge of French, German, English; Striking plate with fork; Glancing at clock; Covering face with hands; Laughing; Lying on sofa; "It's a bore to live in this world,

ANTAGONIST

seem to exist"; One year before retirement & pension; Planning to retire near the Prozorovs; "Ta-ra-ra boom-de-ay... sit on the curb I may."

ANDREI: Violin music offstage; Grown stout; Playing violin; Wiping perspiration from face; Building picture frames & other things out of wood; "The lovelorn violinist" (3); "The lovelorn professor" (3); Reading til four a.m.; Translating book from English; Grown fat after father died, as if weight were removed; Dieting on sour milk for supper; Yawning; Reading by Natasha's candle; Reading old university lecture notes; Dreams of professorship in Moscow; Dreams of eating in Moscow restaurants; Stretching Gambling at the club; Losing 200 rubles; Reading book by candle; "Oh, my maplewood porch" (song); "One university in Moscow" (5); Shortness of breath; Mortgaging the house to the bank; Grown old living with Natasha; Playing the

PROTAGONIST

APEX

↑

ANTAGONIST

PROTAGONIST

to fill it; Long kiss with Masha.

SOLYONY: (="SALTY"); Lifting weights; Sprinkling chest & hands with scent from bottle; "He no sooner cried "Alack" than the bear was on his back"; "Peep, peep, peep"; Wine made of cockroaches; "Two universities in Moscow" (5); Drinking vodka; "Frying & eating" Little Bobik Sitting in corner, Eating all the candy; "I am strange, who is not strange! Benot angry, Aleko! Forget thy dreams..."; "I look like Lermontov"; Pouring scent on hands; "Cheremsha (an onion) (6); Rubbing forehead; Following Irina; Smoking up the drawing room; Only one of the battery leaving on the barge; Has fought two duels; Writes verse like Lermontov; Hands smell like corpse; "And he, rebellious, seeks the storm, as if in storms lay peace"; Sound of gunshot in distance.

[SCHOOL DIRECTOR]: "Most intelligent, but holds certain views"; Meetings; Social

---

APEX

friends" (Gogol); "I don't like civilians;" Yelling at Anfisa; Disarranging Irina's cards; Bed with Screen in Olga's room during fire; Taking pillow out of bedroom; Used to play piano well; Sitting down on sofa; "Ta-ra-ra"; "*Amo, amas, amamus, amatis, amant*;" "Bored, bored, bored"; Lying down; Sleeping, exhausted, during fire; Soul in torment; Clutching head; Taking Irina by hand; "I shall be like Gogol's madman...silence...silence"; "Going behind screen to kiss Irina; Walking in garden; "Is my man here" (quoting former cook); Seething inside; "My dear, happy birds (of passage)"; Sobbing; "Green cat" for "Green oak"; "It doesn't matter."

[MADAM VERSHININ]: Hair in braids like a girl; Sending letter to husband through daughter; Suicide attempts; Poison; Run-

---

ANTAGONIST

violin in his room while the town burns; Yelling at Ferapont; Losing little key to cupboard; Gambling debt of 35,000 rubles; Received no pension like his sisters; Wheeling baby carriage with Bobik outside (2); Compared to fallen & shattered church bell; Moved by Natasha to Irina's room to make place for Sofochka.

TUTZENBACH: Born in cold, idle Petersburg; Had footman to pull off boots; Shielded from work; Does not speak German though of German descent; "Triple-barreled name"; Greek Orthodox faith; Ten or twenty years of visiting Irina at her office; Knocking on floor for Chebutykin; Throwing up hands & laughing; Cranes flying, not knowing where or why; Meaning = It's snowing; "It doesn't matter"; Sending in resignation of army commission; Not good-looking; Drinking cognac with Solyony; Things changing but life remaining just the same; Desire to work in

IMAGE CHART: Chekhov, *The Three Sisters* (cont.):

evenings at his home.

FEDOTIK: Big basket of flowers as present to Irina; Other presents to her—Child's musical top; Crayons & penknife; Notebook; Teaching Irina another kind of patience; Toys for Bobik; "You won't go to Moscow" (to Irina upon playing unlucky card); Taking snapshots of the family; Photography equipment; Singing softly to guitar; Field uniform; "Goodbye, trees"; Teaching gymnastics at local high school on off-duty hours.

RODAY & SOLDIERS: Putting out fire; Driving with firemen through garden to get pumps to the river; Singing; "Birds of passage"; Guitar; Speaking loudly with gutteral "R's"; Military March offstage; Shouting "goodbye!".

APEX

ning to Prozorov house for husband & leaving two daughters standing about in their underwear, Daughters in frail health, their faces full of alarm & entreaty during fire; Shouting in Prozorov kitchen.

IRINA: White dress; Name day the 5th of May—same day as father's death; Sailing before the wind with white birds overhead; Speaking French, German, English, & Italian; Feeling stifled like weeds; Crying; Working at telegraph office; Moved by Natasha to Olga's room to make nursery for Bobik; Exhaustion; Impolite remark to woman in mourning; Woebegone aspect; Face like little boy's; Work without poetry; Dreaming of Moscow every night; Feeling "like a madwoman"; Playing patience; Losing at patience; Yelling for Anfisa; Sending masquers

order to fall exhausted into bed; Envies workmen who sleep soundly; Playing waltzes ("trash") on piano; "Oh, my maplewood porch" (song); Kissing Andrei; Getting drunk; From military uniform to civilian suit; Plan to arrange benefit concert for fire victims; Falling asleep during fire; Plans to work at brick factory; Kissing Irina's hands; Weeping; Wearing straw hat; "Tomorrow we will be rich & happy"; Lost the key to the locked piano of Irina's soul; Compares himself to dead tree swaying in wind; Ordering coffee before duel.

KULYGIN: History of his high school as present to Irina (2nd time he has given it to her); Wrote history because he "had nothing better to do"; Napthaline & Persian powder as rug cleaner; Quoting Latin tags; Putting arm around Masha's waist; Leading organized walk for teachers & families; Looking at watch; "Thirteen at table"; Weeping; "Why bother?" Evening with

IMAGE CHART: Chekhov, *The Three Sisters* (cont.):

PROTAGONIST

APEX

away; Pacing room, deep in thought; "Amazing eyes"; Sobbing loudly; Bed with screen; Forgetting her Italian; Job in Town Council Office; Growing old & ugly; Brain drying up; Weeping quietly; Dream of meeting true love in Moscow; Sitting on bottom step of veranda; "Resembles Masha, same pensiveness"; Soul like fine piano with key lost; Sitting on swing; Observes that the garden is like a public thoroughfare; Giving money to street musicians; Weeping; Teaching job.

OLGA: Exercise books; Teaching at high school; Dark blue teacher's uniform; Grown thin; Crying; Speaks French, German, & English; Head aches; Giving away clothes to fire victims; "I'm tired"; I can hardly stand up"; Drinking water; Bed with screen; Tidying up dressing table; Would marry

ANTAGONIST

high school director (without Masha); School teacher's uniform; "I'm exhausted"; Hiding behind cupboard; Asking for time; Picking up pieces of clock Chebutykin has broken ; "I am content, content, content"; *Omnia mea mecum porto* ("What I have I carry with me"); Violin music offstage; Looking for Masha; Moustache cut off in imitation of school director; Order of Stanislaus, second class, around neck; Receives present of notebook from Roday; Child's false beard & moustache make him look like the German professor.

FERAPONT: Tattered old overcoat; Ears wrapped up; Hard of hearing; Was never in Moscow "by God's will"; Ridiculous stories about Moscow; "Moscow burned down in 1812 ("French were surprised")."

IMAGE CHART: Chekhov, _The Three Sisters_ (cont.):

APEX

even an old man; Going behind screen; Moving to government housing.

ANFISA: Rocking baby: Attending samovar; Laying head on Olga's breast; Sleeping; Pale, tired; "Just sits or sleeps"; Sings to accordian tune; Government apartment with whole room to herself; 80 years old.

(3) *Implicational Dialectic*

Having described the basic pattern of action and counteraction in *The Three Sisters* at the levels of both character and image, it is now possible to engage the protocols for reducing the separate economic units to their essential common attributes, and thus to render into abstract terms the internal conflict that has sought symbolic resolution in the drama's argument (Theorems 13–15). I shall deal first with the protagonists' and antagonists' units, which objectify the work's radical conflict, then with the metastatic unit, which reveals, though much more succinctly, a complex attitude toward women in general.

1. *Activity/Passivity*. Perhaps the most important of all the drama's implicational derivations, this antinomy best expresses the internal struggle at the core of Chekhov's fantasy. For, whatever other idiosyncrasies they exhibit, the play's dominant male characters seize their objectives by resolute action; they do not, like the antagonists, spend their time obsessively on vague hopes that never come to fruition. Written at a time when Chekhov was increasingly restricted in his own activities by the inroads of tuberculosis, yet conducting an affair that was to lead to marriage with the young actress, Olga Knipper, *The Three Sisters* clearly reflects the author's wish to regain that freedom of movement he had so cherished in earlier years, but which he knew would never again be his.[2]

2. *Vitality/Apathy*. "I'm going to work. If only for one day in my life, to work so that I can come home in the evening exhausted, fall into bed, and immediately go to sleep" (267). Baron Tutzenbach's enthusiasm for hard work betrays a deeper yearning for peace and rest—a desire which in his case reaches the ultimate consummation in death. The collective lethargy of the unit to which he belongs receives a fitting theme in Chebutykin's constant refrain, "Ta-ra-ra boom-de-ay, sit on the curb I may" (312). By contrast, Vershinin's gay aria, "To love at every age we yield, and fruitful are its pangs," speaks in general for the protagonists' lust for life in all its vagaries (286).

3. *Maturity/Immaturity*. Whether engaged in military or civic duties, district affairs or love affairs (the latter closely equated), the protagonists behave in what may be characterized broadly as an adult manner—even though certain negative conno-

---

[2]Ernest J. Simmons, *Chekhov: A Biography* (Chicago and London: University of Chicago Press, 1962), p. 491ff.

tations are here attached to that concept. Not so the antagonists, whose activities often appear more appropriate to the kindergarten. Extensive imagistic support lends emphasis to their puerility: pasting newspaper cuttings into notebooks, making wooden knickknacks, stamping on the floor to communicate, breaking "Mama's" china clock, quoting useless bits of information, wearing a false beard and mustache, being given a diet of curdled milk.

4. *Authority/Servility.* All of the play's victors, including the offstage Director of Schools, occupy official positions of authority which they exploit in order to control the destinies of the apex females. The position of the losers is in clear contrast: Tutzenbach resigns his commission so he can wait upon Irina, forever if necessary; Chebutykin looks forward to retiring from military service within a year and returning to live near the three sisters; Andrei sits a subordinate member of the District Council while his wife rules the household; Kulygin achieves minor distinction as a high school teacher by kissing the hems of the Director's garment.

5. *Dominance/Submission.* This antinomy is implicit in every dramatic collision, but requires explicit statement here because it describes an important practical result of the protagonists' authority as opposed to the antagonist's servility: for the former, various means of control over the apex females; for the latter, craven acquiescence in a hopeless situation. Indeed, Kulygin's plea to Masha might stand as a motto for the drama's entire recessive unit: "I am happy, no matter what . . . I don't complain, I make not a single reproach . . . and I won't say a single word to you, nor make any allusion . . ." (305).

6. *Assurance/Uncertainty.* VERSHININ: "I'm almost an old man now, but I know so little, oh, so little! Yet it seems to me that what is most important and real, I do know, firmly know." TUTZENBACH: ". . . in a million years, life will be just the same as it always was; it doesn't change, it remains constant, following its own laws, which do not concern us, or which, in any case, you will never get to know" (365–6). These contradictions as to the certainty of knowledge sum up in words what in deeds distinguishes the reserved confidence of the drama's victorious males from the insecurity and pessimism of their rivals.

7. *Competence/Incompetence.* By contrast with the professional capability of the dominant males, their opposite numbers appear mere bunglers. Chebutykin openly confesses his incompetence as a physician; Andrei never realizes his dream of teaching at a university; Tutzenbach gives up an army career for a business in which

he has no practical experience; and Kulygin's mannerisms reveal a teacher more popular with his superior than with his students. More importantly, each of the characters in the recessive group fails to gain, or to retain, the affection of the woman he loves.

8. *Independence/Depencency.* The military officers' departure at the end of the play is symbolically linked to the flight of happy birds of passage. But Chebutykin, who must stay on for another day and who hopes to return for good the following year, tells Irina that he feels "like a bird of passage that has grown old and cannot fly" (301). His simile applies as well to the other antagonists, whose real or premature old age has created in them a childish dependency on the familiar and the established. Yet even such local civilians as Protopopov and the School Director possess a freedom of action and elusiveness (enhanced by their failure to appear on stage) which connects them spiritually to their military doubles. Both Masha and Irina vocalize their identification with these independent birds of passage.

9. *Restiveness/Domesticity.* The protagonists distinguish themselves from their docile adversaries by a marked impatience of spirit. General Prozorov never remarries after his wife's death, yet sternly disciplines his children, and also, apparently, his subordinates; Protopopov flaunts social convention to seek physical and financial comforts from Natasha; Vershinin argues with his wife all morning, then finds solace in the evening with Masha; Solyony feels uneasy in company and absolutely refuses to brook either contradiction or rivalry in love; the School Director intimidates Kulygin by expressing "certain views"; while Fedotik and Roday run about as if life were an eternal party, and the latter thinks it quite a lark that his quarters have burned down in the fire.

10. *Extroversion/Introversion.* Though depicted as superficially social beings, the members of the recessive unit all betray an essential self-absorption and consequent lack of interest in the external events that engulf them. During the fire that provides the most important metaphor for these events, Andrei wanders off to his room and the solace of his violin; Chebutykin seeks escape in drink and self-pity; Kulygin goes meekly home without his wife; Tutzenbach falls asleep under Solyony's hostile gaze; and ancient Ferapont recalls helpfully that in 1812 Moscow burned down. All this while the soldiers under Vershinin's command assist the fire brigade (presumably answerable to Protopopov) in bringing the conflagration under control.

11. *Attentiveness/Distraction.* Natural extensions of the previous dichotomy, these attributes explain perhaps better than any others the protagonists' ability to control

the destiny of the apex females—a business in which the absent-minded antagonists fail miserably.

12. *Self-assertion/Self-abnegation.* The second term of this set describes the Hamletian manner in which the drama's losers openly express their sense of inadequacy. One has only to recall Chebutykin's confession of professional incompetence, Andrei's unfulfilled dream of fame as a scholar, Tutzenbach's admission of unsuitability as a soldier, or Kulygin's abject servility both to employer and wife. No such crippling self-doubts assail the protagonists, whose confidence expresses itself in action rather than self-pitying reverie.

13. *Attractiveness/Ugliness.* The good-looking officers, with their military bearing, dashing uniforms, and aura of adventure, carry irresistible allure for the drama's bored provincial females. As Masha expresses it in a more sublimated flutter, "the most decent, the most honorable and well-bred people, are all in the military" (261). As the highest district official, Protopopov would also wear the uniform of a civil servant; and it is clear that his allure for Natasha is primarily physical. The losers, on the other hand, are all unprepossessing: Chebutykin too old for romance; Andrei stout, short-winded, and prematurely old; Tutzenbach ugly by his own admission; Kulygin foolish looking, especially without his mustache. But beyond mere physical attractiveness, that which most contributes to the success of the dominant males is the unfailing allure of vitality and enthusiasm.

14. *Potency/Impotence.* Intended here in their widest sense, these terms inform an argument in which freedom of action, not only in regard to the female sex but also to the business of life in general, assumes a special urgency. Once an extremely active and adventurous young man with an eye for the ladies, Chekhov now consciously faced middle age and the prospect of marriage in full awareness that the illness he had so long ignored was incurable, and that it would increasingly restrict his powers of action, making him ever more dependent upon mother, sister, and wife-to-be.[3] The avoidance of such dependency, with its accompanying sense of general impotence, is clearly an urgent part of the drama's motivating wish—a wish objectified in the dynamism and virility of its protagonists.

15. *Unpredictability/Predictability.* Much of the dominant characters' hold over the apex females derives from the unexpected and often capricious nature of their

---

[3]Simmons, Chapter XXI.

actions—a mercurial quality enhanced by the ghostly or behind-the-scenes influence exerted by three members of this unit. Contrariwise, the doggedly faithful and longsuffering disposition of the losers is the very aspect of their character that most annoys the restless and fickle women whose love they seek to gain or retain.

16. *Lust/Love*. Chebutykin was "madly in love" with Madam Prozorov before her marriage, and remained a close friend of the family ever afterward; Andrei, though deeply disillusioned with marriage, persists in defending the wayward Natasha as a "fine, honest person, straightforward and noble," and demands that his sisters show respect for the woman he so clearly loved in Act One; Tutzenbach's adoration of Irina verges on the Renaissance ideal of eternal and hopeless devotion; Kulygin will forgive Masha's infidelity if only she will not leave him. By contrast, the drama's protagonists assume a much more cavalier attitude toward the women who attract them: Protopopov has no scruples against conducting an affair with Natasha even after she has broken off an engagement with him to marry the wealthy Andrei; Vershinin, though married and the father of two little girls, drives his wife to despair by chasing Masha; Solyony cares not a whit for Irina's peace of mind, permitting "no happy rivals" to disturb his peculiar sense of personal honor. Inferentially, one is led to wonder about the romantic proclivities of the late General Prozorov, and about the quality of his marriage to a lady whose short life is never once specifically characterized by those who have known her.

17. *Infidelity/Fidelity*. These attributes speak for themselves—except perhaps in the case of the two offstage protagonists, Sergei Prozorov and the School Director. Yet the general's unpopularity with his own children, and the gloomy memories they associate with him, cast vague shadows upon his moral character—as does the fact that very few people attended his funeral. Nor should one forget that the School Director's advancement of Olga to the position of headmistress has apparently been engineered by Natasha through Protopopov, in which case the Director has not necessarily adhered strictly to the duties of his office in making such an appointment.

18. *Selfishness/Generosity*. Paradigmatic of this dichotomy are the nameday gifts presented to Irina by the affluent Protopopov and the penurious Chebutykin: from the former a cake, from the latter a sterling silver samovar. More curious still is the fact that General Prozorov died on his daughter's nameday, May 5th, and that this anniversary brings to Irina happy thoughts, not of her father, but of "when Mama was still alive" (237).

19. *Impropriety/Propriety.* A passage from Simmons' biography of Chekhov provides a revealing sidelight on this dichotomy. Chekhov, it seems, "specifically instructed Stanislavsky that the officers must be played realistically and not as typical stage caricatures of the time, for he regarded them as enlightened bearers of culture in the provincial town that was the setting of *The Three Sisters*. And he insisted that his friend, Colonel Viktor Petrov, should attend rehearsals and check on all aspects of military dress and deportment. The colonel, it appears, took his assignment too literally; for in a letter to Chekhov he objected that to permit the married officer, Vershinin, to seduce another man's wife was an act of immorality outside the military code."[4]

20. *Callousness/Sensitivity.* One of the protagonists' secrets of success is their thick skin, a shield which seems to be as helpful to them in government service as in affairs of the heart. This callousness protects not only Vershinin but also the other dominant males from those attacks of self-doubt and guilt that beset the antagonists. It also permits the protagonists to use, abuse, and, if need be, abandon the apex females with utter nonchalance; for these men are secure enough not to be possessive, and selfish enough not to concern themselves with the effect of their actions on others. Solyony's killing of Baron Tutzenbach and Protopopov's open dalliance with Natasha are only the most blatant instances of this happy insensitivity. On the other side, the antagonists may be accused of silliness, triviality, and even negligence, but never of callousness.

21. *The Future/The Past.* While Vershinin argues for the slow but steady advancement of the human condition, his comrades at arms march in and out of the drama's provincial setting, blithely unconcerned about the anguish and devastation they have left behind, and no doubt looking forward to further adventures in other climes. But their unlucky rivals, who cannot face the present, stay behind to recall past hopes vanished; and one hears echoes of the dead baron's voice declaiming on the ultimate meaninglessness of existence.

22. *Affirmation/Negation.* VERSHININ: "Life is hard. It presents itself to many of us as desolate and hopeless, and yet, one must admit that it keeps getting clearer and easier, and the day is not far off when it will be wholly bright"(308). ANDREI: "Our town has been in existence now for two hundred years, there are a hundred thousand people in it, and not one who isn't exactly like all the others, not one saint,

---

[4]*Ibid.*, p. 521.

either in the past or in the present, not one scholar, not one artist, no one in the least remarkable who could inspire envy or a passionate desire to imitate him . . . They just eat, drink, sleep, and then die . . . the divine spark is extinguished in them, and they become the same pitiful, identical corpses as their fathers and mothers"(305).

23. *Hope/Despair.* As the military band plays gaily and the "birds of passage" fly away forever, Chebutykin returns from the fatal duel, sits down on a bench, and softly sings the refrain of a man without hope:

> "Ta ra-ra boom-de-ay, sit on the curb I may" . . . It doesn't matter! It
> doesn't matter! (312).

Just before starting work on *The Three Sisters* Chekhov expressed this internal cleavage between hope and despair in a letter to his fiancée from the health resort of Yalta:

> I'm torn up by the roots; I'm not living a full life; I don't drink although
> I like drink; I love excitement and have none of it; in brief, I'm now in the
> state of a transplanted tree, uncertain of whether to take root or begin to
> wither.[5]

Having abstracted twenty-three sets of antinomies to describe the dominant and recessive voices of the argument objectified in *The Three Sisters,* we must now turn to the object of that argument, namely, the apex females. These seven figures collectively represent not so much the drama's motivating wish as they do the fruits of its fulfillment with the triumph of the protagonists; for the metastatic unit always constitutes an ancillary feature of the central conflict between the major contestants. Rather like the football in a soccer match, the apex unit is the object whose control gauges the relative prowess of the combatants; but the focus of the game is more upon the two rival teams than upon the item over which their strengths are tested. Hence, both the comedic love triangle and its more ambiguous ironic variant require relatively few descriptive terms to qualify their apex units, despite the often detailed portraiture of the contested figures. Indeed, the average comedic love triangle usually demands no more than four or five abstractions to describe the essential common attributes of its apex females. That *The Three Sisters* requires as many as nine terms to qualify its metastatic unit testifies to Chekhov's pains at directing attention to the females of his drama, and thus to some degree away from the males whose contest

---

[5]*Ibid.*, p. 501.

betrays the fantasy's radical cleavage—its wishful and fearful impulses. Here, as elsewhere, the apex unit epitomizes an authorial attitude toward the feminine gender, while at the same time objectifying the sought-after prize to be obtained through the wishful triumph of the protagonists. One of the many ironies of the present fantasy is that the prize is clearly a dubious one, which must be abandoned as soon as possessed.

1. *Selfishness.* All of the onstage females are represented as fundamentally self-seeking, the true object of their desire in every case being a life filled with more social diversion and romance. Their inquiries about the meaning of existence seem to express a sublimated desire for "knowledge" less in the philosophical than the Biblical sense. As the spinster Olga expresses it at the play's conclusion, "If only we knew, if only we knew."

2. *Hysteria.* Uncontrollable outbursts of emotion, irrational fears (for instance, Natasha's constant fretting about the house's catching fire), alternate spells of laughter and weeping, headaches, exhaustion, lapses of memory, and autosuggestion (e.g., the almost magical power associated with repetition of the words "work" and "Moscow,")—these attributes, shared in whole or part by all the apex females, provides a fairly exact catalogue of the classic symptoms of hysteria, a condition whose sexual etiology is well documented.

3. *Restlessness.* Closely allied with the previous derivation, this quality describes what in Natasha and Masha expresses itself in illicit sexual adventure. In Irina and Olga it manifests itself through longings for more meaningful work, for romance, and its equivalent, Moscow.

4. *Resentment.* Dissatisfaction, extending to outright loathing for accustomed surroundings and companions, domestic or job routines, consumes the drama's apex figures. Natasha despises Andrei and ill conceals her contempt for her vaporish sisters-in-law; Masha likewise regards her husband with open contempt and returns Natasha's ill-will; both Irina and Olga are romantically frustrated, jealous of Masha, and dissatisfied with their jobs. Madam Vershinin threatens suicide as a punishment for her wayward husband.

5. *Vanity.* While Natasha awkwardly affects upper-class mannerisms, her sisters-in-law openly complain about the "stifling" of their presumed talents in an unappreciative provincial environment.

6. *Rudeness.* Olga's direct criticism of Natasha's attire and the latter's return compliment epitomize the unkindnesses, large and small, that issue from the women's irritability and frustrated self-esteem.

7. *Hypocrisy*. Though lauding the virtues of hard work, both Irina and Olga complain about their jobs and accept promotion with reluctance, while Irina's final encomium on the redemptive quality of industry comes just after she has lost her rich and titled fiancé. Masha complains of being upset by coarseness in others, yet proceeds to cuckold her husband and make contemptuous remarks about him in public. Natasha pleads her children's welfare as a means of gradually pushing Olga and Irina out of the house.

8. *Negligence*. The overwhelming desire for romantic and sexual fulfillment leads to various forms of dereliction, including outright physical betrayal (Natasha, Masha), disregard for the safety of fiancé or children (Irina, Madam Vershinin), and neglect of family welfare (all).

9. *Boredom*. Masha's "Bored, bored, bored" in response to her husband's "Content, content, content" summarizes the condition of these women, who lack the spiritual resources to discover excitement in their lives without help from sexually adventurous males.

With these derivations abstracting the essential common attritudes of the drama's metastatic unit, we may now proceed to construct an implicational chart showing the derivations for all three functional units. This will permit a more expeditious scansion of both dominant and recessive functions, as well as of the ancillary apex function that eventually "metastisizes" into the dominant unit:

IMPLICATIONAL CHART: Anton Chekhov, *The Three Sisters*:

DOMINANT FUNCTION	RECESSIVE FUNCTION
Activity	Passivity
Vitality	Apathy
Maturity	Immaturity
Authority	Servility
Dominance	Submission
Assurance	Uncertainty
Competence	Incompetence
Independence	Dependency
Restiveness	Domesticity
Extroversion	Introversion
Attentiveness	Distraction
Self-assertion	Self-abnegation

	METASTATIC FUNCTION	
Attractiveness		Ugliness
Potency		Impotence
Unpredictability		Predictability
Lust		Love
Infidelity		Fidelity
Selfishness		Generosity
Impropriety		Propriety
Callousness	Selfishness	Sensitivity
The Future	Hysteria	The Past
Affirmation	Restlessness	Negation
Hope	Resentment	Despair
	Vanity	
	Rudeness	
	Hypocrisy	
	Negligence	
	Boredom	

Scansion of the dominant and recessive functions of *The Three Sisters* permits one to apprehend the special, bitter-sweet character of Chekhov's irony; for both units contain an uncommon admixture of negative with positive qualities. On the dominant side, for instance, such attributes as vitality and maturity are inseparably linked with callousness and infidelity. On the recessive side, incompetence and apathy combine in an equally curious way with fidelity and generosity. This high degree of ambivalence at both poles of the dialectic creates that especially poignant, elusive, and oddly frustrating tone summed up in the adjective "Chekhovian." Nor is the sense of ambivalence lessened in *The Three Sisters* by the symbiosis of entirely negative qualities in the metastatic function with similar or identical attributes in the dominant. The author's cynical attitude toward the feminine gender thus finds wishful reinforcement through the victory of males quite unconcerned about the ultimate happiness of the women they dominate for entirely selfish purposes, while the obvious fear of dependency upon beings perceived to be self-centered and negligent finds expression in the fate of the abandoned antagonists. This fear of vulnerability and neglect, together with its complementary wish to dominate, are perhaps understandable, given the author's physical and domestic situation at the time of composition.

It is important in concluding to repeat our opening caveat, namely, that *The Three*

Sisters presents many more obstacles to structural analysis than the vast majority of metastatic-positive actions. The old formula of "boy-meets-girl-and-defeats-rival" does in fact continue to operate here as the underlying structural pattern, yet when irony infuses this dynamic we may expect to encounter obfuscatory tactics on the part of authors much more cautious about the implications of their dark love songs. In purely comedic instances of the form, however, triangular relationships will not be obscured by so many hidden players at the various corners; moreover, physical possession will coincide with marriage rather than abandonment, while the figurative correspondences between metastatic and dominant units will be more evident, and the contested characters will generate conventionally positive rather than negative attributes. Fortunately, the normal comedic love triangle is so ubiquitous that relief from the ambiguities of this form in its ironic mode is everywhere at hand; and one could do no better than to seek for this underlying pattern in such relatively uncomplicated works as Molière's *School for Wives* or Congreve's *Love for Love*.

FIFTH MODEL
METASTATIC-NEGATIVE

Definition. The second and less common of the two metastatic triangles reverses the dynamic of the first, for in this instance the contested apex figure is ultimately possessed by the antagonist or loser. This seemingly paradoxical situation arises from the fact that "victory" in such struggles for control invariably leads to disaster, often death, for the contested figure and sometimes also for his eventual captor, between whom there exists a common and sinister bond. Consequently, the protagonist's failure to gain or to retain possession of the apex figure assumes the character of an unwitting victory, a fateful release from bondage to unhealthy desires and attributes. Often the contested party's spouse or suitor, the protagonist offers a love that appears dull, even ridiculous by contrast to the seductive appeal of the unconventional antagonist. Further, by waging a minimal, often reluctant fight for control, the protagonist "modestly" veils both the fact of his ultimate victory and also those positive qualities that permit him to survive his contact with the apex character unscathed. In a sense it is the protagonist's very drabness and conventionality, his lack of excessive passion, his incapacity or unwillingness to carry the fight to the bitter end that save him from an emotionally corrosive and potentially destructive misalliance. Thus, as the more seductively appealing antagonist and apex figure go off arm in arm to their ruinous joint fate, the protagonist quietly, if a bit wistfully, picks up the pieces and resumes his most ordinary life—his apparent defeat appearing in retrospect a genuine victory.

Schematic. The apex figure "Z" is enclosed in parentheses to indicate his (her/ their) initially disengaged position between the parties contending for possession. An arrow traces the metastatic shift to the recessive unit, and the letter-symbol without parentheses indicates the contested character's position at the drama's conclusion:

PROTAGONIST   ANTAGONIST

X   Y

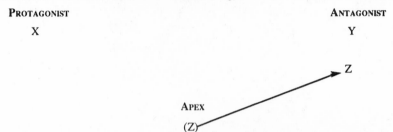

General. The metastatic-negative love triangle is essentially a cautionary morality which, unlike the similarly moralistic apostatic-negative dynamic, usually expresses itself rather in psychological than purely moral terms. From Maeterlinck's *Peleas and Melisande* to the Styron/Pakula screenplay, *Sophie's Choice*, the contested figure of this structure is regularly faced with the alternatives of a decent, safe, but apparently dull alliance on the one hand, and a terribly exciting but thoroughly destructive one on the other. Drawn by a flaw in his (or her) nature, the apex character opts for the unhealthy match, and thus for spiritual bondage, if not always outright physical destruction. The flaw in question is commonly an obsession or dependency with more or less obvious undertones of sexual taboo entailing a heavy burden of guilt. This obsession fixes upon the antagonist as the ideal object of its attachment; and consequently the apex character's negative movement often appears a foregone conclusion once the first electrically charged meeting (or reunion) with the antagonist has taken place.

It is precisely this electricity that often obscures the protagonist's dialectical victory—the fatal attraction between the contested figure and antagonist being so quintessentially dramatic that, by contrast, the true victor not only seems lackluster, he is also perceived (correctly) as a loser of the love contest from the beginning. For who would, on the face of it, prefer the drab Golaud to the romantic Peleas? Or the clean-cut and ordinary Stingo to the complex and urbane Nathan Landau? Usually only at the drama's conclusion, when the full consequences of the apex character's disastrous choice become evident, can the spectator apprehend the true horror of it. And even then the alternatives may appear somewhat of a Hobson's Choice.

Nevertheless, the moral unfolds clearly and simply: Better safe than sorry. The protagonist may not possess tremendous allure; yet one must concede that, given the options, his very drabness offers the key to survival. Hence, the metastatic-negative is at base a deeply conservative, one might even say (in view of the alternatives presented) reactionary, structure. There is always a certain sense here of indulging in a secret vice, letting it run its lurid course, and then violently rejecting it in favor of a reactively conventional morality.

Expressed otherwise, the metastatic-negative triangle is at once a structural and mythical reversal of the conventional love triangle. For instead of the hero's outwitting various abnormal "blocking characters" to lead his prize into the sunset of an implicitly happy future, the protagonist here only just manages to escape a potentially calamitous fate by losing his deeply flawed love (or friend) to a sinister rival. In view of this dark turn of the triangle, it is only natural that the metastatic-negative structure should be dominated by four appropriately picquant and often completely interwoven themes and archetypes: (1) the fatal attraction; (2) the female as siren, or the male as destructively alluring merman; (3) sexual obsession and/or perversion; and (4) regression to infantile dependency.

The fatal attraction motif finds its natural lodging in the metastatic-negative structure, which in fact seems to have evolved specifically to accommodate this cautionary version of the love triangle. Although the same myth may occasionally attach itself to other forms (as, for instance, *Antony and Cleopatra* does to the apostatic-positive, Wagner's *Flying Dutchman* to the metastatic-positive, or Shakespeare's *Romeo and Juliet* to the synthetic-realized), the fatal attraction theme most commonly plays itself out according to the dynamics of the present model. Alice Arden's calamitous love-pact with the depraved Mosbie in the anonymous Elizabethan tragedy *Arden of Feversham*, or Halvard Solness' headlong plunge from the steeple of his church to the feet of Hilde Wangel in Ibsen's *The Master Builder*—both of these actions follow the pattern in question as they work variations on the destructive consequences of a fundamentally unnatural love. For there is always something monstrous and preternatural about the antagonist, something of the siren whose call lures the apex character away from the safe, low ground of a conventional attachment and up to the vertiginous realm of the lovers' leap. And that leap is often quite literal, as in the case of Solness' fall from the church steeple, or of Peleas and Melisande's seeking eternal union in the abyss of a bottomless well. Similarly, in Ibsen's

Rosmersholm, John Rosmer and Rebecca West put the seal on their guilty alliance by leaping together off the footbridge into the millrace, just as in Truffaut's *Jules and Jim* (of which more presently) Catherine lures Jim into her automobile and then drives it off the ruined bridge.

Although the suicidal leap provides an exemplary end for one or both of the negative triangle's doomed lovers, other forms of self-destruction abound in this form. *Arden of Feversham* concludes with the execution of Alice and Mosbie, Ibsen's *Hedda Gabler* with the separate suicides of Loevborg and Hedda, Strindberg's *Miss Julie* with the mesmerized aristocrat's taking her own life on the orders of her hateful servant-lover, while Truffaut's *The Woman Next Door* ends with the murder of the alluring woman and the suicide of the man she had obsessed. Such catastrophes put a fitting period on misalliances fraught with guilt and doomed to failure in the conventional moral world of the living. Nor, in this structure, can the love-death be understood as an exemplary triumph of eros against all odds; for the bond between apex character and antagonist must be counted unnatural by almost any standards, while the actions of the protagonist, however ordinary and undramatic, come to be viewed in retrospect as essentially healthy and life-affirming.

When the primary antagonist of this structure is female, she usually appears in the guise of a siren, or of a black widow spider who poisons and devours any male unfortunate enough to welcome her corrosive love. The man-eating Salomé is virtually synonymous with this archetype; nor is it coincidental that Oscar Wilde's dramatization of her legend conforms to the metastatic-negative pattern. Yet perhaps even more chilling because so "ordinary" an instance of the *femme fatale* is Hedda Gabler, who maliciously plays on her former lover's lingering passion, his delicate sobriety, and his pride, destroying the manuscript of his masterpiece and finally handing her demoralized victim the pistol with which she expects him to do "the beautiful thing." In Wilder's structurally parallel film *Sunset Boulevard* the same archetype appears in the form of the aging but eternally beautiful film star Norma Desmond, who lures a young man into concubinage and then murders him when he belatedly realizes his error and attempts to run off with the female protagonist. As they fish her victim's body out of the swimming pool and the newsreel cameras roll, the demented actress fancies that everyone has come to see her act the part of Salomé.

When the negative triangle's principal antagonist is male, he appears in some appropriate archetypal variant, whether as merman, troll, or vampire, luring his victim to her doom through a conjunction of sexual and other, more preternatural powers of attraction. If Maeterlinck's Peleas provides an unusual instance of this figure in the romance mode, variants of the same archetype abound in more realistic, mythically decomposed forms, and can be seen in Mosbie's relation to Alice Arden, or Jean's to Miss Julie. Such male figures are the exact counterparts of Salomé, Hedda, and Norma Desmond: beings who use their dubious charms for the sadistic pleasure of possessing and then destroying those of the opposite sex gullible enough to fall under their spell.

The conjunction of the contested figure and the antagonist always violates some taboo, usually but not always a sexual one. Adultery is the most popular transgression in plays of this dynamic, and Truffaut's *The Woman Next Door* provides a flagrant example in the married man sexually involved with his neighbor. Yet even when authorial reticence or indirection leaves some doubt as to actual physical consummation, there still often remains a strong hint of impropriety, a suspicion of adultery or at least adulterous proclivities. Frequently, as in several of Ibsen's most famous dramas, this whiff of impropriety is rendered more pungent by the addition of some further disturbing evidence of misalliance, either by reason of disparity of age, social class, or moral background. Thus, Hilde Wangel of *The Master Builder* is a mere child by the side of her middle-aged victim. Similarly, Rebecca West, Hilde's counterpart in *Rosmersolm*, is not only much younger than John Rosmer, the author also hints that she may have been introduced by her father to a sort of knowledge far more liberal than that found in books. An unusual variation on the misalliance theme of this structure appears in Etore Scola's film *Passione D'Amore,* wherein the handsome young Captain is slowly mesmerized and finally won by his superior officer's alarmingly ugly daughter—with appropriately disastrous results.

What was formerly called "depravity" has now become the explicit subject of more recent stage and screen drama assuming the metastatic-negative structure. Whereas playwrights once confined themselves to oblique hints in order to suggest socially proscribed behavior, contemporary authors depict with increasing explicitness the saga of their contested characters' departure from propriety into the forbidden realms of incest, prostitution, drug-addiction, pedophilia, and sadomasochism. In this dynamic, at least, homosexuality and bi-sexuality are also represented as aberrant behaviors. When, on the contrary, contemporary dramatists depict homosexuality in a positive light, they instinctively turn to less inherently conservative structures. For the metastatic-negative, with its phobic stress on ultra-conventional proprieties, seizes upon the slightest deviance from the rigid norm as a fitting cause for the destruction of its mobile characters. Even a metastatic-negative screenplay such as *The Dresser*, which evinces a certain compassion for the homosexual, nevertheless shows the famous Shakespearean actor's demise to have resulted in large part from his attachment to the effete Norman and the latter's fanatical "the show must go on" attitude.

Occasionally the negative triangle depicts its apex character not so much in the light of victim as of co-conspirator and equal partner in vice with the antagonist. In Pinter's *The Homecoming*, for example, when Ruth abandons her university professor husband, Teddy, and their three children to become a prostitute working for her husband's depraved father and brothers, her actions from the outset are clearly provocative and deliberate—fully in accord with the sordid past from which Teddy thought he had rescued her. Teddy is thus well rid of Ruth; and, typical of the protagonists of this structure, he wages a minimal fight for control, eventually leaving his wife to her natural proclivities and returning to America with their three boys and barely a trace of regret. Elsewhere, however, Pinter reverts to the more usual method of depicting the contested figure as a passive and weak victim. Thus, his screenplay *The Servant* shows the slothful and dependent Tony gradually drawn away from the elegant milieu of his fiancée, Susan Stewart, and into the debauched world of "Basher" Barrett, with its moral "muck and slime." Similarly, if somewhat more gently, Williams' *Night of the Iguana* recounts the tale of the ex-priest, Shannon, torn between the ladylike, ethereal Hannah Jelkes and the crass, corporeal Maxine Faulk, and at last falling into the arms of Maxine, who, like Hedda Gabler, secures her victim by inducing him to revert to alcoholic drinking.

In extremely rare instances the apex figure of this dynamic appears in the light of an entirely innocent victim, free of any suggestion of sexual aberrance and doomed only through naïvety and vulnerability to circumstances. Little Hedwig in Ibsen's *The Wild Duck* is the premiere example of the ingénue torn between positive and negative forces, only to sacrifice herself for the latter. The positive, life-affirming side of this triangle consists of Hedwig's natural parents, while the negative pull comes from the weak, idealistic Hjalmar, who, when confronted with the fact that he is not the girl's biological father, causes Hedwig to feel so guilty and unworthy that she commits suicide to atone for her "failure." But although Hedwig is clearly a lamb sacrificed on the altar of Hjalmar's cowardice, even she, with her pubescent vulnerability and affliction by a progressive blindness, bears symbolic traces of those weaknesses which in more mature incarnations of the apex character ripen into fullblown character flaws of less benign aspect.

Because the attraction that draws the contested figure into the arms of the antagonist is almost always unnatural and destructive, the loser of this contest comes to be seen as victorious by the very fact of his defeat. Thus abandoned (and often widowed), the protagonist of the negative triangle is released to get on with his perfectly ordinary life, freed from the distressing melodramatics of an unstable mate who could never have appreciated him or given him peace and security. Professor Tesman is obviously much better off without Hedda, who despises him for the humble and conscientious academic he is. And so, in losing Sophie, is Stingo released to enter manhood, free of a woman so irreparably scarred by the past that she cannot face the future.

Notwithstanding his release from an inappropriate mate, the protagonist of the negative triangle frequently retains some important memento of what was best in his lost love, a legacy symbolizing the life-affirming qualities of the struggle's survivor. Thus both Tesman and Mrs. Elvsted, scorned husband of Hedda and abandoned mistress of Loevberg, quietly join forces to collaborate on restoring Loevberg's manuscript propounding a new general theory of history. The same motif appears in *Sunset Boulevard*, whose protagonist, Betty Schaffer, retains the unfinished screenplay left behind by the doomed Joe Gillis. More often, however, the abandoned protagonist is left not with a brain-child but with a real one, the product of his former union and living symbol of the survivor's appropriateness as guardian of futurity. Teddy's three sons by Ruth in *The Homecoming* or Jules' daughter by Catherine in *Jules and Jim* thus serve at once to stress the self-effacing protagonist's fitness to be a parent and also to point up his quiet victory in an action previously focused on the other two points of the triangle because of their inherently more dramatic nature.

Irony is the dominant mode of metastatic-negative drama, partly because of the lurid relationship between the ill-fated lovers, but principally because the diffident protagonist is in fact the archetypal *eiron* who at first appears to be less than he really is, but later, when the dust has settled, turns out to be the protector of conventional wisdom and the embodiment of the life force which that wisdom seeks to protect. Even when they assume the romance mode, dramas of this sort preserve a highly ironic tone, leaving much doubt as to either the desirability or inevitability of the illicit lovers' union. Consequently, whenever a romantic love-death is represented as a triumph of eros or *agape* (as in Wagner's *The Flying Dutchman* and *Tristan and Isolde*), one can be certain that the drama in question conforms to some other structure; and, in fact, very few negative triangles do adopt the romance mode. Tragedy and comedy are also out of the question here, except in their most ironic phases, wherein the absurdity of the love union can appear as evident as its impropriety. The Italians seem most inclined to see the ridiculous side of the negative triangle and thus to play it in the mode of ironic comedy, as Pirandello does in *Rules of the Game,* or as Latuda somehow manages in his morbidly hilarious film *Come Have a Cup of Coffee With Me.*

However ironic in tone, metastatic-negative dramas are never ironic in the structural sense. For the dominant unit of the protagonist always requires a string of conventionally positive descriptive terms, while the recessive unit of the illicit lovers generates the appropriate row of dialectically opposed negatives. And although the contrastive pairings may vary from work to work, the following eleven sets recur with great regularity in dramas of this structure:

DOMINANT FUNCTION	RECESSIVE FUNCTION
Loyalty	Betrayal
Propriety	Impropriety
Temperance	Intemperance
Humility	Arrogance
Love	Lust/Hatred
Generosity	Selfishness
Caution	Rashness
Normality	Perversion
Health	Sickness
Sanity	Madness
Life	Death

These more or less built-in contrarieties, or their close equivalents, set the tone for works of this type, pointing up the psychologically conservative nature of metastatic-negative actions in general. In the following pages we shall see how most of these complementary opposites conspire with others of a more individual cast to create a unique specimen of this form.

ANALYSIS
François Truffaut, *Jules and Jim* (screenplay)[1]

(1) *Dialectic of Action*:

Adapted by Truffaut and Jean Gruault from the novel by Henri-Pierre Roché, *Jules and Jim* is the story of two friends who love the same woman. This basic situation, together with the fact that Jules and Jim fight on opposite sides of the Great War, might easily lead one to conclude that the screenplay forms a triangle in which the two male figures are the principal combatants, while Catherine, the woman they both love, belongs initially at the apex as the contested character. This impression of Catherine as dialectically disengaged at the outset is enhanced by her characterization as restless and flighty, for she transfers her attentions from Jim to Jules and back again with alarming suddenness, taking on several other lovers during the intermissions.

Despite these initial impressions, the inconstant Catherine does not really belong at the apex of this triangle as its mobile character. In fact it is she, the classic *femme fatale,* insatiably longing to possess men without ever truly loving them, who eventually draws Jim to his death. Like Hedda Gabler before her, Catherine thus functions as the principal antagonist of the piece. And like Hedda's victim Loevborg, Jim is the fly drawn into the spider's web, the collusive apex figure of the triangle. Nor does the analogy end here, for just as the victorious survivors of *Hedda Gabler* include both Professor Tesman and Loevberg's mistress Mrs. Elvsted, so the dominant unit of *Jules and Jim* comprises not only Catherine's tolerant husband Jules, but also Jim's longsuffering mistress Gilberte. Yet these structural similarities result less from any conscious borrowing than from simple engagement of the negative triangle, whose dynamic seems to require that when husband and wife are dialectically opposed, and the apex figure is male, then a female character must be placed alongside the husband to "compete" for the affection of the doomed male in the center. Otherwise Jules' loving-friendship for Jim is insufficient, short of undue homosexual implications, to form a proper triangle without Gilberte's presence in the dominant unit—just as Tesman's great respect for Loevborg's work will not suffice to complete a heterosexual triangle in *Hedda Gabler* in the absence of Mrs. Elvsted. Aside from these structural parallels, there are also certain similarities in portraiture

---

[1]François Truffaut, *Jules and Jim: A Film.* Translated from the French by Nicholas Fry (New York: Simon and Schuster, 1986). All page references are to this text.

between the male protagonists of the two dramas: Tesman, the humble medievalist, and Jules, the self-effacing entomologist, are both perceived by their mates to be dull fellows. But here again, no direct literary influence need account for such likenesses because, as we have indicated, the protagonist of this structure is ever modest and deferential, while his beloved always views him as lackluster by comparison to the third person of the triangle.

The first encounter of Jules and Jim with Catherine is heavily foreshadowed when, at the Paris apartment of their friend Albert, they are shown a magic lantern slide depicting an ancient piece of statuary. It is the crudely sculpted head of a woman with beautiful eyes and slightly disdainful lips forming a nevertheless "tranquil smile which fascinated them." (18) So captivated are Jules and Jim by this bewitching image that they decide forthwith to make a pilgrimage to the Adriatic isle where the figure has recently been unearthed:

> VOICE *off*: They stayed at the statue for an hour. It exceeded all their expectations, and they walked rapidly round and round it, without saying a word. *Circular tracking shot around the statue*. Not until the following day did they talk about it... *Pause*... Had they ever met that smile before? Never!... What would they do if they ever met it one day? They would follow it. (19)

And follow it they do when Catherine enters their life at a garden party, descending the courtyard steps in the company of two other young ladies, and throwing aside her black veil to reveal a face strikingly similar to that of the ancient figure:

> VOICE *off*: The French girl, Catherine, had the same smile as the statue on the island. Her nose, her mouth, her chin, her forehead, had the nobility of a certain province which she had once personified as a child in a religious festival. The occasion took on a dreamlike quality. (25)

Catherine thus first appears to Jules and Jim as a vision, as something almost preternatural, identified both with the alluring but disdainful smile of the ancient statue (of a goddess?) and also with the female personification of a province. Moreover, when she enters together with the two other women (who have no further business in the film), it is as if she were meant to symbolize one of the three Fates, identifiable by her black veil as Atropos, cutter of the thread of life. Catherine's archetypal aspect, together with the "dreamlike quality" of her first appearance, serve to point up the overwhelming impression she makes on the two friends and to hint darkly at the future of their relationship with her. But her unearthly power of attraction also alerts one to suspect that the action of this film will develop a negative triangle in which Catherine is to function as the destructively alluring primary antagonist.

Jules at once begins seeing Catherine alone, "and for his own ends." But when Jim and Jules next meet at the gymnasium, Jules invites his friend to come and visit them: "I've talked a lot about you . . . Catherine is very eager to know you better, but . . . *after some moments*, JULES *turns and looks gravely at* JIM . . . Not this one, Jim, eh?" (26) Truffaut underscores Jules' plea by adding it in French subtitle lest it be obscured by the actor Oscar Werner's foreign accent (for, despite his French name, Jules is German, while Jim, despite his English one, is French). Thus the ordinarily shy Jules shows concern that his friend, the handsome ladies' man, might steal Catherine away from him. This possessiveness appears particularly ironic considering Jules' opening line of the same scene just moments before, as the two gymnasts are first viewed chatting in the shower after their workout: ". . . Dann ist es wohl besser für diesen Mann, nicht zu heiraten (Then it's far better for this man not to get married)." (26) In the light of what follows, the man in question might as well be Jules himself.

That Catherine is not the sort of woman *any* man should consider marrying becomes clear in the next few scenes. The three friends have decided to go off to the seaside together; and when he comes by Catherine's apartment to collect her luggage, Jim finds her still in her nightdress, in the process of dumping a chamber pot full of letters onto the wooden floor. "I'm going to burn these lies," she announces. In the ensuing blaze her nightdress catches fire, and Jim must come to the rescue. As if this were not alarming enough, no sooner are the flames out than Catherine picks up a small bottle to pack in her luggage; and when Jim asks what it is, she replies, "Vitriol, to throw in the eyes of men who tell lies." He dissuades her from taking it along:

> Pan as CATHERINE *goes across the room and empties the bottle down the sink, seen in close-up with smoke rising from it.* (30)

The three friends go off to the seaside, and it is during this pleasant vacation that Jules decides to ask Catherine to marry him. But first he wants Jim's frank opinion of his plan, to which the latter responds cautiously:

> I wonder if she is really made for having a husband and children. I am afraid she will never be happy on this earth. She is an apparition for all to appreciate, perhaps, but not a woman for any one man. (32)

Jules chooses to ignore Jim's warning and proposes to Catherine a few days later. Her response is a tentative affirmative which delights Jules, despite its apparent confirmation of his friend's doubts. "You haven't had much to do with women," she says, "... But I have known a lot of men. We'll cancel each other out, so perhaps we would make a good couple." (33) Just how good a couple is darkly foreshadowed a little while later as the two men play at dominoes while Catherine fondles a bust of Napoleon:

> CATHERINE: When I was fifteen, I was in love with Napoleon . . . I
> dreamed that I met him in a lift. He made me pregnant and I never saw
> him again. Poor Napoleon . . . *She furtively embraces the statue* . . . When
> I was a little girl they taught me "Our Father which art in Heaven" and
> I thought it was "Our Father witch are in Heaven". . . and I imagined my
> father on a broomstick casting spells before the gates of paradise. (34)

Annoyed that she cannot elicit a laugh from the men, she suddenly asks someone to scratch her back. Jules replies facetiously, "Heaven scratches those who scratch themselves." Whereupon she crosses over to the table and "*slaps him hard*", with a "Take that!" Jules is at first stunned, then relieves the tension by bursting out laughing. Jim and Catherine follow suit, and the scene ends merrily.

The extremely problematical nature of any permanent alliance between Jules and Catherine is brought out a few scenes later as the three friends are returning from an evening at the theatre. While Catherine, within earshot, playfully teeters along a narrow parapet beside the Seine, Jules expounds to Jim on the subject of women. "The most important factor in any relationship is the fidelity of the woman," he asserts, adding, "The man's is of secondary importance." Then—whether seriously or just to tease Catherine we do not know—he launches into a series of deeply misogynistic quotations from Baudelaire:

> 'Woman is natural, therefore abominable'. . . What he says of a young girl
> is magnificent: 'Horror, monster, assassin of art, little fool, little slut'
> . . . 'The greatest imbecility coupled with the greatest depravation' . . .
> And this is admirable . . . 'I have always been astonished that women are
> allowed in churches. What can they have to say to God?' (37)

Catherine calls them a "pair of idiots," and when Jim disclaims agreement with Jules' secondhand opinions, she insists that he protest. As Jim utters the words "I protest," Catherine suddenly throws back her veil, stretches out her arms, and flings herself into the Seine. The two astonished men haul her out of the water, experiencing quite divergent reactions. Jules merely thinks she is "crazy." Jim is more deeply moved:

> VOICE *off*: The sight of Catherine plunging into the river made such a
> strong impression on Jim that he did a drawing of it the next day . . . though

> he never normally drew. He felt a surge of admiration for her and
> mentally threw her a kiss. He was quite calm; he imagined himself
> swimming with her . . . holding his breath really to frighten Jules . . . On
> the surface, Catherine's hat drifted along with the current.(38)

Jim has been attracted to Catherine all along, and the latter has given him several signs that she might prefer him to Jules; but hitherto Jim's loyalty to his best friend has prevented him from acting on his feelings. Besides, he has been involved in an apparently longstanding affair with a beautiful woman named Gilberte. However, after the incident of her plunge into the Seine, Catherine invites him to meet her at a café for a tête-à-tête, and Jim (with Jules' encouragement) agrees to see her alone. There is something she wants to ask him. Catherine arrives elegantly dressed, but almost an hour late. Jim has already left, thinking, "A woman like her could quite well have come and gone, not finding me here at one minute past seven." Later that night Jim receives a telephone call from Jules and Catherine, who announce that they are going back to Germany—to get married. (38–40) It almost seems as if Catherine were marrying Jules to spite Jim.

To say that the marriage of Jules and Catherine begins inauspiciously would be rank understatement. On the eve of the wedding Jules' mother deeply offends Catherine by an unspecified piece of "clumsy behavior," and Jules remains characteristically "passive," which from Catherine's perspective is "tantamount to condoning it." Her reaction, as she later describes it to Jim, is swift and brutal:

> I punished him immediately by taking up with an old lover, Harold . . .
> *Yes, lover*. That way I would be quits with Jules, when we were married;
> we could start again from scratch. (59)

The wedding takes place the next day. The bride and bridegroom settle into a chalet on the Rhine, and Jules' family moves permanently to the north of Germany—without bothering to leave Catherine, at least, a forwarding address.

Typical of the protagonists of negative triangles, Jules acquiesces in his mate's outrageous conduct—with the result that her fury only increases. Thus, despite Jules' saintly tolerance, and partly because of it, his marriage with Catherine becomes an essentially adversarial relationship. It is Jim who will be caught in the middle of this conflict and function as the contested character, torn on the one side by his loyalties to Jules and Gilberte and on the other by his fatal attraction to the treacherous Catherine.

Yet just as the plot of this novelistic screenplay begins to reveal its true form, the action is held in suspense by the outbreak of the First World War. Jules and Jim must fight on opposite sides of this conflict, but they do so as unwilling adversaries. While home on leave Jim tells Gilberte that sometimes in the trenches he is afraid of killing his friend. (46) Jules writes to Catherine that he is actually glad of having received orders transferring him to the Russian front, "for otherwise I would live in constant fear of killing Jim." (47) Meanwhile, throwing aside his Bohemian principles, Jim proposes marriage to Gilberte, who responds with characteristic deference, "You don't marry a woman to thank her for sending you parcels . . . Things are fine as they are, I assure you." "As you wish," replies Jim, adding, "Even so, I have the feeling that we shall grow old together."(46)

Jules writes passionate love-letters to Catherine from the front, and she finds that she loves him "more at a distance":

> Once again, I saw him with a halo. Our final misunderstanding, the real
> rupture, came on his first leave. I felt I was in the arms of a stranger . . .
> He went off again. Sabine was born nine months later. (59)

When Jules returns to Catherine at the end of the war, she confronts him with her altered feelings, and once again acts on them with extreme impetuosity. As she later explains to Jim:

> . . . I said to him: ' I have given you a daughter: that is enough for me. This
> chapter is closed. Let's sleep in separate rooms . . . I am taking back my
> liberty.' *A pause*. Do you remember our young friend, Fortunio?...He was
> there, free as air...and so was I. He was kind, he made a good partner.
> What a holiday we had! But he was too young; it wasn't a serious affair.
> And one fine day, to my surprise ...I found that I missed Jules's indulgent
> and leisurely ways. I felt drawn back to my daughter like a magnet. I was
> on the wrong track. So I left. I have only been back for three months. (59)

She has had other lovers as well, including Albert, the man who first showed Jules and Jim the statue, and who also fell in love with the woman it resembled. He has even asked Catherine to leave Jules, marry him, and bring her daughter along. (60)

Catherine reveals all this to Jim during his first visit to see them after the war; and although her news fills him with sadness for Jules, he finds himself unable to condemn Catherine because she is the sort of woman who "could have jumped at other men like she once jumped into the Seine."(55) In fact Jim finds Catherine every bit as alluring as he did the time she made that dramatic plunge. The very moment of their meeting at the railway station, he feels himself once again under the power of her spell; and later during his visit he senses (correctly) that she is trying to seduce him. He knows that he wants her, yet fights against the desire. (60)

It is Jules, ironically, who finally precipitates the affair between his wife and his best friend. Knowing that Catherine has contemplated leaving with Albert, and now sensing the electricity between her and Jim, he approaches the latter in desperation:

> Jim, Catherine has had enough of me. I'm terrified of losing her, that she'll go out of my life altogether. The last time I saw you side by side with Catherine, you were like a married couple. *A pause.* Jim, love her, marry her, and let me see her. I mean to say, if you love her, stop thinking of me as an obstacle. (71)

In relinquishing his wife without so much as a struggle, indeed in making her, as it were, a present to a man whose scruples would probably otherwise have kept him at a respectful distance, Jules reveals his kinship with the passive and deferential protagonists of all other negative triangles. Yet by allowing their wayward mates the freedom to seek presumably greener pastures, these most undemanding of lovers eventually succeed both in regaining peace of mind and also in securing themselves from the very real physical dangers attendant on consorting with sirens (or mermans).

On his part, Jim reveals a kinship with all other contested figures of this structure by betraying both friend and lover to follow the siren call wherever it should lead. Catherine knows that Jim has been in love with Gilberte and asks what she is like. "Sensible and patient. She says she will wait for me forever," he replies.

> CATHERINE: You still love her and she loves you. Don't make her suffer, Jim.
>
> *They stop underneath the balcony.* JIM *moves close to* CATHERINE *and kisses her on the back of the neck.*
>
> JIM: I feel the need for adventures, for risks. And then there is something new. I admire you Catherine, I enjoy coming to see you . . . I am afraid of forgetting about Jules.
>
> CATHERINE: You mustn't forget him, you must warn him. (70)

Jim's compulsion for adventures and risks marks him with the standard character flaw of his fictive breed. Furthermore, his refusal from the beginning to commit himself completely to Gilberte, nor yet to Catherine, indicates that he is dialectically disengaged at the outset, and that his eventual movement to Catherine will be from the apex of the triangle thus created. Any possibility of a full cross-dialectical shift, as in the strictly bi-polar apostatic-negative structure, must therefore be ruled out.

And so Catherine and Jim become lovers, consummating their union under the same roof with Jules:

> VOICE *off*: They did not talk, they reached out towards one another. Towards dawn they reached their goal. Catherine's expression was full

> of curiosity and an extraordinary jubilation ... When Jim got up, he was
> enslaved. Other women no longer existed for him. (72)

With Jules' consent, Jim moves into the chalet where he shares the small bedroom
with Catherine at night. During the days the three friends, together with little Sabine,
continue their usual pastimes as if nothing were altered. "In the village, down at the
bottom of the valley, the trio were known as 'the three lunatics,' but apart from that,
they were well liked."(74)

As might be expected, however, things do not continue long in this blissful state.
One day, on a whim, Catherine decides to seduce her husband. Jim is reading a book
downstairs and can clearly hear Jules saying, "No, no, no!" and Catherine insisting,
"Yes, yes, yes!" Jim begins to develop severe migraine headaches as well as general
fatigue. (75)

This situation is at last relieved when he is called by his newspaper back to Paris,
where he casually renews his affair with Gilberte, telling her at the same time that he
is planning to marry Catherine and wants to have children by her. Jules has agreed to
a quick divorce and has promised to help Jim find work in Germany so that the three
of them will not be separated. (76) Gilberte is jealous, but nevertheless accepts the
situation, even to the extent of carrying Jim's letters for Catherine to the post office.
On his part, Jim begins having qualms about the betrayal of lover and friend:

> VOICE *off*: Jim could no more leave Gilberte than Catherine could Jules.
> Jules must not suffer, nor must Gilberte. They were two different fruits from
> the past, which complemented and counterbalanced each other. (79)

This is a significant passage from a structural point of view, for in linking Jules and
Gilberte together as "complementary" aspects of Jim's past, and in pointing up their
essential similarity as loyal and longsuffering mates, it serves to indicate that both
characters are elements of the same functional unit.

Jim and Catherine continue to correspond throughout the winter. Jim agrees to
return to her, but tells her that he must delay his departure in order to say a few
farewells. Catherine, with some justice, takes this as a betrayal, and so she goes off
to say a farewell of her own—to her old lover, Albert. "I had to do it," she later tells
Jim. "Believe me, it's the only way we can start off on the right footing. Albert equals
Gilberte." (85) And she adds for good measure that now, if she becomes pregnant,
they will never know who the father is. Nonetheless, Catherine tries to conceive a
child by Jim, but without success. Every evening now becomes a nightmare for her:
"I keep thinking about this child we will never have. . . . I feel as if I'm trying to pass

an exam; I can't stand it any longer." (86) Jim tries to reassure her by saying that only their love matters, to which Catherine responds, "No. I count too, and I don't love so much. So let us make an honest attempt to do without each other. . . . Go on, go back to Gilberte, since she writes to you everyday." Jim complains that she is not being fair. "No doubt," she counters, "but I am a heartless person. That is why I don't love you and shall never love anyone."(86–7) The real problem for Catherine, as she explains it to her forbearing husband, is that Jim has not really broken off his affair with Gilberte. And so, after a final night together in a dreary hotel room, where their love is "like a burial, or as if they were already dead," Jim and Catherine part once more. (89)

Jim returns to Paris, and to his old love, Gilberte. He is certain that the affair with Catherine is over. But one day, while Gilberte is helping him nurse a flu, a letter arrives from Catherine announcing that she is pregnant and imploring him to come quickly. He responds that he is unfit for travel, and besides she is probably pregnant by someone else. Jim then receives a letter from Jules writing on Catherine's behalf and reiterating her plea for him to come right away. Catherine follows this up with a passionate appeal, assuring Jim of her love and claiming with absolute certainty that he is the father of her child. Jim can hold out no longer and prepares to leave for Germany. But his plans are brought to a sudden halt by a letter from Jules: "'Your child has died after a third of his pre-natal existence. Catherine wants no further communication from you . . .'"

> VOICE *off*: Thus between the two of them, they had created nothing. Jim
> thought: 'It is a noble thing to want to rediscover the laws of humanity;
> but how convenient it must be to conform to the existing rules. We played
> with the very sources of life, and we failed.' (92)

Jim settles in with Gilberte and, in a belated concession to the existing rules, plans to marry her. (95) Yet it comes as no great surprise when the couple's domestic felicity is shattered once again, and this time permanently, by Catherine's re-entrance. She and Jules have moved back to France and are renting an old mill on the banks of the Seine. This Jim learns when he meets Jules unexpectedly at the gymnasium. He also learns that for a long while Catherine was deeply depressed, even suicidal. "It was as if she were recovering from a serious illness," explains Jules. "She moved around very slowly with the fixed smile of a corpse." (93) But she is feeling better now, and has asked Jules to invite Jim and Gilberte out for a drive in her new car. Jim declines for Gilberte, but accepts for himself.

The two men meet Catherine at the mill. She greets Jim casually, and then, wearing "the secret look which announced one of her evenings of intrigue," carefully folds up a nightdress and wraps it in a paper parcel. With Catherine at the wheel, and Jim holding her parcel, they drive out the Seine valley to have lunch at an inn. No sooner do they alight at their destination than they are met in the doorway by none other than Albert. Catherine feigns surprise, but invites him to dine with them. After the meal, as they are departing through the inn garden, Catherine asks Jim for her parcel, which he hands her. With that, she turns away from Jules and Jim, walks back to Albert, gives him her arm, and tosses the other two a cheerful "Good night!" The astonishment of the abandoned men turns to resignation as they walk off down the road. Jules sums it up with the remark, "Catherine's motto is: in a couple, one person at least must be faithful—the other one." (94–95) Jim chooses this moment to tell Jules that he is planning to marry Gilberte, and his friend responds, "I think she will make a very good wife. She's very attractive." (96)

Early the next morning, as Jim and Gilberte lie in bed asleep, Catherine drives her car by their apartment, sounding the horn and zig-zagging crazily around the square. Jim wakes and sees the car "brushing benches and trees, like a horse without a rider, or a phantom ship." (96) Later the same morning Jim receives a telephone call from Catherine, who tells him that her night with Albert was a disaster, that she is through with that kind of life, that all she could think about was Jim. Before she can even implore him to come straightaway, Jim is out of bed and preparing to rush to her side—leaving Gilberte still asleep in bed.

Jim enters Catherine's room at the mill, and she at once asks him to lie down beside her and kiss her. Instead, he gets up and delivers a speech. " You wanted to invent love from the beginning," he tells her, "but pioneers should be humble, without egoism":

> We have failed, we have made a mess of everything. You wanted to mould me to your needs. On my side, I have brought nothing but suffering to those around me, where I wanted to bring joy . . . The promise I made to Gilberte that we would grow old together is worthless, because I can put it off indefinitely. It's a forgery. I no longer hope to marry you. I have to tell you, Catherine, I'm going to marry Gilberte. She and I can still have children. (97)

Stricken, Catherine sinks down on the bed weeping; but in a moment she recovers enough to reach under the pillow, draw out a revolver, and point it at Jim. "You're going to die. You disgust me . . . I'm going to kill you, Jim," she rasps. He wrests the gun from her and then makes a hurried exit out of the window. (98)

Were Jim truly disenchanted with Catherine, this surely would have been the last episode of their melodramatic affair. But, alas, his attraction to her eludes rational comprehension; and the ultimate fatality, so long foreshadowed, occurs a few months later when Jim meets Jules and Catherine quite by chance at a cinema. Although Jim's heart "no longer leapt on seeing Catherine," he nevertheless agrees to go for a drive with her and Jules. After a few miles of reckless motoring along a country road, Catherine says she has something to say to Jim alone. Jules, obligingly as ever, stays behind as the other two get into the car together. Catherine shouts for her husband to watch them carefully; Jim chooses to ignore this ominous warning and climbs in beside her. As Jules looks on with increasing apprehension, Catherine turns her auto off the road along the river bank and onto a ruined bridge whose middle arch is missing. In horror he sees the car shoot off the bridge, tumble end over end, hit the water, and slowly sink. (99)

The final scene of the film shows Jules at the funeral of Catherine and Jim. A narrator's voice expresses his thoughts about the doomed pair:

> They left nothing behind them. Jules had his daughter. Had Catherine liked struggling for the sake of the struggle? No. But she had sown chaos in Jule's life until he was sick of it . . . A feeling of relief swept over him. His friendship with Jim had no equivalent in love. Together they found amusement and satisfaction in mere trifles; the discovery of their differences did not lessen their affection. From the very beginning of their friendship, they had been called Don Quixote and Sancho Panza. (100)

More articulately than most other protagonists of negative triangles, and in the midst of his grief, Jules expresses his awareness that he has been released from a tremendous burden, that he and his daughter are now free to get on with their lives unencumbered by a wife no wife, and a mother no mother. He is swept with "a feeling of relief."

The basic shape of the triangle is thus clear. Jules, the overly accommodating husband of Catherine, and Gilberte, the equally deferential lover of Jim, are the major protagonists. Their paradoxical victory arises from losing what they had thought they wanted, and, in so doing, gaining what they want even more: peace of mind. Although we are not shown Gilberte's reaction to the death of Jim, it is hard to imagine that her sorrow should not be tempered with the same sense of relief as that of Jules. They both have suffered equally from the fatal attraction between their wayward mates, and both have been released from a hopeless situation that could only have become more desperate with time.

The primary antagonist of the drama is, of course, Catherine, whose overriding motive is to gain a fulfillment in love of which she is constitutionally incapable. Thus doomed to unhappiness from the beginning, she compulsively seeks sexual adventures that never satisfy her. Marriage to Jules, or an offer of marriage from Albert, only make her lose interest because they mark the end of another all-too-easy conquest. Love, for Catherine, is therefore a sort of warfare in which her lovers are perceived as opponents and potential victims. Ultimately, the only opponent she finds truly worthy is the one who shows the most signs of resistance. That one is Jim; and when it appears that he has won the battle by resisting too much, Catherine reveals the essentially anti-erotic quality of her attachment by destroying both herself and him.

Jim therefore stands at the apex of the triangle, dialectically disengaged throughout most of the action because he swings between protagonist and antagonist without ever in fact making a firm commitment to either side—at least not until he impulsively climbs into the car with Catherine for his ride to death. This final, rash action releases the spring which had so long been coiled to propel Jim once and for all into the antagonists' column; and with his movement from the apex of the triangle to the recessive unit, the film's metastatic-negative dynamic fulfills itself.

Before drawing up an action chart, we must account for a few minor characters. Among these, Albert is the most important because he is Catherine's longtime admirer and fitful lover. If, therefore, the metastatic-negative model correctly describes the action of this film, Albert will be "placeable" at one of the three corners of its triangle. That he does not belong with Jim, positioned initially at the apex and then moving to the recessive unit headed by Catherine, seems evident. In the first place, Albert does not experience divided loyalties: there is no other important woman in his life, and thus no contest, however minimal, for his affections. In the second place, he does not suffer Jim's dire fate, but instead remains alive and free at the end of action. His only known motive is to marry Catherine after she has divorced Jules, and to adopt her daughter. In a sense, then, Albert simply desires to replace Jules in Catherine's life. Furthermore, like Jules, he offers a steady loyalty, and wants nothing more exciting than a conventional, monogamous marriage. This is why the adventure-seeking Catherine ultimately rejects him in favor of the more elusive victim. Albert thus unwittingly saves himself from untold distress by failing to hold a lover who is incapable of returning his affection. Like Jules, and Gilberte as well, he wins by losing, and therefore must be counted among the drama's protagonists. "Albert equals Gilberte," says Catherine, in a slightly different context, nevertheless pointing up both the rhyming similarity of their names and their functional equivalence in the dialectic of action. (85)

Catherine has a comic double in the figure of Thérèse, the human dynamo, non-stop talker, and frenetically random manchaser. Jules and Jim first meet Thérèse as they stroll along a street where she and her anarchist boyfriend, Merlin, are painting the slogan "DEATH TO OTHERS" on a hoarding; but having run out of paint, they are unable to add the final "S" (thus leaving the motto ominously in the singular). Merlin blames Thérèse and begins beating her furiously. She runs for help to the passing strangers, and they take her to a café, where, before even introducing herself, she asks them to put her up for the night. Jim has an engagement with Gilberte, so he refers the young woman to Jules, who agrees to take her home. But once there, the shy Jules disappoints Thérèse by treating her rather like a daughter than the sexually available female she is; so the next morning, at the café where they have gone for coffee, Thérèse casually abandons Jules, and picks up with a man named The Aztec. (13–14)

Years later, after the war, Jim runs into Thérèse again and asks her what became of the man she ran off with. This unleashes a machine-gun narrative: She says she deceived The Aztec so that she could earn the money to buy him a big Meerschaum pipe carved with the head of Vercingetorix. He was so furious when he found out how she got it that he locked her up for three weeks. But she finally managed to escape out a window and down a ladder, seducing en route the house painter to whom the ladder belonged. Later she picked up with a rich man who carried her off to Cairo and installed her in a brothel, where she specialized in playing the virgin. Fortunately, an Englishman took pity on her and spirited her away to his villa on the Red Sea. While in this exotic location, she received a letter from her cousin back in France, announcing that he was about to get married. She had always been attracted to this cousin, so she set off immediately for her home town, where she broke up the marriage and wed the cousin herself. But after only three months she was "fed up" and decided to go back to Paris, where she began an affair with an undertaker. Her husband divorced her for desertion, and she finally married the undertaker. "We make a perfect couple, but we've no children," she breathlessly concludes, reloading to add, "He's the only man I can't deceive . . . because he doesn't leave me the time or the energy." She is now writing her memoirs for the *Sunday Time Magazine*.

Death, of course, is the only man who cannot be deceived, and the one who takes away both time and energy. The story of Thérèse's frenzied progress from man to man, and her ultimate satisfaction with one whose business is death, thus provides an ironic parallel to Catherine's neurotic inability to find fulfillment in love, except in the act of destroying both herself and her lover. For Catherine's longings have been perverted into the opposite of love; Eros has been replaced by Thanatos, the life instinct by the death instinct. Thérèse and her Undertaker husband must therefore be placed alongside of Catherine in the antagonists' column, yet more as walking symbols of Catherine's disease than as characters who materially affect the plot.

Several other characters, both on stage and off, play similar purely symbolic roles. Their names will also appear in the action-chart as players in the drama; but, because they are even less important to the plot than Thérèse, I shall defer discussion of their figurative significance until the following section dealing with imagery. Here, then, is a schematic for the screenplay's primary level of action:

ACTION-CHART: François Truffaut, *Jules and Jim*:

PROTAGONIST	ANTAGONIST
[Jules' Parents]	[Catherine's
Jules	Parents]
<Sabine>	x Catherine
Gilberte	x [Dead Child]
Albert	Thérèse
[Harold]	Merlin
[Fortunio]	Undertaker
[Mathilde]	<Gunner's Girl>
[Villagers]	x Jim
[T's Ist Husband]	<Gunner>

APEX

(Jim)

The arrow charts Jim's final movement from a dialectically disengaged position to the antagonists' unit dominated by Catherine. Characters who die during the action are marked with an "X" before their names. Offstage characters are designated, as usual, with square brackets, while those who do not materially affect the plot are enclosed in angular brackets.

(2) *Dialectic of Imagery:*

Whether in form purely verbal or cinematically visual, the figurative orchestration of *Jules and Jim* divides into three basic sections. Of these, the protagonists' and antagonists' units set themselves apart by radically dissonant tropes: on the protagonists' side, ordinary daily activities, creative work, tender gestures of selfless love; on the antagonists' side, figures of sexual restlessness, violence, and death. As might be expected, the apex of the triangle generates an assortment of ambivalent images, which at first harmonize largely with those of the dominant unit, but which later progressively adopt the modality of the recessive unit, until they at last abandon their former key altogether. Thus, throughout the first half of the action, Jim is more strongly linked by figuration to Jules and Gilberte; later this tie begins to weaken as he is drawn ever more closely to Catherine; and, in the last, violent series of images his figurative bond with the protagonists is utterly severed.

By far the most heavily charged tropes of the film are those generated by the antagonists' unit headed by Catherine, who from the outset stands apart from the other characters by reason of her transparently archetypal nature. Her entrance as a veiled figure in the company of three other women, and her resemblance to the ancient statue, with its enigmatic smile, indicate at once that she is something more than human. By a complex but fairly obvious network of association Catherine assumes the features of none other than the great Anima in its infernal aspect—the Bitch Goddess so terrifying to the male psyche.

The insular origin of the statue with which Catherine is identified links her to Calypso, the siren enchantress who lures unwary mariners to humiliation and death upon the shores of her island lair. That this association is far from casual is proven by Catherine's aqueous proclivities. She "swims like a fish," boasts Jules. (28) Appropriately, it is to the seaside that she leads Jules and Jim on their first outing as a threesome, and there, on a hillside overlooking the ocean, that Jules proposes marriage. (31ff.) As we have seen, Jim's real obsession with Catherine begins the moment he observes her fling herself into the Seine: he mentally throws her a kiss and imagines himself swimming with her—as her hat drifts along with the current. (37–8) The siren figure is picked up even in Catherine's chatter with her daughter: "Time for bed, sailor, the fleas are hungry." (53) Moreover, after Jim becomes Catherine's lover and moves into the chalet with her and Jules, the three take walks together round a nearby lake, "a stretch of water shrouded in mist at the bottom of a humid and lush valley," (75) The same aquatic trope is repeated when Jules and Catherine come back to France, for they move into a refurbished water mill; and it is in a room of this mill that she tries to shoot Jim with a revolver. (93–4) Catherine's final attempt on his life brings the water imagery to its frightful crescendo: her automobile lurches before his apartment like "a phantom ship" (96), a vessel that eventually carries them both off the ruined bridge and down into the river, where their bodies are later found "entangled in reeds." (100)

The destructive siren or fish-woman archetype is closely related to another composite of woman and various beasts, namely, the sphinx, guardian of the supreme enigma of life, and destroyer of those who divine her secret. Catherine is also repeatedly associated with this figure, which, according to Jung, symbolizes the Terrible Mother. Like the sphinx, Catherine is a composite creature, the trilingual daughter of a Burgundian aristocrat and a lower-class English woman; therefore she "ignores the average" and "teaches those she is drawn to." (28) Her face, with its tranquil, slightly disdainful smile, often expresses a "secret look" that announces her evenings of intrigue. (94) "Catherine only revealed the things she wanted when she had them in her hand," the narrator intones. (60) Accordingly, when Jim tells her that he understands about her various liaisons, she replies with sphinx-like serenity, "I don't want to be understood." (60)

Jim recalls that Catherine came into their lives "like an apparition." (58) For Jules "She is a force of nature, she expresses herself in cataclysms." (80) Albert composes a song about her entitled "The Whirlwind," whose second quatrain sums up the negative power of her allure:

> Elle avait des yeux, des yeux d'opale,
> Qui me fascinaient, qui me fascinaient.
> Y avait l'opale de son visage pâle
> De femme fatale qui m'fut fatale. (67–9)

Catherine's symbolic scaffolding elevates her far above the level of common seductress and murderess, to the point where she reveals herself, in various archetypal guises, as the destructive force of nature itself. Not only siren and sphinx, she is also the Medusa who slays those whose eyes meet her glance. Jim tells her that he has always loved the back of her neck: "The only part of you I could look at without being seen." (73) Then, too, she is the spirit of the forest (symbolizing both the unconscious and death), into which she lures Jim in a footrace, and with which she is associated throughout the film; indeed, at one point when Jim reads a letter from her, the screen shows an *"Aerial view of wooded countryside with an image of Catherine's face superimposed on it."* (57; 91) Finally, as at the beginning, she is Fate in the character of Atropos, cutter of the thread of life; for the motif of her entrance as the veiled third woman recurs later, when Catherine is seen knitting, then interrupting her knitting to tell the "sailor" it's time for bed, and to wish Jim a seductive good night. (53)

Forebodings of death echo and re-echo around Catherine. Throwing one's hat on her bed is bad luck, as Catherine knowingly points out to Jim when he makes this mistake. (29) Jim later senses her presence as a "threat" hanging over the household (55), while Jules goes so far as to equate her with a mortar bomb waiting to explode. (57) After she loses Jim's child, Catherine moves around "very slowly with the fixed smile of a corpse." (93) These thanatoid figures are brought to a powerful finale in the film's penultimate shot, where we are shown the urns containing the ashes of Catherine and Jim being sealed up in the pigeonhole of a columbarium. (100) Like Thérèse, her comic double, Catherine can only find complete satisfaction with the undertaker. Indeed, Catherine comes to be seen as a figure of death itself.

Turning to the protagonists' unit, one is relieved, though not surprised, to find images of a completely different complexion, figures redolent of life, love, and creativity. Jules may have his moments of sorrow—particularly with a mate like Catherine—but in general "his large round eyes are full of gentleness and good humour." (12)

Three of the chief symbols associated with Jules are the big hour-glass by which he prefers to tell time, the rocking chair which appears wherever he lives, and his favorite pastime of dominoes. That the former is a *momento mori* Jules inadvertently confesses as he turns the glass over and tells Thérèse, "When all the sand has run out, I must go to sleep." (14) However, the hour-glass is primarily a marker of time, and therefore equally a symbol of life. Similarly, the rocking chair, with its rhythmic, clock-like motion, may also represent the passage of time; and for Jules it is clearly the locus of secure quietude in the midst of the whirlwinds around him. In fact, he is first shown using the rocking chair as a place to sleep, and thus to avoid sharing a bed with his libidinous guest, Thérèse, the "human steam engine." (14) Later, in the chalet, one hears the sound of a clock ticking as Jules *"sits in a rocking chair with SABINE on his knee, rocking gently."* (50) This figure is repeated with variations, now again with Sabine, now with Jules quietly reading alone by the fire. (55, 74) The game of dominoes is another quiet way of passing the time; and Jules and Jim are shown repeatedly playing this game together in contented silence. (11, 34, 53) However, after Jim and Catherine become lovers, Jules begins to rely on his daughter, Sabine, as a partner. (72) Thus, the hour-glass, rocking chair, and domino set all associate Jules with peace, quietude, and contentment.

Jules' work as a writer is neither so imaginative nor so glamorous as that of Jim; in fact, his early Paris projects seem to consist entirely in translating Jim's poems and unfinished autobiographical novel into German. (20–6) After the war Jules gives up literature entirely to return to his field of entomology, as he explains to his old friend:

> I've been commissioned to write a book on dragon-flies. I am writing the text and fixing up the photographs. Catherine is doing the drawings and prints. Even Sabine helps . . . She comes to the swamps with me . . . I'm going to have an artificial swamp made in the garden.

Then he adds wistfully, and with a touch of irony:

> Perhaps one day I shall return to literature with a novel about love—with insects for characters. I have a bad habit of over-specialisation. You spread your talents wide, Jim. I envy you. (51)

Jules also specializes with respect to women, in the sense of being monogamous. This predictability is what Catherine finds so dull about him, and its absence so exciting about Jim.

But what Catherine really finds troublesome in her husband is his almost saintly love, which permits him to accept her for what she is, infidelities and all. "I don't blame her or Albert," Jules tells Jim, adding significantly, "I am gradually renouncing my claim to her, to everything I have wanted on this earth." (55) When Jim and Catherine at last become lovers, Jules gives them "a kind of blessing"; and later, after witnessing pain they cause each other, Jules begins to see their love as something "relative," while his own love remains "absolute". (72, 76, 88) Jules' project of renunciation carries to other things as well: "I have stopped smoking since I learned to love nature." (50) Indeed, Jim sees a whole side of his friend's character which is that of a "Buddhist monk." (52) Nor is this facet of Jules' nature lost on Catherine, who early in their marriage sees him "with a halo," and later claims that he has their family routine "organised like a monastery's." (55, 59) No wonder, then, if Jules takes pride in the fact that the German word for "life" is neuter. (56) Another, related figure shows Jules not in the role of monk, but in that of unappreciated genius; for on the wall of Catherine's room is a photograph of Jules as a child, dressed up by his father to resemble Mozart. (52) Taken together, these images reinforce the impression of Jules as a person of almost holy innocence, selfless love, and strenuous self-abnegation.

These same qualities are conspicuous, as we have seen, in another of the film's protagonists. For just as Jules accepts Catherine's liaisons without reproach, so Gilberte acquiesces in Jim's affair in full knowledge that she will eventually lose him to Catherine. Gilberte's selfless love is revealed in simple actions that do not require orchestrations with richer symbolism: sending Jim parcels during the war, giving him his inhaler when he is sick, lying in bed with him while he talks of Catherine, even carrying Catherine's letters to him (46, 76, 78–9, 90–1). When, at the café, Jim tells her that he is going to marry Catherine, Gilberte simply picks up her handbag and leaves without fuss. Shortly thereafter she welcomes Jim back to her arms, confessing her jealousy as a simple fact, and pleading for only a little more time with him: "She will have you for the rest of her life. Give me one more week" (79). Gilberte's humility is not only remarkable in itself; by contrast to Catherine's bottomless egocentrism, it appears downright saintly.

"Saintly" is perhaps not an adjective one would apply readily to Jules' early friend and Catherine's occasional lover, Albert. For one thing, Albert is a sensualist who regards Jules' rocking chair not as a place of quiet sanctuary, but as an "invitation to the pleasures of the flesh", and who, in reference to having been wounded during the war, quotes Oscar Wilde's saying, "My God, spare me the ills of the flesh; I will answer for the ills of the soul" (65, 67). Furthermore, Catherine finds Albert attractive because "he was the natural authority which Jules lacks" (60). These facts would seem to militate against placing him alongside the self-sacrificing Jules and Gilberte. However, one must always credit actions above words (Theorem 3); and if this rule is applied in the case of Albert, his character will be seen to resemble that of the other protagonists in essential respects.

Albert is the effective cause of Jules' and Jim's enchantment, for it is by means of his magic lantern (shades of the motion picture camera) that they first see the enigmatic statue. (18) Yet Albert falls under its spell just as much as his friends do; and, like them, he is later bewitched by the woman it resembles. The few times we see this "friend of painters and sculptors" after he has become Catherine's lover, Albert appears as a relaxed and friendly figure, cheerily wheeling his bicycle up to the chalet, his guitar slung over his shoulder; kneeling down to give little Sabine a kiss; sitting on the grass in conversation with Jules and Jim; accompanying Catherine as she sings the ballad he has composed for her. (18, 60–1, 66–7) During his last appearance, when Catherine meets him at the inn for an assignation, Albert seems embarrassed by the unexpected presence of Jules and Jim, whom he nonetheless manages to greet with a friendly smile and shake of the hand (95). Like them, he is Catherine's plaything. But unlike Jim, Albert has no other woman in the background and wants only to marry Catherine. As the last verses of his song for Catherine reveal, Albert envisions a love that endures:

> Quand on s'est retrouvé
> Quand on s'est réchauffé
> Pourquoi se séparer?
>
> Alors tous deux on est reparti
> Dans le tourbillon de la vie
>
> On a continué á tourner
> Tous les deux enlacés
> Tous les deux enlacés (69)

Albert's creative work, his collection of art specimens (Jules collects insect specimens), his congenial nature and monogamous instincts all link him with Catherine's husband.

Caught between protagonist and antagonist at the apex of the triangle, Jim is a traveler in both worlds. Indeed, on the advice of an admired teacher, he has followed his natural bent and become a "professional tourist" and curiosity seeker, that is to say, a foreign correspondent for a Paris newspaper. (51–2) Just as he divides his professional time between France and Germany, so Jim attempts to divide his literary labors between writing fiction and social commentary, with the result that he has been unable to finish his novel because of the obligation to churn out articles on post-war Germany. (51) He is also translating a Viennese play into French for a Paris production. (76) "You spread your talents wide," says Jules admiringly, to which Jim demurs, "Oh, me! I'm a failure." (51) Catherine tries to cheer him up by affirming that she and Jules both think he has a great career ahead of him—"though," she adds, "I don't say it will necessarily be spectacular." (52)

Jim's eclectic professional career parallels his love life, in which he is also the curiosity seeker, wandering back and forth between the loyal mistress and the neurotic married woman who resembles a piece of ancient statuary. His casual and catholic taste in these matters reveals itself early on, when he advises Jules not to take Thérèse seriously: "No, Jules . . . let her go . . . You lose one and you find ten more." (17) His impulsiveness also betrays itself in an amusing way when he tries, unsuccessfully, to buy from a café owner the marble-top table upon which Jules has drawn a woman's face in the style of Matisse. (17)

The essential similarity between Jim's and Catherine's restive sexuality is revealed by their common taste in reading. Thus, the book Jim is most eager to borrow from Jules' library is *Elective Affinities,* Goethe's novel of tragically crossed love among friends; but before he can finish it, Catherine insists on having it back to read herself. This transaction occurs just before Jim and Catherine become lovers; and as the narrator describes their first night together, the camera pans across to this book, whose title is clearly visible. (71) At another point Jim borrows from Catherine a volume in which he discovers a passage she has marked, and which he finds revealing enough to mention to her:

> It was about a woman on a ship who gave herself in imagination to a passenger she does not know. That struck me as a confession on your part. It's your method of exploring the universe. I have this lightning curiosity too; perhaps everyone has. But I control it for your sake, and I'm not convinced that you control yours for mine. (97)

Jim may be less sexually random than Catherine, but his claim to restraint has a disingenuous ring in view of his during-the-intermissions affair with Gilberte. Indeed, Truffaut stresses Jim's flightiness by cross-cutting between shots of him in bed with Gilberte, and then of Catherine reading his latest letter (78–9); and again of Jim and Catherine together in the dreary hotel room, followed by an image of Jim back once more in his bedroom with Gilberte (89–90). As the plot reaches its climax there are two shots of Jim leaving Gilberte in bed as he rushes off to Catherine, first in response to her letter and then to the sound of her automobile horn outside. (89–90, 96)

Jim's impulsive and predatory impulses are underscored figuratively throughout the film. He is the friend who would be loyal, who honors Jules and his lady with delightful presents including an original canvas by Picasso, but who cannot resist adding as a suggestive gift to Catherine an elegantly carved back-scratcher. (35) It is Jim who keeps his foot a moment too long on Catherine's under the table, who throws his hat upon her bed, and who puts out the flames devouring her night-dress. (25–29) It is he, not Jules, who regards Catherine with admiration when she flings herself into the Seine. (37-8) Nor, at the end, can Jim resist the fatal invitation to climb into

Catherine's auto, although she is behaving most strangely and has already made one attempt on his life. (99) Jim and Catherine are "both drawn to each other by the same force," explains the narrator, who points up the essentially destructive nature of this force by the metaphor he uses to describe their transports of mutual passion: "they soared upwards like great birds of prey." (85-6) Finally, predator and prey become one as, drawn by the same wild and restless power, they bring each each other down:

> *Long shot of the inside of the crematorium.* JULES *steps to one side and, in close-up, anonymous hands uncover the coffins and push each of them into an oven. Doors close behind each coffin. Dissolve to the hands opening the double doors of the ovens....then dissolve again to the ashes and charred remains which are ground up and put into small urns...*
>
> VOICE *off:* The ashes were collected in urns and put into a pigeon-hole which was then sealed up. If he had been alone, Jules would have mixed them together. Catherine had always wished hers to the scattered to the winds from the top of a hill...but it was not allowed. (100)

Before drawing up an image-chart of *Jules and Jim* it is necessary to consider a somewhat problematical cluster of tropes, namely, the First World War sequences created from archival newsreel footage. The purpose of this montage would seem to be primarily narrative: rapid alternate shots of the French and German sides of the war as it progresses from mobilization to armistice, interspersed with scenes of Jules and Jim as soldiers on opposite sides of the conflict, permit Truffaut to evoke this episode of history and his hero's reluctant parts in it with dispatch. However, the mere fact that Jules and Jim are shown to be formal opponents in a conflict so momentous would lead one to suspect that the World War is a metaphor for a personal collision of equally radical character, in short, that Jules and Jim are dialectically opposed throughout the film. But because our protocols have strongly suggested that this is not the case, indeed that Jim is dialectically disengaged throughout most of the action, questions remain as to both the placement and symbolic import of these martial images within the metastatic-negative framework.

As we have seen, the main concern of both Jules and Jim during their tours of duty is not that they themselves will be killed, but that they might inadvertently kill each other. (46-7) Thus, the war poses a threat to the physical rather than to the spiritual continuance of their friendship; ideology and nationalism are not factors here. Jules and Jim accept the conflagration as a force of history to which they must submit— much as they submit to Catherine as to a "force of nature," even though she too threatens their friendship. The symbolic connection between Catherine and the war is not gratuitous, for as we have also seen, she is represented as nothing less than the destructive principle in nature itself: she, the lover of Napoleon, the mortar bomb about to explode, the revolver under the pillow, and bottle of vitriol in the luggage; she whose car is the chariot of death. This motif is repeated in Jim's war story about the gunner who, returning on the train from leave, meets a young girl who gives him her address, and to whom, as the mortar bombs rain down, he writes more and more intimate letters until he proposes marriage, is accepted, and at last finds himself writing such things as "I take your adorable breasts....I press you against me quite naked." Jim moralizes this anecdote in a most revealing way:

> You see, Jules, to understand this extraordinary deflowering by corre-
> spondence, one must have experienced all the violence of the war in the
> trenches, its particular kind of collective madness, with death constantly
> present. So there was a man who, at the same time as taking part in the
> Great War, managed to conduct his own little parallel war, his individual
> struggle, and completely conquer the heart of a woman from a distance
> ... He died after being trepanned, just the day before the armistice. In his
> last letter to the fiancée he hardly knew, he wrote: 'Your breasts are the
> only bombs I love.' (65–6)

The battle of the sexes is thus explicitly interpreted as a "parallel war" to the military conflict, and the conquest of a woman tacitly equated with the subduing of a country. Equally significant is the irony that victory in this parallel war corresponds with violent death, both for the gunner and, eventually, for the man who tells his story. This connection seems to bring us near to the symbolic core of the film, in which the desire for mere sexual conquest is viewed as a deadly form of combat, while renunciation of the war of the sexes is felt to be the corollary principle of survival. Thus, the newsreel footage from the Great War serves not only as a narrative device but also as a metaphor in which the French victory foreshadows Jim's conquest of Catherine, while the German loss prefigures Jules' giving her up. And since loss/renunciation are here equated with survival, the German side of the war belongs, by a curious twist, to the film's protagonists' unit. The victorious French side qualifies Jim's apex unit as a harbinger of his eventual movement to Catherine, at which time Jim and Jules finally become dialectically opposed as exemplars of self-preservation and self-destruction.

The following schematic provides a brief overview of the figurative patterns of the film's three functional units. In the interest of economy, images are here grouped under general headings, with an approximate count of figures for each group, followed by an example or two of each type:

IMAGE-CHART: Truffaut, *Jules and Jim*:

PROTAGONIST	APEX CHARACTER →	ANTAGONIST
1. LOVE, LOYALTY, KINDNESS.	1. OBSESSION, SUFFERING, ILLNESS.	1. VIOLENCE, ANARCHY, WAR, CRUELTY, DEATH.
Approximate count: 27 images.	*Approximate count:* 27 images.	*Approximate count:* 61 images.
"JULES *walking in the meadow WITH HIS DAUGHTER,* SABINE, *holding her by the hand.*" GILBERTE: "Jim, just for once, you could stay here and sleep beside me." CATHERINE: "(Albert) wants me to leave everything, to marry him. He would take the mother and daughter together."	"Catherine had a migraine, which passed. Jim, who was worn out, had a succession of them which were worse. He thought: if we had children they would all be tall and thin and would suffer from migraines."	(CATHERINE writing to JIM): "This paper is your skin, this ink my blood. I am pressing hard so that it may enter in." ("The meeting between CATHERINE and JIM at the inn) "was like a burial, as if they were already dead."
2. HUMOR, INNOCENCE. VULNERABILITY.	2. FRIENDSHIP FOR JULES.	2. LAMIA ARCHETYPE VARIANTS.
Approximate count: 24 images.	*Approximate count:* 26 images.	*Approximate count:* 38 images.
"Jules looked on quietly, his large round eyes full of gentleness and good humour."	"From the beginning of their friendship they had been called Don Quixote and Sancho Panza."	"She came into our lives like an apparition." "*Close-up of* CATHERINE *looking in at the two men and tapping on the window pane.*"
3. ART, SCIENCE, WORK.	3. VICTORY IN LOVE AND WAR, SEDUCTIVE BEHAVIOR.	3. SEXUAL RANDOMNESS.
Approximate count: 25 images. "Jules writes his books, chases after his insects and all kinds of other little creatures." ALBERT (showing slides): "This one is more exotic; it looks rather like an Inca statue."	*Approximate count:* 19 images. "JIM takes (CATHERINE) *by the chin, and with his other hand draws a moustache on her upper lip. Then he gives her a small cigar and lights it for her.*"	*Approximate count:* 37 images. CATHERINE: Do you remember our young friend, Fortunio? . . . He was there, as free as air...and so was I . . . What a holiday we had!" THÉRÈSE: "...So I hopped through a window with a ladder belonging to a house painter who I seduced."
4. FASCINATION WITH WOMEN.	4. AMBIVALENCE, IMPULSIVENESS.	
Approximate count: 16 images. "Jules turned to the professionals . . . *Shot*	*Approximate count:* 18 images.	

IMAGE-CHART: Truffaut, *Jules and Jim* (cont.):

PROTAGONIST	APEX CHARACTER ⟶	ANTAGONIST

through a window of a man kissing a woman's hand; then cut to a close-up of a leg, clad in a black stocking . . . but without satisfying himself there.

5. FRIENDSHIP FOR JIM.

Approximate count: 17 images.

"(JULES and JIM) *playing at the blindman and the cripple.* JULES, *as the cripple, is* perched on the shoulders of JIM, *as the blind* man."

6. SPIRITUALITY, DETACHMENT, ACCEPTANCE.

Approximate count: 18 images.

JULES (during a pause in conversation): "There's an angel passing by." JULES (to JIM): *smiling:* So you won the war, you scoundrel."

7. CONTENTED PASSAGE OF TIME.

Approximate count: 9 images.

"JULES *has settled himself in his rocking chair in front of the log fire.*"

JULES: " (Catherine) invites you out for a drive. I would like you to accept, and perhaps Gilberte as well? JIM: No, she wouldn't come. But I will."

5. ART, LITERATURE, WORK.

Approximate count: 14 images.

"An important Paris daily newspaper was publishing his articles on Germany."

---

4. WATER, FOREST, WIND, NIGHT, WILD ANIMALS.

Approximate count: 32 images.

"*Aerial view of wooded countryside with an image of Catherine's face superimposed on it.*"

5. MENTAL IMBALANCE, ILLUSION, DISTORTED VISION.

Approximate count: 9 images.

" . . . she invented a game they called 'the village idiot'. " "I dreamed I met (Napoleon) in a lift. He made me pregnant and I never saw him again. Poor Napoleon."

(3) *Implicational Dialectic*

In attempting to abstract the essential common features of the three functional units of *Jules and Jim* I shall follow the same procedure as in the previous chapter, dealing first with the major colliding forces of protagonist and antagonist, then with the apex unit, which in this case projects certain traits as being especially vulnerable to the negative syndrome objectified by the antagonists' unit.

1. *Love/Lust-Hatred.* When Catherine asks Jules if he despises her for her affair with Jim, her husband replies, "No, Catherine, I never despise you. . . . I shall always love you, whatever you do, whatever happens." (88) Thus, Jules' love for Catherine, like Gilberte's for Jim, is unqualified and transcends the egotism of possession. Catherine's affections, on the contrary, depend entirely upon self-satisfaction and whim. When she fails to conceive the child she wants by Jim, she dismisses him in frustration. He protests, "But we love each other, Catherine, and that's all that matters." To which she responds, "No. I count too, and I don't love so much...I am a heartless person. That is why I don't love you and shall never love anyone."(86–7)

2. *Fidelity/Infidelity.* Jules allows nothing to alter his loyalty to friend or wife, neither Catherine's several casual affairs, nor the more serious one with Jim; indeed, in order to keep them both close to him, he gives his blessing to their union. As a consequence, Jules finds the love between Jim and his wife becoming something "relative," while his own remains "absolute." (88) Similarly, Gilberte says she will wait for Jim "forever," and is grateful merely for the little time she has with him before he must leave her for Catherine. (70) Even the unsuccessful Albert offers the loyalty of a monogamous marriage. But this sort of loyalty is not in Catherine's repertoire. As Jules succinctly puts it, "Catherine's motto is: 'In a couple, one person at least must be faithful——the other one.' " (95) This random tendency is parodied in the serial sexual adventures of Thérèse, the ultimate trollop.

3. *Civility/Anarchy.* The early scene of Thérèse and her anarchist boyfriend, Merlin, trying to paint the slogan "DEATH TO OTHERS" on a hoarding serves as the first major leitmotif for the action's negative pole. For the initial meeting of Jules and Jim with Thérèse, the walking symbol of lust and neurotic instability, occurs only a few scenes before they first see the slide of the ancient statue, and then encounter its living double, Catherine. The motifs of anarchy and death thus herald the entrance of a woman who comes to be seen as a menacing "force of nature," a more-than-human figure who

"expresses herself in cataclysms." (80) As the archetypal Terrible Mother, it is she who creates psychic disturbances which manifest themselves in chaotic and self-destructive patterns of behavior. Jim eventually succumbs to this force; Jules survives it by means of a loving detachment, intense concentration on his scientific work, and strict ordering of his (psychic) household.

4. *Domesticity/Wildness*. Metaphorically, Catherine is the "whirlwind," the "great bird of prey"; literally, when she dies she wants her ashes "to be scattered to the winds from the top of a hill." When Jim meets her again after the war, he sees her as "the radiant queen of the household, ready to take flight at any moment." (55) These images epitomize Catherine's restless, unpredictable, and petulant nature. She herself identifies with a female character in a play who wants to be completely free, and who therefore "invents her life every moment." (36) All this adds up to a woman constitutionally incapable of bearing the domestic burdens of marriage and mother-hood. On the other side, Jules, Albert, and Gilberte desire precisely that domestic felicity which neither Catherine nor Jim can offer. The domesticity/wildness di-chotomy is a primary motive in at least one other Truffaut film, which bears the second term of the set in its title: *The Wild Child*.

5. *Responsibility/Irresponsibility*. Little comment is required here, except to say that Catherine's irresponsibility approaches the absolute, that her utter lack of compassion for those around her is crowned by the love- and life-negating act of murder–suicide. Her victims include not only lover and husband, but also her innocent daughter, Sabine.

6. *Openness/Mystery*. Jules talks quite candidly to Jim about the most intimate matters, including his wife's lovers; and Jim returns the compliment, though to a somewhat lesser degree. Albert speaks to Jules "quite freely" about his desire to marry Catherine and adopt Sabine. (55) Similarly, Gilberte puts her cards on the table with Jim, even though confessing that she will wait for him forever makes her extremely vulnerable to his whims. Thus, neither Jules, Albert, nor Gilberte employ secrecy for strategic purposes. Unlike these, however, Catherine attempts to conceal her motives and plans, revealing them only after they are already accomplished, when she has them "in her hand." Occasionally she inadvertently betrays herself to Jules by wearing a secret look that announces an evening of intrigue; but for the most part both Jim and Jules are moved by Catherine "as if by a symbol which they did not understand." (27)

7. *Moderation/Excess.* "Normally she is sweet and kind," says Jules of Catherine, "but if she feels that she is not being sufficiently appreciated, she becomes terrifying. She passes suddenly and violently from one extreme to another." "Napoleon was the same," responds Jim. (55) Earlier Jules speculates that it is her upper-class/lower-class background that inclines Catherine to "ignore the average." (28) She is also attracted by excesses of passion in others, as Jules explains to Jim just before the final calamity: "For Catherine, you were easy to get in the first place and difficult to keep. Your love fell to zero, then rose to a hundred again with that of Catherine. I have never known your zeros . . . nor your hundreds." (99)

8. *Restraint/Impetuosity.* A slightly different shading of the previous antinomy, this set is helpful because its second term defines a quality in Catherine that Jim finds so attractive, perhaps because he shares it with her. In fact, his obsession with Catherine begins the moment she impulsively throws herself into the Seine. The first term of the set applies with equal justice to the protagonists, except (one might quibble) inasmuch as they continue to love in spite of everything.

9. *Detachment/Obsession.* As we have seen, Jules defends himself against Catherine's infidelities by spiritual detachment: "I am gradually renouncing my claim to her, to everything I have wanted on this earth." (55) The disciplined aspect of his detachment is indicated by references to Buddhism and monasticism. In a more casual way, Gilberte also renounces her claim to Jim, delighting in his presence when he grants it, but accepting the fact that he will eventually leave her for Catherine. Albert, too, simply withdraws without protest once Catherine has abandoned him as lover and rejected his offer of marriage. However, detachment is hardly one of Catherine's outstanding qualities; for although she is flighty, her "grasshopper" movements are totally in the service of her compulsion for sexual conquest and domination. "I had to do it," is her excuse to Jim for yet another amorous encounter with Albert. (85) Finally, it is Jim's inability to detach himself from Catherine, despite all the danger signs, that causes his destruction.

10. *Acceptance/Rejection.* Detachment involves accepting life on its own terms, without trying to change things to suit one's personal desires. Jules does this when, having observed that Jim and Catherine together are "like a married couple," he gives Jim leave to possess her and, after they have become lovers, offers them both "a kind of blessing." (71, 76) Unlike her husband, Catherine rejects anything that does not suit her current whim; and ultimately she rejects life itself because she cannot have it her own way.

11. *Humility/Egoism.* "Why, after all, should a woman as sought-after as Catherine have chosen to grace us with her presence?" Jules asks Jim rhetorically."Because we give her our undivided attention, as we would to a queen." (80) The same theme emerges when Jim summarizes for Catherine the reasons why their experiment in love has failed: "You wanted to construct something better, refusing hypocrisy and resignation. You wanted to invent love from the beginning . . . but pioneers should be humble, without egoism. . . . You wanted to change me, to mould me to your needs. On my side, I have brought nothing but suffering to those around me, where I wanted to bring them joy." (97) If the essential egoism of their attraction is the cause of their failure, it is also the quality that separates them so widely from the selfless Jules and Gilberte.

12. *Self-sacrifice/Self-indulgence.* Catherine admits to Jim that part of what attracted her to Jules was his "indulgent and leisurely ways." (59) A rather delicate match of complements, it would seem, for as Jim senses from the beginning, "Catherine was terribly demanding . . . She could have jumped at other men like she once jumped into the Seine." (55) But he rationalizes this quality in her as a virtue: ". . . once Catherine wants to do something, so long as she thinks it won't hurt anyone else—she can be mistaken, of course—she does it for her own enjoyment, and to learn something from it. That way she hopes to become wise." (78) Just how mistaken she can be Jim will learn at great cost.

13. *Vulnerability/Callousness.* "It was Jules's generosity, his innocence, his vulnerability which dazzled me, conquered me," explains Catherine, adding, "He was so different from other men." (58) Yet Jules' reticence and "passivity" soon begin to infuriate her when, for instance, he will not defend her against slights (real or imagined) from his own family; and she takes immediate revenge by sleeping with an old boyfriend on the very day before her wedding to Jules. For Catherine cannot tolerate even the hint of disapproval or lack of deference to her queenly dominance; that others may have their reasons does not concern her in the least.

14. *Timidity/Boldness.* The second term of this set defines a quality that draws Jim and Catherine together, for they are both adventurers, experimentalists, and curiosity seekers in the dangerous land of sexuality. Jules too is attracted by this wild territory; but when he cannot reclaim and domesticate it to suit his more conventional needs, he is forced to relinquish it to bolder spirits. This has been Jules' pattern from the beginning: around women he has always been "shy," "timid," and "a little dull." (12, 13, 25)

15. *Gentleness/Violence*. As we have seen, images of mutilation and violent death—the bottle of vitriol, the statue of Napoleon, the breasts like bombs, the impulsive jump into the Seine, the presented revolver—heavily prefigure Catherine's final act of driving herself and Jim off the bridge. For violence, both emotional and physical, is the signature of one who "expresses herself in cataclysms." Those who escape the "whirlwind" are the gentle, timid, and selfless souls who do not long attract this ungovernable force.

16. *Forgiveness/Vindictiveness*. When Jim delays his return to Germany, pleading work and farewells yet to be made, and incautiously mentioning having seen Thérèse, Catherine becomes suspicious. Resolving to even the score, she takes up again with her old lover, Albert. As she explains it later to Jim, "You talked about saying good-bye to your old loves, so I went to say good-bye to mine." (85) The longsuffering Jules sees it a bit differently: "Catherine doesn't like people being away from her. You have been away too long. When she has the slightest doubt, she always goes much further than the other person." (79)

17. *Kindness/Cruelty*. Catherine's final act is her masterpiece of cruelty: with Jim beside her in the car, she calls out to Jules to watch them carefully as she prepares to drive the vehicle off the ruined bridge; and thus the entirely unsuspecting Jules, who has forgiven them everything and loved them both in spite of all, is forced to witness the sudden death of both his wife and best friend. (99) This is how Catherine rewards Jules' saintly kindness, and how Jim, albeit inadvertently, rewards the patient love of Gilberte.

18. *Stability/Instability*. Jules' patient entomological research—the "over-specialisation" to which he modestly confesses—together with his loyal, undemanding love for wife and child, bespeak an essential steadiness of character. By contrast, his wife's agitated mental condition is symbolized by the automobile she drives so recklessly, zig-zagging from side to side, or veering around the deserted square, "brushing the benches and trees, like a horse without a rider or a phantom ship." (96, 97)

19. *Order/Chaos*. Jules' desire for a disciplined, harmonious life is exemplified not only by his organization of the household routine "like a monastery's", but also by the ordering of his mental household like that of a "Buddhist monk". (52, 55) The chief threat to this order is Catherine, but only after her suicide does Jules fully realize that "she had sown chaos in his life until he was sick of it." At last freed of her, he is

swept by a feeling of relief. (100)

20. *Reality/Illusion*. Everything about Catherine partakes of the "dreamlike," the mysterious, the phantasmal; as a result, the obsession she inspires in men assumes the quality of a delusion. Thus, when Jules and Jim regard her dressed up to resemble Charlie Chaplin's The Kid, they are "moved as if by a symbol which they did not understand." (27) But just as Jules begins to detach himself, to renounce his claim to this being of mythical aspect, his friend becomes increasingly, and fatally, obsessed with her. The realistic acceptance of life on life's terms is thus equated with renunciation of the Anima in her infernal aspect; or, as in the case of Gilberte, a corresponding detachment from the Animus (Jim) in his negative mode.

21. *Innocence/Experience*. The marriage of Jules and Catherine is clearly a case of the attraction of opposites. To a woman who has "known a lot of men," Jules' sexual inexperience and general "innocence" are not only novelties in themselves, they also offer a possible antidote for her own worldliness: "We'll cancel each other out, so perhaps we'll make a good couple." (33, 58) But in close quarters the opposites fail to neutralize each other; instead they begin to repel. Annoyed by Jules' passivity and bored by his loyalty, Catherine returns to her old ways with a vengeance; and, in order to avoid constant anguish, Jules frees himself of the desire to possess her.

22. *Spirituality/Bestiality*. The spiritual nature of Jules' eventual detachment from Catherine is underscored, as we have seen, by allusions to sainthood, monasticism, and Buddhism—things which connote the renunciation of personal and especially of physical desires. Thus, Jules voluntarily sleeps alone while Jim and Catherine consort together by his leave. And although not figuratively associated with monasticism, Gilberte too accepts the loss of her beloved to another woman almost without complaint. By contrast, the possessive and essentially animal attraction between Jim and Catherine transforms them into "great birds of prey."

23. *Health/Sickness*. Shortly after Jim and Catherine become lovers they both start having migraine headaches. Moreover, during an outing to a nearby lake Catherine urges an already "worn out" Jim to throw pebbles across the water until he is truly "exhausted." (75) Later, when the two break up for the second time, Jim returns to Paris and promptly comes down with a flu, which Gilberte helps him to nurse—just as Jules nurses his wife after she loses the child by Jim. (90, 93)

24. *Contentment/Discontent*. According to Jules, when things go "too well" for Catherine, "she begins to feel discontented. Her manner changes and she only says

or does anything to lash out at everything." (54) What Jules fails to perceive is that his boundlessly patient love and his urge for domestic order are precisely the qualities least likely to satisfy Catherine's need for drama, for the challenge of conquest—just as Jim's itch for adventure and risks disqualify him from finding contentment with the "sensible and patient" Gilberte.

25. *Sanity/Madness*. Catherine's feeble grip on reality is suggested at the outset by her advocacy of a crazily inverted cosmology, according to which the universe is a hollow sphere on whose inside wall humans walk upright with their heads towards the center. (33) Later her distorted view of the world comes to be symbolized, appropriately, by the progressive failure of her eyesight. (55ff) Yet these metaphors seem almost redundant in view of Catherine's actions, which almost from the beginning suggest grave imbalance, and at the end prove it beyond all doubt.

26. *Creativity/Destructiveness*. In the midst of the turmoil brought into his life by marriage, Jules continues to work patiently on his book on dragonflies. (87) Similarly, Gilberte goes off to her (unspecified) job, calmly carrying a letter from Jim to Catherine on her way out. (91) Presumably Albert too continues his work of collecting art, composing songs, and befriending painters and sculptors even after Catherine has rejected his offer of marriage. By contrast, the overextended Jim never does complete the novel he has been working on fitfully. The major symbolic dyad for this opposition between creation and destruction are Catherine's two children— the first a healthy daughter by Jules, and the second a stillborn infant by Jim. The narrator provides a grim epitaph for Catherine's and Jim's experiment in love: "Thus between the two of them, they had created nothing". (92)

27. *Success/Failure*. Jim regards the death in utero of his child by Catherine as a sort of natural retribution for their having tampered with the "laws of humanity" and "the existing rules": "We played with the very sources of life, and we failed." (92) He also communicates to Catherine his awareness of the pain they have brought upon each other, and also upon Jules and Gilberte, summing it up with the admission, "We have failed, we have made a mess of everything." (97) Among the antagonists, only Thérèse seems to have attained a measure of "success," in that the lurid story of her amours has become so notorious that she has been asked to write it all down for a London newspaper. But when we recall that Catherine's comic double finds contentment at last only with the Undertaker, the one man she cannot deceive, her apparent good fortune must be regarded symbolically as the ultimate failure. (76–7) For in this

fantasy blind Eros is indeed the chore boy of Thanatos.

28. *Freedom/Slavery*. When Jim arises from Catherine's bed after their first night together as lovers, he knows that he is "enslaved." (72) Although he later makes two attempts to break his shackles and return to Gilberte, Catherine has only to pull on the chains to remind him of his enthrallment. Given Catherine's powerfully archetypal aspect, it is difficult to interpret Jim's bondage other than as a fixation to the Dark Mother, the Negative Anima, or whatever one chooses to call this destructive psychological force. Jules too is drawn by this power; but realizing that he cannot control it, he manages to stay away from the center of the vortex by an act of renunciation. Yet he still loves her, and she remains a disturbing element in his life. Therefore, Catherine's death comes to him as a sudden liberation: "No longer would Jules suffer from the fear he had had from the very beginning, first that Catherine would be unfaithful to him, and then only that she might die . . . for now it had happened . . . A feeling of relief swept over him." (99–100)

29. *Temporality/Eternity*. Curiously, Jules' spiritual detachment is accompanied by an acute sense of the fleetingness of time. Thus, his attention to the large hour-glass, and his awareness that when the sand has run out, he must go to sleep. (14) Gilberte also seems to share this sense of the evanescence of life when she asks Jim to stay with her just a little while longer; for, after all, Catherine will have him for the rest of her life. (79) In fact, Catherine represents the force of nature which possesses everyone in the end, and which it is therefore most foolish to deny. One may either accept this force for what it is, or merely flirt with it and thus risk provoking its ire.

30. *Life/Death*. The old equation between illicit sexuality and death operates as a controlling element in this fantasy. For Catherine is at once the personification of sexual allure and the lamia who destroys those who attract her: the woman "whom all men desire" and the "*femme fatale qui m'fut fatale*." (80, 67) Catherine's extra-marital offspring is significantly stillborn, and after its loss she withdraws into herself "like a widow" and moves around "very slowly with the fixed smile of a corpse." (93) Like death itself, she is unpredictable, incomprehensible. Catherine's overdetermined association with such archetypes as Atropos, the Gorgon, the Sphinx, Calypso, and the Spirit of the Forest serves both to bind the sex–death equation and to associate it with the negative forces of the unconscious. The bottom of the river and the crematorium oven are the logical terminals for the instincts she represents. Jules too is greatly drawn to this force; but when he finds that he cannot domesticate it, he is

obliged to let go: his freedom and indeed his very life depend at once upon loving acceptance and detachment. This power must neither be denied, controlled, nor provoked.

The apex character of the metastatic-negative structure is rather like the tail of a lizard: an appendage to be sacrificed as a decoy in order that the vital organs may escape the predator. In the case of *Jules and Jim* the vital parts are the motives objectified by its protagonists: the desire for such things as love and loyalty, domesticity and stability, health and creativity. The predator, of course, is Catherine, who represents the negation of these qualities. Jim is the lizard's tail, bonded at first to Jules through all the ties of friendship and common interest, later offered up as a sacrifice to Catherine so that Jules and the other protagonists may survive. Yet the simile is imprecise because, like all other apex figures of this structure, Jim is actually disengaged from the outset: the lizard's tail has been released before the action begins. Furthermore, at the characterological level, Jules has no intention of harming Jim when he gives him leave to woo Catherine. It is important to understand that the real detachment here is on the part of the screenwriters, who objectify in Jim certain qualities sensed to be destructive because of their symbiosis with the frightening attributes of the antagonist.

As in all metastatic actions, whether positive or negative, the distinguishing qualities of the apex character will be far fewer in number than those generated by the major colliding forces. Moreover, although this initially disengaged figure will share certain traits in common with both sides of the dramatic equation, only those qualities which render him particularly vulnerable to the functional unit to which he finally moves need concern us here. For what sets Jim apart from Jules are those traits which make him a desirable victim for Catherine:

1. *Adventurousness.* Jim's most deadly flaw is undoubtedly his self-proclaimed "need for adventures, for risks." (70) His thirst for danger first attracts him to the unpredictable Catherine, subsequently leads him to join her in the attempt to "rediscover the laws of humanity," and finally lures him into her chariot of death.

2. *Sexual Curiosity.* Jim confesses that he has a "lightning curiosity" about females who attract him, and that his instincts are not really monogamous. As he puts it, "I think that, in love, the couple is not ideal." (97) He shares this prurient instinct with Catherine, but at the same time tries to "control" it for her sake while complaining that she does not return the favor.

3. *Obsession.* " 'A woman like her . . . A woman like her . . . But what is she like?' And for the first time he began to think directly of Catherine." (39) As Jules begins to detach himself emotionally from Catherine, Jim's obsession with her grows; and precisely when Jules lets her go, Jim finds himself utterly "enslaved." Despite his later doubts about Catherine, his guilty feelings toward Gilberte, and his efforts to return to a more settled life, Jim remains Catherine's slave, and thus becomes her victim.

4. *Ambivalence.* When Jim is with Gilberte, he thinks of Catherine; when he is with Catherine, he thinks of Gilberte. For neither the steady, loyal woman nor the wayward, dangerous one can fully satisfy a fundamental inconsistency in his nature. Jim's complaint is in fact the common male dysfunction of being alternately attracted to the feminine extremes of Madonna and whore. In Freudian parlance these extremes are sometimes referred to as the "spilt mother."

5. *Self-destructiveness.* Jim is much more experienced with women than Jules. Moreover, it is Jim, not Jules, who has early warnings of Catherine's wayward and vindictive nature; he who sees her packing the bottle of vitriol to throw in the eyes of men who tell lies, and he who later looks down the barrel of the revolver she pulls out from underneath her pillow. Yet despite, or more likely because of his awareness that she is a classic *femme fatale*, Jim enjoys the dangerous adventure of being pulled into her web. The self-proclaimed lover of risks knows that he is flirting with death, and his flirtation is ultimately successful.

Having rationalized thirty sets of antinomies for the dominant and recessive functions of *Jules and Jim*, together with five qualities connecting the apex figure with the recessive unit, we are now in a position to print out a schematic whose function is to abstract at a glance the argument at the heart of this fantasy. The alert reader may perhaps wish to supply a few terms that have been overlooked, but it is hoped that the following implicational chart will afford a fairly complete and accurate summary of the film's motivational polarity:

IMPLICATIONAL CHART: Truffaut, *Jules and Jim*:

Dominant Function	Recessive Function
Love	Lust/Hatred
Fidelity	Infidelity
Civility	Anarchy
Domesticity	Wildness
Responsibility	Irresponsibility
Predictability	Unpredictability
Openness	Mystery
Moderation	Excess
Restraint	Impetuosity
Detachment	Obsession
Acceptance	Rejection
Humility	Egoism
Self-sacrifice	Self-indulgence
Vulnerability	Callousness
Timidity	Boldness
Gentleness	Violence
Forgiveness	Vindictiveness
Kindness	Cruelty
Stability	Instability
Order	Chaos
Reality	Illusion
Innocence	Experience
Spirituality	Bestiality
Health	Sickness
Contentment	Discontent
Sanity	Madness
Creativity	Destructiveness
Success	Failure
Freedom	Slavery
Temporality	Eternity
Life	Death

Apex

Function
Adventurousness
Sexual Curiosity
Obsession
Ambivalence
Self-destructiveness

Among the striking features of this motivational opposition, perhaps the most singular is the odd mixture of qualities comprising the film's dominant or wishful function. For despite the presence of many conventionally positive ideals such as love, fidelity, kindness, and stability, there also appear a significant number of others which, taken together, might seem to vitiate the image of an artist trying to break new ground in the cinema. Thus, cheek by jowl with the desire for freedom and creativity occur such ideals as innocence, timidity, moderation, predictability, restraint, and humility—qualities not normally associated with creative innovation. The artist's vaunted boldness and impetuosity, his sense of mystery and his obsession with the world of illusion are here relegated to the category of tendencies to be repressed at all cost. Moreover, one of the most ominous traits of the apex function, a quality perceived to represent perhaps the greatest of all threats to creativity, is, paradoxically, adventurousness. Indeed, the generally diffident and conservative motives of this screenplay add weight to the judgement of critics who have found Truffaut to be an "*enfant terrible* confined within the bounds of bourgeois respectability," and who have noted "the absence in his films of revolutionary innovation on either a technical or a political level."[2] At the same time, the dominant motives of *Jules and Jim* are clearly in accord with the quality Truffaut cherished above all others in cinematic art—*tendresse.*[3]

From a psychological perspective the dialectic of this film reveals, as we have seen, a clear equation between sexuality and annihilation. With a sense of urgency unsuccessfully masked by the lightly ironic tone of his narrator's voice, Truffaut predicates survival—physical, mental, and creative—upon the renunciation of sexual instincts which are bound to the negative female image. Thus the film's recessive terms descend almost exclusively from Catherine and her double, Thérèse, while the only on-camera masculine figures in the same unit fill the entirely symbolic supporting roles of Anarchist and Undertaker (destruction and death). What could easily be interpreted as a misogynistic streak in this fantasy is to some degree offset by the presence in the dominant unit of the lovely Gilberte; but her almost abject passivity and deference to Jim's wishes would hardly qualify her as a feminist's role model. Another screenwriter working with this material might have found it appro-

---

[2]Jean Curtelin, quoted in Don Allen, *Finally Truffaut* (New York: Beaufort Books, 1985), p.18.
[3]Allen, *ibid.*, p.18.

priate to bring Gilberte and Jules together at the end, for they represent the same values of loyalty and gentleness. However, Truffaut allows these two protagonists only one brief meeting, during which Jules says nothing and Gilberte leaves the room after a single pleasantry. (93) Instead Truffaut underlines the moral of sexual renunciation by placing the Madonna-like Gilberte on a pedestal beside the saintly Jules, but also at a discrete distance from him.

Among the ten or so wishful motives which appear with great frequency in the dominant function of metastatic-negative dramas, only two are conspicuously absent from *Jules and Jim*: propriety and normality. For Jules' triangular arrangement with Catherine and Jim could hardly be said to meet conventional standards of propriety. Nor can his Buddha-like renunciation of all he ever wanted in life, and his consequent detachment from sexual love, be taken as normative adjustments. Aside from these peculiarities, however, all the other more or less built-in motives of the form are there, from restraint and humility to health and sanity. So is the structure's invariable moral— that illict sexuality is the greatest of all threats to sanity, and indeed to life itself.

SIXTH MODEL
SYNTHETIC-REALIZED

Definition. The synthetic-realized structure occurs whenever a standoff between two equally extreme and intransigent forces is broken by a moderating character who eventually draws one or both of the initial contestants to his apex position, thus forming a dominant group that restores order in a rational manner. This dynamic presents at the outset a deadlocked conflict between two factions unable either to resolve or to give over the struggle; though superficially at variance, their stances are found to be qualitatively identical and invariably dysfunctional. The original source of trouble is always the initial antagonist, a plainly villainous figure who commits a severe infraction of the common sense of order and decency; in so doing, he provokes the initial protagonist to a righteous fury that leads him in turn to violate the very same rational and ethical norms. At this point the moderator or raisonneur steps in, and, as the minimum condition for the synthetic-realized action, convinces at least one of the initial protagonists to see the light of reason. Thus augmented by converts to the Middle Way, the apex unit gains sufficient strength to defeat the initial antagonist. Often, however, all of the initial protagonists together with several members of the initial antagonists' unit will also be drawn to the rational center; less frequently both units will shift in their entireties to the apex position, thereby creating the comparatively unusual situation of complete dialectical collapse.

Unlike the metastatic triangle whose apex figure eventually moves to one of the primary warring camps, the synthetic-realized dynamic evinces movement to the center, where a new protagonist displaces yet at the same time incorporates the initial one. Often closely allied by family or other ties to the initial protagonist, the raisonneur may be present onstage from the beginning or may appear, deus ex machina, *to impose a rational compromise at the penultimate moment.*

Schematic. Our diagram illustrates the most common synthetic-realized situation, in which all of the initial protagonists ("X") shift to the apex position of the moderating character ("W"), while only some of the antagonists ("Z") do likewise. The primary antagonist and original cause of the conflict ("Y") remains unmoved in defeat. In cases of complete dialectical collapse, however, all initial combatants, including the principal antagonist, eventually converge upon the center. Yet the minimum condition for this dynamic is the movement of but a single personage from the initial protagonists' unit to the apex:

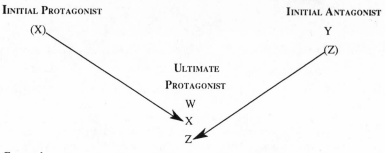

Iinitial Protagonist

(X)

Iinitial Antagonist

Y

(Z)

Ultimate
Protagonist
W
X
Z

General.

> Good sense views all extremes with detestation,
> And bids us be noble in moderation.

> Molière, *The Misanthrope*

"Comedy of the Golden Mean" provides an apposite cognomen for the synthetic-realized dynamic, both because all actions conforming to this model resolve themselves happily and thus constitute specimens of *commedia* (no matter how tragically they begin), and also because the ideals of rationality, moderation, and compromise form the spiritual tripod upon which the whole structure rests. These ideals being quintessentially classical ones, it comes as little surprise that the dramatic form most naturally embodying them should figure prominently in the plays of ancient Greece, the Renaissance, and the Baroque.

It is entirely fitting, therefore, that Aeschylus' *Oresteia* should provide our first known example of the synthetic-realized dynamic in its concluding drama, *Eumenides.*

Although the first two parts of this trilogy conform to the static structure (Model 1), its final drama brings the conflict between mutually exclusive ethical claims of the preceding works to a synthetic resolution when Orestes and his pursuers, the Furies, submit their argument to the arbitration of the divine *raisonneur*, Athena. Casting the deciding ballot in a previously deadlocked vote, the goddess thereby effects a compromise between the conflicting justices of earth and sky gods, matriarchy and patriarchy, the old *lex talionis* and the newer taboo against shedding kindred blood. The syncretism here is total, with both sides of the initial conflict relinquishing their right to administer justice in such cases, and both acquiescing in a rule of law under which homicides must henceforth be tried before the Court of the Aeriopagus. Thus, even the initial antagonists move to the rational center, and through this movement find themselves metamorphosed from avenging Furies into "Kindly Ones" (Eumenides).

Much of the exigetical mist that envelops Sophocles' *Ajax* and *Philoctetes* vanishes once these works are also understood as conforming to the synthetic-realized model; for in both dramas a stalemated ethical confrontation between equally irrational opponents is broken by moderating figures who advocate the pious, humane Middle Way. Odysseus assumes the *raissoneur*'s function in *Ajax*, employing the argument of enlightened self-interest to break a deadlocked struggle between Ajax's brother Teucer and Agamemnon over the issue of whether the title-character deserves honorable burial. When it is understood that the drama's first half, depicting at length Ajax's madness and suicide, constitutes a strategy for setting up the more critical confrontation and eventual compromise that follow, the play's bipartite form does not appear so strange as it is sometimes made out, nor its second half so anti-climactic; for Ajax's passion and death presage a much more important, if less physical, conflict, at the end of which reason and humanity prevail over false pride and pure self-interest.

Like Odysseus in *Ajax,* young Neoptolemus plays the moderator's part in *Philoctetes.* Unwilling to accept the Greek leaders' advice to use deception or force to take Philoctetes from his island, yet equally loathe to oppose the gods' will for the great archer to play a decisive role in the war against Troy, Neoptolemus eventually attracts this strange figure to the pious Middle Way by examples of his own courage, honesty, and compassion. Yet neither Sophoclean drama permits the apex character to function alone; for Neoptolemus eventually receives critical aid from Heracles sent at Zeus' command, just as the Odysseus of *Ajax* relies upon the advice of Athena. The moderators of both works thus operate as agents of the divine *raisonneurs*, whose intercession permits their mortal counterparts to achieve an essentially holy purpose. (That Odysseus appears as a moderator in *Ajax* while acting the villain's part in *Philoctetes* has been a natural source of confusion to later commentators; yet the Greeks' attitude toward this wily hero was highly ambivalent, and Sophocles exploited contrary versions as they suited his purpose. Hence, despite their divergent portraits of Odysseus, these tragedies—or, rather, averted tragedies—remain both ethically and dynamically consistent.)

The fiercely satirical Old Comedy of Aristophanes does not easily lend itself to a pattern stressing compromise; but in *Lysistrata,* at least, the playwright's desire to show Athens and Sparta concluding a just peace finds ideal expression in the synthetic-realized dynamic. Supported by three offstage goddesses (Demeter, Athena, and Artemis), Lysistrata and her Spartan counterpart, Kalonike, succeed in contriving the women's sex-strike which forces the initial combatants to lay down the arms of war and open those of peace. Here the hemichorus of Athenian women also functions as a collective moderating agent, whereas the men's hemichorus eventually moves, along with the other Athenian warriors, from the initial protagonists' position to the rational and loving center. And because the Spartan soldiers likewise shift to the apex from their initial antagonists' position, *Lysistrata* provides another instance of total syncretism, with no intransigent characters left to sustain dialectical tension at the end of action.

Still yet another case of complete dialectical collapse is to be found in Menander's *Diskolos.* The chief moderating character of this highly sophisticated pastoral is the god Pan, whose shrine appropriately stands between the two warring houses which the deity eventually reconciles by casting love's spell upon the young hero, Sostratos. At the play's conclusion all previously feuding characters, including old Cnemon, the misanthropic primary antagonist, enter the god's sacred grotto to drink libations in celebration of the double wedding that unites rich with poor and restores harmony to a house previously subject to jarring discord. A later play of Menander's survives only in large fragments but remains complete enough to reveal that it follows the same dynamic of compromise—as its title, *The Arbitration,* indicates. This apparent tendency of later Greek comedy toward synthetic formations stressing moderation and compromise may possibly provide an answer as to why Aristotle, the philosopher of the Middle Way, found the laughing genre's greatest formal as well as ethical perfection in New Comedy, of which Menander was the leading exponent.

The synthetic-realized dynamic is virtually absent from medieval drama—the Corpus Christi cycles, the saints', miracle, morality, and Passion plays of England and Continental Europe. For, among the various dynamic patterns, Christian drama of this era naturally favors three: the static (good and evil irreconcilable), the apostatic-positive (movement from damnation to salvation), or the apostatic-negative (cautionary moral depicting a fall from grace). Only in the Renaissance does the inherently classical synthetic pattern reappear with signal effect, and nowhere more than in Shakespeare, four of whose major plays assume this form: *Romeo and Juliet, A Midsummer Night's Dream, A Winter's Tale,* and *The Tempest.*

That this revitalization of the synthetic-realized dynamic during the late sixteenth century does not reflect, at least in Shakespeare, an abandonment of the religious ethos informing earlier Christian drama is well exemplified in *Romeo and Juliet,* where the indirect technique of allegory now takes up the cross to carry an old argument in a new way. For here a doubled Satan lurks offstage as prime motivator of both sides of the initial conflict, while God works mysteriously but surely behind the scenes as the chief moderating figure of the ultimately triumphant apex unit. As a result of this divine intervention the lovers' "tragic" movement to the center effects a complete reconciliation between the previously feuding Capulets and Montagues, a conversion to the ideals of amity and justice advocated from the beginning by Prince Escalus and implemented by Friar Lawrence, the onstage representatives of the drama's heavenly *raisonneur.* Hence, according to the religious ethos governing this work, the lovers' death cannot be taken as defeat: the personal reward for their devotion lies not in the dust of the Capulet vault but in heaven, just as the social import of their acts resides in the blessing of peace they have conferred upon Verona (though here, as elsewhere, Shakespeare takes a somewhat unorthodox tack on suicide). Consequently, although this work may approach the tragic by representing death onstage, *Romeo and Juliet* nevertheless stands as a specimen of religious *commedia.*

The same is more transparently true of such metaphysical comedies as *A Winter's Tale* and *The Tempest.* In the former the characters of Hermione, Mamillus, Paulina, and Camillo all function as mediating agents of God, whose will eventually brings about a reconciliation between Leontes and Polixines; in the latter Prospero, the earthly representative of an all-powerful deity, employs his magical (read spiritual) powers to heal wounds of political and personal injustice by effecting a lovematch between his daughter and the son of his old betrayer. Both allegories posit Satanical motives as the cause of the initial conflict, and convergence upon the center as the result of miraculous events clearly to be interpreted as the work of Divine Providence.

Although entirely secular in implication, *A Midsummer Night's Dream* yet stands as Shakespeare's most intricate and masterful employment of the dynamic under consideration, for this play contains three structurally parallel synthetic-realized actions descending in levels of decorum and rhetoric through the orders of the gods, human gentlefolk, and simple rustics. The happy resolution of the jealous quarrel between Titania and Oberon thus sounds a double echo in the conundrums of two progressively broader underplots which conclude with the "tragic" reunion of Pyramus and Thisbe. And because the perennial opposition of God and Satan does not figure in the argument of this fretwork comedy, dialectical collapse here is total, with all formerly opposed characters converging upon the apex—a position occupied from the outset by all the rustics, including Snug, the "joiner."

As one might expect, the neo-classical drama of seventeenth-century France gravitates naturally towards Comedy of the Golden Mean—at least in its moments of most exquisite pathos or humor. Among Racine's works it is thus his *Phaedra* that assumes the synthetic-realized dynamic. This paean to faith, fidelity, and temperance places the captive Princess Aricia at the apex position between the initially warring camps, which comprise on the protagonists' side Theseus and Hippolytus, and on the antagonists' Phaedra and Oenone. For the purely internal conflict between father and son touched off by Phaedra's unnatural passion can only be resolved when both of the initial protagonists give up their reactively extreme positions and move to that advocated by the innocent and trusting Aricia. Hippolytus' shift occurs at the moment he offers himself in marriage to the princess, while Theseus belatedly seeks the center when, after learning of his son's death and hearing Phaedra's dying confession, he vows to honor Hippolytus' spirit and to adopt Aricia as his own child. And although Hippolytus meets death on the way to his wedding with Aricia, such an event following a character's movement to the ultimate protagonists' unit is not without precedent, as a backwards glance at *Romeo and Juliet* confirms.

Undoubtedly the greatest refulgence of the synthetic-realized dynamic during the neo-classical period occurs in the works of Racine's contemporary, Molière, four of whose major comedies conform most delightfully to this model: *Tartuffe, The Misanthrope, The*

Learned Ladies, and *The Imaginary Invalid.* Each of these works pits two unacceptable and qualitatively identical "extremes" against each other, gradually amplifies the squabbling to a level at which their common irrationality becomes hilariously apparent, and finally draws one or more of the initial protagonists (the originally offended parties) to the rational center through the offices of various numbers of moderators, headed in each case by the offstage cultural *raisonneur*, Louis XIV. Thus augmented by new converts to the Middle Way, the apex unit empowers itself through rational persuasion to discredit and thereby to disarm the original source of the disturbance, the initial antagonist.

Of *Tartuffe* I shall presently speak at length; yet a brief examination of the three other Molière works conforming to the synthetic-realized model provides some idea of the relative flexibility this dynamic permits without in the least abandoning its salient features as a distinct, coherent structure. Thus, among these comedies, *The Misanthrope* alone fulfills the bare minimum requirement of the form by depicting the movement to the apex unit of but a single initial protagonist and none of the antagonists; for Éliante's shift to the center leaves the intransigent Alceste behind in the initial protagonists' camp, still in opposition to Célèmene and the rest of the comedy's hypersocial antagonists. In *The Imaginary Invalid,* however, the author depicts the convergence upon the rational center of all four initial protagonists (Argan, Angelique, Cléante, and Louison) but none of the antagonists, while in *The Learned Ladies* he propels one character from each of the initially opposing units (the protagonist Chrysale and the antagonist Philaminte) to the apex position. Moreover, the number of onstage *raisonneurs* varies in each comedy, from the sole moderator, Philinte, of *The Misanthrope,* through the twosome, Béralde and Toinette, of *The Imaginary Invalid,* to the quartet of moderators in *The Learned Ladies,* Ariste, Henriette, Clitandre, and Martine. Though somewhat dryly statistical, these comparisons serve both to reveal several possible variations on the same basic kinetic pattern, and also to indicate the dynamic range of a form that ratifies its philosophical predeliction for flexibility by the multiple strategies it allows its practitioners.

Following its resurgence in the sixteenth and seventeenth centuries, the impulse toward the syncretism of this form appears to decline rather abruptly. Even later adaptations of Molière's works in this vein often seek other dynamic configurations— a process that can be seen as early as Wycherley's restructuring of *The Misanthrope* into the *The Plain Dealer*, which assumes the apostatic-positive configuration (Model 2).

With occasional exceptions, such as Arthur Murphy's *Know Your Own Mind,* most English comedies of the Augustan age favor the more common and less overtly philosophical metastatic-positive triangle (Model 4), a dynamic which also appears to dominate Continental drama of the eighteenth century. Yet a most noteworthy exception to this trend, a sort of belated apotheosis of the baroque urge for syncretism appears early in the next century with Goethe's completion of the second part of *Faust.* For the hero of this drama, previously torn between conflicting urges and philosophical claims, at last achieves spiritual redemption in the presence of Eternal Womanhood, the Mater Gloriosa whose power at once comprehends and synthesizes the oppositional pulls upon man's soul.

Notwithstanding its relative decline after the seventeenth century, the synthetic-realized remains a permanent dynamic option that continues to be taken up now and again, often in conscious imitation of neo-classical models, but always as the most congenial vehicle for the symbolic resolution of social conflicts perceived to be founded upon false and therefore mutually destructive premises. Such a work is Wilde's *An Ideal Husband,* where an initial opposition between those espousing conventional rectitude on the one hand, and cynical depravity on the other, is eventually exposed as a struggle between closely related evils by the witty Lord Goring, a moderator who (much like Menander's god Pan) personifies the reconciling power of love. The same Dionysian aura surrounds Madam Desmemortes of Anouilh's *Invitation to the Chateau,* where this almost mystical figure serves as the magnet drawing the lovers together from their reactively extreme and equally foolish initial bickering. Even such a comparatively recent work as Milinaro's farce *La Cage aux Folle* is capable of replicating not only the dynamic pattern of both *Romeo and Juliet* and *Tartuffe* but also of embodying many of the same motives as its illustrious predecessors. And because these implicational similarities constitute the rule rather than the exception in the present model, it is necessary to conclude our survey with a brief discussion of this phenomenon.

Like its close relative, the synthetic-implied (Model 7), the synthetic-realized structure contains certain built-in motives, unavoidable implications inherent in the kinetics of the dynamic itself. Indeed, it would be odd if a form so solidly founded as this upon the principles of love, moderation, and rationality did not reflect these motives in its entire building. Consequently, although the majority of implicational derivations required by dramas of this type may vary considerably from work to work (thereby revealing the motivational idiosyncrasies of each), yet certain specific antinomies will be universally implicit and certain others commonly so, regardless of author, era, or opus. Among this structure's motivational constants, at least six sets of antinomies will be required without exception for any work conforming to its symmetry:

DOMINANT FUNCTION	RECESSIVE FUNCTION
Moderation	Excess
Flexibility	Rigidity
Rationality	Irrationality
Compromise	Dissention
Wisdom	Ignorance
Love	Hatred

Aside from these motivational invariables, seven other complementary opposites crop up more often than not:

Trust	Suspicion
Honesty	Hypocrisy
Tolerance	Intolerance
Maturity	Childishness
Humor	Dourness
Beauty	Ugliness
Serenity	Strife

Beyond these omnipresent or at least frequent antinomies, the remaining derivations for separate works conforming to this model may differ widely in number and kind, displaying unique variations—but always on the same basic theme established by the five invariable sets, with the dominant value of "moderation" as the keynote. Although in this respect it is motivationally normative and thus "conservative," the synthetic-realized dynamic nevertheless permits much greater latitude of implication than does the second synthetic model, of which I shall speak in the next chapter.

Whenever a dramatist addresses an objective social conflict between what he perceives to be equally dysfunctional but at the same time avoidable "extremes," he will tend naturally and unconsciously to adopt this model, for it allows him to draw at least one side of the argument to a new and more rational ground from which it can effectively neutralize its former oppressor and corrupter. That longstanding social stresses continue to seek this sort of metaphorical adjustment is evident from such topical films as Reiner's *The Russians are Coming* and Forsythe's *Local Hero*, which symbolically resolve in turn the problems of cold war and environmental exploitation by working variations on the Comedy of the Golden Mean. In a more sweeping and elevated manner, Attenborough's *Gandhi* propounds the Indian martyr's ideals of universal brotherhood and tolerance by placing its title-character at the apex of a synthetic triangle, from whose two other corners all but the most ignorant eventually converge.

ANALYSIS
Molière, *Tartuffe, or The Impostor*[1]

(1) *Dialectic of Action*:

Molière's most illustrious opus provides a splendid instance of the Comedy of the Golden Mean in one of its regular dynamic variants, namely, that in which all of the initial protagonists but none of the antagonists move to the apex position of the *raisonneurs*. For although the moderators of this comedy eventually convince the originally offended parties to quit behaving every bit as irrationally as the primary antagonist, and thus to escape his machinations, yet the argument's chief instigator and his cohorts remain impervious to reason and therefore irredeemable to the very end.

The play's well-known argument has begun prior to the opening curtain with the intrusion into Orgon's prosperous household of a professional confidence man posing as a religious zealot. Feigning the most saintly and austere observance (including self-scourging), Tartuffe succeeds in utterly hoodwinking the credulous paterfamilias, while in reality intending to dispossess him of his wealth, marry his daughter, and seduce his wife into the bargain. Molière "builds" the entrance of this dissimulated man of God by delaying it for two entire acts, during which the audience witnesses instead the domestic brushfires already ignited by his presence; for, as is customary in dramas of this structure, the initial protagonists have grossly over-reacted to their uncomfortable pass. Thus, when Orgon foolishly seeks to break off his daughter's engagement to young Valère so as to free her hand for Tartuffe's febrile grasp, Marianne at once falls into despair, first proposing suicide and then taking the

---

[1]Molière, *Jean Baptiste Poquelin Molière: Four Comdies*. Translated into English Verse by Richard Wilbur. (New York: Harcourt Brace Jovanovich, 1978). All line references are to this text.

veil as the only logical escapes from such a revolting alliance. In this distracted state the girl then proceeds to fight with her inamorato, Valère, who on his part rashly presumes that she has willingly consented to her father's altered plans. Furthermore, Mariane's brother, the hot-headed Damis, has lapsed into a customary dither over the prospect of her engagement's being broken off; for, as he succinctly phrases it,

> Unless my sister and Valère can marry
> My hopes to wed *his* sister will miscarry (1.2.325).

As if these headaches were insufficient, Orgon's prudish mother, Madam Pernelle, has also been taken in by Tartuffe's false piety and, possessed by her new-found fanaticism, drops in to berate at wearying length the other members of her son's household for supposedly leading a wanton, irreligious life, preoccupied with worldly show and "costly fripperies."

Thus, even before the title-character's first appearance on stage, his creator has accomplished two impressive feats simultaneously, providing at once an indirect composite portrait of Tartuffe (a likeness whose accuracy will be verified after the malefactor makes his entrance) and also a lively first-hand picture of the excessive reaction to his machinations on the part of his intended victims, several of whom have already become engaged in an intense and hilarious internal conflict. This *tour de force* most artfully sets up the characteristic enantiodromia or mirror effect of all synthetic-realized actions, whose initial victims invariably come to reflect, through in somewhat paler tones, the essential colors of the principal antagonist. For Tartuffe's intemperance, hypocrisy, childishness, and (most significantly) his disloyalty act as lodestones to identical qualities latent in his adversaries, so that the play's initial conflict comes to be seen obliquely as a collision by mutual attraction. Though less obviously than its synthetic-implied cousin (Model 7), the synthetic-realized structure thus develops an argument between manifest opponents who upon closer inspection turn out to be none other than Tweedledee and Tweedledum. Yet the unique feature of this dynamic lies in the fact that, with the aid of more rational spirits, one of the nasty twins eventually alters his attitude, withdraws from the projective-reactive game, and as a consequence drives his former double from the stage. Prior even to Tartuffe's belated entrance in Act Three Molière has already placed his initial protagonists in a position so uncomfortable that only a few more turns of the screw will set them in motion toward a synthetic transformation.

Before charting this metamorphosis, however, it is necessary to anticipate a potential objection concerning our dialectical placement of Orgon in the initial protagonists' column, alongside his mother, son, daughter, and the latter's fiancé. For if he falls so deeply under the spell of Tartuffe that he becomes the latter's minion in opposition to his own family, does not Orgon (and for that matter also his similarly spellbound mother) more properly belong beside Tartuffe in the initial antagonists' column, moving from thence to the apex at the *denouement*? At first glance this alternative description appears promising, for it seems to tally both with our "Deeds, Not Words" theorem and also with the fact that numerous works of this class (including the author's own *Learned Ladies*) do represent a convergence upon the center from two directions at once, thereby also incorporating some of the initial antagonists in the formation of synthesis and new thesis. Yet certain critical facts militate against this dynamic possibility, not least among them that Tartuffe's designs upon Orgon are purely adversarial, and that the latter has been grossly deceived as to the title-character's true-meant design. Orgon could not possibly share Tartuffe's overriding wish if he knew what it really were; and when undeceived he reacts with understandable outrage. Although gullible in the extreme and slavishly subservient to the principal antagonist, the head of the family nevertheless falls willing victim only to Tartuffe's false mask, not his true visage; as a consequence Orgon's temporary opposition to his own wife and children while under the impostor's spell invites description rather as a strictly internal *agon* among those whose true interests are in fact identical. More significant dialectically than this internecine warfare in the initial protagonists' camp is what its members do in concert, namely, overreact to Tartuffe, whether pro or contra.

What is the nature of the title-character's villainy that it provokes such extreme responses from his initial victims? Molière dwells without mercy on the discrepancy between Tartuffe's pretensions to strict Christian morality—his outward show of piety—and his utterly selfish and immoral behavior. Listed baldly, his offenses against Orgon are rank: (1) sponging off him and setting about to indulge in every sensual pleasure the well-endowed household affords; (2) distracting him from, indeed temporarily corrupting, his sense of duty and loyalty as husband, father, and head of the family; (3) coveting marriage with his daughter and contriving to break off her engagement to Valère; (4) lusting after his wife, Elmire, and attempting to extort her favors by using her stepdaughter as a pawn (if Elmire yields, he will not hinder Mariane's match with Valère); (5) encouraging Orgon to disinherit his own son, Damis, and make him (Tartuffe) sole heir instead; (6) accepting Orgon's house and fortune as an "offering" conveyed to him by deed of gift and then, after being exposed as a fraud, trying to have the giver and his family summarily evicted; and (7) seeking to ruin Orgon utterly by revealing presumably incriminating private papers of his to the king. Apart from their egregious villainy, these betrayals of trust central to the age-old confidence game also produce a reactive breakdown of trust among the game's victims, thereby creating the typical doubling effect alluded to above—the process of inversion by which apparent polarities eventually show themselves to be reversed images of the same ugly figure. And whenever these combative twins materialize, it falls to the lot of the *raisonneurs* to convince the originally offended party that his behavior has become as extreme and dysfunctional, if not quite as coldly malicious, as that of the catalytic agent himself—that he is in fact thrusting and parrying at his own distorted image in a fun-house mirror.

Opposing this ludicrous fencing match and occupying the apex of the action's triangle from the outset, the onstage moderators of *Tartuffe* include three figures: the maidservant, Dorine; Orgon's wife, Elmire; and the latter's brother, Cléante. As one might expect in a Molière comedy, it is the sharp-witted soubrette who first smells a rat and at once springs into action, attempting to repair the damage wrought by the vermin's foraging and laying the first trap to catch it. When, in Act Two, Marianne and Valère begin squabbling because they misinterpret Orgon's refusal to honor their engagement as a sign of disloyalty on each other's part, Dorine tries to ridicule them out of their vexatious humour; but, this proving bootless, she quite literally pulls them back together, joining their hands in a physical gesture that epitomizes her function as moderator. Having accomplished a reconciliation, she promptly sets in motion the first concerted effort to bring Orgon back to his senses, exhorting Valère,

> Go to your friends, and tell them what's occurred, And have them urge
> her father to keep his word. Meanwhile, we'll stir her brother into action
> And get Elmire, as well, to join our faction (2.4.380).

By the end of the second act Dorine has thus produced the play's first synthetic movement by drawing Mariane and Valère to the rational center, from which position they will henceforth also act as moderators. At the same time she has alerted the two other *raisonneurs,* Elmire and Cléante, to the far more arduous task of dealing with Orgon on the one side, and Tartuffe on the other. Yet Dorine's hopes that Mariane's brother, Damis, will also act as a conciliator do not bear fruit; for this intemperate young man seeks instead to end the initial conflict by main force, threatening at every turn to execute corporal punishment on Tartuffe. It therefore becomes one of Dorine's principal tasks to prevent Orgon's son—equally excessive in the right—from disrupting the moderators' plans by committing murder. The simple burden of her advice to him might be taken as the rallying cry of all the comedy's apex characters: "Now don't give way to violent emotion" (3.1.385).

If Dorine flexes the hard muscle of deeds to combat the madness of the initial conflict (with its resultant internal conflicts on the initial protagonists' side), Orgon's brother-in-law, Cléante, chooses rather to stride the high road of reasoned argument, attempting by measured discourse to persuade the engaged parties above all to exercise caution, charity, and moderation. And although his exhortations are at first largely ineffective, Cléante nevertheless affords the author a highly articulate spokesman for the ethical principles upon which the actions of the other, more successful moderators are founded. Elmire's elegant brother thus functions largely as a walking abstraction of uniquely baroque cast—a *raisonneur* possessed of entire confidence in the godlike power of reason. Yet his attempts to argue the initial belligerents into sanity constitute positive action not only in the limited sense of advocacy but also as material contributions to the holding action waged by the beleaguered moderators, pending unexpected assistance from a far more powerful quarter.

Cléante immediately senses that Tartuffe's religiosity is so much "hocus-pocus" and cautions Orgon against his infatuation with the intruder, warning him also against unethically breaking his pledge to give Mariane in marriage to Valère; and when his words fall on deaf ears he hastens to convert principles into action by going at once to warn Mariane's fiancé of the trouble brewing (1.5.339). After this scene Cléante does not return again until the fourth act, this time to confront Tartuffe in private and at length, challenging the self-proclaimed man of God to act with truly Christian charity towards Damis—disinherited by Organ for offending the impostor—and putting him on notice that all of Paris is following his motions:

> Ought not a Christian to forgive, and ought
> He not stifle every vengeful thought?
> Should you stand by and watch a father make
> His only son an exile for your sake?

Again I'll tell you frankly, be advised:

The whole town, high and low, is scandalized (4.1.415).

For the very reason that it fails either to reform or intimidate the title-character, this interview serves the better to highlight Tartuffe's intransigence and to remove any lingering doubt that his hypocrisy is entirely of the conscious, first-degree variety. Yet Cléante's most effective work remains to be done in the last act, where he prevents Orgon from lapsing into rage and despair after his abrupt disenchantment with his erstwhile brother in the faith; and this time the moderator's advice not only eloquently recapitulates the essential philosophy of all the *raisonneurs* but also produces the desired result by calming Orgon down so that contingency plans can be made:

> ORGON
>
> Enough by God! I'm through with pious men:
> Henceforth I'll hate the whole false brotherhood,
> And persecute them worse than Satan could.
>
> CLEANTE
>
> Ah, there you go—extravagant as ever!
> Why can you not be rational? You never
> Manage to take the middle course, it seems,
> But jump, instead, between absurd extremes.
> You've recognized your recent grave mistake
> In falling victim to a pious fake;
> Now, to correct that error, must you embrace
> An even greater error in its place,
> And judge our worthy neighbors as a whole
> By what you've learned of one corrupted soul? (5.1.445).

But if Cléante operates as the comedy's spokesman for the Middle Way, it is his sister, Elmire, who most effectively carries the principles of this philosophy into action, remaining cool and permitting her head to govern her responses in trying situations. Orgon's wife enters the first of her two celebrated interviews with Tartuffe intending to convince the malefactor to step aside and permit the marriage between Mariane and Valère to go forward; but even before she can raise the subject, she finds herself being palpated and openly propositioned by the feigned Puritan. Instead of reacting with outrage to this turn of events, however, she senses an opportunity to use his indiscretion as a lever for advancing her original purpose:

> Some women might do otherwise, perhaps,
> But I shall be discreet about your lapse;
> I'll tell my husband nothing of what's occurred
> If, in return, you'll give your solemn word
> To advocate as forcefully as you can
> The marriage of Valère and Mariane,
> Renouncing all desire to dispossess
> Another of his rightful happiness (3.3.398–9).

Although her ploy fails because Tartuffe remains confident of Orgon's utter enchant-ment, Elmire gains from this initial *tête-à-tête* an invaluable bit of information about the impostor's concupiscence—a weakness she exploits in her second interview so far as to discredit him completely in her husband's eyes. This is the famous scene in which Orgon hides beneath the dining table and witnesses Tartuffe's making unambiguous sexual advances on the seemingly cooperative Elmire, who has cooly staged the whole charade for her mate's education. She suspects that the intruder will fall for the trap because "amorous men are gullible"; and topple he does, openly forswearing every principle he has heretofore pretended to espouse, and providing along the way a burlesque of Puritan morality:

> There is a science, lately formulated,
> Whereby one's conscience may be liberated,
> And any wrongful act you care to mention
> May be redeemed by purity of intention.
> I'll teach you, Madam, the secrets of that science;
> Meanwhile, just place on me your full reliance.
> Assuage my keen desire, and feel no dread:
> The sin, if any shall be on my head (4.5.432).

Executed with admirable finesse, Elmire's stratagem renders Orgon's disenchant-ment sudden and complete; nor is it without significance that as her husband rushes out of hiding, he immediately demands that Tartuffe begin to exercise "a little more restraint" (4.7.436). By the next and final act Orgon has calmed down far enough to ratify his shift to the moderate center by attempting to reason his still infatuated mother into making the same move (5.3.447ff).

Yet despite the onstage moderators' heroic efforts, Tartuffe still holds the high cards: Orgon's deed of gift to his entire estate and the strongbox containing the personal papers of a friend (Argas) who was exiled for complicity in an uprising against the crown. Molière has contrived events in this way so as to necessitate the *deus ex machina* intervention of Louis XIV, who sends his officer to arrest Tartuffe just as it appears that the latter will succeed in having Orgon's family evicted by a bailiff. The king's mercy extends to forgiving the head of the household in consideration of his war record:

> The king, by royal order, invalidates
> The deed which gave this rascal your estates,
> And pardons, furthermore, your grave offense
> In harboring an exile's documents.
> By these decrees, our Prince rewards you for
> Your loyalty in the late civil war,
> And shows how heartfelt is his satisfaction
> In recompensing any worthy action,
> How much he prizes merit, and how he makes
> More of men's virtues than their mistakes (5.7.468).

The final shifts from the initial protagonists' unit to the comedy's apex occur almost unnoticed. Indeed, the sudden reticence of Damis provides the best possible evidence that Orgon's irascible son has at last regained his senses; for after yet another threat of violence in the fourth scene of Act Five he lapses into a profound and refreshing silence, though present on stage until the end. As one might suspect, Orgon's prudish mother delays longest in admitting her error, gasping perfunctorily almost as the final curtain descends, "I breathe again, at last" (5.7.469).

With Tartuffe's arrest and these belated movements to the rational center (now augmented by the unseen Royal Presence), we are very nearly in a position to draw up the play's action-chart. Before such a project can claim thoroughness, however, it must account for two other unobtrusive but far from unimportant players. And it comes as something of a surprise that a work so anti-Puritanical, and one reputed in its own day to be even anticlerical, should reflect at its core the Christian duality of God and Satan after all. Yet this old conflict—urbanely soft-pedalled and suavely harmonized with such neo-classical values as reason, humanity, and Nature— nevertheless supplies this comedy with its principal characters. For lurking in the wings on either side of the stage the shadowy figure of Old Nick operates as an unseen prompter for both parties to the initial conflict, while hovering discreetly behind and ever so slightly above Louis' throne at center stage appears the outline of the Divine

Raisonneur. This motivational polarity becomes explicit at various points in the dialogue, yet nowhere more so than in Cléante's speech cautioning Orgon against the specious piety of men like Tartuffe, who proceed "by way of Heaven, toward earthly goals" and who "crucify their foe in Heaven's cause." To such knaves he contrasts instances of genuinely pious men whose religion is both "moderate and humane":

> They show by deeds how Christians should behave.
>
> They think no evil of their fellow man,
>
> But judge of him as kindly as they can.
>
> They don't intrigue and wrangle and conspire;
>
> To lead a good life is their one desire;
>
> The sinner wakes no rancorous hate in them;
>
> It is the sin alone which they condemn;
>
> Nor do they try to show a fiercer zeal
>
> For Heaven's cause than Heaven itself could feel.
>
> These men I honor, these men I advocate
>
> As models for all to emulate (1.5.335–6)

Clearly articulating the Christian, if latitudinarian, viewpoint of Molière's spokesman for the dominant unit, this discourse also serves the dual purpose of identifying religious zealotry with the sin of pride (Lucifer's primary failing) and of contrasting this "rancorous" self-inflation with the specifically Christian virtues of humility, forgiveness, and love. If the positive side of the moral dichotomy receives greater emphasis in the passage quoted, its negative face dominates the speech's first half and appears throughout the dialogue in pointed references to the "evil" that proceeds from willful contravention of Heaven's most reasonable decrees—a perversion that Tartuffe recommends to Elmire with Mephistophelean candor:

> . . . there's no evil till the act is known;
>
> It's scandal, Madam, which makes it an offense,
>
> And it's no sin to sin in confidence (4.5.433).

Elsewhere Tartuffe's malefactions are more bluntly linked to diabolical motives, as when the flabbergasted Orgon says of him that "Hell never harbored anything to vicious!" (4.6.435). Such abundant and unambiguous references to the Christian duality leave no doubt that, however decomposed through amalgamation with neo-classical humanism, God and Satan nevertheless stand as the primary adversaries of *Tartuffe*—just as they do in the contemporaneous *Phaedra*, and as they did a century earlier in *Romeo and Juliet.*

With the addition of Satan doubled on both sides of the opening conflict, and of the Christian deity at the summit of the comedy's apex, we are now prepared to draw up an action-chart for *Tartuffe*. The two flanking columns of this diagram show the opposing forces of the initial battle, while the center file comprises the action's moderators. An arrow indicates the shift of the (collectively bracketed) initial protagonists to the rational center—a redistribution of forces resulting in the ultimate dominance of the apex unit. Under the banner of Satan, the initial antagonists remain unmoved; for dialectical collapse can never be complete in the presence of a theological dualism such as this:

ACTION–CHART: Molière, *Tartuffe*:

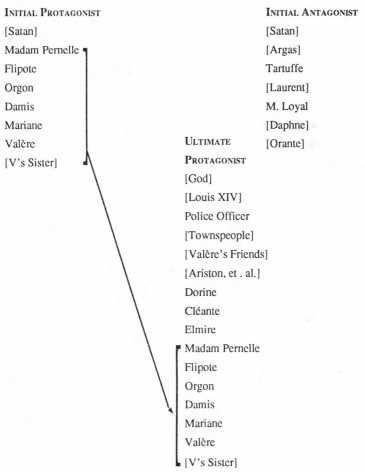

Initial Protagonist		Initial Antagonist
[Satan]		[Satan]
Madam Pernelle		[Argas]
Flipote		Tartuffe
Orgon		[Laurent]
Damis		M. Loyal
Mariane		[Daphne]
Valère	Ultimate	[Orante]
[V's Sister]	Protagonist	
	[God]	
	[Louis XIV]	
	Police Officer	
	[Townspeople]	
	[Valère's Friends]	
	[Ariston, et . al.]	
	Dorine	
	Cléante	
	Elmire	
	Madam Pernelle	
	Flipote	
	Orgon	
	Damis	
	Mariane	
	Valère	
	[V's Sister]	

(2) *Dialectic of Imagery*:

Like most other plays of its age, *Tartuffe* favors the abstraction over the metaphor, the conventional symbol over the contextual image; indeed, there seems a certain urgency here to supply qualitative glosses for rhetorical figures, as if their ethical bearings might otherwise get lost in the emotional wilderness of allusion. Owing to this intellectual specificity, the text of *Tartuffe* guides us from the dialectic of imagery to that of implication at nearly every step of the way, rendering it difficult to mistake the qualitative meanings that stand behind its rhetorical figures. And as is typical of works obeying the synthetic-realized dynamic, these figures all adhere to one of three larger constellations, each coloring a single point of the play's action-triangle: (1) negatively charged images attaching to Tartuffe and the other initial antagonists; (2) negative figures, often mirroring those of the first cluster, generated by the initial protagonists in response to their adversary; and (3) contrasting positive images qualifying the *raisonneurs* at the comedy's apex, and later also those initial protagonists who shift to the apex position.

The initial antagonists' constellation of *Tartuffe* consists principally of dark figures generated by the title-character himself, although to these must be added a much smaller number of equally negative tropes attaching to his manservant, Laurent, and to the bailiff, Monsiuer Loyal, as well as to three other hidden players—the traitor, Argas, and the local gossips, Daphne and Orante. Rounding out this cluster, a few discretely placed yet unmistakable allusions to the comedy's primary (though invisible) antagonist supply conventional symbolic coordinates pointing from Tartuffe's lurid imagery to the hellfires of Satan. Topically considered, the figuration of the antagonists' unit breaks down into several subdivisions distinguished according to the sundry moral (or rather immoral) qualities they exemplify; and since these attributes are usually spelled out in close proximate relation to the specific images themselves, it becomes possible to assign abstract headings to them with a high degree of assurance. Thus, the first and largest of these categories includes all the activities, physical properties, and figures of speech indicative of hypocrisy and deceit. Under this heading belong the many references to Tartuffe as one to make a "flashy show of being holy," to "weep and pray and swindle and extort." Molière hammers away at this contradiction between the pious façade and the venial inward of his title-character, and nowhere more resoundingly than through Dorine's acid judgments:

> A man whose spirit spurns the dungy earth
> Ought not to brag of lands and noble birth;
> Such worldly arrogance will hardly square
> With meek devotion and a life of prayer (2.2.350).

As usual, however, it is Cléante who introduces the dominating figure of this important sub-group, yet not before prefacing it with the familiar qualitative gloss that leaves no doubt as to its moral significance:

> There's a vast difference, so it seems to me
> Between true piety and hypocrisy:
> How do you fail to see it, may I ask?
> Is not a face quite different from a mask? (1.5.333).

The forthright signification of "hypocrisy" for "mask" and "true piety" for "face" permits us to anticipate one or two important sets of qualitative complements at the next stage of analysis, while indicating that a contextual definition of "true piety" will become necessary to understanding the play's dominant unit. Although the mask/face opposition is repeated with little modification at several points in the text, many cognate forms of the "mask" figure are also developed to qualify not only Tartuffe himself but also but also minor offstage antagonists as well. Thus, if the title-character feigns self-scourging while lusting after the gentlewomen of the house, his manservant engages in similar hypocrisy with the household domestics:

> He sermonizes us in thundering tones
> And confiscates our ribbons and colognes (1.2.324).

To this same rhetorical group also belong certain images specifically identified with that near relation to hypocrisy, disloyalty—in particular the incriminating private papers left with Orgon by the traitor Argas during his exile, papers later used by Tartuffe as instruments of blackmail against Orgon.

Closely allied with these "mask" tropes effectively coloring the hypocritical behavior of the antagonists, several related subgroups throw light on other facets of Tartuffe's unsavory character. A second cluster dwells upon his physical ugliness, his base origins, and his criminal record; a third depicts him in attitudes of sloth, gluttony, and lust; while a fourth particularizes his inclination to cruelty and violence. Yet another star of this constellation illuminates an aspect of the malefactor's deceitfulness that crosses over into downright blasphemy: his raising a "hymn and a hosanna" to Elmire in anticipation of her favors and claiming that upon her consent depends his "salvation"; his using the excuse of "pious duties" to cut short the uncomfortable interview with Cléante; and his kneeling in feigned humility while pretending to beg Damis for mercy (3.3.396; 4.1.418; 3.6.404). With a characteristic twist of irony, Molière permits the most damning tropes in this category to issue from the title-character's own mouth. When, for instance, Damis makes public the hypocrite's attempt to seduce Elmire, Tartuffe seeks to disarm her husband by dissimulating an utter contrition and castigating himself with only slightly exaggerated verity:

> Yes, Brother, I'm a wicked man, I fear:
>
> A wretched sinner, all depraved and twisted,
>
> The greatest villain that has ever existed.
>
> My life's one heap of crimes, which grows each minute;
>
> There's nought but foulness and corruption in it;
>
> And I perceive that Heaven, outraged by me,
>
> Has chosen this occasion to mortify me (3.6.403).

Indeed it has.

If at the primary level of action the impostor's villainy provokes reactive excesses on the part of his victims, so at the secondary level of imagery his diabolical "foulness and corruption" give rise to visions of disorder and madness among those he has imposed upon. Several clusters of coordinate tropes standing in mirror image relationship to Tartuffe's figures (Theorem 11) qualify not only the credulous Orgon but also his mother, son, daughter, and the latter's fiancé.Corresponding to the title-character's "mask" group signifying hypocrisy and deceit, the first of these clusters can be abstracted as figures of gullibility and irrationality. Orgon is described as having fallen beneath Tartuffe's "infatuating spell," and being "led by the nose." In this "dazed," "bewitched," and "addled" condition, having "quite lost his senses," he has begun acting like a "dunce" and "talking rot." "In short," concludes Dorine, "he's mad." Orgon's home is "like a madhouse with the keeper gone," claims his mother, who herself adds to the din by storming, haranguing, and making a "scene" in the drawing room. And even though Orgon's children are not beguiled by the feigned Puritan, they too begin to behave foolishly under the pressure of their father's unreasonable demands. The volatile Damis acts like a "dunce" (the same term used to describe Orgon), while Mariane "talks drivel" and she and her fiancé together turn into "great fools," Valère receiving the addition of "simpleton." More important to this cluster than mere epithets, however, are the many figures that spring directly from action itself—all the arguing, the repeated turnings-away-from and comings-back-together-again, the storming, ranting, whining, pleading, and threatening with blows. These frenzied activities link the initial protagonists together in the emotional and moral contagion that spreads to all those family members who are not inoculated by reason.

For each of the other figurative categories generated by the title-character Molière provides a corresponding set of mirror images to qualify his victims in the initial protagonists' unit: figures of excess for excess, disloyalty for disloyalty, cruelty for cruelty, and despair for evil. The impostor's viciousness thus finds its reflection in Orgon's harsh commands to Mariane, Pernelle's slapping of her servant, Mariane's and Valère's hurtful words to each other, not to mention Damis' constant threats of physical violence. And so for the remaining categories, which need not be elaborated here beyond noting that at several points the mirroring becomes too explicit to escape even casual regard, as when Orgon kneels to the already kneeling Tartuffe and demands that the unwilling Damis likewise implore the hypocrite's pardon (ORGON. How he blasphemed against your goodness! What a son! TARTUFFE. Forgive him, Lord, as I've already done.)

At the apex of the *Tartuffe*'s synthetic triangle, and providing emotional orchestration for the alternative thesis advocated by those who moderate between the play's increasingly look-alike thesis and antithesis, the dramatist has disposed a figurative constellation consisting of five principal subsystems. By far the largest of these component networks is made up of conventional symbols referring to the Christian faith and to Christian piety and charity. The text literally swarms with references to the "great God in Heaven," "the law of Heaven," and "the Lord," as well as to "salvation," "the Bible," "the Church," "Christian love," and "Christian forgiveness." While many of these phrases are uttered by the impostor himself, their extreme inappropriateness in his mouth clearly indicates that they must point elsewhere; yet it is evident that they cannot refer to Tartuffe's principal victims, some of whom also mouth such pieties in the service of their own unworthy ends. Rather it is to the comedy's moderators, chiefest among them the unseen Lord himself, that all such allusions apply without perversion of their sense; and it is to Cleánte, the spokesman for the apex unit, that Molière assigns the task of correcting Tartuffe's vindictive and impious constructions:

Why put yourself in charge of Heaven's cause?
Does heaven need our help to enforce its laws?

> Leave vengeance to the Lord, Sir; while we live,
> Our duty's not to punish, but forgive;
> And what the Lord commands, we should obey
> Without regard to what the world may say.
> What! Shall the fear of being misunderstood
> Prevent our doing what is right and good?
> No, no; let's simply do what Heaven ordains,
> And let no other thoughts perplex our brains (4.1.416).

If Cléante becomes the play's most voluble pleader of "Heaven's cause," the remaining two onstage moderators advocate the same cause primarily through pious deeds. Yet little things they let slip provide guides to the morality of their actions, as when Dorine insists that she will continue to love Orgon despite his nastiness to her and despite the "sinful marriage" he has planned for his daughter, or when Elmire attempts to fend off Tartuffe's advances with the caution that to yield would be an "offense to Heaven." Similarly, the purely ornamental offstage figures of Ariston, Periandre, Oronte, Alcidamus, and Clitandre provide, we are told, examples of "true piety" in showing "by deeds how Christians should behave," just as, at the denouement, King Louis acts in the name of "Heaven's justice" when he orders Tartuffe's arrest. This wealth of pious allusion—bolstered indirectly by the title-character's outrageous misappropriation of religious sentiment—leaves no room whatever for mistaking either the deepest motives of the *raisonneurs* or the identity of the comedy's Ultimate Moderator.

The four remaining categories generated by the apex unit may be abstracted as figures of moderation and circumspection, rationality and common sense, love and loyalty, and, lastly, humor. In this quintessentially baroque scheme the dominant radiance of Christian piety has been tempered with the pastel shades of neo-classical Aristotelianism and embellished in gilt with arabesques of urbane levity and worldly affections. Without particularizing these categories beyond saying that their most piquant figures emanate largely from action rather than dialogue, we must nevertheless point out that the initial protagonists also begin to generate a few images of this type once they have made their moves to the rational center. Valère offers Orgon material assistance in the form of money and a coach to escape the anticipated storm caused by Tartuffe's perfidy; Orgon himself begins to appeal to ocular evidence of the hypocrite's concupiscence in order to convince his mother of the truth; Mariane gives up her former whimpering and exclamations of despair; Damis falls into an unaccustomed silence; while Madam Pernelle, the most stubborn holdout, finally gasps, "I breathe at last"—an image bursts forth at moments of happy resolution in other works of the consumptive dramatist, notably in his *Imaginary Invalid*.

The following image-chart for *Tartuffe* makes no attempt at an exhaustive listing of individual tropes; rather it provides an overview of the major figurative categories in each of the comedy's three functional units, together with an approximate numerical count of the images in every group and one or two typical examples of each type. The enantiodromia characteristic of all synthetic actions will be evident from the similarity between figures in the initial protagonists' and antagonists' units (Theorem 11); for the real contrast, as indeed the true radical conflict itself, consists not in the collision between these two irrational forces, but between them on the one hand and the ultimately dominant apex unit of the other. The opening struggle thus comes to be seen as a contest between elements of almost equally negative symbolic value, the main difference being one of degree rather than kind.

IMAGE CHART: Molière, *Tartuffe*:

INITIAL PROTAGONIST	ULTIMATE PROTAGONIST	INITIAL ANTAGONIST
1. CREDULITY, GULLIBILITY, IRRATIONALITY: *Approximate count*: 37 images. *Example*: DORINE to ORGON: "How can you possibly be such a goose? / Are you so dazed by this man's hocus-pocus / That all the world, save him, is out of focus?	**1. GOD, PIETY, CHRISTIANITY:** *Approximate count*: 99 images. *Example*: CLÉANTE: "... there is nothing I more revere / Than a soul whose faith is steadfast and sincere, / Nothing that I more cherish and admire / Than "honest zeal and true religious fire."	**1. HYPOCRISY, DECEIT, BLASPHEMY:** *Approximate count*: 66 images. *Example*: TARTUFFE: "A love of heavenly beauty does not preclude / A proper love for earthly pulchritude; / Our senses are quite rightly captivated / By perfect works our Maker has created."
2. EXCESS: *Approximate count*: 27 images. *Example*: MARIANE: "I'll kill myself, if I'm forced to wed that man."	**2. MODERATION, CIRCUMSPECTION, RESTRAINT:** *Approximate count*: 26 images. *Example*: CLÉANTE: "... man's a strangely fashioned creature/Who seldom is content to follow Nature, / But recklessly pursues his inclination / Beyond the narrow bounds of moderation."	**2. EXCESS (LUST, GLUTTONY, SLOTH):** *Approximate count*: 60 images. *Examples*: DORINE: "He [Tartuffe] drank, at lunch, four beakers full of port." "He ate his meal with relish / And zealously devoured ... / A leg of mutton and a brace of pheasants."
3. DISLOYALTY, FALSEHOOD, SUSPICION, NEGLIGENCE: *Apporixmate count*: 42 images. *Example*: VALÈRE: "Would you prefer it if I pined away / In hopeless passion till my dying day? / Am I to yield you to a rival's	**3. RATIONALITY, COMMON SENSE:** *Approximate count*: 26 images. *Example*: ELMIRE: "The Lord preserve me from such honor as that, / which bites and scratches like an like and alley-cat! / I've	**3. CRIMINALITY, BASENESS, UGLINESS:** *Approximate count*: 35 images. *Example*: OFFICER: "The King soon recognized Tartuffe as one / Notorious by another name, who'd done / So many vi-

IMAGE CHART: Molière, *Tartuffe* (cont.):

INITIAL PROTAGONIST	ULTIMATE PROTAGONIST	INITIAL ANTAGONIST
arms / And not console myself with another's charms? / MARIANE: Go then: console yourself; don't hesitate. / I wish you to; indeed I cannot wait."	found that a polite and cool rebuff/Discourages a lover quite enough."	cious crimes that one could fill / Ten volumes with them, and be writing still."
4. CRUELTY, VIOLENCE: *Approximate count:* 49 images. *Example:* ORGON: "Under his tutelage my soul's been freed / From earthly loves, and every human tie: / My mother, children, brother, and wife could die./ And I'd not feel a single moment's pain."	4. LOVE, LOYALTY: *Approximate count:* 17 images. *Example:* DORINE: "True love requires a heart that's firm and strong."	4. CRUELTY, VIOLENCE: *Approximate count:* 17 images. *Example:* TARTUFFE to ORGON: "Gently, Sir, gently; stay right where you are./ No need for haste; your lodging isn't far. / You're off to prison."
5. SATAN, SINFULNESS: *Approximate count:* 7 images. *Example:* CLÉANTE to ORGON: "Being blind, you'd have all others blind as well; / The clear-eyed man you call an infidel / And he who sees through humbug and pretense / Is charged, by you, with want of reverence."	5. HUMOR, JOY: *Approximate count:* 10 images. *Example:* DORINE to ORGON: "There's lately been a rumor going about— / Based on some hunch or chance remark, no doubt— / That you mean Mariane to wed Tartuffe. / I've laughed it off, of course, as just a spoof." CLÉANTE to PERNELLE: "Madam. this world would be a joyless place/If, fearing what malicious tongues might say,/We locked our doors and turned our friends away."	5. SATAN, SINFULNESS: *Approximate count:* 10 images. *Example:* ORGON, of TARTUFFE: "Hell never harbored anything so vicious!" TARTUFFE, of DAMIS: "The mere thought of such ingratitude / Plunges my soul into so dark a mood . . . Such horror grips my heart . . . I gasp for breath, /And cannot speak, and feel myself near death."

(3) *Implicational Dialectic*:

Our third level descriptive reduction of *Tartuffe* will employ a single column of abstractions to qualify both the initial protagonists and antagonists, for in the synthetic realized dynamic these apparently conflicting units operate as qualitatively identical mirror-functions. Each recessive term derived in common from these two units will be preceded by its dominant opposite, qualifying the *raisonneurs* at the comedy's ultimately triumphant apex:

1. *Moderation/Excess*. If moderation is the quintessential motive for Comedy of the Golden Mean, it is also the most clearly manifest implication of the dominant apex unit of *Tartuffe*. Cléante's advice to Orgon, "Be cautious in bestowing admiration / And cultivate a sober moderation (*Et soyez pour cela dans le milieu qu'il fait*)," is but one of many in the same vein employing this same term and its cognates—in the original, *milieu, doux temperament, limite, traitabilité*. Indeed, few other works of this structure permit a moderator to advocate so openly the concept for which he himself is the objectification; and while this comedy's other apex characters voice their *raison d'être* less frequently or directly, their actions are just as evidently based upon its most classical regulatory principle.

2. *Restraint/Rashness*. Sympathetically resonating with the comedy's primary set of antinomies, this pair describes those emotional qualities requisite for either the exercise of moderation or the yielding to excess. For extreme impulsiveness characterizes the behavior of both sides of the initial conflict. Thus, Elmire's rebuke to Tartuffe, "You'd have done better to restrain your passion / And think before you spoke in such a fashion," is echoed in Dorine's warning to Damis, "Now don't give way to violent emotion . . . Do calm down and be practical" (3.3.396; 3.1.385).

3. *Temperance/Intemperance*. More or less synonymous in common usage with our first two sets of antinomies, this pair here expresses the physical and active sides of "moderation/excess" as philosophical attitudes and "restraint/rashness" as emotional predispositions. For Tartuffe's boundless appetite for various sensual delights leads him to commission of each of the Seven Deadly Sins, just as his victims' inability to temper their own passions makes them so vulnerable to his designs. Thus, Orgon abuses his family in his zeal to be thought a holy man, his son threatens murder when frustrated, and his daughter contemplates suicide when thwarted in her marriage plans.

4. *Rationality / Irrationality*. If moderation is the keynote of the synthetic-realized dynamic, rationality is one of its principal harmonics; and it is to reason that all the

moderators of *Tartuffe* appeal in their efforts to end a conflict in which both the title-character's "corruption of soul" and his victims' excessive reaction to that corruption are viewed primarily as lapses of rationality. From Dorine's exhortations to Mariane ("Do listen to reason won't you?"), to Cléante's eloquent speeches, and Elmire's calculated demonstrations to Orgon, the *raisonneurs* rely, true to form, upon reasoned argument. Ultimately, however, it is left to the monarch, whose "sovereign reason is not lightly swayed" ("*sa ferme raison ne tombe en nul exces*"), to punish the hypocrite and release his victims from his spell (5.7.467).

5. *Reality / Illusion.* "Cannot sincerity and cunning art, / Reality and semblance, be told apart?" asks Cléante of the "bewitched" Orgon, whose aspiration to a saintliness quite beyond his compass renders him such an ideal victim for the confidence man that only ocular evidence of the most damning sort can jolt him out of his illusion (1.5.333).

6. *Common sense / Foolishness.* Wishing Tartuffe to be a true saint and instrument of his own beatification, Orgon willfully denies the reality beneath the impostor's transparent mask. "You're a fool, brother " ("*vous êtes fou, mon frère*"), exclaims Cléante; and our English text quite properly renders this term as a negation of its opposite: "Have you lost your common sense?" (1.5.332). Any false posture of excessive reaction is here viewed as a lapse of common sense, which always humbly honors the limits that Nature has imposed upon her forms. This dichotomy represents a slight tonal modification of the structure's ever-present "wisdom/ignorance" opposition.

7. *Maturity / Childishness.* This spat between Tweedledee and Tweedledum is accented with imagery redolent of the kindergarten: Mariane "whines" and "snivels," her brother stamps the floor with his foot and hides in a closet, their father falls weeping before his idol, their grandmother talks incessantly but cannot bear interruption, while their persecutor carries about with him a little paper bag containing licorice bits.

8. *Circumspection / Gullibility.* Orgon's extreme credulity appears but as a reflection of an even greater gullibility in his oppressor; for despite Tartuffe's cunning, his inordinate appetites—especially his taste for the ladies—render him highly vulnerable to exposure. His overly fastidious request of Dorine, "Cover that bosom, girl. The flesh is weak, / And unclean thoughts are difficult to control," leads the maidservant to suspect his designs upon Elmire, who in turn plays upon his lust to

expose him: "...amorous men are gullible. Their conceit / So blinds them that they're never difficult to cheat" (3.2.389; 4.3.425).

9. *Discretion / Indiscretion*. If Orgon is nearly ruined by his indiscretions in the matters of the strong box and the deed of gift, Tartuffe is at last utterly foiled by his own foolhardy proposition to Elmire and subsequent action of eviction against the family. The first indiscretion exposes the impostor in his true colors to Orgon, while the second brings him to the attention of a monarch who has forgotten neither his *modus operandi* nor his previous criminal record.

10. *Piety/Impiety*. In order to avoid being thought anti-religious, the playwright is careful to express this important dichotomy as "true piety" and "false piety." Of truly pious men his Cléante offers the clearest description:

> They're never ostentatious, never vain,
> And their religion's moderate and humane;
> It's not their way to criticize and chide:
> They think censoriousness a mark of pride,
> And therefore, letting others preach and rave,
> They show, by deeds, how Christians should behave (1.5.335).

Moderation has thus become the hallmark even of piety: zealotry is to be eschewed like sin, and quiet virtue in action preferred to outward show and the trappings of faith. It is neither genteel nor humble to wear one's religion on one's sleeve, and doing so puts one under suspicion of harboring ulterior, impious motives.

11. *Arrogance / Humility*. Tartuffe's sanctimoniousness is but a screen for self-will driven by pride—Lucifer's flaw and the deadliest of the cardinal sins. Under the promptings of this motive the impostor arrogates to himself the rights of both man and God, until Divine Justice, operating though the agency of royal justice, brings him down.

12. *Trust / Suspicion*. Tartuffe's confidence trick produces a reactive breakdown of trust among the members of Orgon's family—and by extension the king's, and ultimately God's family. Hence, when the belatedly enlightened Orgon tries to tell his mother that he saw Tartuffe making advances on Elmire, the old lady refuses to believe him; and in this Dorine finds poetical justice:

> It's your turn now, Sir, not to be listened to;
> You'd not trust us, and now she won't trust you (5.3.451).

13. *Honesty / Hypocrisy*. In ordering Orgon to vacate his own house forthwith,

Tartuffe seeks to disarm his victim's wrath with typical sanctimony: "You needn't try to provoke me; it's no use. / Those who serve Heaven must expect abuse." At which Dorine gasps, "How he exploits the name of Heaven! It's shameless" (5.7.464–5). The very egregiousness of the title-character's hypocrisy renders that of his victims slightly less obvious; yet Orgon's near calamity is the direct result of his desire to appear more holy than he really is. In the same manner, his daughter threatens to take the veil only when it appears that she cannot have the lover of her choice; and his son meanwhile asserts that since Heaven prompted him to hide in the closet and overhear Tartuffe's proposition to Elmire, it is now his right to seek "sweet revenge" (3.4.401).

14. *Loyalty / Disloyalty.* Disloyalty and oath breaking are special issues of great concern in this comedy. Just as the curious offstage figure of Argas had been disloyal to the crown by joining in the nobles' uprising against the father of Louis XIV, now Tartuffe betrays his own benefactor by a calculated breach of trust; and in reaction to that betrayal Orgon ignores his wife's illness (not to mention her honor), disinherits his son, and breaks his word to give his daughter in marriage to Valère. Orgon regains his senses and moves to the rational center only after he has given (and kept) his word not to interrupt Elmire's interview with Tartuffe until he is convinced that she is in real danger; and at the conclusion the king forgives Orgon in consideration of his "loyal deeds in the late civil war." Ironically, the bailiff brought by Tartuffe to carry out the eviction is named Loyal. There is a real urgency here to link puritanism with treason and disorder, both civil and domestic.

15. *Justice / Injustice.* The title-character's actions are based upon fraud, a calculated injustice to which his victims respond so outrageously as to begin perpetrating injustices upon each other. Their eventual salvation and the impostor's defeat are represented to be the direct results of "Heaven's justice" (*"un juste trait de l'équite suprême"*) (5.7.468).

16. *Urbanity / Rudeness.* At first refusing to believe that Tartuffe has actually made a pass at Elmire, Orgon asserts that if his wife's story were true she would have 'looked more angry, more upset." To which she responds,

> Myself, I find such offers merely amusing,
> And make no scenes and fusses in refusing. . . .
> I've found that a polite and cool rebuff
> Discourages a lover quite enough (4.3.423).

Her urbanity typifies the cool-headedness of the moderators as a group and contrasts most markedly with the churlishness and impetuosity of the parties to the initial conflict.

17. *Civility / Incivility*. Madame Pernelle's long-winded public criticism of Elmire (her son's second wife) sets the tone in the play's opening scene for other lapses of good manners on the part of the old woman's blood-relations. Elmire wisely refrains from defending herself against these charges of frivolity and wantonness, but her brother Cléante gallantly comes to her defense:

> Madam, this world would be a joyless place
> If, fearing what malicious tongues might say,
> We locked our doors and turned our friends away (1.1.319).

18. *Humor / Dourness.*

> MADAM PERNELLE
> As a wise preacher said on Sunday last,
> Parties are Towers of Babylon, because
> The guests all babble on with never a pause,
> And then he told a story which, I think . . .
> (*To Cléante*)
> I heard that laugh, Sir, and I saw that wink!
> Go find your silly friends and laugh some more! (1.1.321)

19. *Serenity / Irascibility*. The second term of this set characterizes both sides of the opening conflict and receives constant reinforcement on the initial protagonists' part from active images of yelling, slapping, rushing about, pouting, weeping, stamping the floor, calling for a stick, etc. On the other side there are such outbursts as Tartuffe's partly feigned, partly genuine reaction to the accusations of Damis:

> The mere thought of such ingratitude
> Plunges my soul into so dark a mood . . .
> Such horror grips my heart . . . I gasp for breath
> And cannot speak, and feel myself near death. . . . (3.7.409).

In the midst of all this touchwood and gunpowder, the moderators constantly appeal for calm.

20. *Compromise / Dissention*. Like its twin brother "moderation," "compromise" stands as one of the motivational constants of the synthetic-realized structure; and its spirit animates *Tartuffe* most particularly when, even after Orgon is threatened with eviction from his home, Cléante still seeks some accommodation between opressor

and enraged victim, cautioning his brother-in-law to control his anger and consider patiently any offer of "fair adjustment" *(et s'il parlé d'accord, il le faut écouter)* (5.4.454).

21. *Gentleness / Violence.*

> What a display of hot headedness!
> Do learn to moderate your fits of rage.
> In this just kingdom, this enlightened age,
> One does not settle things by violence (5.2.446).

Cléante utters this caution when Damis threatens to cut short Tartuffe's life—an over-reaction typical of the other initial protagonists' violent responses to Tartuffe's own "extreme rascality." Madam Pernelle slaps her servant, the gentle Mariane threatens suicide, her lover rushes off to find consolation in another's arms, while Orgon repeatedly tries to slap Dorine and later vows to persecute all pious men "worse than Satan could." Cléante's appeal for calm specifically points to the rule of civil law under King Louis, the enlightenment of the age, and, as usual, the spirit of moderation.

22. *Flexibility / Stubbornness.* A slight modification of the second term of this structure's ever-present "flexibility/rigidity" dichotomy permits us to epitomize the willful, self-defeating stupidity of everyone engaged in the opening conflict, and none more than Orgon's mother, who responds to the revelations about Tartuffe's imposture with typically arrant disregard for the facts. "You can't shake me," she insists, "I don't believe it, and you shall not make me" (5.3.451).

23. *Tolerance / Intolerance.* The puritanism that Tartuffe dissimulates and Orgon and his mother uncritically embrace is an ethic that seeks to exclude those who deviate from its rigid code, whereas the Catholicism of the moderators is inclusive and tolerant. In eschewing extremes and advocating compromise, *Tartuffe* follows the disposition of its structure by favoring both/and over either/or—the former set being naturally dominant because it comprehends and synthesizes the extremes. This helps to explain why the synthetic-realized structure duplicates its negative values as mirror-functions, for its task is to demonstrate the inadequacy and essential likeness of exclusive either/or alternatives.

24. *Forgiveness / Vindictiveness.* To Tartuffe's disingenuous suggestion that, in light of recent accusations, it might be better for him to avoid Elmire's company, the latter's husband protests reassuringly,

> It pleases me to vex them, and for spite
> I'd have them see you with her day and night.

What's more, I'm going to drive them to despair

By making you my only son and heir (3.7.412).

Yet at the end, when Tartuffe has been arrested and Orgon begins to savor the idea of vengeance against his former idol, Cléante urges benevolence:

... don't say anything to aggravate

His present woes; but rather hope that he

Will soon embrace an honest piety,

And mend his ways, and by a true repentance

Move our just King to moderate his sentence (5.7.469).

25. *Love / Hatred.*

DORINE

If I didn't love you . . .

ORGON

Spare me your affection.

DORINE

I'll love you, Sir, in spite of your objection.

ORGON

Blast! (2.2.353).

26. *Beauty / Ugliness.* The negative term of this common pair aptly qualifies the behavior of the initial belligerents, who in the art of life are most ungainly actors; and images they generate heighten the impression of things unsightly and distasteful. Thus, Tartuffe has red ears, a dishonest face with pale complexion, and "distended guts"; he gorges like a swine, belches, and then snores all night, yet claims to scourge himself and to wear a hair shirt. Under the impostor's influence Orgon comes to view the world as a dunghill (*fumier*). Appropriately enough, the sham piety that gives rise to this excremental vision is exploded through the agency of Elmire's dazzling beauty.

27. *Normality / Perversion.* If Tartuffe is a self-styled "wretched sinner, all depraved and twisted," his principal victim has been released, under his tutelage, from all "earthly loves, and every human tie"—so far as to contemplate with equanimity the death of his whole family (1.5.331). By contrast, the sober rationality of the moderators is identified with the boundaries defined by rational law itself, as Cléante points out:

Ah, Brother, man's a strangely fashioned creature

Who seldom is content to follow nature,

> But recklessly pursues his inclination
>
> Beyond the sober bounds of moderation
>
> And often, by transgressing Reason's laws,
>
> Perverts a lofty aim or noble cause (1.5.333).

28. *Sanity / Madness*. Tartuffe's reasoning has become "badly warped and stretched" in the service of his venality. This aberration has also spread to his victims, for Orgon has "lost his senses" and gone stark "mad" since he fell beneath the impostor's spell; and as a result of his bewitchment Pernelle, Mariane, Damis, and Valère have also succumbed to sundry forms of extravagance and obsession, from which they will not be released until they learn to take reason's middle course and quit "jumping between absurd extremes."

29. *Dignity / Indignity*. Nothing better exemplifies the dignity of the comedy's moderators than the urbane way in which Elmire parries Tartuffe's advances during their first interview, or the cool manner in which, by seeming to yield in their second meeting, she elicits a full declaration for Orgon to hear from his hiding place; and even then she protects herself from unnecessary indignity by making her husband promise not to expose her to the hypocrite's "odious lust" but to intervene as soon as Tartuffe's intentions become clear to him. To crown all, she actually apologizes to Tartuffe for the necessity of employing deception to trap him! (4.7.436).

30. *Innocence / Guilt*. This antinomy scarcely requires comment, beyond mentioning that the title-character's crimes are the greater for being premeditated and habitual—as the eventual revelation of his criminal record makes clear. The term "guilt" applies here not only in its ethical and legal connotations but also in its theological sense, for at bottom the play is concerned with Judas' sin—the betrayal of friendship and trust.

31. *Humanity/Inhumanity*. The religion of truly pious men, says Cléante, is "moderate and humane" (*est humaine, est traitable*) (1.5.335). Condemning the sin but not the sinner, such men never "crucify their foes in Heaven's cause"—as Tartuffe does Orgon, or, indeed, as the latter does his own family and subsequently wishes to do to his erstwhile oppressor. Like all other virtues advocated in the play, humanity is predicated upon restraint and moderation.

32. *Virtue / Evil*. When Orgon exclaims that "Hell never harbored anything so vicious" as Tartuffe (*rien de plus mechant n'est sortie de l'enfer*), he is not at all wide of the mark; for the impostors' trespasses are premeditated crimes of commission,

conscious violations of the most fundamental laws of God and man. Moreover, like Satan, he tempts others to commit evils of their own; and his power can only be broken through God's mercy—here conveyed through the channel of Heaven's anointed on earth.

33. *Gratitude / Ingratitude.* Only after his shift to the moderate center does the head of the household begin to express gratitude where it is truly owed—to Valère for offering to secure his escape from arrest, and to the king for his deliverance (5.6.463; 5.7.470). Curiously enough, God is omitted from Orgon's final acknowledgments of thanks—presumably because King Louis has acted as intercessor on behalf of Divine Justice, and also because the comedy's modality must not be wrenched by sounding too solemn a chord in its last cadence.

34. *Hope / Despair.* Tartuffe is capable of fraudently impersonating a holy man because he himself has no faith in God, and consequently "despair" applies to him in its strict theological sense. To his victims, however, "despair" must assume a more secular usage to designate their temporary loss of hope (not faith) when confronted by evil.

With thirty-four sets of antinomies to qualify the comedy's ultimately dominant apex unit on the one hand, and its recessive mirror-functions on the other, the descriptive possibilities seem about exhausted. Although additional sets could possibly be squeezed out, it is perhaps unwise to apply further pressure at this stage; and major omissions will be readily supplied by the alert reader. The following implicational chart—this time repeating the mirror-functions in both the left and right hand columns to show their descent from the initial protagonists and antagonists, while listing the apex derivations in the central column—will permit rapid scansion of the comedy's motivational polarity. Double asterisks indicate antinomies or variants of antinomies universally implicit in synthetic-realized dramas, while single asterisks distinguish those commonly present:

IMPLICATIONAL CHART: Molière, *Tartuffe*:

RECESSIVE FUNCTION(I)	DOMINANT FUNCTION	RECESSIVE FUNCTION(II)
Excess**	Moderation**	Excess**
Rashness	Restraint	Rashness
Intemperance	Temperance	Intemperance
Irrationality**	Rationality**	Irrationality**

Illusion	Reality	Illusion
Foolishness**	Common Sense**	Foolishness**
Childishness*	Maturity*	Childishness*
Gullibility	Circumspection	Gullibility
Indiscretion	Discretion	Indiscretion
Impiety	Piety	Impiety
Arrogance	Humility	Arrogance
Suspicion*	Trust*	Suspicion*
Hypocrisy*	Honesty*	Hypocrisy*
Disloyalty	Loyalty	Disloyalty
Injustice	Justice	Injustice
Rudeness	Urbanity	Rudeness
Incivility	Civility	Incivility
Dourness*	Humor*	Dourness*
Irascibility*	Serenity*	Irascibility*
Dissention**	Compromise**	Dissention**
Violence	Gentleness	Violence
Stubbornness**	Flexibility**	Stubbornness**
Intolerance*	Tolerance*	Intolerance*
Vindictiveness	Forgiveness	Vindictiveness
Hatred**	Love**	Hatred**
Ugliness*	Beauty*	Ugliness*
Perversion	Normality	Perversion
Madness	Sanity	Madness
Indignity	Dignity	Indignity
Guilt	Innocence	Guilt
Inhumanity	Humanity	Inhumanity
Evil	Virtue	Evil
Ingratitude	Gratitude	Ingratitude
Despair	Hope	Despair

Perhaps the most salient feature of the implicational dialectic of *Tartuffe* is its utter lack of irony; for the dominant function generates a long string of exclusively positive terms, while the mirrored recessive functions consequently produce an equal number of wholly negative qualities. This strict segregation of conventional polarities, this eschewal of the ironic tendency to contaminate both units by mixing up the positives and negatives, characterizes not only *Tartuffe* but all other plays conforming to the synthetic-realized dynamic. By choosing to supplant two irrational "antitheses" with a more moderate and reasonable thesis, writers in this form commit themselves in advance to a highly normative differentiation of motives; and this inherent conservatism of the structure no doubt explains its appeal to the classical temper, whose clearly defined system of values results in a confident and thoroughgoing distinction between good and evil, functional and dysfunctional.

If at first glance the play's dominant unit appears to recommend a series of virtues to which no sane person could possibly object, a closer inspection reveals numerous motives that would offer but bland fare for the palate of an inveterate romanticist. The work's classicism manifests itself not only in such structurally requisite derivations as "moderation" and "rationality" but also through such exceptional terms as "restraint," "piety," "discretion," "circumspection," "civility," and "normality." This concatenation of staid virtues, coupled with the play's utter lack of self-doubting irony, would seem to render *Tartuffe* appealing chiefly to the nostalgic inclinations of modern audiences, for whom motives are usually more mixed and a commonly shared ethic more elusive. Yet it is significant that the synthetic-realized structure still appeals to writers who seek an ethic of accommodation in a fictive world ultimately animated by universal brotherhood and tolerance.

Although the dominant unit of this comedy invites commentary in terms of historical ethos, its twin recessive functions—containing such distressing terms as "intemperance," "indiscretion," "suspicion," "disloyalty," "vindictiveness," "guilt," and "madness"—appear to provide startling insight into the private fears of a dramatist whose life was far from serene. For at the time of composition Molière and his wife, a flirtatious actress many years his junior, were living under the same roof with his former mistress, who was reputed in some quarters to be his wife's mother. Malicious tongues even rumored—on no solid evidence—that Molière was married to his own daughter. Whatever the precise relationship among these three, it seems probable that the comedy's almost obsessive emphasis on the loyalty/disloyalty opposition derives its force as much from private as from public conflicts, and further, that such recessive motives as "hypocrisy," "injustice," "intolerance," "ingratitude," and "indignity" reflect not just a strong philosophical aversion for these qualities but also the fear of personal vulnerability to them. This likelihood opens the way, in turn, for a more intimate construction of the tolerant and loving virtues so forcefully advocated by the play's *raisonneurs*.

Despite its archaically strict segregation of conventional polarities, *Tartuffe* exhibits a richness and complexity that are reflected in the large number of implicational derivations required for adequate description of its action and counteraction (Theorem 18). That the play demands more antithetical pairs than some works of Sophocles and Shakespeare belies the common prejudice that comedy cannot possibly spring from spiritual depths comparable to those of tragedy or other forms of so-called serious drama—especially a comedy such as this, which unfashionably expresses its motives quite freely in open discussion rather than merely implying them through the bare metaphor of action clothed skimpily in figurative allusion. Yet when it is recalled that *Tartuffe* assumes the same dynamic pattern as *Oedipus at Colonus* or *A Winter's Tale*, and therefore also shares with those plays the most essential built-in motives of their common structure, such richness of texture is no more surprising than Molière's special fondness for a play that got him into so much hot water. This is not to say that other works conforming to the synthetic-realized model are always as deeply textured, or that the Comedy of the Golden Mean cannot be rendered more allusive and oblique; but it does provide confirmation of a high degree of motivational complexity in a play that is both comic and explicit.

SEVENTH MODEL
SYNTHETIC-IMPLIED

Definition. The synthetic-implied structure develops an oppressive conflict between two equally dysfunctional forces—often rationalized as discordant political systems—and leaves the struggle either stalemated or so unhappily concluded that, in either case, the auditor is drawn to supply in his own mind an acceptable alternative. The nature of this "synthetic" resolution is suggested by the presence of a dialectically disengaged character whose actions point to a just and humane solution, a course rendered possible only by adopting terms entirely different from the brutalized vocabularies of the major combatants. For although their conflict may appear to arise from the clash of highly articulated conventional polarities, it is in reality a nasty spat between Tweedledum and Tweedledee. Standing apart from this struggle, the apex or indicator character offers an alternative to the apparently opposite but in fact qualitatively identical modes of action persued by the initial protagonist and antagonist. Yet unlike the raisonneur of the synthetic–realized structure (Model 6), the apex figure of the synthetic-implied remains powerless to alter a course of events in which he is often the principal victim; for the engaged parties continue their benighted struggle to the bitter end without a single character on either side shifting to his central position. Bringing down the curtain on an inconclusive war where victory and defeat have utterly lost significance, the dramatist calls attention to the disengaged figure who has remained spiritually aloof.

Synthetic-implied actions are always highly ironic in tone, if not in implication, expressing authorial awareness that however inevitable the conflict's manifest polarities appear in the conventional order of things, they are nonetheless unendurable. Both sides are therefore allowed to carry the logic of their arguments to such irrational extremes that their dialectical interdependence, indeed collusion, becomes obvious; and when at last they are no longer perceived as viable alternatives, a dialectical collapse occurs in the spectator's mind, which then fixes upon the apex character as both synthesis and new thesis.

Schematic. The initial protagonist ("X") and initial antagonist ("Y") remain dialectically immobile, but the broken arrows from them to the apex figure ("Z") indicate the direction of a new thesis, made necessary by the recognition of an implied dialectical collapse:

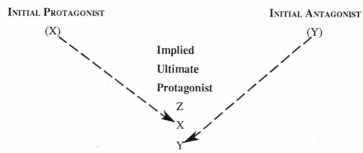

General.

> And we are here as on a darkling plain
> Swept with confused alarms of struggle and flight,
> Where ignorant armies clash by night.

The concluding lines from Arnold's "Dover Beach" might serve in general as an epigraph for the synthetic-implied structure, whose central mythos is a perennial and deadly struggle between unacceptable alternatives, apparent polarities ultimately revealed to be opposite faces of the same counterfeit coin. Easily misconstrued as the drama's only (and therefore definitive) dialectic, this seemingly all-consuming conflict is often based upon a familiar dichotomy drawn from the noisy storehouse of the more violent episodes of history and myth. Indeed, a disproportionate number of works obeying this structure is set at notable moments of actual armed conflict, as between Trojan and Greek in Shakespeare's *Troilus and Cressida*, Protestant and Catholic in Brecht's *Mother Courage*, the I.R.A. and the British in Behan's *The*

Hostage, or Robin Hood and the Sheriff in Goldman's screenplay *Robin and Marion*. More generalized but no less violent collisions also occasionally serve the purpose, as revolutionary versus reactionary in Ghelderode's *Pantagleize*. Whatever the particular encounter, the color of the uniforms, or the rationalizations for engaging, each of these battles between well-publicized opponents provides a metaphor for an obsessive argument of which the dramatist has grown weary, and to which his only sane response eventually must be "A plague on both your houses."

Although there is descriptive value in drawing a clear distinction between initial protagonist and antagonist in synthetic-realized actions (Model 6), this taxonomy becomes superfluous in the synthetic-implied because here both sides of the manifest conflict remain dialectically immobile, permanently fixed in their mirror image relationship. While writers employing the synthetic-realized dynamic wish to elicit some sympathy for the initial protagonist in order to motivate his eventual shift to the moderator's position, those employing the synthetic-implied are under no such obligation. On the contrary, any ties that for convenience often link the sympathetic apex character with one or another side of the manifest argument must not be permitted to distract from that side's essential repellancy and intractibility, nor from the indicator figure's dialectical disengagement from it. Consequently, apart from distinguishing the look-alike engaged parties, it makes no difference at all which of the initial adversaries we designate as "protagonist" and "antagonist." For when the implicit dialectical collapse becomes apparent, the auditor will perceive the disengaged figure to be the drama's real protagonist, and the true conflict to exist between him on the one hand and *both* sides of the manifest conflict on the other. The latter are therefore belatedly understood to be antagonists unwittingly locked in an internal war.

Allowing the bitter manifest conflict between unacceptable alternatives (in truth no alternatives at all) to grind maddeningly on, the author works a *reductio ad absurdum* through the use of intentionally frustrating repetition. Yet to erase any doubt as to the irrationality of the argument, he will often epitomize it in one or two highly metaphorical set-scenes showing the adversaries, sometimes separately, other times together, demonstrating the egregious folly of their interlocking obsessions. Such a set-piece is the famous "china scene" of Wycherley's *The Country Wife*, where the male and female adversaries engage in a sort of stylized game of hide and seek that highlights both the manic extremity and the ultimate depravity of their sexual preoccupation. A similar purpose is served in Brecht's *Mahagonny* by the fatal prizefight between Joe and Trinity Moses, who exemplify the apparently eternal war between haves and have-nots in a world brutalized by profit. Fellini's *City of Women* juxtaposes separate set-pieces for thesis and antithesis, epitomizing the male mystique in a fête at which the ultimate rake celebrates his ten-thousandth conquest, and its distaff counterpart in a nearby convention of frenzied feminists. The purpose of all such set-scenes, whether solitary of paired, is to point up the chilling likeness between Tweedledum and Tweedledee.

Having made us acutely uncomfortable with both voices of the debate, and at least vaguely aware that thesis and antithesis are both ruinously extreme, the author prepares us emotionally, and to some degree intellectually, for acceptance of a new thesis. The shape and quality of this alternate ethical postulate is suggested by the actions of the apex character, a figure represented as a good-hearted simpleton, a sort of holy idiot whose constitutional inability to attach himself to either side of the argument makes him seem mentally deficient in the face of the others' passionate commitment and polarized logic. Yet his foolishness comes to be seen, obliquely, as a higher wisdom, his vulnerable, exploitable humanity as a superior form of life. The mute and self-sacrificing Kattrin of Brecht's *Mother Courage* supplies perhaps the most notable modern instance of the indicator character of this structure; and of her, as well as the play as a whole, more shall be said presently. Yet it should be noted that Brecht has created even more complex representatives of this type in two other plays: *The Good Person of Szechwan* and *Puntilla and Matti, His Hired Man*. The title-characters of these contemporaneous works both suffer from personality splits so extreme that their opposing aspects do not even belong in the same dialectical unit. Thus, the simple and humane Shen Teh functions as the apex figure of *The Good Woman,* while her other, self-serving persona, Shui Ta, joins with the initial protagonists in their war against the lower orders who constitute the play's antagonists. An almost identical split occurs in *Puntilla,* whose title-character serves, when drunk, as the apex figure representing man's more benign social instincts, but operates, when sober, as the primary agent of the ruling class in its seemingly eternal conflict with the peasantry and proletariat. Because Brecht views the relationship between exploiters and exploited as essentially symbiotic and thus degrading to both of these adversaries, he is inhibited from positioning his title-characters' positive, exemplary personae on either side of the manifest conflict; instead, he finds for them a neutral corner where they may function uncontaminated by the selfish motives of the others—including their own shadows in the initial protagonists' units!

The indicator-character of this dynamic may occasionally move in the spotlight, dominating the stage and providing a constant emotional and moral point of reference. One such figure is Ghelderode's Pantagleize, a holy idiot who quite accidentally triggers the initial conflict, and through whose eyes, as it were, most of the subsequent events are viewed. Yet the apex character may just as often fill a supporting role that supplies rather a steady pedalpoint to the frenzied rhythms of the major combatants, as do Harcourt and Alithea, the rational couple of Wycherley's *The Country Wife*, or the heroic Minnie Powell of O'Casey's *Shadow of a Gunman*. The implied protagonist may even appear as a minor character in but one or two scenes calculated to provide a sudden glimpse of moral vistas outside the purview of the blindly impassioned others. This more oblique hint of alternatives to the moral deadlock is afforded twice by Euripides in his portraits of the humble Farmer of *Electra* and the rational Tutor of *Hyppolytus*. Shakespeare creates a vision of the synthetic character even more fugitive in *Troilus and Cressida,* permitting the foolish and immoral struggle between Greek and Trojan to be punctuated only twice by the prophetess Cassandra, who interrupts the Trojan war council first to foretell general disaster and finally to accuse Hector of betraying Troy by accepting Achilles' challenge. Cassandra's "madness" (from Apollo) replicates the holy idiocy characterizing many other synthetic figures—all of whose passages across the stage, whether brief or sustained, sweep the scene with breezes of sanity as refreshing to the auditor as they are annoying to the dialectically engaged characters.

Nor does the apex character always function alone. As we have already seen in the case of Wycherley's normative couple, Harcourt and Alithea, instances of two or even more dialectically disengaged characters do occur with fair regularity in works of this dynamic. The Farmer of Euripides' *Electra* walks in the sympathetic company of the villagers (represented by the chorus); Racine's *Britannicus* contains at its apex not only the title-character but also his friends Junia and Burrhus; while De Brocca's screenplay *The King of Hearts* disengages all the inhabitants of an insane asylum to crown the absent-minded title-character as their monarch. Yet even when a crowd forms at the apex, its members stick out like stranded tourists from another universe: in this one they are but refugees and victims whose compassion and good sense appear as folly to those surrounding them in the alien landscape.

The imagery of this landscape is dominated by figures of chaos, violence, useless repetition, and beleaguered wretchedness. The action itself often takes place in a no man's-land strewn with the smoking rubble of recent battles past and reverberating with the offstage alarms and cracklings of battles present—for these wars seemingly have no beginning or end. Knights of the opposing armies periodically return here to engage in single or group combat: this is where Hector and Achilles must meet to settle an ancient argument over "a cuckold and a whore" (*Troilus and Cressida*); where the Sheriff and Robin Hood engage in what seems the world's longest and most wearying combat at arms (*Robin and Marion*); here that the brutal prizefight symbolizing the ethic of dog-eat-dog takes place (*Mahagonny*), as well as the gladiatorial contest between representatives of captors and captives (*Escape from New York*); this the town square where, puppet-like, the German and English rifle companies kill each other to the last man (*King of Hearts*). Even when the dominating metaphor is not a military one, a closely related imagery will nevertheless often develop, as it does, for instance, in Sheppard's *True West,* whose middle-class kitchen progressively assumes the aspect of a battlefield, strewn with burned manuscripts, broken typewriter, stolen appliances, dead houseplants, torn-out telephone, and other rubble generated by the clash between two brothers over (significantly) control of the screenplay they are jointly writing. Similarly, a satire such as *The Country Wife,* whose primary tropes are bestial and medical rather than martial, still finds room for the military figure to add a certain acerbity to its war of the sexes:

> . . . hark you, Sir, before you go, a little of your advice, and old maim'd
> General, when unfit for action is the fittest Counsel; I have other designs
> upon Women, then eating and drinking with them; I am in love with
> *Sparkish*'s Mistress . . . now how shall I get her?

Figuratively allied to the martial trope, images of decay, disease, mutilation, deformity, bestiality, and cannibalism regularly attach themselves to both of the initial belligerents of this structure. Thus, when Shakespeare attributes the manifest conflict of *Troilus and Cressida* to the sin of pride, he declines pride to anarchy, and when "anarchy becomes the rule,"

> Then every thing includes itself in power,
> Power into will, will into appetite,
> Appetite, an universal wolf,
> So doubly seconded with will and power,

> Must make perforce an universal prey,
> and last eat up himself (1.3.119–24).

This moral ill at the root of Shakespeare's Trojan War generates the seemingly endless list of consumptive diseases that Thersites ascribes to the Greeks, as well as Hector's admission that the Trojan plight results from the "hot passion of a distempered blood." Similarly paired mirror-images almost always accompany the opposing forces of the manifest conflict in these plays: Phaedra's lust-corrupted flesh and the broken body of the puritanical Hyppolytus dragged behind his horses (*Hyppolytus*); the "beastliness" of Horner's feigned self-castration and the characterization of his female adversaries as "more ridiculous than their Monkeys . . . and almost as ugly" (*The Country Wife*); poor Mr. Luckerniddle sliced up for bacon while the capitalists on the meat exchange hit each other in the stomach (*Saint Joan of the Stockyards*); the picture of the Martyrdom of Saint Sebastian in Carrie's house and the image of her persecutors slaughtering a pig for a bucket of its blood (*Carrie*). If no other structure exhibits such consistently repellent figuration, it is because creators in this form wish to alienate us so thoroughly from both sides of the initial conflict that we will instinctively flee them, taking in our retreat the escape hatch held ajar by the indicator character.

Irony is the invariable mode of plays conforming to the synthetic-implied dynamic. But within that general tonality these dramas range, in Northrop Frye's taxonomy, through the various phases of satire, from "low norm" (in which a normative system of values is clearly implicit), to "Quixotic" (in which the positive values are carried by an eccentric character in defiance of an abnormal society), to "high norm" (in which a general beastliness makes it very difficult to perceive the moral alternative). The "lower" and therefore more obvious the implicit norm, the more comedic the drama's tone; the "higher" and thus more obscure the norm, the more melodramatic or "tragic" its aspect. Consequently, synthetic-implied dramas may range from rollicking satirical farces such as the 1950's British film satire on union-management conflict, *I'm All Right, Jack,* to high-strung tragi-comedies such as Brecht's *The Good Person of Szechuan*; or, as we have seen among classical dramas, from *The Country Wife* to *Troilus and Cressida*. Despite this tonal variability, however, dramas of the synthetic-implied class never really stray from the province of satire, and therefore of irony; for the underlying motive of this dynamic is to expose the utter folly of both of the major combatants.

The synthetic-implied is remarkable among the seven structural models in being the only one whose implications are largely predictable from play to play, author to author; for to employ this dynamic is to commit oneself in advance to specific meanings inseparable from its dialectical logic. While its close relative, the synthetic-realized, always yields certain specific antinomies (as "moderation/excess" and "flexibility/rigidity") yet permits reasonable latitude in the remaining motives of any particular work, the synthetic-implied, on the contrary, allows room for relatively few embellishments of an implicational pattern fairly predetermined as to specific motives. Because of this inherent tendentiousness of the structure, a collation of the implicational charts of various plays and screenplays assuming this form (ranking descriptive pairs in order of frequency and omitting pairs that occur only once) will yield a composite model for the implicational pattern of any other work of this class. In Figure One a collation of the qualitative abstractions of twenty synthetic-implied dramas duplicates the recessive functions in both left and right hand columns because those terms apply equally to the look-alike adversaries of the manifest conflict; the dominant function, derived by inference from the actions of the apex figure, stands isolated between the initial combatants.

FIGURE 1

Composite Implicational Chart for Synthetic-Implied Drama:

RECESSIVE FUNCTION (I)	IMPLIED DOMINANT FUNCTION	RECESSIVE FUNCTION (II)
Hatred	Love	Hatred
Ignorance	Wisdom	Ignorance
Hypocrisy	Honesty	Hypocrisy
Selfishness	Generosity	Selfishness
Cruelty	Kindness	Cruelty
Competition	Cooperation	Competition
Cowardice	Courage	Cowardice
Excess	Moderation	Excess
Conflict	Peace	Conflict
Guilt	Innocence	Guilt
Suspicion	Trust	Suspicion
Betrayal	Loyalty	Betrayal

Ugliness	Beauty	Ugliness
Dourness	Humor	Dourness
Arrogance	Humility	Arrogance
Delusion	Rationality	Delusion
Ruthlessness	Compassion	Ruthlessness
Injustice	Justice	Injustice
Inhumanity	Humanity	Inhumanity
Inflexibility	Flexibility	Inflexibility
Violence	Gentleness	Violence
Chaos	Order	Chaos
Intolerance	Tolerance	Intolerance
Bondage	Freedom	Bondage
Unhappiness	Happiness	Unhappiness
Death	Life	Death

It is clear from this chart that, while synthetic-implied dramas are highly ironic in the modal sense, they are never truly ironic from a structural point of view because the descriptive abstractions required for the implied dominant function always remain conventionally positive, reflecting the race's most lip-honored values. These works' regular depiction of both of the initial combatants as stupid, cruel, and hateful (with all the other negative qualities attendant upon this dreary threesome) renders it dialectically inevitable that the apex figure seem wise, kindly, loving, etc. There is no room here for Chekhovian shadings of positive and negative within the same function, nor indeed for much individuality at all in the sense of admixtures of moral strengths and weaknesses within the same character. This accounts for the uniformly schematic nature of these plays, which represent an indirect clash between radicals of good and evil. For if the apparent polarities of the manifest conflict must at last come to be seen as essentially identical, and their true opposites can only be suggested by the actions of a lonely "eccentric" or two at the apex of the triangle, then the former and the latter must be drawn in the strongest possible colors. Hence, the subtlety of this dynamic consists not in delicate portraiture but rather in bold strokes applied to keep the oblique from seeming merely obscure. Despite its largely fixed pattern of values, however, the synthetic-implied structure does permit a certain leeway for auxiliary motives which create, as we shall presently see, shadings of meaning from instance to instance.

ANALYSIS
Bertolt Brecht, *Mother Courage and Her Children*[1]

(1) *Dialectic of Action*:

Contests between unacceptable alternatives held a particular fascination for Bertholt Brecht, among whose major plays no fewer than five assume the synthetic-implied structure: *Mahagonny, Saint Joan of the Stockyards, Mother Courage and Her Children, Puntilla and Matti, His Hired Man,* and *The Good Person of Szechwan.* Of these, the most celebrated as well as the most typical of its dynamic class is *Mother Courage,* which, though less complex than the author's later creations in the same form, still poses a number of problems for the structural analyst. Perhaps the greatest of these difficulties is the dialectical placement of Mother Courage herself—although this issue has been somewhat artificially confused by layers of misreading imposed upon the character by those who find her attractive in a way that her creator clearly did not.

The manifest conflict between mirror-image opponents that dominates *Mother Courage* from first to last can be expressed very simply as "Protestant against Catholic." For the Thirty Years' War between anti-Papist states and the Holy Roman Empire supplies an historical context in which the title-character and her children play out their tale of woe, moving involuntarily from the Swedish camp where they begin, to that of the Catholic Emperor, and finally returning to the Protestant fold. This war has already begun when the drama opens and is still going on when the lights dim on the final scene—a situation reminiscent of *Troilus and Cressida* and other works of this structure wherein the focal characters' ironic stories also alternate between both sides of a larger and apparently interminable military conflict. Yet Brecht's version of this historical struggle depicts no knightly challenges nor councils of war at which the great issues are aired; instead it paints a worm's-eye view of the battlefield from the lowly vantage of Mother Courage's provisioner's wagon at the periphery of the action, leaving the audience to infer both Protestant and Catholic motives largely from what it can see from her humble perspective.

Nevertheless, the dramatist manages to include three set-scenes during which his

---

[1] Bertholt Brecht, *Mother Courage and Her Children.* Translated by Ralph Manheim. In *Bertolt Brecht: Collected Plays*, vol. 5. Edited by Ralph Manheim and John Willet. (New York: Vintage Books, 1972). All scene and page references are to this text.

title-character retreats a little into the background, and with these he epitomizes the rapaciousness and irrationality of both sides of this "war of religion," the drama's manifest conflict. Thus, Scene 2 exposes the Protestant cause when the Swedish General honors Courage's son, Eiliff, for slaughtering peasants and stealing their cattle. Having drunk the General's wine, the young man does a sabre-dance and sings a double-edged song about a rash soldier who joins the fray despite the wise counsel of his elders. This set-piece receives an ironic follow-up in Scene 8, where Eiliff having performed a similar "heroic" deed during a cessation of hostilities, is arrested and executed as a common criminal—his wartime valor suddenly assuming the color of barbarity! (2.144–50; 8.192–5).

If Scene 2 and its reversal in Scene 8 provide heavily ironic commentary on the Protestant cause, Scene 4 epitomizes the Catholic side in equally negative terms. Here we witness a young soldier of the Emperor waiting to receive his promised reward for risking his life to save the battalion commander's horse; but he is refused a hearing by the junior officer, who has embezzled the reward money to spend it on liquor and women. Ready to commit murder over this arrant injustice, the soldier nevertheless eventually backs down after blowing off steam and considering the consequences of acting upon his justifiable anger (8.170–4). These three episodes permit Brecht to demonstrate more pointedly the underlying social irrationality at the root of this "holy war." For the rest, however, he depicts the mirror-image opponents only indirectly and in small segments more intimately connected with Courage's own activities. But as to the shape and character of the manifest conflict, there remains little doubt.

Somewhat less obvious, however, is the position of the title-character herself in relation to this conflict; for by choosing to show both faces of the struggle from Courage's vantage point, the author finds it expedient to have her drift between the Protestant and Catholic camps, easily adjusting to profiteering under either banner, and even flying both flags alternately above her wagon. This apparent independence, coupled with her seemingly heroic adaptability and protectiveness toward her children, raises some question as to Courage's allegiance, and even suspicions that she may be a dialectically disengaged figure representing some alternative mode of behavior. Yet much as the free-agent description seems to accord with her qualities of toughness and resilience, Courage is nonetheless attached, however casually, to the Protestant side of this conflict between mutually unacceptable opponents. Her "business as usual" association with the Catholic forces which momentarily surround her cannot be understood as a dialectical shift, but rather as the enlarged detail of a greater picture of collusion between essentially similar adversaries. Indeed, she herself is quick to distinguish apostasy from opportunism:

> Maybe we stand to gain. We're prisoners, but so are lice on a dog (3.159).
>
> At least they let me carry on my business. Nobody cares about a shop-keeper's religion, all they want to know is the price. Protestant pants are as warm as any other kind (3.160).

More relevant than these minimal expressions of allegiance, however, is Courage's successful effort to circle around and rejoin the Protestant army, to which she thereafter remains attached (9.194).

Therefore, according to our "Order of Ends" and "Unidirectionality" theorems (to the effect that a character's dialectical placement is determined by comparing his initial and final allegiances, and that double-crosses are to be ignored as dynamically irrelevant), Courage must be placed with the Protestants, whom we shall designate as the play's "initial protagonists." In the long view, of course, it would make little difference which side of the argument she took, since both come to be seen as qualitatively identical. The critical matter is her attachment, if any, to some side; and of that there can be no doubt. Her temporary collaboration with the Catholics—the "initial antagonists" of the piece—serves to highlight the disturbing resemblance between the manifest adversaries, but in no way indicates the title-character's detachment from the conflict.

Brecht predicates all of Courage's actions upon one simple overriding motive, which he allows her to voice in Scene 6: "My aim in life," she says, "is to get through, me and my children and my wagon" (6.183). At the drama's end she is still barely alive and still has her provisioner's wagon, but all her children are dead, each lost in part as the result of her obsession with survival and her attendant urge to drive a bargain or turn a profit, even when life is at stake and time of the essence. Based upon fear and reflexivity, her survival instinct is thus shown to be grounded in qualities that render it inadequate for the purpose it would serve. As we have seen, Courage's equation of survival with profit affords a closeup look at the motives animating both Protestants and Catholics; for their larger conflict also grows from the same unqualified urge for mere personal continuity—an urge that turns humans into wolves that prey upon their own kind, and even upon their own children. Courage is a war profiteer, however modest, and firmly believes her survival to be dependent upon the continuance of a struggle whose primary motive she shares:

When you listen to the big wheels talk, they're making war for reasons
of piety, in the name of everything that's fine and noble. But when you
take another look, you see that they're not so dumb; they're making war
for profit. If they weren't, the small fry like me wouldn't have anything
to do with it (3.156).

If Mother Courage belongs with the Protestants of the initial protagonists' unit, so
also do her two illegitimate sons, the half-brothers, Eiliff and Swiss Cheese, whom
she has harnessed up to pull the canteen wagon now that her horse is dead. Although
Courage desperately seeks to keep them out of the army and tied to the family
enterprise, even drawing a knife on a recruiting officer who sidles up to the lads, Eiliff
is nevertheless quickly lured by promises of glory and a ten guilder bonus into joining
the Swedish forces. This event occurs while his distracted mother haggles with the
Sergeant over the price of a belt buckle—the imperiousness of her greed thus
establishing a precedent whereby she will lose each of her children for good. Eiliff's
motive for joining the Swedes is glory; but, as we have seen, this urge leads to his
destruction when a temporary armistice renders his martial daring a criminal offense.
In the scene following his execution Courage sings her famous "Solomon" song
recounting the sundry virtues that become liabilities in an irrational world, and here
we learn that poor Eiliff has met the fate of Caesar:

It's daring that brought him to that pass!

How happy is the man with none! (9.198).

If Eiliff's downfall results from misplaced daring, his half-brother, Swiss Cheese,
meets his own doom owing to the misapplication of yet another virtue: honesty.
Brought up by his mother to be conscientious rather than brave because he isn't very
bright, Swiss Cheese obtains through her efforts the job of paymaster of the Second
Finnish Regiment. But there his single virtue backfires when, after the Emperor's
troops overrun his position, he decides that duty requires him to hang onto the
regimental funds until he can rejoin his unit. Catholic spies promptly arrest him on
suspicion of hiding the cash box; but when they question his mother, she denies
knowing her own son in order to avoid drawing suspicion on herself. Instead, she
desperately tries to mortgage her wagon for money with which to bribe his captors.
Not desperately enough, however; for Swiss Cheese falls before a firing squad while
she is still haggling over the price. When soldiers bring the body to her for
identification, Courage once again refuses to claim her second son, who has died the
foolish death of a Socrates:

His honesty had brought him to that pass.

How happy is man with none! (9.199).

Whatever their sundry virtues, those who live by the sword shall die by it. Thus, Swiss Cheese and Eiliff require dialectical placement beside their mother in the initial protagonists' unit, a camp headed by the offstage King Gustavus Adolphus and including all but one of the other figures from the Protestant side of this great "war of religion." The single exception is their half-sister, Kattrin, whose detachment from the struggle constitutes a critically important element of the play's dynamic structure. Aside from Kattrin, however, the remaining characters of *Mother Courage* must be segregated according as they attach to either the Protestant or Catholic camps; and in order to deal as quickly as possible with the other figures of this populous and eventful drama, we shall hasten our discussion by listing their names and offering a brief rationale for the placement of each, beginning with the Protestant side:

1. [*King Gustavus Adolphus*]. Offstage. King of Sweden and leader of the Protestant armies. After he enters Poland, says Courage, "the Poles start butting into their own affairs and attack the king while he's quietly marching through the landscape. That was a breach of the peace and the blood is on the Poles' head." "In the beginning," she continues, "he only wanted to protect Poland against the wicked people, especially the emperor, but the more he ate the more he wanted, and pretty soon he was protecting all of Germany" (3.156). His death at the Battle of Lützen proclaimed by banner in Scene 8. Motives: power, greed.

2. *The Recruiter*. Swedish Officer. Recruits men he admits are unfit for service; lures Eiliff into the army with money and promises of glory. Maintains, in the play's opening speech, that there is no order or morality without a war. (Scene 1). End not given. Motives: fear (survival), power.

3. *The Sergeant*. Swedish. The Recruiter's N.C.O. Distracts Courage with the hope of a small sale while the officer approaches Eiliff. Superstitious, and so frightened of being killed in battle that he always stays in the rear ranks; draws Courage's black cross signifying death. Exits with the couplet, directed at Courage, "If you want the war to work for you / You've got to give the war its due" (1.144). (Scene 1). End not given. Motive: fear (survival).

4. *The General*. Swedish regimental commander. Rewards Eiliff for slaughtering peasants and stealing their cattle, calling him a "young Caesar." Makes fun of the Chaplain and his pious rationalizations for the war. "Eats like a pig," although his cook claims that his taste in sauces is

deficient. (Scene 2). End not given. Motives: power, greed, gluttony.

5. *The Chaplain*. Attached to Swedish regiment. Rationalizes the Protestant cause with sanctimonious lies; claims that since the war is about faith it is therefore pleasing to God. Later joins up with Courage for security; removes his canonicals when the Swedes are overrun by Catholic forces, but puts them back on again when they rejoin the Protestants. Tries to lure Courage into a marriage of convenience; competes for her with Pete and loses. Goes off in defeat. End not given. (Scenes 2–3, 5–8). Motives: fear (survival), greed, lust.

6. *The Ordinance Officer*. Finnish. Puts the army in jeopardy by selling bullets to Courage in order to buy liquor for his colonel; won't sell them to a fellow ordinance officer whom he doesn't trust "because he's a friend of mine"; takes less than he originally asks for the ammunition and exits disappointed; later advises Courage to get rid of a nearby cannon because the Catholics are approaching, then runs off. (Scene 3). End not given. Motives: fear (survival), greed.

7. *The Cook (Pieter Lamb, alias "Pete the Pipe")*. The Swedish General's cook who fails to bargain Courage down on the price of a capon; later invites her to join up with him to run a small pub he claims to have inherited, but is turned down when he excludes her daughter from the deal as *de trop*. A former ladies' man; "ruined" Yvette Pottier, who calls him the "worst rotter that ever infested the coast of Flanders." Believes that "all men are sinners from the cradle, fire and sword their natural lot" (8.192). Winds up begging for food with Courage, and is finally left standing "dumbfounded" at being abandoned by her. (Scenes 2-3, 8-9). End not given. Motives: fear, (survival), greed, lust.

8. *Yvette Pottier*. Protestant camp follower. "Ruined" by The Cook ("Pete the Pipe"), for whom she still carries a torch. Tries unsuccessfully to buy Courage's canteen wagon. Later marries an old colonel's elder brother and becomes a countess. At last re-encounters Pete the Pipe and warns Courage against him; goes off angrily with her ancient husband. End not given. (Scenes 3, 8). Motives: fear (survival), greed, revenge.

9. *The Old Colonel*. Protestant. Yvette's companion, described as "doddering," but then "colonels make money by the bushel." Agrees to buy Courage's wagon as a present for Yvette; warns her away from a young Lieutenant she claims will also give her money. By Scene 8 has been dead for "a few years." (Scene 3). Motives: lust, greed.

10. *[The Count Starhemberg]*. Offstage. The Old Colonel's elder brother,

whom Yvette marries for money and a title following the colonel's death. End not given. (Ref. Scene 8). Motive: lust.

11. *The Peasant Woman*. Protestant. Pleads with the Catholic soldiers to spare her livestock, telling her son to show their officer the way to Halle, as he demands. Wants to warn the citizens of Halle of the sneak attack, but is afraid of being killed; decides to pray for them instead, and tells Kattrin to join her. Suggests that the soldiers smash the canteen wagon in order to get Kattrin to stop drumming the alarm; pleads with the Lieutenant not to kill them because of Kattrin. Loses her defiant son. End not given. (Scene 11). Motive: fear (survival).

With the exception of several offstage figures (including the various fathers of Courage's children) who function rather as images than as actors in the drama, the above characters round out the Protestant camp, which we have designated as the initial protagonists' unit of *Mother Courage*. The following figures comprise the Catholic camp and initial antagonists' unit of the play:

1. [*The Pope*]. Offstage. Spiritual leader of the Catholic forces. Having enumerated the reasons why it takes gumption for the poor to survive a war, the title-character adds, "And putting up with an emperor and a pope takes a whale of a lot of courage, because these two are death to the poor." End not given. (Ref. Scene 6). Motives: power, greed.

2. [*The Emperor*]. Offstage. Temporal leader of the Catholic forces. "The Emperor had everybody under his yoke, the Poles as much as the Germans; the King had to set them free." When the war shows alarming signs of grinding to a halt, the Chaplain reassures Courage: "But the kings and emperors, not to mention the pope, will always come to help in adversity." Courage: "Even an emperor can't do anything by himself, he needs the support of his soldiers and his people." End not given. (Ref..Scene 6). Motives: power, greed.

3. [*Marshall Tilly*]. Offstage. Imperial Field Marshall. His funeral is proclaimed by banner and described in Scene 6. Killed "by accident" after getting lost in the fog and mistakenly riding forward into the thick of battle. At his funeral the church bells cannot be rung because they had all been shot out on his orders. "It seems the general had been having his troubles. Mutiny in the Second Regiment because he hadn't paid them. It's a war of religion, he says, should they profit by their faith?" (Ref..Scene 6). Motives: power, greed.

4. [*Polish Peasants*]. Offstage. Catholic. Killed defending their cattle

against Swedish soldiers led by Eiliff. Armed with clubs, they almost succeed in "making hash" of the Swedes, but stop fighting when Eiliff begins bargaining with them; thus distracted by the prospect of gain, they are quickly mowed down. (Ref. Scene 2). Motives: fear (survival), greed.

5. *Man with Eye-Patch*. Catholic spy. A "little runt." Stalks Swiss Cheese and has him arrested on suspicion of secreting the Finnish regimental cash box. Swiss Cheese is executed, but the cash box is never found. End not given. (Scene 3). Motives: power, greed.

6. *The Sergeant*. The spy's N.C.O. Arrests Swiss Cheese for hiding the Finnish regimental cash box and orders his body thrown on a dump when Courage refuses to identify it. The cash box is never located. End not given. (Scene 3). Motives: power, greed.

7. *[The General]*. Offstage. Catholic. Ordered his troops to cut across wheat fields and trample down the grain, an act later resulting in the starvation of his own troops. Gives his soldiers permission to loot a conquered city for just one hour, claiming he's not a monster—although Courage says "the Mayor must have bribed him." End not given. (Refs. Scenes 4, 5). Motives: power, greed.

8. *[The Captain]*. Offstage. Catholic. Company commander who spends reward money belonging to The Young Soldier on liquor and women. End not given. (Ref. Scene 4). Motives: greed, lust, gluttony.

9. *The Young Soldier*. Catholic. Distinguishes himself by jumping in the river to save the colonel's horse, but is denied his due reward by the captain; storms about in the latter's office threatening to murder him if the money isn't forthcoming, yet finally gives up and sits down just before the officer enters. Courage tells him that he "can't start a riot sitting down" and that his temper is too short for him to fight for justice (whereupon she gives up her own complaint and sings "The Great Capitulation" song). End not given. (Scene 4). Motives: fear (survival), greed, revenge.

10. *The Clerk*. Catholic. The Captain's N.C.O. Tries to restrain Courage and The Young Soldier from voicing their complaints to the Captain. "Keep your trap shut," he growls to Courage, "We haven't got many provisioners and we'll let you keep on with your business, especially if you've got a guilty conscience and pay a fine now and then." (Scene 4). Motives: power, fear (survival), greed.

11. *The Older Soldier*. Catholic. Attempts to restrain the Young Soldier from voicing his complaints to the Captain. End not given. (Scene 4). Motive: fear (survival).

12. *The Soldier*. Catholic. Wants to drown his sorrow in drink because he

came too late to loot a conquered city. Admits having shot at peasants from his own side because you can't tell Protestant from Catholic peasants when you're shooting. Borrows a woman's coat from Courage, but she rips it off his back when he can't pay. End not given. (Scene 5). Motives: fear (survival), greed.

13. *The Second Soldier*. Catholic. Helps Kattrin and the Chaplain rescue some peasants whose farm is set ablaze; and when the first soldier objects that they're Protestant peasants, he contends that they're "Catholics like us." End not given. (Scene 5). Motives: fear (survival), partisan aid.

14. *Peasant Woman (and Family)*. Catholic. Risked their lives to stay on their farm and protect their property during a skirmish; shot at and wounded by their own side; burned out of their farm. Motive: fear (survival).

15. *The Old Woman & Young Son*. Catholic. Try to sell bedding to Courage to pay taxes on their house. The old woman faints when she hears that "peace has broken out," but her son helps her up and they rush back with the bedding. (Scene 8). Motive: fear (survival).

16. *The Lieutenant*. Catholic. Leader of a platoon about to storm the city of Halle by surprise. Forces The Young Peasant to show him the path to the city; threatens to cut Kattrin to pieces when she starts drumming the alarm; also threatens to kill the peasant family if they do not stop her; offers his word as an officer that Kattrin's mother will be spared in the city if she stops drumming; finally shoots her from her perch; her alarm succeeds anyway. End not given. (Scene 11). Motives: power, fear (survival).

17. *The First Soldier*. Catholic. Threatens to cut down a peasant family's ox and cows if they do not cooperate by showing him the path to Halle. Claims that with peasants "it's the animals that come first." Tells Kattrin they will spare her mother in the city if she stops drumming; chops wood to drown out the sounds of her beating; all in vain. End not given. (Scene 11). Motives: power, fear (survival).

This necessarily telegraphic overview of the initial protagonists and antagonists of *Mother Courage* nevertheless reveals an obvious identity of motive for the war's opposing forces. The only noticeable variance occurs at the highest levels on both sides of these fictive hierarchies where the urge for mere survival is supplanted by the dual incentives of power and greed—more comfortable attenuations of the same drive in those for whom bare subsistence does not pose an immediate concern. Thus, while class antagonisms form an important aspect of the internecine conflicts occurring in both the Protestant and Catholic camps, these internal differences have not been radicalized: the little fish still continue to define themselves either as sharks or barracudas, and accept being devoured by larger members of their own species as an unfortunate but perfectly natural consequence of being predators. Those most easily succumb who, like Eiliff and Swiss Cheese, would like to play the game but are handicapped by their inability to control at will such occasionally useful virtues as bravery and honesty. So long as the characters of both sides persist in viewing the war as divinely ordained or inevitable in the course of nature, the small fry like Courage will continue to identify with the motives of those having bigger mouths and longer teeth. No one, it seems, possesses the natural insight and true courage to alter the terms of the brutal argument by adopting a radically different course of action. No one, that is, except the title-character's apparently retarded daughter, Kattrin.

To this frustrating spectacle of unremitting oppugnancy and all-too-human selfishness, Kattrin's actions supply a sharply contrasting counterpoint and an increasingly insistent throbbing of the moral alternative—of compassion, self-sacrifice, and a deep courage that none of the others can consistently muster. Kattrin's spiritual disengagement from the manifest conflict is symbolized by her physical difference; for she is mute and unable to communicate except by gestures and animal-like grunts, a fact that causes the other characters to regard her as simple-minded and something less than human. This "holy idiocy" of hers comes not from Apollo, like Cassandra's, but from "a soldier who stuffed something in her mouth when she was little" (6.183–4). Unemployable except by her mother, homely and unmarried at twenty-five—though she dearly wants to wed and raise children—Kattrin waits on soldiers, washes dishes, runs errands, and helps her mother pull the canteen wagon (9.194, 196–8). Traumatized by the war early on, she continues to be terrified of its bestiality, although the others around her accept it at worst as a necessary evil and at best as a splendid occasion for profit. Even her usually unsentimental mother offers this intimate portrait of Kattrin:

> How could she pull the wagon by herself? She's afraid of the war. She couldn't stand it. The dreams she must have had! I hear her groaning at night. Especially after the battles. What she sees in her dreams, God knows. It's pity that makes her suffer so. The other day the wagon ran over a hedgehog, I found it hidden under her blanket (9.197).

The play's early and sporadic hints of Kattrin's compassionate nature do not reveal at once her essential moral difference from those around her, but they do strike the first chords of a swelling theme as she makes raucous sounds to warn her mother that Eiliff has gone off with the recruiter, or gesticulates wildly and howls to alert Swiss Cheese and Courage to the spies who have come looking for the cash box (1.143–4;

3.161–2). That such actions flow from a source deeper than mere filial obedience becomes more evident in Scene 5 where Kattrin actually threatens to hit her mother with a board for refusing to allow her stock of shirts to be torn up as bandages for wounded peasants. When the girl rushes into a burning house to rescue a baby and then tries to calm it by singing a lullaby, the exasperated Courage marvels, "there she sits, happy in all this misery" (5.175–6). Subsequent scenes add further sympathetic, indeed sentimental notes to Kattrin's theme: the desire of a poor and plain girl to make herself attractive in order to get married come peacetime; her mute despair at the cruelties of war; the horror and grief at Eiliff's execution; the assault and disfigurement by soldiers; the touching willingness to release her mother to marry the cook (6.180–4; 9.194–8). Yet as qualitatively different as these strains make Courage's daughter sound, they nevertheless issue largely from the passive sufferings of a victim and therefore bear a vague tonal relationship to the other characters' grudging acceptance of the war. Kattrin is clearly an unusual and sympathetic type, but not until near the drama's end does the author cause his apex figure to perform a deed that puts her spiritual singularity beyond all doubt. Then, in Scene 11, she is made to do something completely out of context, utterly at variance with the motives of the other characters: in a last suicidal act she defies the Catholic soldiers and beats a drum to warn the inhabitants of Halle that they are about to be slaughtered, thus reminding the audience that compassion and self-sacrifice are still possible, even in a world brutalized by the seemingly eternal war between religious sects. Carefully placed at the drama's penultimate moment, Kattrin's courageous deed—triggered by her compassion for the children of Halle—provides the only sovereign and unambiguous act of altruism in the entire play; and coming thus after ten scenes of unmitigated selfishness and barbarity on both sides of the conflict, it provides not only a powerful emotional release but also the sudden vision of an alternative mode of behavior.

Scene 11 also contains what at first glance appears to be a dialectical movement— that of the young peasant who realizes that Kattrin is drumming to save not only her mother but all the inhabitants of Halle, and who eventually forfeits his own life by shouting encouragement to her. Not uncommon to dramas of the synthetic-implied order, such fleeting moments remind us of its near kinship to the synthetic-realized. Yet the young peasant's apparent shift does not radically affect the outcome of the drama as a whole, as actual movements always do in the synthetic-realized; his action, like Kattrin's, rather constitutes pure gesture, significant but contextually futile. Moreover, since the author has represented this figure as openly defiant of authority and thus exceptional from the outset, we are obliged to include him in the apex unit all along, a fitting anonymous companion for Kattrin and necessary reminder that her sacrifice is not inimitable.

These acts of compassion and courage bring into focus an alternative that before was present only in the blurred outline of hints and indirection: the picture that began slowly to seek resolution through Kattrin's eccentric behavior, now becomes clear. A dialectical collapse, if it has not already occurred in the spectator's mind, must happen now or never. In the following action-chart the broken arrows indicate the dynamics of this implosion:

ACTION-CHART: Bertolt Brecht, *Mother Courage and Her Children***:**

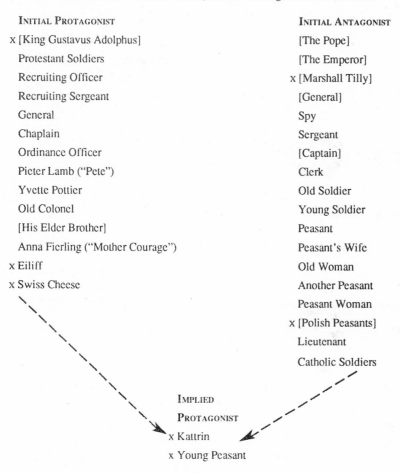

INITIAL PROTAGONIST	INITIAL ANTAGONIST
x [King Gustavus Adolphus]	[The Pope]
Protestant Soldiers	[The Emperor]
Recruiting Officer	x [Marshall Tilly]
Recruiting Sergeant	[General]
General	Spy
Chaplain	Sergeant
Ordinance Officer	[Captain]
Pieter Lamb ("Pete")	Clerk
Yvette Pottier	Old Soldier
Old Colonel	Young Soldier
[His Elder Brother]	Peasant
Anna Fierling ("Mother Courage")	Peasant's Wife
x Eiliff	Old Woman
x Swiss Cheese	Another Peasant
	Peasant Woman
	x [Polish Peasants]
	Lieutenant
	Catholic Soldiers

IMPLIED
PROTAGONIST
x Kattrin
x Young Peasant

(2) *Dialectic of Imagery*:

Brecht deploys a truly extraordinary number of images in *Mother Courage*. Whether projected as physical properties, word-pictures, or activities, these figures express a meticulous concern with the details of his characters' interactions, as with those tangible things great and small that provide instruments of such exchange; and along with all this particularity come arresting landscapes flashed onto the mind's screen by a continuous barrage of epithets, exclamations, and sayings, as well as parodistically colored settings of religious and military iconography. Owing to this monumental profusion (greater than in most plays by Shakespeare) our analysis must restrict itself to the very general, citing but a few instances as typical. Structurally, then, the play's images divide into three principal sets, each qualifying one of the points of the action's "synthetic" triangle: (1) negatively charged figures generated by the Protestant side; (2) repellent figures, similar in kind and identical in effect, qualifying the Catholic side; and (3) emotionally contrasting positive figures associated with the apex unit. For practical purposes this figurative triad may be reduced to binary form by taking the dramatist's hint and collapsing the first two sets in which the Protestant and Catholic image-clusters produce specular doubles of one another and eventually come to be experienced as a single rhetorical unit.

The emblematic disposition of this war between Tweedledum and Tweedledee resembles others of the same structure: a desolate no-man's land where nearby armies attack and counterattack across the rubble-heaps of former strife, where fire-eaters seem to breathe while the gentle suffocate, and the loud curse drowns out the soft blessing, sarcasm the tender gesture—until voraciousness seems at last to consume itself. Bombarding the spectator from either side of the manifest conflict, these repellent attacks upon sense and sensibility come in seven major varieties, without essential distinction between Protestant and Catholic: (1) images of violence, pain, and death; (2) expressions of profanity, hostility, and derision; (3) contextually inverted allusions to the Bible and religion; (4) activities centered on profit-making, cheating, lust, gluttony, and starvation; (5) images of social control, regimentation, order, and chaos; (6) references to the passage of many hard seasons and years; and (7) songs epitomizing these categories while moralizing them ironically. Falling in a withering hail, these figures often explode in tightly compacted clusters of powerfully negative resonance; and as a consequence the strict segregation of such tropes into logical groupings more than occasionally seems an arbitrary process.

Under our fourth heading, for instance, one cannot really separate images of profit-making from those of gluttony and lust because the three sorts often adhere not only logically but also topologically, as when Eiliff exuberantly remarks that cutting down peasants whets the appetite, or when the recruiting officer justly accuses Courage of wanting the war "to eat the core and spit out the apple" (i.e., be profitable rather than costly to her) (2.146; 1.140). That even our very broad categories frequently collapse into composite structures is well exemplified by the Swedish General's command, "Food, Lamb, you lousy, no-good cook, or I'll kill you," which runs a rapid-fire sequence of our groups 4, 2, and 1, respectively, combining as it does figures of gluttony and violent death with expressions of derision. Considering the prolonged and numbing flurry of images generated by all this shadow-boxing (repetition with slight variation being sought here for its saturation effect) and in light of the fact that these tropes ultimately collapse to form a larger mirror-system reflecting misery and mendacity either way, we shall allow the play's concluding song to stand as our chief example for both units. Sung by the now childless Courage, this lyric neatly compacts most of the war's major figurative categories and epitomizes the tone of the manifest conflict in one last jarringly ironic salvo:

> With all the killing and recruiting
> The war will worry on a while.
> In ninety years they'll still be shooting.
> It's hardest on the rank-and-file.
> Our food is swill, our pants all patches
> And still we dream of God-sent riches.
> Tomorrow is another day!
>
> > The spring is come! Christians, revive!
> > The snowdrifts melt, the dead lie dead!
> > And if by chance you're still alive
> > It's time to rise and shake a leg (12.210).

Compared to the profusion of lurid figures issuing from the initial protagonists and antagonists, Kattrin's apex unit generates at spacious intervals a smaller constellation of radiant signs whose emotional pull is sharply in the other direction and vastly out of proportion to the sum of its constituent elements. The gradually countervailing weight of these tropes derives in large part from the girl's very muteness, which requires that most of her images be active ones, that she express her compassion through deeds rather than those slippery words mouthed by the others primarily for purposes of deception and self-deception. By insisting that her figuration resonate almost exclusively at the primary level of action, the dramatist at once frees it from the ambiguity of common speech and grants it the substantiality and dramatic priority that the deed always carries over the word; in the process he endows all her gestures with one overriding motive: love. Whether she signals wildly to save her brothers from the army and death, threatens her recalcitrant mother in order to rescue peasants, sings to a homeless infant, takes a dead hedgehog to bed with her, or steals off in the night to seek companionship—all of Kattrin's inarticulate motions eloquently bespeak their spiritual origin, and thereby reveal themselves to stand in diametrical opposition to all the harsh voices barking their fear and hatred. Her sign language thus grows into a mighty semiology of spiritual detachment and ultimate liberation from the conventional, cowardly grammar of the other characters.

While Kattrin's last action is clearly her grandest, the final crescendo of mute gestures begins as early as Scene 9, when, hidden in the wagon, the girl overhears her mother reluctantly declining the cook's tempting offer because it excludes her daughter—one of Courage's all-too-few acts of real self-sacrifice. Following the couple's exit, Kattrin rises to meet this affirmation of mother-love by performing a telling pantomime:

> Kattrin climbs out of the wagon. She is carrying a bundle. She looks around to make sure the others are gone. Then she spreads out an old pair of the cook's trousers and a skirt belonging to her mother side by side on a wheel of the wagon so they can easily be seen. She is about to leave with her bundle when Mother Courage comes out of the house (9.200).

This utterly articulate sign-language, so at variance with the noisy haggling of the others, sets Kattrin even more clearly apart and prepares the audience to accept her final gesture of love at face value.

Then, in Scene 11, this swelling of the moral alternative undergoes a sudden and radical figurative modulation; for Kattrin's *gestus*, previously confined to the languages of silence, now assumes an entirely new and imperative auditory dimension, and, as the scene's banner proclaims in advance, "THE STONE SPEAKS" (11.203). This allusion to the Philosophers' Stone, the mystical speaking rock that has the power to transmute any imperfect earthly matter into its utmost degree of perfection, provides a rich metaphor for Kattrin's final work of compassion. For as her language of the spirit responds to its greatest challenge, it breaks forth into sound, no longer audible only to the few within range of her former gesticulations and strangled groans, but boldly to the world at large. Still insulated from the forked meanings of ordinary discourse and elevated to the plane of pure action, Kattrin's warning drumbeats to the citizens of Halle proclaim for all to hear that an instrument normally used to count war's cadence may also be employed to amplify the beating of a merciful heart. And although a Catholic bullet finally silences her utterly, Kattrin has nevertheless prevented the surprise attack and saved Halle's children, as the answering roar of the city's cannon announces in the distance. It must be added at once, however, that the apex figure has not thereby ended the manifest conflict, which will continue its dismal course, with the bereaved Courage once again trudging off to its old drumbeats. Yet it is the thunder of the mute girl's alarm (like the anguished cry of Shen Teh at the end of *The Good Person of Szechwan*) that will ring in the ears of the audience as it leaves the theatre; and this resonance, operating simultaneously at the levels of catalytic action and figurative accompaniment, most powerfully suggests an alternative to the seemingly endless hostilities between the drama's initial combatants.

Owing to the profusion of tropes attaching to the initial protagonists' and antagonists' units of *Mother Courage* our image-chart must radically abbreviate its listings, offering only general headings for the major figurative categories followed by a few typical examples and an approximate numerical count of the individual tropes under each—approximate because the frequency of composite figures renders highly subjective the task of determining when images must be counted separately or as parts of larger units. Mother Courage's images have been placed in the initial antagonists' unit whenever they refer to her activities as a collaborator with the Catholics, but in the initial protagonists' unit whenever they clearly allude to her former business on the Protestant side; and so for the Chaplain and the Cook. Only in the implied protagonists' central column have I attempted a fairly comprehensive (though telegraphic) listing of the separate figures under each general heading:

IMAGE-CHART: Brecht, *Mother Courage and Her Children:*

INITIAL PROTAGONIST (PROTESTANT)	IMPLIED PROTAGONIST	INITIAL ANTAGONIST (CATHOLIC)
1. VIOLENCE, PAIN, DEATH: *Approximate count:* 125 images, *Example:* "GERMANY HAS LOST MORE THAN HALF ITS POPULATION. THOSE WHOM THE SLAUGHTER HAS SPARED HAVE BEEN LAID LOW BY EPIDEMIC. ONCE-FLOURISHING COUNTRYSIDES ARE RAVAGED BY FAMINE. WOLVES PROWL THROUGH THE CHARRED RUINS OF CITIES" (banner).	1. MUTENESS: "It's the war that made her dumb too, a soldier stuffed something into her mouth when she was little;" "It's a gift of God to be dumb;" "She was like a stone … The people used to say: We don't see the cripple; "THE STONE SPEAKS" (banner). 2. LOVING GESTURES: Making sounds to warn Courage that the recruiter has gone off with Eiliff; Gestures & sounds warning Swiss Cheese of the spy; Forcing Courage to tear up shirts as bandages for wounded peasants; Running into burning house to rescue baby; Rocking baby & singing to it; "She's crazy about children"; Pantomime with cook's trousers and Courage's skirt; Beating the drum to warn the city of Halle of the surprise attack; The young peasant's shouts of encouragement to her & his own death as a result; The city's alarm bells & cannon fire indicating Kattrin's success. 3. DISTRESS AT WAR: Running behind wagon & sobbing when Swiss Cheese is lost; throwing down bottles & running out	1. VIOLENCE, PAIN, DEATH: *Approximate count:* 116 images. *Example:* "A lieutenant and three soldiers in heavy arms step out of the woods." THE LIEUTENANT: I don't want any noise. If anybody yells, run him through with your pike."
2. PROFANITY, HOSTILITY, DERISION: *Approximate count:* 55 images. *Example:* "Shut up you depressing wreck! Watch your step with him, his kind are dangerous even when they've gone to seed."		2. PROFANITY, HOSTILITY, DERISION: *Approximate count:* 38 images. *Example:* "Boque la Madonne! Where's the stinking captain? He embezzled my reward money and now he's drinking it up with his whores. I'm going to get him."
3. INVERTED ALLUSIONS TO RELIGION: *Approximate count:* 50 images. *Example:* "You mowed down [the peasants], splendid, so my troops could have a		3. INVERTED ALLUSIONS TO RELIGION: *Approximate count:* 33 images. *Examples:* (a) "Bribe-taking is the same thing as mercy in God." (b) "Don't stand

INITIAL PROTAGONIST (PROTESTANT)	IMPLIED PROTAGONIST	INITIAL ANTAGONIST (CATHOLIC)
decent bite to eat. Doesn't the Good Book say: "Whatsoever thou doest for the least of my brethren, thou doest for me'?"	when Courage starts talking about buying in expectation of renewed war; Sustaining a wound across forehead & one eye when assaulted by soldiers: "There'll be a scar." She can stop waiting for peace";Burying her head in a blanket after Eilif is taken off; Bad dreams & groaning after battles; Taking a dead hedgehog to bed with her; "Crawling with lice"; Groaning upon hearing of innocent children in besieged city; Sobbing as she beats the alarm drum; Her body being covered by her mother and carried off by peasants.	around like Jesus on the Mount of Olives, bestir yourself, wash those glasses . . ." (c) "Maybe she'll give us three guilders if we throw in the cross."
4. PROFIT, GREED, CHEATING, GLUTTONY, STARVATION: *Approximate count:* 103, images. *Example:*(a) "Maybe you'll scare up a rat, maybe, I say, 'cause they've all been eaten, I've seen five men chasing a starved rat for hours. Fifty hellers for a giant capon in the middle of a siege." (b) "One time in Livornia our general got such a shellacking from the enemy that in the confusion I laid hands on a beautiful white horse from the baggage train."	**4. REGENERATIVE ACTIVITIES:** Washing dishes; Folding washing; Scouring knives & glasses; Cleaning dirty dishes; Pointing to lovely yellow leaves on tree; Offering Swiss Cheese a drink; Waiting on soldiers; Helping take inventory; Bandaging the wounds of peasants; Going out to pick up provisions & carrying packages back despite being assaulted; Pulling wagon after her brothers are gone.	**4. PROFIT, GREED, CHEATING, GLUTTONY, STARVATION:** *Approximate count:* 117 images. *Example:* (a) "Her mother's gone to town on business.—Buying up people's belongings, they're selling cheap because they're getting out." (b) "Ah, peace! What becomes of the hole when the cheese has been eaten?"
5. REGIMENTATION, ORDER, CHAOS: *Approximate count:* 24 images. *Example:* "It takes a war before you get decent lists and records; then your boots are done up in bales and your grain in sacks, man and beast are properly counted and		**5. REGIMENTATION, ORDER, CHAOS:** *Approximate count:* 23 images. *Example:* THE YOUNG SOLDIER . . .When the captain comes out I'll cut him to pieces. THE CLERK (*looks out*) The captain will be here in a moment. Sit down.

IMAGE-CHART: Brecht, *Mother Courage and Her Children* (cont.):

INITIAL PROTAGONIST (PROTESTANT)

marched away, because people realize that without order they can't have a war."

6. HARD SEASONS, DETERIORATION:

Approximate count: 25 images.

Example: "The winter will go by like all the rest. Harness up, it looks like snow."

IMPLIED PROTAGONIST

5. DRESSING UP: Putting on Yvette's hat & red shoes; Strutting in imitation of Y's gait; "she [Y] ruins herself for money. But you'd like to do it free of charge, for pleasure"; Rejecting gift of red shoes after she is assaulted & crawling into wagon; Afraid to appear outside with her scar; Stealing off at night to be with soldier; [K] "in silk gown / Cut from an angel's / Best party gown."

6. PEACETIME IMAGES (INDIRECTLY ASSOCIATED WITH KATTRIN):

Stopping for a beer between battles; Taking a little nap by the roadside; Plowing in the middle of war; Bells ringing for peace; Raising children; "The rose bush in our garden" (song).

INITIAL ANTAGONIST (CATHOLIC)

(The young soldier sits down)"

6. HARD SEASONS, DETERIORATION:

Approximate count: 23 images

Example: "From Ulm to Metz, from Metz to Pilsen/Courage is right there in the van./ The war both in and out of season / With shot and shell will feed its men."

(3) *Implicational Dialectic:*

Because the initial protagonist and antagonist of the synthetic-implied dynamic generate identical descriptive terms, we shall simplify our rationale for the third-level abstraction of *Mother Courage* by permitting in each case a single term to stand for both of the recessive mirror-functions. Preceding this term and separated from it by a stroke mark will appear in parentheses its antinomy, derived by inference from the action and imagery of the drama's implicitly dominant apex unit:

1. *(Courage)/Fear.* Although nicknamed "Courage" for her intrepidity at spiriting fifty loaves of bread out of the besieged city of Riga, the title-character comes to be seen, ironically, as exemplifying the most fundamental underlying motive of the entire manifest conflict, namely, fear. As it is employed in the drama's dialogue, the term "courage" refers not to a moral virtue but rather to that gumption and resiliency that permit its victims to tolerate war; and this "virtue," like all the other negative tendencies that keep both Protestant and Catholic locked in their mutual stranglehold, springs from the wormy root of insecurity. Fear of starvation and premature death is thus paradoxically demonstrated to be the effective cause of these very afflictions. Among the whole cast of characters only Kattrin and the Young Peasant summon up the true moral courage to put their life on the line for a humane principle.

2. *(Security)/Insecurity.* Intimately related to the drama's primary set of motives, this pair distinguishes the general mental state of those who in moments of crisis can or cannot overcome their reflexive hesitations grounded in fear. Those afraid to lose life, let alone house or cattle, for the greater good are condemned to remain permanent hostage to any person or group capable of threatening such loss. Insecurity is therefore represented as the dehumanizing bind, the original, self-perpetuating social sin. When Kattrin pleads with her mother for shirts with which to make bandages and the latter replies, "I can't give you a thing. What with all my taxes, duties, fees and bribes!" her excuse provides a candid admission of this bind (5.175).

3. *(Aspiration)/Resignation.* "My aim in life is to get through, me and my children and my wagon" (6.183). With this statement of grimly constricted motive the title-character expresses her resignation to a life of mere survival, nothing more. Contextually, this motive appears to be not only the result but also the cause of the manifest conflict, which turns around the axle of a cowardly and hopeless outlook on life.

4. *(Assertion)/Submission.*

Sit down! And down we sit. You can't start a riot sitting down... We were

full of piss and vinegar, but they've bought if off. Look at me. No back
talk, it's bad for business (4.172).

Speaking to the angry soldier cheated of his reward, Courage follows this confession
by singing the theme for all the drama's manifest adversaries: "The Song of the Great
Capitulation." In contrast to this craven submissiveness, Kattrin's gestures constitute
selfless assertions of her humanity in the very teeth of authority.

5. (*Activity*)/*Passivity*. Notwithstanding all their grumbling and bluster, the engaged characters adopt an essentially passive attitude toward their difficulties; for
with mere survival the primary motive, all energies turn toward accommodation to
present circumstances, however degrading. When Courage curses the war, or the
peace, she does so only because events have once again forced her to make a painful
business adjustment, not because she takes a moral stand for or against either state.
By implication, the ethics of survival and accommodation must be abandoned in
order for man to assume an active (and thus moral) role in his own history—an
alternative to which Kattrin's courageous defiance points the way.

6. (*Wisdom*)/*Ignorance*.

> You saw the wise king Solomon
> You knew what came of him.
> To him all hidden things were plain.
> He cursed the hour that gave birth to him
> And saw that everything was vain.
> How great and wise was Solomon!
> Now think about his case. Alas
> A useful lesson can be won.
> It's wisdom that has brought him to that pass!
> How happy is the man with none! (9.198).

"Our beautiful song proves that virtues are dangerous things," expostulates the Cook,
underscoring the injunction against rational thought and insight so crucial to the
continuance of the manifest conflict. Those who attain wisdom, like Kattrin, will be
as disposed as she (and Solomon) to tears, as well as to self-sacrifice. Thus, Kattrin
weeps as she beats the alarm in her last scene (11.208).

7. (*Rationality*)/*Superstition*. "Don't be sentimental, cook," exhorts the Chaplain,

> There's nothing wrong with dying in battle, its' a blessing, and I'll tell
> you why. This is a war of religion. Not a common war, but a war for the

faith, and therefore pleasing to God. (3.155).

Superstition in its most elaborated, institutional form provides the chief instrument for rationalizing a passive acceptance of the status quo. True rationality, on the contrary, is equated with an instinctive refusal to play the game. Thus, when in Scene 11 the terrified peasant woman pleads with Kattrin to kneel down and pray to save the people of Halle, the girl at first complies; but upon hearing the woman's supplication for her brother-in-law and his four innocent children, Kattrin suddenly forgets all about prayer and runs to sound the alarm (11.205).

8. (*Flexibility*)/*Inflexibility*. "Don't tell me peace has broken out when I've just taken in supplies," laments Courage on hearing of the King of Sweden's death. For notwithstanding her intermittent damning of war and constant extolling of resiliency, mobility, and flexible morality, the prospect of peace throws her into a state of panic (8.186ff). Eiliff's execution for pillaging during a temporary cessation of hostilities underscores this fixation on war as the status quo, for the drama's manifest opponents have all grown so inured to conflict and aggression as a way of life that they have difficulty operating without them. Only Kattrin constantly dreams of peace and makes plans for a happy life after the war is over.

9. (*Selflessness*)/*Selfishness*. "Wanting a reward is perfectly natural. Why else would he distinguish himself?" asks Courage about the soldier who saved the colonel's horse (4.171). Carrying social Darwinism to its illogical conclusion, the manifest adversaries seem to take as their motto the first part of the Mishnaic saying, "If I am not for myself, who will be for me?" forgetting the closure, "And when I am only for myself what am I? And if not now, when?" Kattrin does not forget.

10. (*Generosity*)/*Greed*. Like Shakespeare, Brecht is fond of drawing truths from the mouths of the unworthy. Thus the hypocritical Chaplain justly upbraids Courage for claiming that the war was a "dud":

> . . . when I see you picking up peace with thumb and forefinger like a snotty handkerchief, it revolts my humanity; you don't want peace, you want war, because you profit by it, but don't forget the old saying: "He hath need of a long spoon that eateth with the devil" (8.189).

Yet this same greed in one way or another animates the actions of every member of the cast except the apex character, whose generosity extends to the gift of her life.

11. (*Moderation*)/*Insatiability*. Like the offstage King of Sweden, who "the more he ate the more he wanted," Mother Courage and the other engaged parties suffer

from an insecurity that grows hungrier with the feeding: undue fear of loss rendering all desires immoderate, compulsive. And while only relinquishment of fear would correct the process, this very trepidation naturally construes such letting-go as foolishness. The moral vicious cycle is analogous to the drug addict, compelled by the poison he consumes to rationalize his own destruction. Repeated images linking gluttony with greed and violence reinforce the negative term of this set.

12. (*Constancy*)/*Equivocation*. "God damn the war," exclaims Courage in the last line of Scene 6. Yet her opening line of the very next episode is "Stop running down the war. I won't have it" (6.184; 7.185). Like the other belligerents, the title-character speaks out of both sides of her mouth in the attempt to rationalize her accommodations to current circumstances. This equivocation in the cause of survival (and profit) confuses even Courage:

> Sometimes I have visions of myself driving through hell, selling sulphur and
> brimstone, or through heaven peddling refreshments to wandering souls
> (9.196).

13. (*Humility*)/*Arrogance*. Gripped by fear, suspicion, and selfishness, the initial protagonists and antagonists arrogate to themselves any object or right, and abandon any trust or responsibility at will; for to do otherwise, as Swiss Cheese discovers, leads to destruction as soon as the definition of "responsibility" mutates according to altered circumstances. Even when Courage finds herself unable to abandon Kattrin in order to accept a tempting offer, she shows acute embarrassment at her foolish sentimentality: "It's the wagon. I won't part with the wagon, I'm used to it, it's not you, it's the wagon" (9.210). The constant vollies of sarcasm and epithets of derision (at first grimly humorous) soon render this universal arrogance highly repugnant, thus pointing by indirection to its dialectical opposite.

14. (*Love*)/*Hatred*. Like all other related virtues, love becomes a liability in a World dominated by competition and violence, as the embittered prostitute Yvette laments in her "Song of Fraternization":

> The love which came upon me
> Was wished upon me by fate.
> My friends could never grasp why
> I found it hard to share their hate.
>> The fields were wet with dew
>> When sorrow first I knew.

> The regiment dressed by the right
> Then drums were beaten, that's the drill
> And then the foe, my lover still
> Went marching from our sight (3.154).

Upon which Mother Courage exhorts her daughter, "Let that be a lesson for you, Kattrin. Have no truck with soldiers. It's love that makes the world go round, so you'd better watch out" (3.154). Despite this and many other warnings, however, Kattrin sneaks out at night to seek male companionship (6.184).

15. (*Cooperation*)/*Exploitation.* Hammered by insecurity and insatiable self-seeking, the wedge of greed cracks every human bond, even that of parent to child—as we see when Courage loses each of her offspring while preoccupied trying to drive bargains. For in this world almost all relationships have become instrumental and exploitative. The only exception to this tiresome rule occurs when the Young Peasant risks his own life by encouraging Kattrin to continue sounding the alarm that will save the children of Halle.

16. (*Trust*)/*Suspicion.* The equation of suspicion with self-defeat receives bold formulation in the opening scene where Courage gets distracted from her task of saving Eiliff from going off with the Recruiting Officer:

> (*Mute Kattrin jumps down from the wagon and emits raucous sounds*)
> MOTHER COURAGE: Just a minute, Kattrin, just a minute. The
>   sergeant is paying up. (*Bites the half guider*) I'm always suspicious
>   of money. I'm a burnt child, sergeant. But your coin is good. And
>   now we'll be going. Where's Eiliff?
> SWISS CHEESE: He's gone off with the recruiter (1.143).

17. (*Loyalty*)/*Betrayal.* Just as the Ordinance Officer betrays his comrades by selling their ammunition, Courage plays false to her second son by haggling over the selling-price of her wagon when Swiss Cheese's life depends upon an immediate bribe; and she betrays her own feelings by allowing his body to be thrown on the garbage heap rather than implicate herself by claiming it as kindred. The exchanging at will of Protestant for Catholic banners and clerical for civilian clothes, depending on the fortunes of war, provides vivid heraldry for the mercurial loyalties of everyone engaged in this "holy war."

18. (*Justice*)/*Injustice.* The perversion of justice, as of all humane values, caused by the universally accepted dog-eat-dog ethic receives ironic commentary from the

Cook in his direct address to the audience between the stanzas of the "Song of Solomon":

> We're God-fearing folk, we stick together, we don't steal, we don't murder, we don't set fire to anything! You could say that we set an example . . . yet we sink lower and lower, we seldom see any soup, but if it were different, if we were thieves and murderers, maybe our bellies would be full. Because virtue isn't rewarded, only wickedness, the world needn't be like this, but it is (9.199).

19. *(Compassion)/Ruthlessness.*

> St. Martin couldn't bear to see
> His fellows in distress.
> He saw a poor man in the snow.
> "Take half my cloak!" He did, and lo!
> They both of them froze none the less (9.199).

St. Martin's pity is the quality that the manifest adversaries strive hardest to suppress, for they view it, rightly, as a fatal weakness in a world dominated by competition and struggle for survival. Compassion can undoubtedly be costly, as Kattrin knows: "It's pity that makes her suffer so"—and pity that costs her her life (9.197).

20. *(Normality)/Perversion.* The negative term of this set speaks for itself. However, in the context of a general perversion of all humane values, Kattrin's behavior does not appear to be indubitably normative. This difficulty appears to account for the presence in the text of scattered reminders of everyday peacetime activities—references not directly associated with Kattrin but whose functional position can only lie alongside her images in the apex unit. Thus, for instance, the beautiful offstage song of the peasant which Courage and her daughter overhear in Scene 10 ("The rose bush in our garden") (10.202).

21. *(Integrity)/Depravity.* In his notes to the play Brecht suggests that "In no other scene is Courage so depraved as in Scene 4, where she instructs the young man in capitulation to the higher-ups and then puts her own teaching into effect." The dramatist goes on to assert that this is a problem of her class in general ("The Mother Courage Model," 361). Yet his portrayal here of the other social orders offers little to suggest their own freedom from depravity in its broad sense; for while the peasants knuckle under for fear of losing a hut or cow, the rulers capitulate to their own excessive appetites, and all consequently dwell in chaos. Class conflict is therefore represented as but one of the inevitable concomitants of the depravity of both recessive mirror-functions. The absence of such conflict is symbolized by the

cooperation of a peasant and daughter of a petty bourgeois to save a whole population, regardless of class.

22. (*Pride*)/*Shamelessness*. "Pride isn't for us," claims the prostitute Yvette. "If we can't put up with shit, we're through" (3.153). With this she echoes all the drama's belligerents, whom fear of insecurity or insufficiency drives to violate all the moral principles they claim to hold dear.

23. (*Gentleness*)/*Violence*.

> THE COOK . . . In a way you could call it a war, because of all the extortion and killing and looting, not to mention a bit of rape . . . But it makes a man thirsty all the same, you've got to admit that (3.155).

> SWISS CHEESE: Won't be many more days when I can sit in the sun in my shirtsleeves (*Kattrin points to a tree*). Yes the leaves are yellow. (*Kattrin asks him by means of gestures, whether he wants a drink*) (3.161).

24. (*Peace*)/*Conflict*. The ethic of survival at all costs generates a permanent state of hostilities, not only between the manifest adversaries (churches and kingdoms) but also between classes and individuals associated with the same cause; for all human intercourse has become instrumental, self-serving. The contention between Chaplain and Cook for the security of Courage's provisioner's business exemplifies this degradation of social life in the arena of love between man and woman, where the war of the sexes is shown to be a natural off-shoot of the competitiveness and bellicosity of society at large (8.187-94). The characters envision peace as a transitory, unnatural state because its maintenance depends upon the suppressed and therefore atrophied virtues of self-sacrifice and cooperation.

25. (*Regeneration*)/*Degeneration*. A gradual decline in physical appearance parallels the steady moral decline of the survivors of the drama's manifest conflict. This spiritual deterioration receives figurative emphasis everywhere, from Courage's wagon, latterly "much the worse for wear," to the increasingly deplorable condition of the principal characters' dress. By contrast, Kattrin's regenerative instincts are accented figuratively by her actions of serving, cleaning, dressing up, bandaging wounds, etc. And while she does sustain a disfigurement, this image is immediately offset by others signifying renewal: "*Enter Kattrin out of breath, with a wound across her forehead and over one eye. She is carrying all sorts of things, packages, leather goods, a drum, etc*" (6.183). As Kattrin lies dead in the last scene her ragged and distraught mother sings over her body:

Lullaby baby

What stirs in the hay?

The neighbor brats whimper

Mine are happy and gay.

They go in tatters

And you in silk gown

Cut from an angel's

Best party gown (12. 209).

26. (*The Future*)/*The Past*. Infants and children figure large in Brecht's dramas as symbols of that which in life they are the literal bearers: the future. Thus, Kattrin's great and tender concern for the young, which leads her at last to an extraordinary act of self-sacrifice, invests her apex function with the quality necessary for the proper care of mankind's future. Posterity cannot thrive under the timeworn survival ethic of Mother Courage, who loses all her children while compulsively obeying this timorous principle.

27. (*Plenty*)/*Poverty*. The banner for Scene 9 proclaims in general what the action has shown in small particulars:

> The great war of religion has been going on for sixteen years. Germany has lost more than half its population. Those whom slaughter has spared have been laid low by epidemics. Once flourishing countrysides are ravaged by famine. Wolves prowl through the charred ruins of the cities...Business is bad, begging is the only resort (9.175).

28. (*Beauty*)/Ugliness. Mother Courage constantly tries to protect her daughter from the soldiers by various stratagems to make her unattractive: "The girls that attract them get the worst of it. They drag them around till there's nothing left...It's like trees. The straight tall one gets chopped down for ridgepoles, the crooked ones enjoy life" (6.183). Like virtue, strength and beauty also become liabilities in this monstrous conflict which runs on the doubly perverse principle of the survival of the unfittest. In utter contrast to all this, however, Scene 10 is entirely devoted to a brief interlude during which Courage and Kattrin, much the worse for wear and in the train of "increasingly bedraggled armies," pause to listen to a voice singing from within a peasant's hut. Its simple lyric offers a hauntingly poignant reminder of the beauties of peacetime, felicities almost entirely forgotten after all the preceding violence and beastliness:

> The rose bush in our garden
>
> Rejoiced our hearts in spring
>
> It bore such lovely flowers.

> We planted it last season
>
> Before the April showers.
>
> A garden is a blessed thing
>
> It bore such lovely flowers (10.209).

This almost transfigured scene provides a sort of quiet overture to Kattrin's final and most beautiful gesture in the following episode.

29. *(Order)/Chaos.* "Peace is a mess, it takes a war to put things in order," grumbles the Recruiting Sergeant, adding "In peacetime the human race goes to the dogs" (1.135). One of the play's many ironies is that while the engaged parties equate security with the regimentation of war (and the profits to be had from it), this conflict brings them to a state of utter desperation and chaos:

> In Saxony a man in rags tried to foist a cord of books on me for two eggs,
> and in Württemberg they'd have let their plow go for a little bag of salt.
> What's the good of plowing? Nothing grows but brambles. In Pomerania
> they say the villagers have eaten up all the babies, and that the nuns have
> been caught at highway robbery. . . . It's the end of the world (9.196).

30. *(Innocence)/Guilt.* Kattrin's behavior appears extremely näive as the world wags in this fictive realm, a place where knowledge of how to survive equates with betrayal and collective guilt, and where loving self-sacrifice therefore becomes a manifestly dysfunctional characteristic. The drama's chief irony resides in the fact that the prevalent values of this realm are themselves dysfunctional, and that innocence of the way of the world in fact offers the only alternative to its destruction. There is here an almost Biblical equation of knowledge with "sin" and innocence with "salvation"—the latter connection being enhanced by Kattrin's identification with children and animals, the conflict's most innocent victims.

31. *(Freedom)/Bondage.* Brecht equates freedom with the letting go of fear and all its attendant personal and collective disorders, from insecurity, greed, exploitation, and conflict, to utter chaos and destruction. The willingness to die if necessary for the common welfare is shown to be the essential condition for individual and social liberation.

32. *(Self-fulfillment)/Self-defeat.* We shall permit the text to speak for itself here, with two examples of the negative term followed by one of the implied positive:

> Last year your general made you cut across the fields to trample
> down the grain. . . . He thought he'd be someplace else this year, but

now he's still here and everybody's starving (4.171).

It seems they wanted to ring the bells [at Marshall Tilly's funeral] naturally, but it turned out the churches had all been shot to pieces by his orders, so the poor general won't hear any bells when they lower him into his grave. (6.177).

(. . . *Kattrin's last drumbeats are answered by the city's cannon. A confused hubbub of alarm bells and cannon is heard in the distance.*)

FIRST SOLDIER: She's done it (11.208).

33. (*Humanity*)/*Inhumanity.* The engaged parties cannot act on humane principles because they are possessed by fear, which makes them selfish and therefore essentially animals of prey. Kattrin's fearless readiness for self-sacrifice is shown by indirection to be the necessary quality for a truly humane bond of man to man.

34. (*Life*)/*Death.* The action presents a double irony in the discrepancy between Courage's bootless attempts to shield her offspring from the maw of war and Kattrin's successful move to save the children of Halle from the same voracious engine. Courage fails because fear and greed inhibit her from offering the ultimate sacrifice of security, and even perhaps her life; yet at the end she is left alive to suffer her bereavement without understanding its cause. Kattrin's symbolic motherhood is crowned with victory, however transitory, precisely because she operates in the absence of these reflexive motives; yet her life-preserving act for others costs her her own. Courage's dispensing slips of paper marked with black crosses signifying "death" provides heraldry in the opening scene for the title-character as the personification of man's thanatotic urges.

With the rather large total of thirty-four derivations briefly rationalized, we are now in a position to lay out an implicational chart for the purpose of scanning the dominant and recessive functions, both across and downward, in order to acquire a more instantaneous impression of the action's motives. This time the mirror recessive functions will appear in both the extreme right and left hand columns, as they properly descend from the manifest opponents. In the middle, and again in parentheses, we shall place the column deriving from the implicitly dominant apex function:

IMPLICATIONAL CHART: Brecht, *Mother Courage and Her Children*:

RECESSIVE FUNCTION (I)	IMPLIED DOMINANT FUNCTION	RECESSIVE FUNCTION (II)
Fear	(Courage)	Fear

Insecurity	(Security)	Insecurity
Resignation	(Aspiration)	Resignation
Submission	(Assertion)	Submission
Passivity	(Activity)	Passivity
Ignorance	(Wisdom)	Ignorance
Superstition	(Rationality)	Superstition
Fixation	(Flexibility)	Fixation
Selfishness	(Selflessness)	Selfishness
Greed	(Generosity)	Greed
Insatiability	(Moderation)	Insatiability
Equivocation	(Constancy)	Equivocation
Arrogance	(Humility)	Arrogance
Hatred	(Love)	Hatred
Exploitation	(Cooperation)	Exploitation
Suspicion	(Trust)	Suspicion
Betrayal	(Loyalty)	Betrayal
Injustice	(Justice)	Injustice
Ruthlessness	(Compassion)	Ruthlessness
Perversion	(Normality)	Perversion
Depravity	(Integrity)	Depravity
Shamelessness	(Pride)	Shamelessness
Violence	(Gentleness)	Violence
Conflict	(Peace)	Conflict
Degeneration	(Regeneration)	Degeneration
The Past	(The Future)	The Past
Poverty	(Plenty)	Poverty
Ugliness	(Beauty)	Ugliness
Chaos	(Order)	Chaos
Bondage	(Freedom)	Bondage
Guilt	(Innocence)	Guilt
Self-defeat	(Self-fulfillment)	Self-defeat
Inhumanity	(Humanity)	Inhumanity
Death	(Life)	Death

If the implicational dialectic of *Mother Courage* yields few surprises it is evidently because Brecht writes in full consciousness of his motives, seeking to veil them neither from himself nor his audience. Consequently, what one senses in this drama is very much what it gives, however oblique the manner of representation . This same quality of forthrightness adheres to all other works of this type, for the synthetic-implied dynamic seems to demand that the author proceed in complete awareness of the internal argument seeking symbolic resolution through its offices. The very indirectness of the form requires the dramatist to hammer away at the various inhumanities of the recessive mirror functions, until the audience is made so acutely uncomfortable that they are willing at last to embrace the "eccentric" indicator-character with relief. The case is far different, however, with many didactic works assuming other structures, dramas which often appear to champion one cause by the advocacy of false "persona" figures while recommending quite another through the management of that touchstone for motive in all cases, namely, action. (Shaw's apostatic-positive *Major Barbara* springs to mind as an instance of this sort of double message). It is entirely fitting, however, that a dramatist who despises equivocation as much as Brecht does should decline to engage in such tactics.

The only thing here that might raise a few eyebrows is the fact that Mother Courage herself turns out to be the principal representative of the immoral and self-defeating recessive functions. For a few influential critics have preferred to see her as the exemplar of true courage on the score of mere endurance, and thus to champion her as a "tragic" figure. That Brecht motivates her with the same fear and greed that possesses almost everyone else in this wasteful conflict would seem to be obvious even without systematic analysis, and it is clear that the dramatist regarded her minimal aspiration to mere survival, at best, as pathetic. The interpretation of Courage as an exemplary or "tragic" figure must therefore be discounted as another instance of the tendency of critics (and directors) to project their own values onto those of the text.

Of more moment for a joint understanding of *Mother Courage* and the synthetic-implied dynamic are those oppositional pairs that distinguish Brecht's play from others of the same structure, with its largely predetermined motivational pattern. Thus, of the thirty-four antinomies seemingly requisite to this work, a majority of twenty coincide with those on the composite implicational chart for synthetic-implied drama (See p. 316), while a minority of fourteen are unique to Brecht. And although these exceptional antinomies are insufficient of themselves to describe the play's motivational complexity (which greatly depends upon the built-in oppositions of this particular dynamic), they do show precisely where Brecht differs from other dramatists who follow this structure. Moreover, the first seven of these atypical pairs constitute important causal factors, revealing on the positive side the author's teleological vision as well as his political activism, and on the negative side his diagnosis of the social ill:

(Security)	Insecurity
(Aspiration)	Resignation
(Assertion)	Submission
(Activity)	Passivity
(Rationality)	Superstition
(The Future)	The Past

The remaining exceptional antinomies describe the combination of effects, positive and negative, that descend from these opposed motives:

(Constancy)	Equivocation
(Normality)	Perversion
(Integrity)	Depravity
(Regeneration)	Degeneration
(Plenty)	Poverty
(Self-fulfillment)	Self-defeat

Self-fulfillment and regeneration, both moral and material, are thus shown to be intimately connected with optimism regarding the future and a rational assertiveness issuing from inward security. Humanity cannot aspire either to general prosperity or to moral integrity under the threadbare and ultimately depraved ethic of mere survival, with its cowardly inclination to accept the errors of the past as permanent and unavoidable elements of the human condition. This, in a nutshell, is what the exceptional descriptive pairs to *Mother Courage* tell us of the motivational variance of this work from dramas of the same structure by other authors, and indeed of the coherence and complexity that such networks may attain even within the somewhat rigid system of meaning inherent in this dynamic.

For the most part, however, the values championed in *Mother Courage* are identical to those advocated by all other works of its structural class. By invariably demonstrating the dehumanizing effects of conflict itself, and by elevating such qualities as trust, compassion, tolerance, and cooperation to positions of supreme importance, these dramas seek to draw us away from any sectarian loyalty for which we would feel obliged to sacrifice the lives and happiness of others.

AFTERWORD

In the preceding pages I have set forth a general theory of dramatic form together with a complete system of textual analysis. I believe that this approach offers an objective and practicable method for comprehending the underlying binary organization of dramatic works, and therefore a new and fruitful way of perceiving essential relationships between the myriad details of the individual text—actions, characters, motives, scenes, speeches, images, and even locutions. This in turn should make possible the generalization of those details into an abstract description of the opposing values at the heart of the drama's conflict. Any such abstraction is, of course, also a reduction; but a good model reduces in such a way as to integrate and explain many processes which before were understood only piecemeal, if at all, and without clear relationship to their functioning within the larger dynamic structure. The present study, then, is an attempt to unify the various elements of the dramatic enterprise through a workable model which clarifies more than it obscures, and which I trust will have general value to students in the field.